Simon

The Promised Mates of Monktona Wood

Vera Foxx

Foxx Fantasy Publishing

Publisher: Foxx Fantasy Publishing

Editing by: MarcEdits

CONTENTS

DEDICATION

This book is dedicated to the real Simon. An actual fainting goat.
Yes, Simon started out as a joke in Calliope's book. I thought it would be hilarious for a little fainting goat to follow around a human that thought she was a fairy. A rather good friend and author, Emm E. Goshald told me about her friends who owned a goat named Simon. Thus, Simon's name was born.

Thank you, Emm's friends for letting me use his name. I didn't plan on making him shift into a bulked up Mr. Tumnus but here we are.

My apologies.

Thanks also to Pam who put the idea out there to turn him into faun. Way to go and make me change course for awhile. I appreciated it. It was fun and naughty. :)

Just for clarification, the real Simon does not shift into a faun or human and does not have an insatiable appetite for women named Lucy.

SIMON

SIMON IS A FAUN and human rom-com, with Tarzan and Jane vibes and fated mates; he falls first and instant attraction. While this story is part of a series, you can read this spicy story as a stand-alone.

Simon hadn't always walked on two legs. In fact, he had spent most of his life on four legs, as a goat and companion to a human raised by fae. He hadn't seen himself as a pet; he had been much too smart for that. Simon had grasped human speech, surpassing the intelligence of the average goat, a concept beyond his comprehension.

His companion knew and treated him as her equal, and when it came time to protect her, he literally jumped at the chance, which resulted in him changing him into what he was that day... a two-legged 'monster'.

Simon ran away from his human and wandered Monktona Wood alone. He learned to walk on two legs, used his hands, made tools, and built a home. He was more than an animal then, but speaking had been the last thing on his mind.

That changed when he stumbled upon a human female who made his heart beat faster and stirred something in his pouch.

Lucy was shy around males, mostly thanks to her father being over protective, which lead to her emotional disinterest towards the opposite sex. Her curiosity about how the world worked, and a desire to *know all the things,* sparked something new inside her during a feverish dream with a not so human male.

While Lucy was there to gather information and map out the Monktona Wood, an ogre attacked their camp but a mysterious faun rescued her first.

He was mute, touchy-feely, demanding, and he would not let her go.

He scented her, claimed her, and it would have taken the Moon Goddess herself to rip them apart.

Monktona Wood History

TEN YEARS AGO, IN the serene land of Bergarian, a sinister force crept in. The once harmonious continent was plunged into darkness by a malevolent power. The sorcerer, who had delved deep into the art of necromancy, had let the evil spirits take over his body. The sorcerer's ultimate goal was not just to conquer Bergarian but the entire Earth.

The clash of swords echoed through the battlefield as the four kingdoms fought bravely against the rogue enemies. But the air was thick with the stench of death and defeat as the enemies, aided by dark magic, had gained the upper hand. Just when all hope seemed lost, King Osirus and a dragon named Creed stumbled upon a group of green monsters called orcs. These strangers were all too excited to lend a helping hand in saving the continent by going to war.

The sounds of their determined voices filled the air, their eyes ablaze with a fierce determination to make things right. They set off without question.

The sturdy wall that had long divided the uncharted terrain from the rest of Bergarian finally crumbled. The deafening sound of the collapse echoed across the land, followed by the thunderous footsteps of the orcs, impervious to magic, as they charged into the realm of Bergarian. The acrid smell of burning magic filled the air as the last line of defense gave way to the orc's relentless assault.

With the orcs' help, the people of Bergarian became the heroes of their own story. They forged deep bonds of friendship with all the inhabitants of the land, including the shapeshifters, fae, pixies, sirens, and other races of Bergarian. The feeling of unity and solidarity was palpable as the different factions came together to celebrate victory over the dark forces that had once threatened to overwhelm them. As national heroes, the wall was permanently destroyed, a treaty was signed, and they were granted rights to search for their own mates across each of the kingdoms.

These are their stories along with the new creatures that reside within.

GLOSSARY

Monktona Wood- Name of orcs' home

Dark Forest- What everyone else called Monktona Wood before they knew of the orcs beyond the wall.

The Dark War- When Bergarian went through dark times and had to fight through a dark entity. A wall was discovered, revealing the orcs and with their help the Bergarians were able to win the war.

Orgamo- Father

Seeded orgamo- Sired father

Ogamie- Mother

Clan- A small family that holds one orc female and several males. Each male has their own cabin, while the female visits one male every night. Clans are no longer in practice because all the female orcs have died.

Tribe- The orc race as a whole

Miresa- Orc word for mates

Moon Fairy- Moon Goddess

Bassza- Curse word equivalent to *fuck*

Fattyu- Bastard

Guardard snap- Curse word equivalent to *damn it.*

Orcling- Orc child or child in general

DEAR READER

This story may contain content that might be disturbing to some readers. Please take the time to check out this list before reading. While this is a romcom, it does have dark undertones due to some of its content.

This can also be considered a list spoilers.

Breaking and Entering

Unconsented Scenting

Kidnapping

Unconsented Touching from MMC & FMC (SA)

Possessive (animalistic male)

Biting

Large Faun Peen

Ruts

Fight Scene, Some Gore

Drugged Male (not my FMC)

Somnophilia

FMC performing acts on drugged MMC (DubCon)

Chapter One

Lucy

I HELD MY SPIRAL notebook to my chest, clutching it tighter by the second. The double suns–*light sources,* I reminded myself–bore down on the naked skin of the shifters, with the hot summer day. They were loading the open wagons, filling them with supplies: tents, dry food, fire starters and so on. It was more than I thought we really needed, but the queen and my father wanted to be sure that I was comfortable.

Dutton slung a bag of rice over the wagon like it was a small bean bag. Dust flew into the air, and he slapped his hands together. Dirt swirled around him and clung to the sweat on his bare chest. He turned his body to face me, and he smiled widely as droplets of water ran down his neck and between his pectoral muscles.

My eyes widened, and I looked away. He was a good-looking man. They all were in this realm; the women, the men, and even the children looked like tiny little models running around.

This place was magical. There was no doubt about that. From the multi-colored sky to the palace I've stayed in. I've been there as a guest for several weeks, hoping to understand the basics of this realm, down to the animals they are used to seeing in this part of the land.

I couldn't get over how lucky I was to get this job.

I met every criteria they needed. Which was a scientist who understood basic botany, but mostly, with the discovery of new species of animals and insects and anything else that I may deem important.

Especially in a new area to explore where no other scientist had ever been.

It was like being a kid in a candy store.

This was better than any holiday I'd ever encountered. A whole new world for the taking. I wouldn't be able to share it with Earth—we left that world behind—but this world, Bergarian, seemed to appreciate how I have an excitement to understand it all from fresh eyes and a scientific point of view.

This place was magnificent and seemed to contradict everything I had learned. It could be slightly infuriating but also delightfully exciting at the same time.

"That's the last of it." Dutton took a rag from his waistband and wiped away his forehead. He kept his eyes on me as he did, and I looked for my father to keep away from the wolf shifter.

I buried my head in books most of my life, and when I wasn't working on a research paper or thesis, I was out with my father in a remote area doing archeological digs. I had little finesse with talking to the opposite sex. In fact, I hardly had any experience talking to men. My cheeks would flush red, and I would stumble over my words. It didn't matter if they were young, old, single or married. Father did his best to keep me protected.

My father was the only man I talked to, and he'd been fiercely protective of me since my youth. Unfortunately, it made me socially awkward. I didn't blame him in the slightest, though; he loved me, and I loved him back just as fiercely. He'd homeschooled me and let me travel with him since I could walk. I'd seen plants, animals, and cultures that many scientists would kill to see.

Now that he was older, he wouldn't be able to travel on this journey. He'd been very supportive, though, and said I would be fine on my own. I had some apprehension. This trek resembled our previous treks, but it ventured into uncharted territory, encountering unseen animals and plants, unknown to humans and even to the shifters accompanying me.

The thought thrilled me. I'd be able to record everything. Not by camera, however, just by sight and with my pencils. Just like the great explorers in the past, on Earth. It was so primitive, so old-fashioned.

It was how they liked it here. They wanted to keep the land pure and free of trash. Most of its products were biodegradable. The realm's inhabitants permitted very few electronics, and technological communication with the other side was very limited.

Fascinating, simply fascinating.

My heart fluttered, and I stood up on my tippy toes while I bit my lip.

And I was doing this trek on my own. I was in charge!

"Someone is excited." Dutton strode over. His gait was wide, and the linen pants he wore were thin. It left little to the imagination. To see people strip naked out of the blue was the norm here, especially for shifters. I still wasn't used to it and would pivot away each time.

I received a warning that this world was a little freer with nudity due to necessity. Shifting with clothes on would just be a waste of clothing. It made sense, and it was something I just had to get used to.

The males laughed when they heard me shriek as they threw their pants off, and now I thought they did it on purpose.

But the thin linen pants that Dutton was wearing grew tighter. The pants bunched and gathered right at an area I did not need to see.

Don't look, Lucy. Why do you have to look?

Because you are both depraved and deprived. Too worried about pleasing your father with your studies and not taking care of yourself.

I whimpered in the back of my mind.

"I... uh... yes, that's excellent. Thank you very much, Mr. Dutton." I turned my face, not looking at him at all, and swallowed.

I could see the smirk in my peripheral as he dusted off his hands once again. "You don't need to call me mister. That's so formal. Dutton is fine." He tilted his head and came closer.

Shifters, who were predominantly in the Cerulean Moon Kingdom, were very warm-blooded. Even though I was a good three feet away from his massive body, I could still feel the heat radiating off of him. I tried to look him in his eyes. It was like he was wanting attention, perhaps demanding. I wasn't sure, but he kept looking me up and down.

I gazed around his body, seeing my father with his cane coming in my direction, along with the king and queen. *Please hurry and get here.*

"Lucy. Is it alright if I call you that?" I peered up at Dutton, seeing him stand above me. His darker hair, wet from sweat, fell onto his forehead. That crooked smile was still on his face. He was handsome, I'd give him that, but he wasn't anything that lit my world on fire.

No man ever could. I was starting to think I was broken. I'd just never had a feeling or desire for anyone in particular. I've tried to look it up, of course. The scientist in me wanted to make sure my body wasn't broken. The results were… inconclusive.

My face went pink again. *Kitty whiskers! I hope he didn't think I liked him or anything.*

"L-Lucy is fine. We will travel for six weeks, right? Miss won't be required." I nervously chuckled and stood up straight to step away.

Six weeks. It would be the longest I had ever been away from my father. Before this, I'd only been away from him for four days, when I came down with dengue fever. Even that didn't really count because I was asleep and he was at my side, but that was beside the point.

Dutton rubbed the back of his neck. "Yeah, we will be. The other warriors are excited. The females especially. They want to know all about your travels on Earth. One wants to explore there once this expedition is over."

I nodded, and my ears perked up. "Yeah, do they like science and discovering new species, too?"

Dutton threw out a boisterous laugh. "No, she is looking for her mate. She is nearly thirty. They get antsy, you know? She thinks she will find them on Earth."

Right, the mate thing. The *soul mates* idea that I found absolutely intriguing. This realm seemed to revolve their whole lives around the notion that a soul was not complete unless they found their other half.

Some humans talked about soul mates on Earth. Finding the perfect person who complimented you in every way. In Bergarian, there was a common belief that was centered upon a Moon Goddess who gifted each person a soul mate. I was still trying to understand this religion, but it was hard for my mind to grasp. Father taught me to be more scientific. He raised me to see how things were and how things worked.

The study of religious cultures never tickled my fancy. I was very hands-on, I loved to touch and feel what I was studying. The thought of a higher form was hard for me to grasp, but I knew they were important.

Here, this Moon Goddess was prevalent. More than that I even realized, and I would need to study it further while I was on the trek to the Monktona Woods.

"There you are!" I heard my father call around the wall, I mean Dutton, who was still standing in front of me.

My father, a shorter man of just five foot five, a head full of white hair and an equally white mustache, approached. "You are too close to her. Back away." Father took his cane to separate Dutton and me.

Dutton put his hands up in surrender and smiled. "Professor Watts, I meant no disrespect."

My father huffed in annoyance and held his arm out for me. I was taller than him by at least four inches. I let him lead me away, relieved to be away from the source of my anxiety. "Perhaps I should go, too. I don't know if I trust some of these men that are going to be around you."

"Father, it's going to be alright. They won't lay a hand on me. Besides, I took those self-defense courses you wanted, and the king and queen trust these warriors the most."

The queen, a short, petite woman who looked much younger than me, pranced over with her tall, imposing husband—mate. "Trust me, none of them will harm you. They know what consent is." She raised a brow over at Dutton, who bowed with one arm over his chest.

My father bristled and shook his head. "I don't..."

"Father, I don't plan on consenting, but even if I did, it would be my decision." I stood up straight and held my notebook closer to my chest.

The people here do date, but it was never for the long term, and I wasn't one for a one-night stand. I had never even been on a date, never had the desire nor interest, and that made my father all the more happy.

"No one is good enough for my daughter," he would say.

"There, you see. She has a backbone." Dutton chuckled and stalked off back toward the wagon. My father bristled. He took a step to try and catch up with Dutton, all the while, having to use his cane for support. I grabbed him by the wrist and pulled him back toward me.

"Father, I will be fine. It was a joke."

The light that was filtering through the branches of the trees was suddenly blocked, and when I turned my head, a large male stood beside us. The king was large. His forearms, covered in tattoos, were crossed over his bulging chest, making his tunic stretch so much it was in danger of ripping to pieces.

"I will speak with him," the king, known as Kane, said. "He, nor anyone else, will cause you problems." He walked past us, and I wanted to stop him, but Queen Clara put her hand on my forearm.

"Let him boss someone around." She sighed as she stared off, looking at his backside. "He is practicing his daddy skills now that he has a daughter. He will make sure that Dutton and the other warriors leave you alone. This is strictly business."

I bit my lip. "I don't want to cause trouble or have people hate me. I don't want..."

The queen shook her head. "Lucy, it is not your problem to deal with. People don't need to be pushing themselves on you when you haven't shown interest. You are not Dutton's mate or anyone else's mate on this trek. They would have made it known by now. Not trying to hurt your feelings in any way." She sighed. "You are a gorgeous woman, and yes, we have mates here, but some decide to date and do... other things before they meet who belongs to them. I highly discourage it because it gets messy, but I cannot control people's lives. I do emphasize consent, though, and that's what Kane is reminding them of."

I nodded in understanding. She hooked her arm around mine and led me closer to the bustling marketplace. The trees stood tall. They were thick with branches that overhung the area, with beautiful vines that cascaded downward. It kept the area cool, and the breeze was ever constant. It wasn't humid, and the thick mosses and damp soil filtered all the dust, allowing my lungs to expand to their fullest extent.

Goodbye, asthma!

"We are so excited that you are able to do this. It was fate. I truly believe it was. You are meant to be here." She gave me a side-eye and a wink.

I looked everywhere but her after that statement. I hoped she didn't think that someone was going to think I was their soul mate, because soul mates was a strange concept for me. How can you just fall for someone so fast? Was it like lightning? How could you truly know?

None of it made sense. Was it a biological chemical in the brain? Was it a scent the body released? Did it have to do with reproduction? There were too many questions, and for now, as a human, I did not find it logical that it could happen to someone like me. Interspecies relationships did not seem that common. The humans I had seen here were single.

I swallowed again as we stopped at a food cart. They were selling something similar to a hot dog, but instead of those buns with infected chemicals, it was on freshly baked bread with spices that didn't even need ketchup and mustard. The meat was a large sausage that I knew I wouldn't be able to eat all on my own, but every portion of food was shifter-sized.

Big. Everything was big.

Clara handed it to me and motioned for me to start eating.

"I want her safe," my father chimed in as he grabbed his Bergarian hotdog and took a bite. "Oh, that's good stuff," he mumbled around the food. "And I know this Dutton character is the head of security, but I swear if he puts one hand on my daughter…"

Clara put a calming hand on my father's shoulder. "She is in excellent paws. Five males and five females; all top warriors. Then, two orcs will accompany her when they arrive. Sugha is extra excited for you to be there. His brothers have all found mates, and he's hoping you might be his."

The food I just shoved in my mouth went down the wrong pipe, and I choked. Immediately, my hands went to my throat. My father came up behind me and immediately did the Heimlich maneuver. It wasn't necessary. It only took one good jerk of his fist into my stomach, and it flew out and hit the bottom of the cart.

The people around us looked in horror, and my face turned so red, I was sure I could make a car stop. If there were cars around here.

Father kept doing the Heimlich, and I pushed away from his hold. "I'm fine!" I squeaked and wiped away the spit-dribble on my chin. "And what do you mean, an orc as a mate?"

Clara giggled. "I'm sorry, I shouldn't have said that. Sugha mentioned he was hoping you were his mate. He may not be, you never know. Those orcs are very eager. They won't touch you, though, just like the rest of the wolves traveling with you. If you aren't theirs, they won't bother. Trust me."

My mouth opened and closed while my father studied Clara. He said nothing but picked up his cane. "These mates, they can just steal my daughter if they think that she belongs to them? If they think she is their soul mate?"

Clara nodded cheerfully. "Yes, and they will take care of her, love her, and make sure she is satisfied in all ways. It's truly romantic." Clara swooned and looked toward the king in longing. The large king was currently yelling at his warriors, his shaking fist coming close to their faces. They all looked like they might pee their pants.

I swallowed and rubbed my throat. I grabbed a paper napkin from the cart and patted the corner of my lips.

"That's it; I'm going with you." Father shook his head and hobbled with his cane back toward the wagons. From there, he would find the road back to the palace.

Clara watched me as I took several steps to catch up to him, and I tugged on his arm. "Father, no. I am fine. I can do this. Please, let me do this."

He stopped and pursed his lips.

I didn't believe in divine intervention, but I did believe I was here for a reason. Who knew, maybe by the end, I might believe in something.

"Father, as noble as you are trying to be. I am an adult." I tried to reason with him. His brows furrowed, and the already deep lines in his face further deepened. "You are here to learn about shifter anatomy. You won't be able to handle the terrain in the Monktona Woods. I will draw as many pictures as I can and tell you everything when I get back."

My father swallowed. "You will come back. And be safe." He said, more to himself. "You will."

My smile trembled. "Of course I will. You taught me everything I know for the last twenty-nine years of my life."

He let out a shaky breath and ran his fingers through his hair. "Right."

Father wasn't one for emotion. He was logical and practical and always looking at things from a realistic point of view. But standing in this mystical land of shifters, fae, elves, and who knew what else, anything seemed possible. With the mysteries of the unknown all around us, I thought it must all be hitting him right now.

Clara, with her gentle smile and wise eyes, stood beside us. "Your father will be safe here, too, Lucy. He will learn much from our healers and scholars, while you embark on your journey through the Monktona Woods, and you will bring us just as much knowledge as we have been wanting to know about that place. Orcs aren't great at explaining things. They are a little"—she bobbed her head back and forth—"basic. They just aren't great with words."

I stared up into the sky, which was a canvas of pastel shades, a watercolor masterpiece blending pinks, purples, and blues in a harmonious symphony, each shade swirling and dancing with the others in a cosmic tie-dye.

It was beautiful.

This place was absolutely stunning, and I was here ready to explore it all.

Chapter Two

Lucy

THE ENORMOUS HORSES GALLOPED–yes, galloped–along the smooth pathways to our destination. The road was well maintained, especially the main roads between kingdoms. It was the perfect sand, dirt, and ground rock ratio. They really thought of everything. Especially when they don't use concrete.

When we first arrived in Bergarian, I poked and stared at the dirt for too long for everyone's comfort. They must have questioned my sanity. The shifters stared in shock when I took teaspoons of samples in a glass jar so I could study it later.

"How does the trip fare, so far?" I was abruptly startled by the captivating presence of Elmira, the breathtaking female warrior with luscious chestnut hair. Her arms, adorned with lean muscles, rippled beneath the snug, sleeveless tunic she donned, which emphasized her sculpted physique. With a graceful flick of the reins, the horses let off a squeal of excitement and jumped forward again.

I was grateful that Elmira was up here, in the front of the wagon, with me leading the horses. I felt more at ease with her here than one of the men.

"It's wonderful," I said as I stared out over the road. To the left of us, we passed by the Vermillion Kingdom. It was completely destroyed during a terrible war a decade ago, but you couldn't even tell now.

Towering trees that looked ancient, though I knew they were actually very young, stretched towards the sky, dominating the landscape. They cast a shadow of mystery to the place. A sense of foreboding hung in the air, as the dense canopy blocked out most of the light from the light sources, inside the forest that hid the kingdom within. Perched atop a hill, just like in a fairytale, was a palace shrouded in darkness, emanating an eerie presence. It was rumored it was built the same as the previous palace, with only minor changes.

I couldn't tear my gaze away from the ominous silhouette of the palace atop the hill. Legends and myths surrounded the ruins of the Vermillion Kingdom, and stories of curses and restless spirits haunted its grounds. The air seemed to grow colder as we passed by, the horses snorting nervously as if they sensed the lingering darkness.

Elmira must have noticed my unease, as she cast me a reassuring smile. "Don't worry, Lucy. The Vermillion Kingdom may look dark, but we are at peace. The temporary rulers, until the prince comes of age, are very close friends with Queen Clara. Nothing will harm us."

The other shifters running alongside the wagon took off into the woods, snarling and barking at each other's heels. They came back out moments later, rolling into the tall, deep green grasses with red tip blades, and jumped in front of the horses. The horses let out a whine, stomping their feet harder into the dirt, and jerked the wagon along faster.

I wanted to ask more questions about Vermillion, but my attention was brought back to the horses. More time for Bergarian history later.

My ADHD just can't, right now.

"Why are the horses so big?" I gripped my seat, my short hair flying backward and my body leaning against the polished wood.

"Didn't you know? Everything in Bergarian is bigger. Just like they say about Texas on Earth. Bigger is better, am I right?" Elmira winked at me, and we sped along. "This world is just naturally stronger. You can call it evolution, as you believe with your scientific mumbo jumbo, but I think it was out of necessity that the gods gave us these things. We were built different ourselves, so why would they give us weaker animals to work with?" She shrugged.

That was true. These horses had been at it for nearly a day and they showed no signs of being tired. Neither had the shifters that pranced and ran alongside us. This was just a walk to them, while I was tired from sitting on this wagon full of supplies.

The closest I had come to working out was carting a bunch of books in my arms from one table to another.

"Yeah," I said shakily. Perhaps I was too confident coming on this expedition alone. I was really out of my element, but I was just so excited to come out here. This was every researcher's dream, and it was mine for the taking.

I gripped hold of the wagon again when we hit a hole in the road, and I let out a squeal. A wolf with dark gray fur and a white chest darted toward me. It was Dutton. I made sure to know what his wolf looked like before we started our journey. He got closer to the wagon and sounded off a playful bark, warning me to push myself up.

Yes, the books I could handle, as well as the research and having my two feet on the ground, but not the extra adventurous thrill ride that came with it.

Was I that boring?

Elmira grabbed my elbow and pulled me closer to her. She gave me a confident smirk and wrapped her arm around mine to keep me in place.

"You've got this, Lucy. I've been around many humans that have come through the portal and have trouble adjusting. Children don't have any problem, their minds are full of curiosity. You actually remind me of them."

"I do?" I questioned as I noticed a fast moving cloud, or at least I thought it was a cloud that went over us, causing a shadow. Once I looked up, I realized I was mistaken.

I gasped. *It was a dragon!*

I squealed and stood from my seat. Elmira grabbed the back of my dress to hold me steady, along with the horse's reins. "It's a dragon! Did you see that?!"

Elmira laughed, and my heart raced when I realized I just confirmed what she meant.

Ah, yes. I guess I exuded child-like excitement.

Anyone would be excited to see that, though. It was a freaking dragon!

I sat back down, and she continued to laugh. I put my hands on my lap and tried to contain myself, but the further away we got from the Cerulean Moon Kingdom, the more things I saw and wanted to explore.

A month living in the palace, visiting the local pack houses, playing around in the marketplace wasn't enough time to get acclimated. Especially before I was thrown into an area like the Monktona Woods that hadn't been explored at all.

Of course, the orcs have explored some of it, but they weren't great at writing. The shifters accompanying me are strong and very capable, but they had their reservations about going into the Wood alone. Orcs had alpha-like personalities, as if they are on high amounts of steroids like King Kane—Kane, I reminded myself. Kane and Clara don't like to be referred to by their titles often, and since they said they were more like family to my father and me, we were to address them as such.

Kane was nothing but raw power. He was a beast. His nickname suited him. The Beast. When he transformed into his animalistic body, he was a gigantic wolf-beast creature that stood up on two legs. It was by far the most horrifying thing I'd ever seen, and thankfully, he didn't see me gasp in horror when I watched from my guest room window as he sparred with his warriors.

He sparred and taught them. He wasn't a king who sat around the palace doing political things. Kane was very much a person and had a sweet personality that many do not see. He was loving and caring to his wife—mate?—and their daughter.

Now that we are traveling to a land with orcs, with more personalities like Kane, the possessive, grunty sort, I could only wonder what conflicts might arise. These alpha orcs had trouble being around each other, and we would have two traveling with us. How will that affect them and the shifters who were reluctant to be traveling into the Wood?

All these guys are just full of testosterone.

I nervously tugged at the delicate fabric of my dress, feeling the smooth texture between my fingers. Simultaneously, I gently scratched my neck, relieving an itch that had been bothering me.

Great, now I'm gonna get a rash.

Now that we were getting closer, I was rethinking everything.

"Hey!" Elmira grabbed my hand and pulled it away from my neck. "You keep doing that and the vampires will come out of the forest."

I gasped and slapped my neck with my hand.

My actions threw Elmira into a fit of giggles. "Honey, I'm kidding you. They don't eat humans. Well, not anymore."

I felt the color drain from my face.

"Okay," she drawled. "I think you're overstimulated. How about you hop in the back of the wagon and shut your eyes, hmm? Get away from the males?"

I frowned. "My father told you about that?"

She sighed and had me lean closer. "Your father said you weren't used to being around a lot of males. Said it was his fault. This trip is to help you. Every male here except for Dutton is mated to one of the females here. Dutton is just a flirt, but he means you no harm. I promise my life on it." She patted my knee and took both reins again.

There were five males, five females, so that must have meant that one female was not mated. Mated pairs stuck together; they couldn't be apart for long. "Are you not mated?"

Elmira's smile widened, her canine fangs dropping into a mischievous grin. "No, I'm not."

⁓

When we arrived at the wall that the entrance of the Monktona Wood lay beyond, it was a sight I didn't think I could ever imagine on my own. It was such a massive difference from the forests we had come across so far, that my brain couldn't process.

Thick, large leaves resembling dinner plates, possessing a waxy texture that not only appeared green, but exuded a mesmerizing blue hue, creating a captivating twinkle in the fading light. As my gaze delved deeper into the woods, a surge of excitement ran through me.

Darkness has already enveloped the surroundings. The air was dense with the scent of foliage, as bushes, underbrush, and towering trees, surpassing even the redwood forests from Earth, dominated the landscape.

I sat on the wagon in awe. The shifters were changing back into their human forms as a precaution, while Elmira clicked her tongue for the gigantic horses to move forward. They did hesitantly, with jagged trots and jerking heads. Their movements were not as graceful or smooth as during the first part of our journey.

They sensed this place was different, too. I was glad it wasn't just me.

"Stay close, Lucy. None of us have been here. The king and queen said to be vigilant. As long as we stay in this clearing, right on the other side of the wall, we should be fine. I'd rather wait for our guides to arrive before we venture any further."

I nodded while we entered through the wide opening of the broken wall. It was ancient, maybe even thousands of years old—no one could know for sure. No one had dared to cross it or fly over it before, because they thought their ancestors had a good reason to keep whatever was in the woods there. So, it had lain forgotten.

Discovering the orcs was a consequence of the war. The enemy tried to hide in the orcs' lands, and the orcs were not happy about it. The war in Bergarian ultimately concluded with the orcs joining the fight and bringing a hard-won peace to all kingdoms after years of conflict. The wall was mostly in ruins now, crumbled remnants of stone and magic that set apart two worlds. The orcs were free.

This land contained a lot of history, and fortunately, the kingdoms maintained impressive records of their past wars. I'd spent the past several nights of our journey sleeping under the stars and using the firelight to dig deeper into it, reading all I could about it.

"Stay here. I'm going to unhitch the horses and get them to the troughs." Elmira left no room for argument when she gave me a condescending glare and hopped off the wagon. I would not argue. I felt like an ant around her and everyone here.

The rest of the shifters came up behind the wagon, now clothed, thankfully, and pulled sleeping pads, food, and tents from the wagon. While we were safe to sleep under the stars while we traveled here, we were warned to sleep inside the tents in the Wood. We weren't sure what animals or insects we would cross, and it would be best while we were awake to be on the lookout and sleep well into the night.

"Coast is clear," Elmira said when she tied the horses to the post. "Come on, Lucy, stretch your legs."

I went to the side of the wagon, being careful not to trip. I was still getting used to wearing the moveable, breathable, and comfortable corset dress that most of the non-shifter women wore, which I felt at odds with. Once I reached the edge, Dutton was there with his hand held out.

"Come on, I don't bite..." he chuckled, "... hard."

Elmira let out an enormous sigh and crossed her arms. "Stop fucking around Dutton!" She glared at him and flipped him off. Elmira stomped over and put out her hand for me, then led me off the wagon. "Can't find good help these days. It's a damn shame. Come on, I'll grab your tent." She shot one more warning glare at Dutton, who smiled back and held his hands up in mock surrender.

"I'm gonna gut him from navel to nose," Elmira said under her breath.

I looked back and forth between the two. Was I sensing something there? He was staring at her even though she had already turned. She had a swing in her hips and tossed her hair over her shoulder.

Mating rituals were not my forte, but that was something I was going to have to watch. Are they mates or just sexual partners?

I covered my mouth and laughed, as we walked away and saw the campsite being set up. Tents for each couple, except for Dutton and Elmira, who were stealing glances at each other. Mine was nearly finished and just in time because darkness was falling.

When I put the finishing touches on my bed, we heard stomping coming through the woods. Then, a deep barrel of laughs came from the other end of the clearing. The horses tightened up on their reins, neighing and pulling, trying to get away from their posts. Two of the males went over to settle them, while I stood from my tent and held on to one of the poles for comfort.

A large, orc male was pushed into the clearing first, stumbling to one knee. He was large, like I expected, with a long braid down to his waist with both sides shaved. A loin cloth was the only thing covering his private areas, and straps of leather covered either side of his chest. He roared in anger and stood up quickly, facing the woods, only for another orc to stride out confidently. He was leaner than the first, with short hair, with no braid- reminded me of an ordinary, popular haircut the shifters had- and a wide smile on his face.

Definitely more approachable than the first.

"Greetings!" The one smiling raised his hand to wave at us. "I am Sugha, son of Eman, and this is Durz, son of Forge."

Durz stood, the dirt flying up around his bare feet. He patted himself down and strode forward. "Yes, I am Durz. Where is the human female, so I may smell her?"

Mary freaking Poppins!

Chapter Three

Simon

The wind had shifted.

I laid down the tool I used to dig under the soil and got the nutrient-rich roots I had been craving. I didn't know what they were called, but they bled a deep red and my mouth watered when I saw the bright liquid gush from the ground.

The root was sweet with sugar. It reminded me of the mouth-watering treats Calliope, the human I had protected for such a long time, would feed me beneath the table of her former home.

I perked one ear up to listen for any unfamiliar sounds, and my other hand reached inside the hole, too hungry to wait. Wetness seeped onto my fingers. I never thought I would have had such body parts, but here I was.

I took the handful of roots, letting the liquid drip down my wrist, arm and elbow, and trotted to the stream. My hooves, which I now only had two, were easier to walk on, as it had been some moons. I used to have four. I was so sturdy and confident with four, but now with two hands—with thumbs—I could do many tasks I never thought I would be able to.

I wasn't human, but not quite animal.

I pushed the roots into the stream, letting the dirt wash away. My taste buds changed when my appearance did. I could not eat everything in sight anymore. Food tasted dirty, when before I did not care about taste. Now, grit gets into my teeth, and it stays for days and hurts my stomach.

I pushed the roots into my mouth and let them crunch under my back teeth. My front teeth now had sharper points. They were no longer flat for me to be able to pull up the grasses from the soil. No, I can do much more now, such as tear and rip into food that I had no desire to eat before.

Like meat.

I had gained a new craving, one that I would have found repulsive in my past life. The texture and taste had been enlightening. Preparing it had been difficult, so I had resorted to stealing it from others who had prepared the bloody material. The enjoyment of seeing orcs blaming one another and trying to figure out who had stolen their prized food had been entertaining.

I let the last of the root slither down my throat. That was when the wind shifted again and new smells filled my lungs.

I had become attuned with the Wood. The shadows, the smells, tastes, and sounds, and there was a change that was quite unfamiliar.

The orcs were the primary beings that lived here besides the two human females. One was Ellie, mate to the leader of the tribe, and the other was Calliope—my best friend in my former life. I knew their smells quite well, but these unfamiliar scents were new to the Wood.

I raised my head with a sense of anticipation, my ears perking up as I trotted towards the destination the Wood guided me to. The vibrant leaves rustled and the branches swayed, their inviting gestures and gentle whispers seemed to call out specifically to me. In that moment, a peculiar sensation washed over me - as if the foliage was communicating, speaking directly to my very essence. These natural elements had become my steadfast companions ever since my transformation into what I was now.

I felt as if I was connected with nature, and a good thing too, since I could not communicate with anyone else. My face just could not form the words that I wanted.

Not that I had tried.

I had spent most of my time thus far learning to walk, using my hands, and making tools. I knew how to by watching the orcs from afar. It was difficult, but I tried to make them myself, so I did not have to steal them. I only borrowed what I needed. Most of it was from Calliope and her male.

Speaking? I did not have time for it.

Now, I was getting lonely. Being a full animal, I enjoyed companionship with my human. Watching over Calliope for so long had ingrained in me a sense of belonging, and now I did not know what to do with myself.

I wanted...someone else to take care of.

I trotted toward where the trees beckoned me. My hooves gently prodded the soil while I sought the strange noises and scents that came from within. I got closer to the mouth of the Wood where the orcs came and went, and I heard boisterous laughter.

I stiffened and bolted toward the thickest shrubbery I could find. I peered through the dense leaves and saw that this wasn't just a party of orcs to leave the Wood in search of females, but a group of shifters who had come inside.

I sniffed several times. The trees moved, wafting the scent of the group toward me. Wolves. Most of them smelled of wolves, but there was another smell that was intertwined within them. It smelled of fresh rain and damp grass. It was a natural scent, intensified, and my mouth salivated.

My elongated tongue glided slowly over the rough surface of my parted upper lip. The foreign presence of a newly formed fang startled me, and I felt it tear a wound into my tongue. A sharp breath filled my lungs as the taste of my own blood danced on my taste buds.

I hummed softly, pressing my fingers into the rich soil, feeling its coolness against my skin. The scent enveloped me, mingling with the tantalizing aroma that filled the air. I longed to sink my teeth into whatever was emitting that irresistible smell, but where it was coming from eluded me. Frustrated, I continued my search, my senses heightened, hoping to uncover the source of this mouthwatering temptation.

I patiently expected the rumble of my stomach, but it failed to make a sound. Instead, a taut sensation formed at the juncture between my legs, causing me to emit a low groan. I could feel my shaft, often referred to by the orcs as a cock or shaft, emerging from its hidden pocket between my legs and brushing against the balmy air.

It was hard, so painfully hard, and I wrapped my hand around the thick body part to ease the pain. Instead, a clear white fluid formed at the head, and when I took my hand up and down its length, I shuddered, as an amazing tingle ran down my spine.

The more I breathed in the scent, the more I wanted it.

What was it?

As I crept closer to the group of shifters, my senses were on high alert. The scent of rain and sweet dewy grass grew stronger, pulling me towards its source. My heart raced with anticipation and excitement, the temptation nearly overpowering me.

As I came as close as I could without being noticed, my hand still gripping my throbbing cock, I caught a glimpse of a single figure that seemed to be the focal point of the gathering. Her back was to me, and she was staring at the two orcs. One I knew to be Sugha and the other—it wasn't important. All I knew was that their eyes were on the female, and I didn't like it. A growl erupted in my throat, and my lip went into a snarl.

This female was tall and slender, with long limbs and short yellow hair falling around her face like a shadowy halo. The side of her face showed fear, and it took everything in me not to burst from the trees to save her.

I licked my lips, tasting blood again as I tried to decipher the complex feelings swirling within me. Was it because of my loneliness? Was this curiosity? Desire? Hunger? The line between them was blurred, and it seemed that every fiber of my being thirsted for this female.

Before I could make a decision, another shifter female stood in front of my female. She berated the unnamed orc, shoving a finger up in his face until she pushed him away. My shoulders relaxed, but the hand on my cock didn't.

Did I just say she was mine?

With each passing moment, my cock grew harder and more demanding, throbbing with every heartbeat. I couldn't help but wonder if this was how Calliope felt about her male—the orc she had claimed. Did it mean this female could be mine?

I shook my head and stroked the hair that grew on my chin. Couldn't possibly be? I was a monster. A half-human, half goat creature. I was not meant to be here.

Even so, I stroked my cock, watching her.

Does this female have hair that smells like soft, sweet hay? Does her skin feel like silky flower petals?

Her head turned toward my section of the Wood, and I froze.

"Hey?" her voice, like a song, broke me from my trance.

"Do you see that over there?" She pointed in my direction and my eyes widened. My heart quickened in my chest too much, and I felt my body seize.

No, not now, anytime but now.

My body went rigid, and my body fell to the ground. My cock was still hard and exposed, and my body lay frozen on the soft ground.

"Did you hear that?" I heard a male say out loud.

I grunted in my throat. I could already feel my muscles loosening. My body didn't stay frozen for long, and I felt my fingertips and limbs coming back to life as I heard footsteps approaching. I scrambled up when my body began functioning again, and I took light, hooved steps deeper into the Wood. My heart raced, but I didn't let it reach high levels. I calmed myself and let the Wood guide where I should go.

The wind pushed at my back, the branches bent for me as I was led further away, and the voices became distant.

That was close, too close, but her voice was so strong within my mind that it was as if she was whispering in my ear.

She had taken over my body, and I had not even come close to her.

What did this mean?

As I continued deeper into the wood, I couldn't shake the feeling that seeing her was no accident. This was far from over. The Wood around me seemed alive, and I couldn't help but feel drawn back to her. My mind returned to the human. My thoughts were consumed by the image of her face, her voice echoing in my ears, and the unmistakable sensation that our paths were destined to cross again.

The familiar stream that ran across the Wood came across my path. I came closer, my mouth parched. The closer I got to the water, the idea of drinking its waters was not as appealing as drinking in her presence. I felt an undeniable pull towards the female surrounded by shifters. It was as if an unseen force was drawing me towards her, and I found myself resisting the urge to turn back and confront her once more.

I leaned over the clear stream to drink, hoping that its cool water would quench both my thirst and my confusion. As I bent over the water, I caught my reflection on the still surface. My sharp fangs glinted in the dim light, and I couldn't help but think of how they might have looked to her - a terrifying sight for a defenseless human.

The human I once looked after did not see me as a threat. She was different and did not find many creatures terrifying. Her orc mate was a testimony to that. Calliope was different, though.

She found beauty in everything.

Even after I transformed, she sought me out. Now, I was afraid of what this female may see me as. A monster?

My fingers trailed along my mouth, touching my fangs, then I felt the ears that dangled on the side of my head. Even the orcs looked somewhat like a human. I was different, half goat, half human, and when the female gazed at the orcs, she looked at them in fear.

What would she do if she saw me?

A lump formed in my throat, and I slapped the water in front of me.

Would she find me hideous?

Was I worse than an orc? Orcs were repulsive to look at.

They were large, loud, annoying, and they smelled of rotten moss. They believed they owned the Wood. No one owned the Wood; the Wood owned itself.

The wind blew, and the gentle caress of the leaves fanned my back. What should I do about the female?

I huffed, feeling the heat of my breath on my lip.

Her smell came to me tenfold, and I knew what the Wood wanted me to do without having to say a word.

It wanted me to follow her, to ignore my thoughts, find the female and take her as my own.

I felt the bulge in my pouch that held my shaft. It's heavy, and I could feel my cock's head poke out of its safe compartment. It was hard and tight, and my body reacted to just the thought of her smell and the way she looked in my direction.

I hummed, taking in the fresh scent of her, as the Wood continued to bring in her smell.

The Wood silently tortured me. It would not let me retreat into its safe embrace. I would have to seek out the female once again. Perhaps next time, I would take her and bring her to my home.

CHAPTER FOUR

Lucy

Durz' thick thighs rubbed against each other when he stepped forward. His loincloth moved in a way that kept his private parts covered, but my face went red at the thought of a brisk breeze.

My head snapped up, and I looked his way when realization hit me.

Did he just say he was going to smell me?

"I beg your finest pardon!" I raised my hand to my chest and couldn't help but notice its small and delicate appearance. It was a stark contrast to his, which was large and robust. I found it surprising because my hand was typically swollen and bruised from my day-to-day activities of collecting plant samples, caring for animals, and occasionally dropping heavy objects on it.

I was clumsy.

"You will not be smelling any part of me!"

The wolves behind me chuckled, and Elmira bolted from an unknown location, standing in front of me to use herself as a shield. "You heard the human. Back off." Elmira stepped forward, shoving her finger to the giant's chest. "It seems you haven't learned your manners yet. Haven't you learned anything from the manual our gracious queen made for you?"

Sugha snickered from behind him. His shoulders rose and fell. "Does Durz strike you as a male that would want to read?" Sugha lifted an eyebrow and smiled.

No, I didn't believe so. Durz was the exact type of orc I pictured in my head: large, muscular, and his brain the size of a pea.

"Suppose not." Elmira shared the thoughts in my head and backed away but still kept my body covered. "You stay away from Lucy. She is my charge, and I won't have you making her feel uncomfortable. It's under order of the queen."

Durz didn't care. He still stared at me like I was a puzzle he was trying to figure out. I was the same. I stared at him with questions. This was the first time I'd seen an orc in person. When I first heard that orcs lived in this realm, I thought them to be hideous, like in the *Lord of the Rings*. Thank heavens he didn't look like those orcs. Sugha and Durz were the opposite. They were easier on the eyes.

I also didn't feel threatened by them as I should've been. The more human-like males were who I had trouble with. I could see having conversations with Sugha was going to be easier than Dutton, or any of the other men around me. I couldn't put my finger on why that was, but I was already relaxing at the thought of it.

"I won't bother her," Durz said to both of us when he turned away. "She isn't my miresa—er, mate as you all call them. But if she was, I would have carted her off and made her mine, no matter what your order was."

My face grew red, and I looked away. Shifters were similar in their actions. One could construe their acts as barbaric, but that was the way the cultures were in this realm. It could also vary from couple to couple.

When my face was turned away, I saw a shimmer in the darkened part of the wood. I tilted my head to get a better look.

Elmira and Durz argued, but I blocked them out when the bushes moved and the light sources reflected off something inside the darkness of the brush.

"Hey?" My voice came out stronger than I intended, but it made the arguing stop behind me. "Do you see that over there?" I pointed in the general direction of the shrubs. It was a reasonable distance away, but there was no denying something was there. A thump sounded, and all the wolves behind me stiffened.

"I'll check." Durz removed the blade at his side and widened his stance. The males took off with him and fanned out around to give him space.

As they arrived at the location, they parted the dense undergrowth, their weapons slicing through the foliage with a sharp swish. The leaves rustled and twigs snapped, accompanied by the earthy scent of crushed vegetation.

"Anything?" I stood on my tiptoes as I tried to see over the wall of female shifters that gathered around me.

Sugha stood by my side with his arms crossed.

"Strange," Durz said when he sheathed his sword. "No scent, but there was something there. You can see where someone broke the branches and indented the soil. The only remains was some fur on the branches." He came back with the rest of the crew and held up a minuscule amount of hair in his claws.

I squinted my eyes and saw it was only a few threads. "So, an animal?" I rose to my tiptoes again and plucked it from him.

He grunted and turned away. "Aye, no smell, though. Strange."

I concentrated on the fur, my eyes crossing as I felt its fibers. It was soft and smooth, not coarse like most animals you would find in a jungle. Normally, you find fur to be slightly coarse from living outside. I was also surprised that the orc and shifter, with their exceptionally strong noses, couldn't detect a scent.

Dutton came closer and took to sniff from my fingers. I shied away but held it out for him.

He tutted. "Yeah, no smell."

"That's what I said, wolf. No scent," Durz snapped.

Dutton's muscles tensed, emitting a low growl that reverberated through the air. With a rigid posture, his back stood straight like a steel rod. A mixture of disdain and revulsion twisted his lip, emanating a palpable sense of disgust. "Wolves' noses are better; I'm just making sure."

Durz scoffed and slammed an arm over his chest. "Orcs are stronger. We know the Wood. What we say goes."

Feeling the tension rise and watching the shifters gathering around with bags of peanuts and jerky to watch a fight, I stepped between them.

"Isn't there a rare plant that can cancel out the smells and scents of beings? Shifter, fae, and animal?" I held onto the fur with my fingers and glanced between the two heavily breathing males.

Durz grunted in response and nodded once. "Aye, yellowcress. It grows in the northern mountains with the dragons, but we have grown it here in the south as of late. Helps keep the ogres away from the human females. We should grab a sack from the farm keepers," he told Sugha, who was wiping a tear from his eye from the earlier scuffle.

"I already brought some. Can never be too prepared." He held up a bag. "Now leave the human bean alone. Give the poor thing some space."

Elmira blinked several times. "Bean? What do you mean, bean? Who is a bean?"

I giggled. "I think he means human *be-ing*."

Sugha's face turns a deep shade of green. "Ah, right. *Be-ing*. I am still learning the human sayings. My apologies."

Despite him being a green man—male—and larger than the shifters, I felt better with the *monsters*, as everyone in Bergarian seemed to call them. Even Durz, with his habit of smelling and his aggression over Dutton, I found comical.

The idea that an animal or another being covered themselves in yellowcress meant that we were being watched, and it unlocked a new fear inside me. Something was out there, watching, and it did not want to be found. With the fibers in my hand, I knew I had to figure out if it was really an animal that was particularly smart or something different entirely.

"It's no matter, a large group like us won't have any problems dealing with whatever it was," Dutton said. "As long as Lucy adheres to the rules, there should be no problems."

I gave a slow nod. It wasn't like they could go after whoever was hiding. There was no scent, and splitting up now would not be wise. The light sources were setting, and as long as I stayed with at least two or three shifters or an orc, I should be safe.

The group worked quickly to unload most of the supplies. Despite leaving a lot of my gear in the wagon, I retrieved a rudimentary microscope, one that was easy to travel with and not completely electric like back on Earth. I had to make do with no electricity and use a small candle to use as light to see through it.

When the bonfire was at full roar, I unfolded my small worktable and got to work with the strands I still held tight to. I didn't have much to work with, and I would not lose them.

I placed the five that I had between the glass slides and carefully slid them under the microscope. My heart raced with the prospect that I could find out what animal that was staring at us from the bush.

I closed one eye, and my tongue poked out at the side of my mouth. It was a terrible habit, but it was the only way to get the microscope to adjust just right, so I could get it into focus.

I clicked my tongue. Huh.

I wasn't looking at just animal fur or hair.

It was both.

Human hair is pigmented evenly and has a greater density towards the cuticle, while animal hair tends to have more centralized pigmentation and a higher overall density.

My hair color was similar to the fur. Did I somehow contaminate my sample? I plucked some hair from the top of my head and pushed it under the microscope.

The color was close to identical.

I let out a puff of air and shook my head.

Possible cross-contamination.

That meant it must have been an animal because an animal couldn't have both. No worries about a being trying to hurt us, then.

I heard a loud smack, and Dutton jumped over the fire to run away from Elmira, who was rubbing her butt. She let out a playful growl, and her claws lengthened as she chased after him.

Hmm, yes, strange courting practices.

The soft, setting light sources cast a warm, golden glow over the shaded area, painting the sky with hues of orange and pink. As I stood there, a gentle breeze rustled the leaves, creating a soothing melody. The delicious aroma of food wafted through the air, inviting me to indulge. However, a shadow hovered over me, and I stared up to see Sugha smiling down at me.

"Lucy, why don't you come eat? The exploring hasn't even started yet, and you've started working."

"Right, sorry. I was trying to figure out if it was an animal or person that was in the bushes."

Sugha hummed thoughtfully. "I'm sure it isn't anything to worry about. Besides, with two orcs at your party, I doubt they would even try to come close. Whatever it may be. Animals stay away, and if it was an ogre, they'd make themselves known."

Yes, ogres. Ogres are large, smelly creatures and, luckily, are loud. We should know when they were coming. They have a taste for humans specifically and want to 'use' them in not such wholesome ways.

I wanted to throw up at the thought of that.

Ogres aren't too bright though, so outsmarting them would be my best way to evade them. I was not worried.

"And with two orcs here in the party, that won't cause tension?"

Sugha huffed a laugh. "I am the smarter orc. I know when to pick my battles. Have no worries, dear Lucy, I will let Durz think he is in charge, for the sake of the mission." He cupped his large hand to his face and whispered, "We all really know who is in charge, though."

I snorted and stood, brushing off my skirt. "Indeed. Thank you. You've made me feel comfortable. That's hard to do."

Sugha's eyes softened. "Of course. We may look like monsters to everyone else here, but really, we only wish to keep the ones we care about safe."

CHAPTER FIVE

Simon

I COULDN'T RESIST FOR long, returning swiftly after my initial escape from the group. The allure of her scent enveloped me, leaving me utterly captivated. It consumed my senses, overpowering even the most tempting of food to fill my belly.

When I was fully an animal, that was all I cared about: having my belly full and satisfied. To have something in my mouth, to chew, and wander aimlessly through life. I had no worries except to make sure the human I watched over had me to pet when she wanted.

I inhaled deeply, the cool breeze from the Wood brushing against my skin, carrying with it the sweet scent of her presence. The distant group of shifters, orcs, and the female were oblivious to my presence, too far away to hear or catch a whiff of my scent. A smirk formed on my lips, satisfaction washing over me.

I could be sneaky, too.

From my position, I could see her clearly. Always with a notebook in her hand, a satchel at her side, and pencils filled with color. She fiddled with the straps often, flipping them back and forth between her fingers.

She looked so soft, so delicate. Humans were, but I didn't know how much. I had fur before, now that I had my own skin, I wanted to touch her with my fingers.

Would she like my touch? Would she like my smell?

As my chest thumped wildly, causing the heat of my body to rise, I couldn't help but notice the gentle rise and fall of her chest as she breathed. Her skin appeared so smooth.

Touch, I wanted touch.

With each step closer to her, I couldn't help but wonder if she would welcome getting to know me. Would she feel the same fire current that surged through me at the mere thought of it?

Would she appreciate my unique scent, the remnants of my previous life, as a creature of fur? Would it intrigue her or would she just find me strange? Or would she want to be near me at all, for I was the only creature like me.

The desire to bridge the gap between us grew stronger, as if an invisible force pulled me toward her. I yearned to be closer.

This female never stayed still. Her feet tapped on the purple moss before her, making the lights fly into the air. Her eyes darted through the scene before her, memorizing everything in her sight.

They had discarded the horses and left them other orcs when they first came to the Wood, and the shifters had become mules, carrying all of their belongings. They dropped the supplies unceremoniously and worked to set up the tents.

Durz stretched his back and reached behind him, pulling his sword from his sheath and stabbing it into the ground. "Here is good. Lucy will find many things here to record. There is a hot spring up ahead, and plenty of animals that have not seen shifters. They will be curious, and we won't have to hunt for them to come near."

I tilted my head, but my horns got caught on a nearby branch, and I had to tug them away.

They were staying.

The female's radiant smile stretched across her face, reaching her sparkling eyes as she aimed it at Sugha. With a swift motion, my sharp claws scraped against the rough surface of a weathered tree stump, sending fragments of wood soaring through the air, before falling to the ground. Inhaling deeply, my nostrils widened, capturing the pungent scent once more, and igniting my senses.

I didn't like her smiles directed toward another male, especially to an orc. I'd already had one orc take away a companion; I would not have this orc take away what should be mine.

Yet, he has not claimed her, unless he was trying to be subtle. He was one of the smarter orcs. Sugha let the other do what he wanted, while he nodded and did not start a fight.

I scratched at the base of my horns and decided to get closer.

I'd kept my distance from the group, afraid of getting caught, but these past few days had been excruciating. The sight of her, the sound of her laughter, her scent - they all called to me, making it harder to resist.

I licked my lips when her scent penetrated my nose, and my treacherous body responded immediately. How could I have never known what this feeling was before? I had seen males like me, when I was a goat, mount a female, but I never had the desire.

But with this female, I feel the need to do it to her.

I shook my head and got on my hands and knees, so I could stay low and in the thickest part of the greenery.

She was close; so close, I could nearly smell her breath.

How could I think about mounting her?

I was not an animal.

But I was.

Partly.

The animal part of me wanted it, demanded it. My human side held me back.

No, what would Calliope think of me if I ever did such a thing to another female like her? I couldn't– wouldn't– let the animal in me do that. Never.

But if she were willing?

I held in the whimper that lingered in the back of my throat.

"Look at this!" I heard her whisper-yell across the campsite.

I froze in fear, thinking she'd caught me, but her smile widened and her eyes twinkled at the blue light buzzing between us.

"Is this a whisp?" she asked breathlessly and held out her finger to touch it.

Elmira lowered herself to a crouching position, and her eyes darted between the whisp and the female.

"Yeah. It's a whisp. They are pretty important in this realm. Do you know what they are, Lucy?"

Lucy. The name rung in my ears when the other female called the human by her name. Now that I had her name, I tried to whisper it to myself but still was not used to moving my lips and tongue to form the word.

"I was told about them briefly," she said. "There was a lot to learn in just a month." Her finger grazed the light, and it made a whirling sound.

I watched in awe until it jumped into the foliage where I hid, and I reared back.

I shook my head and wanted to crawl away. It danced around atop of my horns and shot right back out of the bush toward Lucy. I quietly got back into position, and looked through the bush again, to see the whisp was keeping Lucy entertained again.

"Are they an insect?" she asked, looking even more enthralled. "Or some type of pixie?" She held her finger out, and the whisp touched it, then danced up her wrist, along her arm, and whirled around her hair. More whisps appeared and dove into her hair, and before long, it looked like an enormous ball of mess until they exploded into thin air.

"What just happened?" Lucy asked, smiling as she pushed her tangled hair back down.

Elmira lay down in the grass, pulled a long wheat blade, and stuck it into her mouth. "Whisps lead you to your fate." She chewed. "And they are also big troublemakers. Males don't like them much because, well, they cause more trouble for them. The females, it just gets them what they need."

Lucy tilted her head and stared at the ground. "Do whisps lead humans to their fate, or just the supernaturals?"

Elmira smiled mischievously. "Aye, they do. Ellie, who is mated to Sugha's brother, Thorn, was brought to him by the whisps. It wasn't a fairytale meeting, but whisps led her to her fate and ultimately, her mate. Thorn knew before Ellie. Supernaturals; it hits different. Smell, possessiveness, we just know."

My heart thundered in my chest, and my smile widened. Then, I must not be imagining things. Lucy, this female, was my mate. I had been gifted a mate, a companion. Someone to love.

This was why my body reacted to her. Her scent, her voice, her beauty, it was because fate had gifted her to me. This Moon Goddess I had heard Calliope speak about all the time, she had given me a mate!

I could barely keep the vibrations of excitement from leaving my body.

I had a female.

Mine.

Night fell, and the embers of the fire smoldered beneath the stars. Snores came from the tents, and even the largest orc was asleep, who'd said he would remain awake through the night. His heavy breathing and his body releasing an awful smell from a relaxed backside, were signs that he was in a deep sleep. Sugha was patrolling, but he had taken off into the Wood. If I had the timing correct, he wouldn't be back for a while.

My body throbbed with exhaustion from remaining crouched in my concealed spot for what felt like an eternity. The longing to catch sight of Lucy grew overwhelming. Slowly, I rose to my full height, feeling the strain in my muscles as I stretched. The sound of my spine cracking echoed through the stillness. As I inhaled deeply, her scent filled me with determination. Cautiously, I crouched, determined to remain hidden, even if the likelihood of being spotted was slim.

Since transforming into this creature, my hearing had increased tenfold. The once-dull sounds now reverberated through my ears, sharpening my senses. With my elongated ears drooping low beside my face, I twitched them several times, ensuring that I could catch even the faintest of whispers behind me.

I went straight toward her tent, her smell permeating the air. The light was dim inside when I got to the entrance, and I folded back the fabric to make sure that she was indeed asleep. She was, her notebook on her chest, her head propped up on several pillows, working late into the night.

I stepped inside and blew out the light. I didn't need anyone outside to see my silhouette. After a moment, my eyes adjusted, and my body began to shake as I drew closer to her.

I couldn't believe I was here. I was so close to what was mine, who was going to be mine.

I would protect her and keep her safe. Just like the orcs do with their mates.

My hands trembled as I cautiously approached. I kneeled silently beside her bed, as she lay there, oblivious to the lurking danger. A surge of anger coursed through me, as the weight of responsibility settled upon me. Sugha, unaware of the impending threat, had failed to safeguard her or the rest of the group. The ease with which I had infiltrated the camp filled me with a mix of frustration and anger.

Maybe I was just too good.

I huffed at that thought. I wasn't that good.

I leaned over her, getting more of her in my sight. It was hard not to touch. My instincts were going wild, telling me to take her while she slept. I should take her to my home, where she would be safe. I could not do that, however. Not when she looked happy with these people.

I didn't know if she would like me. She may find me more like a monster.

I knelt beside her for a long while until my patience ran out. I picked up her arm and held her wrist to my nose. I took a long pull of her scent and sighed, poking my tongue from my lips and taking a tentative lick.

I groaned.

She tasted sweet.

Better than any grass or hay I'd ever tasted.

I delicately grasped her wrist. A sigh escaped me, at enjoying the softness of her soft skin. I pulled her wrist behind my ear and felt the coolness of her skin against my fingertips.

While I have hidden my scent from the Wood, there was one place I could release my scent just enough where I could still keep myself safe and place it on my female.

With a gentle motion, I nuzzled her wrist behind my ear, careful not to disturb her slumber. Slowly, I pulled it away. I brought her delicate wrist closer to me and savored the harmonious blend of our scents.

Mmm, I enjoyed my scent on her.

CHAPTER SIX

Lucy

I FELT THE WARMTH of his breath caressing my exposed breasts, sending tingles down my spine. His hands held onto my hips with a firm grip, as my body arched in response. The anticipation heightened, craving to experience the sensation of his mouth on my sensitive nipples and the gentle brush of his teeth against their peaks. That desire, the one everyone spoke of, the one I had devoured in books for so long, the urge to finally let my body take over, was there.

His warm breath cascaded down the gentle slope between my breasts, caressing my skin and leaving a trail of warm saliva in its wake. As it descended further, it cooled against my delicate navel, sending another shiver of desire coursing through my body. With deliberate tenderness, his hand traced a path upward, exploring every curve, until they found their place, firmly cupping my breast. The touch was electrifying, heightened by the sharpness of his nails.

His nails were sharp, sharper than I ever thought a man would have. I felt it when he gripped my breast firmly, nearly piercing the skin. Surprisingly, the hint of pain ignited a primal response within me, intensifying the growing ache between my thighs. My senses were heightened. My pussy was wet and aching, and my clit begged to be touched. I could feel my heart beating erratically in my chest.

If I prayed to some deity, I'd be screaming their name now, thanking them for finally feeling desire and lust. I've craved it but never had the motivation? The want? The need?

I whimpered when their mouth connected to my nipple, sucking, licking, and flicking their rough tongue against it. Instead of feeling warmth, fire erupted in my belly and went straight to my core. My legs rubbed against each other, trying to get friction.

I panted, needing more, but I couldn't express what.

In my previous experiences, I had engaged in solitary play. However, this encounter was distinctively different. It felt like a collision of fire and ice, engulfing my entire being. The air was thick with steam, rising from my body and creating an even more enjoyable experience.

A low growl came from the being's throat. My head automatically turned, baring my neck. I surrendered completely to this man—creature. It had to be a creature. From my studies of this realm, this was how females bared their necks for their males to bite or claim them.

I had secretly wanted it to happen to me.

It was such a turn-on, to give up, to submit. Eventually, males did the same for the females, but why did I love it so much?

Why, when I was deathly afraid of men in general?

But this was a creature, not just a man; it had to be a creature, I decided.

My heart pounded in my ears like a thunderstorm, as the other hand stealthily ventured down my stomach. His mouth remained locked on my breast. The vibrations of his low hum tingled across my skin, sending shivers down my spine. With a sudden surge of desire, my hands swiftly reached behind his head, entwining themselves in his soft, luscious curls. I tenderly caressed his head, pulling him closer to me. His lower body, enveloped in furred garments, brushed against mine, igniting a greater fire within me. And then, in an electrifying moment, I could feel the weighty, elongated, moist shaft pressing against my leg, intensifying the longing between us.

Catnip almighty! I was a cat in heat.

My leg moved and rubbed against that thickened shaft, as my hands reached higher on his head, and then I knew something was really different. He had horns on top of his head, but before I had time to react, a finger slid into my body.

I gasped, my body experiencing something completely new. I knew what a dildo was; I knew what it was like to put something in my body, but not something warm, hot and, damnit, he was curling his finger in places I didn't even know existed.

Warm lips descended upon mine, hesitant at first, but so was I. They were slightly furred, and I relished how soft they were. I moaned into the kiss, as his tongue swept into my mouth, and my body melted in the moment.

My leg lifted, giving them better access for his finger, which now became two. It was a stretch, but who was I to care when I was feeling this horny for the first time since... ever?

His fingers thrust into me harder, with my body following him. I gasped and moaned, and his tiny growls grew louder.

It wasn't until I felt my body had reached its point and I tumbled over the peak, that I fell apart in his arms, completely spent with the best orgasm of my damn life.

I opened my eyes to see the intruder who had invaded my tent and given me the most mind-blowing orgasm, but I was alone. It was just a dream! I had pleasured myself, with my fingers buried into my own pussy and my other hand on top of my nipple, still pinching it.

Well, that was embarrassing.

I slapped my face with the nipple-pinching hand. I hope no one heard me moan, or coming for that matter.

I pulled my fingers from between my legs and found the evidence of my orgasm coating my fingers. I was wet, soaking actually, and it made me realize I was, in fact, not broken. I just wished I could find someone I was actually attracted to, so I could do this more often.

Who was that in my dreams, though? I wish I had opened my eyes to see his face, but it felt so real I didn't want it to stop. I didn't want to think that once I opened them, they would disappear, or I would freak out.

Of course, it was a dream. No one in their right mind would come into the tent of a sleeping woman and stare down at them.

I scoffed and went to the water basin to wash my hands. It was just absolutely absurd.

After getting dressed and making sure I had cleaned up enough to leave the tent, I grabbed my notebook and stepped outside. The fire was already set for breakfast, and Sugha and Durz were already smoking a boar.

The shifters had gathered wood to put into the fire, and when I approached, they all stopped, the wood they carried dropping to the ground as they spun in my direction.

I stiffened and balled my hand into fists. Crap, did I still smell of my earlier activities?

Dutton sniffed the air, and Elmira gave me a wary glance. "Lucy?" She tilted her head as she approached.

My face turned bright pink, and I shook my head. "Please don't tell me you can smell it. I think I just might die!" I buried my face into my hands and backed away.

Elmira held out her hand, and I jerked away.

"No! Don't touch me! Ugh! I can't believe that you can still smell that after I washed it off! I can't even practice self-care around here. I didn't know shifters and orcs could smell arousal even after you washed it off. I swear I only came once!"

Elmira's eyes widened, and she looked back at the rest of the group.

"You think we can smell your arousal?" she whispered.

I blinked several times and stared back at everyone. "Yes? Why else is everyone looking at me like that?"

White on rice, are you kidding me right now? Did I just tell everyone I masturbated when I didn't have to?

"I'll have you know, masturbating is very normal. I shouldn't feel any shame about it. But, I am feeling uncomfortable talking about it, with people who do not find the scientific ways interesting and just want to poke fun and stare at me."

The group just stared back.

I was ready to crawl back into my tent and die. Maybe even see if I could orgasm once more before I kicked the bucket, because, heck, my body was on a roll right now.

Elmira grabbed my wrist and brought it to her nose.

"Elmira! What in the name of Charles Darwin are you doing?" I tried to pull my arm away, but she held it still.

"You have been scent-marked," she growled. "Someone has marked you as theirs," she snarled and turned back to the rest of the group.

I took my wrist back and smelled it. I didn't smell anything particularly different about it. Maybe a hint of marigold, but I thought it was the soap. I sniffed my other wrist and smelled nothing.

I went back and forth, smelling between each wrist.

Huh, that was weird.

It smelled... nice. I continued to sniff, and I felt dampness between my thighs. My head perked up, and my breasts felt heavy, like they wanted to be held. Great! Now, I was thinking of *them* as sentient beings.

Yes, your pussy wants to be fucked.

Was I ovulating? I must be ovulating.

I needed to check my chart.

"Who scent-marked her?" Elmira growled out. "Was it you, Durz?!"

Durz stood from his log and crunched his iron cup in his hand. "How dare you, dog. I would never! She is not my miresa! I would never!"

Durz spat on the ground, his face red with anger. "I would never mark her without her permission! Monster, I am not!"

Sugha put a hand on his friend's shoulder, trying to calm him down. "Easy, Durz. We don't know who did it. It could have been anyone."

Could it have been the guy in my dreams? Or was there someone that really came into my tent and shoved my fingers up my pussy to cover it up. My face paled.

They touched me so intimately and made me feel things I never thought possible. I felt a stirring in my body, right now when I thought about him, and my cheeks grew warm at the memory of his hands on me.

Maybe I was broken.

I liked creepy dudes that came into my tent!

I had to stop reading dark romance.

Elmira glared at everyone in the group, her eyes narrowing as she searched for the culprit. But no one seemed to confess to the act.

"Can't you just sniff them?" I nudged her. I mean, it could be one of them, but I thought the man might have horns if my memory served me correctly.

Dutton crossed his arms. "You just don't go around sniffing shifters. It isn't polite. We aren't dogs." He glanced over at Durz. "You can smell me to check. I'm the only unmated male shifter here. I don't mind proving my innocence. Everyone else has a mate."

Elmira took in a whiff and shook her head. "I knew it wasn't you, just had to be sure. For precaution," she added.

Dutton winked at her and stepped back.

Their flirting was something else.

"What about you two?" Dutton jerked his head to the orcs. They came up to Elmira, just to placate her, too. I knew it wasn't them; they wouldn't have been able to fit in my tent.

They also didn't have horns.

Hard, male horns that would feel good to rub up against my thighs—

Crap. I was in trouble. I sniffed my wrist again and then quickly pushed it to my side.

I stood there and didn't dare to look at anyone. Instead, I kept my eyes on the pot of porridge that sat on a stump nearby, and that was when I saw the faint ripples that came from the middle.

Elmira, Dutton, and the orcs were discussing their next move, but all I could concentrate on were the vibrations I could now feel from the ground. "Uh, guys?" I went over to them and patted Elmira on the shoulder. "Guys!"

They all stopped talking and stared down at me. "Look." I pointed to the thick porridge, where the ripples were now sloshing in the pot.

Everyone went quiet, and the trees of the Wood swayed, although the birds were quiet. Animals started running through the camp, uncaring about who we were.

"Shit," Dutton said as he grabbed me and threw me over his shoulder.

"What's going on?" I screamed, holding onto my notebook for dear life.

"Ogre," Sugha growled. "A big one. Get everyone out of here, grab what you can carry, and go. We don't need Lucy to be seen, or he won't stop."

Durz unsheathed his massive sword from his back, causing a resounding 'shing' through the clearing.

Dutton hurriedly guided me towards the opposite end of the camp. An ear-splitting roar erupted from the ogre, and fear pierced my heart as soon as I saw the creature. An overpowering stench, so repugnant and indescribable, engulfed the entire camp. The nauseating odor was so intense that everyone instinctively gagged, desperately covering their mouths with their hands.

"Orcs and wolves," the ogre snarled. He took a deep breath in, even with the snot falling down his nose and into his mouth. The loin cloth he wore dragged on the ground, and his feet were massive, and his toenails were full of trash. The cloth only covered his privates, and his enormous belly hung over it. He didn't even need the cloth; his belly would cover his privates just fine.

"And, hu-man."

"Time to go." Dutton took off into the woods, his arms wrapped around my legs. I watched as the ogre didn't even flinch as the shifters changed into wolves, and the ogre began his attack.

Chapter Seven

Lucy

Dutton raced through the trees like his butt was on fire.

The gnarled branches scraped relentlessly against my trembling arms and stinging thighs, their sharp edges leaving faint red trails. Yet, with every ounce of strength, I clung desperately to Dutton, my heart pounding in my chest. I had no qualms about Dutton holding onto me or worrying about a man touching me. Not when that ogre was back there fighting against the entire camp.

The repulsive ogre, with his grotesque features, had a repugnant stench emanating from his hulking frame. His enormous, wicked, yellow eyes fixated on me as if I were his next meal.

I dry heaved at the thought of that thing coming any closer to me and gripped onto Dutton's tunic a little tighter.

"Try to keep quiet," he whispered as he ran through the thicket. More scrapes slid across my skin, and I tried not to wince.

Sure, I was used to the outdoors, sleeping, roughing it, but I hadn't done a lot of manual labor. I was a spoiled researcher because of my father. No ill will toward him, at all, but I now wished my skin was toughened up, just a little.

Dutton effortlessly leaped over a fallen log, causing my stomach to collide with his strong, muscled shoulder. The air filled with the sound of rustling leaves and my empty stomach trying to come up my throat.

Good thing I hadn't eaten breakfast yet, because it would be all over his back by now.

Dutton stopped, his body turned to look from left to right. As he did, my body was slung like a rag doll. He trotted over to a large, hollow log and threw me off his shoulder, my head dizzy. He set me down at the mouth of the log, and I put my hand over my head to steady myself.

Dutton didn't check on me; instead, his eyes were on the surroundings. "Get in and don't make a sound," he ordered through gritted teeth.

I did as he said, keeping my dress over my body, and scooted inside.

"No matter what you hear, you don't come out, do you understand?"

He stared at me. The command was final, and I nodded to appease him. I didn't want to be an ogre's fudging toy then his breakfast, lunch, and dinner. I thought these ogres were stupid, but something told me that this ogre meant business.

"I thought..." I went to say, but Dutton pinned me with a look. "This one is different, Lucy. He's the oldest, biggest. The orcs warned us about this one. He will be hard to get rid of."

A horn blasted in the distance, and my stomach dropped. If that horn was blown, it meant that Sugha was calling for more orcs, for help.

Orcs didn't like calling for help, so it must have been serious.

"I need to go back." He stood up, growled under his breath, and grabbed bushes from ten feet away to put them in front of the trunk of the tree.

I crawled toward him. I could feel the blood draining from my face when I grabbed his wrist, but I needed to know.

"Elmira... is she your mate?" I barely got it out when his demeanor softened, and his lip curled into a smile.

"That she is." Dutton continued to pack shrubs around me and pushed my head back into the log.

I shook my head. "Then why haven't you mated with her? Don't you want her?"

Dutton scoffed and kneeled at the base of the trunk. "I suppose you wouldn't get it. You're human and just arrived in this realm, but just because she's my mate doesn't mean she will automatically accept the bond." He stared off into the distance from where we came. "We are destined to be together, but the journey to get there is part of the fun. Besides,"—he winked—"I enjoy riling her up, pulling out the bond. Stretching the bond longer intensifies the pleasure, until one day she will jump my bones and fuck me into oblivion."

My face regained its color as the blood that had drained from it was replenished, turning my face crimson.

"I see." I ducked back inside the log to contemplate what he just said when I heard a roar.

"Stay in the log until I come back." He pulled a sack from his pocket and untied the twine. He sprinkled the powder around the trunk and where his feet had been. The yellowcress was the only thing keeping me safe right now.

I leaned back into the damp wood. The moss and various plants that grew inside were being trampled by me, but I didn't have it in my heart to care. I was hiding for my life and felt silly for doing it.

The orcs and the shifters were fighting for me, and I was hiding like a tiny child. I wiped my hand down my face, feeling the guilt weighing heavy on my chest. They knew this could be a dangerous excursion, but it didn't make me feel any better. We hadn't been out here for a full week and were already facing problems.

What if someone died? If one person died who was mated, their partner would follow because two souls bound cannot live without each other. That was hard for me to grasp because I hadn't seen it before, but if someone died because of this ogre, I would see it firsthand.

Mates could live for a long while here, too. Everything lives a long time, even eternity if they didn't get killed with a weapon or another person in a spar. I couldn't believe that people here didn't age past thirty as well.

There are a few humans who live here. We will grow old and die, unless we find a mate. Like my father, or me. I giggled at that thought. My father, nearly eighty years old, finding a mate. They say coming to this realm is no mistake, that every human that arrives is destined, fated for something greater.

I had yet to believe that, but then again, the dream from last night was still stuck in my head. If that orgasm was my destiny, I'd die a smiling woman.

I let out a puff of breath.

Why was I thinking about that when an ogre was attacking the camp?

A branch snapped from outside, and my heart stopped. The notebook that I had carried like a security blanket crinkled under my weight. I stopped breathing, thinking that it would help whatever was outside to walk away.

The yellowcress would keep my scent hidden, but moving, talking, and breathing? They could listen and find me without question.

The small taps of movement came closer, and my eyes widened when I saw a shadow at the entrance of the log. I closed my eyes, curled my legs up toward me, and wrapped my arms around them. I hoped that by acting as if I wasn't there, they would think I wasn't there. Because I had nowhere else to go. The other end of the log was crushed, leaving my entry as my only exit.

Branches moved, and the greenery slipped away. I could see it in my mind, even though my eyes were closed. The breeze came inside, moving away the musty scent of the log.

Maybe it was Dutton?

No, Dutton would have made an announcement. He was too cocky. He wouldn't scare me. At least, try not to scare me.

A warm breath fell on the scratches I got from being hurled through the Wood, and a growl came from the creature, which sounded so familiar. It was the same growl from my dreams.

My eyes opened, staring down into my lap, and I knew I had to look.

I raised my head, turning it slowly, ready to meet the creature that had its nose sniffing my arm. So far, they hadn't hurt me, but I wasn't about to rush my movements and make a grave mistake.

As a rough tongue cautiously brushed against a scratch, a tingling sensation spread through my body, eliciting an intense shiver of pleasure. From the periphery of my vision, I caught sight of a pair of horns gracefully bending down, their tips gently grazing my skin, accompanied by the sound of delicate licking.

Was it a goat? A ram?

The curls on top of its head were blocking my view.

"Um, hello?" I spoke shakily, and then I saw the most golden eyes I had ever seen. The pupils weren't human, reminding me of an animal. His pupils were like a goat's, which were rectangular in shape. The nose was also more animal like, with slits going upward and with fur on. Their lips were similar to a human's, but the top lip had a split just as a ram or a goat, with whiskers and soft hair.

I wasn't sure what I was looking at, but it was no creature I had ever heard of in all of Bergarian. All creatures looked human-like. Even the orcs, except they were green, and their private parts were yet to be talked about openly.

This... was an animal with human-like qualities.

"Hello there." I laughed nervously.

Although I hadn't seen their body yet, I was quite disturbed by the way my body reacted when they leaned back down and continued licking the scratches on my arms.

Oh, this was bad, so bad.

This was an animal, right? I should not have these sorts of feelings.

I pulled my arm away slowly, but the creature whined and grabbed hold of it. Four fingers and an opposable thumb with claws, wrapped around my wrist and pulled it back. I didn't fight; too shocked to see that this thing had an actual hand.

I mean, what did I expect? A hoof?

I laughed internally, hoping not to spook the thing.

"Hey, um, can you stop?" The creature stopped and tilted his head up at me like he understood, then backed away. He was on his knees, and his lower body was fur, no pants. The fur was part of his body.

He studied me with those piercing golden eyes, and a wave of unease washed over me as I realized this creature seemed to comprehend my words. How was this possible? No one told me there were beings like this. The creature's partially human, partially animal appearance unsettled me further.

As it backed away, I climbed out of the log and scrambled to my feet, putting some distance between us. My heart raced in my chest, unsure of what to do next. Was this creature a threat or something else entirely?

I studied it, now that it wasn't right in front of me, noting the seamless transition from fur to skin on its lower body. Its physique was lean and muscular. The hooves for feet had me gawking, and I raised my hand to cover my mouth.

A satyr, a faun? Those were myths, mostly in Greek mythology, and this creature was standing right here in front me.

I went with faun because when I thought of a satyr, I thought of those things with a musical instrument at their lips, drunk, mischievous, maybe not as beautiful. After checking this male out and gaining some footing of who this was, I found him utterly breathtaking.

I squeezed my notebook to my chest as I stood before him. "Can you understand me?" I asked because I couldn't be sure. He could have just stopped just because I spoke.

He nodded his head once and took a step forward, and my eyes zeroed in on the front part of his body. There was a pouch where his private parts should be, and it looked well stocked.

Maybe he has some food in there, berries? You know, like a fanny pack. *Or maybe his big, fat sausage.*

I'm going to hell, no wait, the Underworld. Now, I know all these creature myths exist, I'm beginning to believe *something* beyond science exists.

"Easy." I put my hand out to keep him away.

I wasn't afraid because he was male, as I very much knew he was, by his sculpted physique. The fact that he was a faun, very different from me and the way my body was reacting, made me uncomfortable.

What were his intentions besides licking my wounds?

Did he wanna…

It made me clutch my pearls.

Was he helping?

Did he drink blood?

I didn't know what this thing liked to eat.

Maybe my pussy? That rough tongue might feel good down there.

Immediately, I clamped my thighs together.

No, no, no. Intrusive thoughts, bad. We do not want to think about that tongue anywhere.

Sure I do, those horns scraping against my thighs while he vigorously lapped at my clit.

It's an animal, Lucy.

Well, he is mostly animal.

We don't even know if it talks, but he understands.

Wait, he has an opposable thumb!

Ugh, so do monkeys, but that doesn't mean humans—

I was so lost in my own thoughts, I didn't notice that he'd stepped closer to me, and both his hands were cupping my face. I was too stunned to move when he came nose-to-nose with me.

"Ucy."

Charles fudging Darwin.

CHAPTER EIGHT

Simon

SHE DIDN'T PUSH ME away.

Instead, she stumbled back into a sturdy tree while I followed. I refused to release my grip on her face, my selfishness overpowering any urge to let go. The sight of her arms, covered in scrapes, some with dots of blood, filled me with anger. The metallic scent filled my lungs, which intensified my frustration towards Dutton for treating her less than the precious female she was.

However, amidst his sins, I couldn't deny the excitement that I felt being here with my Lucy.

I would not let my anger surface for her to see. I concealed it beneath a calm façade so she wouldn't be more afraid than she already was. Instead,

I would reveal my care for her through tender actions, tending to her wounds with gentle hands and easing her pain with a soft touch.

Her shock was clear. She had seen an ogre today; they were beastly monsters, and I was a new... creature? Another monster?

Internally, I shook my head. I was a true monster—the only one of my kind. The way she had studied me these last few minutes, I didn't know if she thought of me that way.

Over the past few days, I'd practiced saying her name. I could not make the sound that started it. I tried my best, but my best was not good enough. With time running out, I was only able to give her "Ucy."

That was when I had really gotten her attention, and her eyes widened in surprise. A sharp gasp escaped her lips as I came closer, our noses almost touching. In that moment, her intoxicating scent engulfed me, overwhelming my desire for her.

The yellowcress root I had seen Dutton spread around her was laughable. I thought I might be the only being in all of Bergarian who could sniff through it. Her scent was so strong, and I could smell it and the faintness of mine on her wrist, where I'd left it the night before as if the root wasn't there.

There was also another scent. It twisted with the fresh grass and rain but also a hint of sweet musk that made me drool. My body warmed when I leaned close to sniff her neck, and her body trembled as I let go of her face so my hands could travel lower down her body.

Since she was awake, surely this was more appropriate.

My hands traveled lower and landed on her chest. My head perked up, feeling the soft curve and the plumpness to it. I felt mine at the same time. Hmm, mine was firmer, while hers was soft.

She was female. This must be her teat, then.

I squeezed her chest again, and she pushed me. I stumbled back in shock. "I beg your finest pardon!" She glared at me, holding her teats.

I grunted and stepped towards her. She was my mate. I was allowed to touch her, to feel her, just like she could feel me. Perhaps she did not know. I grabbed her wrist and put it on my chest. I let her rub the skin and gripped her fingers to squeeze. Mine was hard, but I showed her it was okay.

Her face turned a bright red, and she looked away. "Yes, a very nice... chest you have. But you cannot squeeze my breast. It isn't proper!" She pulled her hand away and rubbed it on her clothing.

I lifted my arm. *Did I stink?*

I tilted my head and stared at her breast, closer. Why could I not squeeze it? I liked it and wanted to do it again. I lifted my hand to cup it, and she slapped my hand.

I shook my hand to take away the sting, and I let out a bleat of annoyance.

She laughed and covered her mouth with her hand.

I stomped my hoof and blew my tongue at her.

How can she be laughing at me? I was not funny.

She cannot hit my hand away from her. I may touch her.

She is mine.

She laughed again and watched me curiously. My ears twitched back and forth, and she smiled. "You have no boundaries, do you?"

Boundaries? I remember Calliope was told she had none. What was wrong with not having boundaries?

I stepped forward again, this time not touching her, since she didn't want to be touched... for now. I gazed up and down her arms, and she wrapped them around her body. She was hiding from me, hiding her teats. I didn't like it.

I huffed out through my nose and saw the scrapes on her skin. My tongue pressed forward, and I licked them again to clean her wounds.

She squealed and jumped away. "What, what are you doing? You can't just go about licking people!"

I grabbed her arm and pulled her back to the tree. She didn't fight me when I pinned her back there. Instead, her breath hitched when she stared at my hand as it touched her skin. There was a heat in our contact, which had entranced us both, that I could not deny.

She felt it too, I knew she did. Otherwise, she would have run away by now.

I extended my tongue and gently caressed her scrapes, eliciting a soft moan that escaped her throat. Looking up, I could see her captivating gaze as my body drew nearer, pressing her against the sturdy tree.

The flavor was exquisite. As I meticulously cleaned her, I closed my eyes, relishing the blend of her taste with the faint scent of blood. My breath quickened, and I pressed against her chest, attuned to her beating heart.

"I'm going to hell," she muttered. Her head leaned against the tree, and her musk blossomed below the waist.

I whimpered, and my hands landed on her hips to restrain myself from going any lower. I could not rut her here. I was not an animal anymore; I could not do what the animals did.

Yet, I licked her to tend to her wounds.

The orcs did that—maybe I was not terrible.

I licked up her arm to catch a large scratch. She gasped, and my hands traveled higher so she didn't struggle. To my surprise, she didn't, maybe because I kept my hands away from her *breasts*.

The dress she was wearing, similar to my companion in style, was dark, but it was still revealing around her shoulder. My mouth watered when I looked at the curve of her shoulder and neck. My teeth tingled with eagerness to sink them into her flesh.

"Oh... oh, dear!" She pushed for me to back away.

I listened and stepped back slightly. My eyes gazed into hers, but she wasn't looking into mine. Instead, she stared down my body.

I knew my upper half could be more appealing if I did not have as much hair, but my lower could ruin it all. Lucy had said nothing, but her mouth was opening and closing while her body was trying to back away but could not go any further back into the tree.

What was she... oh.

My cock was hanging out of its pouch, dripping, and my mate was speechless.

I stood up straighter, proud that I could render her so. This goddess that everyone talks about has blessed me. She gave me a girthy shaft. I will please my mate when the time comes to claim her.

"Can you put that thing away?" she squeaked and looked away. "It's just hanging out of your fanny pack. Where does that thing go?"

I stared down at it. It was too large to stick it back inside. The only way for it to go down was to take care of it or—

An enormous roar came from the distance, and a faint smell of ogre came from the wind where the Wood had brought it to me.

Yes, that would make my shaft go down in an instant.

I shoved it back inside my pouch and pulled my mate to my side. Her head was spinning in all directions, looking for the ogre.

"Wait, it's coming here!" She went to run, but I pulled her back to my side, bent over and put my arm under her legs, her back leaning against the other. Her arms went around my neck, and I puffed out my chest to show her my strength.

"Where are we going? You need to put me down. I don't know you!"

You let me lick all up your arm, and now you want to talk about me not knowing you?

Another roar came from the Wood, and she squeezed my neck tighter. "Okay, get going, let's go!" She kicked her legs in demand.

I let out a bleat of laughter and took off. My run was quick, faster than any ogre, and with the yellowcress on me and my mate, those shifters or orcs would never find Lucy.

This worked out far better than I had originally planned, and I couldn't wait to take her back to my home.

We traveled deeper into the Wood. The wind swirled around us, so that if there were any smells, especially of her arousal, they were mixed in with the musky scent of the humid soil. No one would find us where I was taking her, not even Calliope and her orc had found me so far, and it had been months.

My mate still clung to me like I would drop her, but that was unnecessary. I may look thin, but my strength was great, and my legs—well, they could climb any mountain, which was exactly what we were about to do.

The Wood had foothills, not tall enough to be mountains, but steep enough to be trouble for an orc or shifter to climb. I picked my home on the steepest part for my safety, never knowing I would bring home a female for myself. Now, I could pat myself on the back for a job well done.

I stopped at the base, getting a better grip on my mate, and she wiggled in my arms.

"What are you doing? The ogre is gone now. You can put me down."

I huffed, then put my hoof on the side of the mountain, and her eyes widened. "You will not climb this!"

Ah, now I could show her my skill. I smiled at her, and she shook her head.

"Don't you dare!"

With ease, I climbed as she held me tight with her head buried into my chest. I tried not to think pleasurable thoughts of her holding me tight, while I sunk into her cunt for the first time, giving us both the pleasure we wanted.

"This was not on my list of things to do today," she mumbled under her breath, as I skipped from rock to rock. It was nearly a vertical climb, and she hardly breathed.

"Ucy," I said, and she held onto me tighter. Her hot breath slithered down my body, and it took everything inside me not to shudder in delight. "Ucy, okay."

She whimpered, and I kept climbing until we reached the cliff. Once I straightened I moved safely away from the ledge, and closer to our home. It was carved into the rock, and although not a deep cave, it was large enough to keep out the weather and have a large living space.

"Ucy, eeeere." I rubbed her back up and down, but her body still clung to me. I did not know if I should be upset or excited that she did not want to leave my body.

"Are we on the ground?" she asked. I looked around and stomped my foot.

She poked her head out from my chest, and I gently lowered her to the ground. Her face was flushed red as she straightened her dress. "Thanks, uh." She brushed her hair back. "I don't like heights."

Good, she won't be able to leave.

I motioned her to the cave, and she shook her head.

"Nah, no thanks. I think I'll go meet up with the camp. It was great meeting you, uh, Mr. Tumnus. C. S. Lewis would get a real kick out of this." She backed away from me. "Except, this Mr. Tumnus is attractive, and I'm having impure thoughts. Am I dreaming?" she muttered under her breath and pinched herself.

Who was Mr. Tumnus? Does she think my name is Mr. Tumnus?

I did not need her to yell another male's name during our mating. I needed to learn to say my name. Before I could think any further, I realized my mate was backing up and was not aware there was a cliff behind her.

"Ucy!" I shouted, running toward her.

She saw me as a threat and walked backward faster. Before she fell over, I grabbed her by the waist and pulled her away. She spun around into my arms, but her sight caught the massive drop, and she squealed.

She didn't fight me anymore when she looked over the side. Instead, her body went limp, and I caught her before she fell to the ground.

CHAPTER NINE

Lucy

"Mr. Tumnus, I didn't know you had such a big dick." I shook my head from where it rested comfortably in the blankets.

That was the wildest dream I'd ever had.

I dreamed I confessed about masturbating in my tent to the whole campsite. I rode on the back of a shifter, ended up meeting a sexy Mr. Tumnus and his giant penis, which was hanging out of his fanny pack. Not to mention the licking; lots of licking and then he carried me up a mountain.

I'm so glad it had all just been a dream.

I let out a shuddering breath, the sound escaping softly. I smacked my parched lips and could almost taste the dryness lingering on my tongue.

Immediately, my hand reached out, seeking the familiar coolness of my water bottle on the side table. But to my surprise, it wasn't there. Instead, my fingertips brushed against something unexpected; a softness, like fur, gently curled beneath my touch. As I explored further, I could sense the strength beneath it.

Thick muscles.

Galileo, no! Please no. Let the gravity suck me down into the soil because I do not want to be here right now.

Lies. You wanted to get up close and personal with that faun sausage.

"Ucy?"

I still hadn't opened my eyes yet. I wasn't sure if I wanted to. I had hoped that this was still a dream.

"Ucy?"

But no, he said my name again. This meant he was not an animal at all; he had a brain and could understand me. He hadn't touched my breast again after I told him not to. Even though he wanted to, he had restrained himself. Which meant he was capable of complicated thoughts, even restraining himself.

I let out another sigh, one of many I would let out I was sure, and opened my eyes. As soon as I did, the faun stared down at me.

"Ucy, o-kay?"

I let out a high-pitched squeak, my heart pounding, as I hastily scooted away from him.

With his hands supporting his weight, he leaned over me, his presence looming. He wasn't on his knees, but he sat in an odd position. Do fauns have knees? Or was it technically an elbow? No, they were hocks. Similar to a horse's back leg.

"Ucy?"

"It's Lucy," I corrected. "Lucy. Can you pronounce the L?"

The faun's cheeks turned a rosy hue as he reared his head back. I settled on the soft blanket, as I watched as his tongue gingerly emerge from his lips, probing the air. It dawned on me why he seemed to struggle. His textured tongue, which resembled that of a goat, stretched out.

If I had a tongue like that in my mouth, I would have trouble with placement, too.

"Here, watch," I spoke to him gently. His face was still red as he flashed his long lashes at me and looked so ashamed. "It's alright. You can understand me, can't you?"

He nodded and wrung his hands together.

"Okay then, this isn't so bad. Watch where I put my tongue when I make the *L* sound. We will have you saying my name in no time, okay?"

If I was friendly enough with him, maybe I could get him to take me back down the cliff. Saying my name could work, right?

"Okay, you ready? Watch." I showed him where to place my tongue by pointing right at the roof of my mouth. "Then, let out the sound. Just like this."

As I made the sound, he watched intently, coming far too close and showing he had no boundaries at all. He leaned closer to my mouth as he looked inside. My body felt the heat of his when he placed both his hands on my thighs, leaning on me to get a better look. I held the sound for longer until he backed away, and I could catch my breath.

"You try?" I motioned for him, and he cleared his throat. It took him several times, and I even placed my hand to help move his jaw. By the fifth time, he'd got it. He had to maneuver his tongue. It wasn't quite like mine, but he made the sound perfectly and then added the rest of the letters to it.

"Lucy."

My heart suddenly fluttered when he said my name. His voice lacked the deep resonance that typically captivates women in romance novels or movies. Instead, it was velvety, gentle, and seemed to be exclusively meant for me. Every syllable he spoke felt like a tender caress, like a whispered prayer.

"You did it," I whispered.

He crawled closer to me and grabbed both of my hands. "Lucy."

What was he doing?

We were on a bed. A well-made bed, actually, and this was not a good place for me to be. What if he attacked me, tried to push me onto the blankets and do something to me? He already proved that he was stronger than me, by carrying me through the forest and then climbing a mountain.

I scooted farther away from him, ripping my hands from him, and his face dropped in utter disappointment.

Why did my heart hurt at the sight of that?

The faun backed away, giving me space, and stood up. He didn't stay near me but went over to a table, poured water into a steel cup, and pushed it across the floor to me. He had a cave filled with items that were rather quite civilized.

Tools hung on the walls. There were cups, eating utensils, and places to sit. He could have stolen all these things, but he knew what to do with them. He even placed the bed on a raised platform, not on the ground. The cave was clean and well-ventilated, mostly because there was no door, just a gaping wide area where you could walk in and out of the cave.

Overall, it was comfortable in here.

He saved you, Lucy, and you just acted like he was going to assault you.

He is only curious. The lack of boundaries is completely normal in this realm, anyway. The poor thing has probably lived here alone for ages and just needs someone to talk to him.

I rubbed my forehead and slid off the bed. The faun sat in the chair to appear less intimidating because, let's face it, he was.

If fact, he was rather adorable.

His hair was in disarray, and his ears were drooped like I'd kicked is puppy.

Wow, great way to thank your rescuer.

He was trying, so I had to be a little more understanding. He was trying to understand me, and I wasn't giving him a chance.

"I am sorry. This is new to me." I walked closer to him, being extra careful not to make any sudden movements. The light sources were setting, and gold and pink lights were filtering into the cave. "I don't know why you saved me or how you even found me. I've also never seen a creature like you before."

The faun lowered his head, and I heard a grunt.

"Hey." I rushed toward him and got on my knees. "It isn't a bad thing. I don't know many species around here. I just came to Bergarian a month ago. I'm here to record all the species I can."

The faun shook his head.

"Have others seen you before?"

He shrugged his shoulders.

That wasn't much of an answer. I frowned, put my hands on either side of his face, and had him look at me as he had done to me before. "How many know that you live here in the Wood?"

Faun held up six fingers and shrugged his shoulders. "You think six people have seen you? Ever?"

He nodded and looked away.

Why has no one said anything? That there was a faun running in the woods and it was all alone? He appeared to be sociable and was obviously lonely.

"Are there others like you? With horns and pretty little hooves?" I smiled and poked at his cheek.

He let out a bleat when I tickled him under his chin, but he narrowed his eyes and shook his head.

"No one? What about a mom? Dad? Sibling?"

He shook his head again.

"No wonder you don't have any manners or social boundaries." I crossed my arms and tapped my lip.

He jerked his head toward me and let out a bleat.

Okay, he had an extensive vocabulary if he could understand that. So, where did he learn it?

"It's alright; I'm not blaming you. It upset me in the beginning. All the touching, you just need to ask permission first. It isn't right to put your hands on someone without their consent. Do you understand?" I wagged my finger at him.

The faun nodded and reached out his hand. "Lucy tou-ch." His teeth whistled, and I smiled.

"Where are you going to touch?" I eyed him up and down.

The faun leaned forward and pointed at my arm. I held it up to him to give him my consent, and he took it. He gently pulled me to stand and led me over to a table that had an assortment of jars. None of them looked familiar to me. They could hold medicine or food.

He took his finger and dipped his claw inside a glass purple one, then put it over one scratch. The rest already looked healed; only small, red marks remained.

Could his spit already be healing my wounds?

He smeared a small amount on the wound, which was deeper than all the others, and a cool sensation came over the scratch. The faun concentrated solely on my arm, and that was when I could really look at his face.

He was an animal in his looks and movements, but he had human-like qualities. And my body was reacting to him more than any male that I had come into contact with.

He was handsome, even beautiful. I liked the warmth of his hand holding my arm, and how tender he was. It was innocent, and for once, I felt completely at ease being with someone other than my father.

Of course, I didn't like him like he was my father; I liked him a different way. More. That scared me the most.

And that little voice in the back of my head that wouldn't mind if he *was* rough with me one day.

We would call her Lucy the Hoe.

As I watched him blow on the wound, careful to ensure it was dry, I realized that our earlier encounter was all a misunderstanding.

He didn't grab my breast because he wanted me. He was just curious. He didn't know what he wanted. His penis, which sprung free earlier, was just his body reacting. He probably didn't even know what to do with it.

So, stop getting your panties in a twist, Whore Lucy. He's a sweet, innocent little faun who just needs some guidance.

And that was exactly what we were going to do. We were going to get patched up, get him to talk, and he would then lead me back to camp.

Easy peasy.

Chapter Ten

Simon

I RUBBED THE REST of the cream onto her arm, which would take away any left-over pain she might have. I had hoped to lick more of her soft skin, but this whole 'asking for permission to touch her' is what she wanted. I could not lick her. If touching her breasts were not proper, then using a cream instead of a tongue would be better.

I didn't like it!

For now, I would do as she asked. She does not know me, and she *was* new to all things in this world.

I knew Bergarian wasn't the only realm, and there was another that did not hold many creatures like shifters and orcs. It was mostly humans who knew nothing about them.

If those humans wanted to live in ignorance, then that was on them. My female was smart. She came to this realm and was not afraid. She was not even afraid of me, and let me far closer than I ever thought she would.

Lucy did slap my hand, but at least it was not my face. My face was sensitive, and I might have fainted if she had done so.

"I need a name. I can't keep calling you Mr. Tumnus in my head."

I let out a bleat of disgust.

Was she serious? She was still calling me Mr. Tumnus?

Who was that?

My mate snickered, and as much as I enjoyed seeing her smile and show joy, I didn't like it when it was at my expense.

I wanted to make her laugh *in my own way.*

"It's from a book." She bobbed her head. "It's about a girl named Lucy, actually." She scratched the side of her head with her finger. "How ironic. Anyway, she meets a faun. Much like yourself." She waved her hand up and down my body.

I stared at her in confusion. How could she speak so casually? A faun? Was that what I was?

I gently placed my hand on my chest and felt my heartbeat at her words. The soft touch of my hand glided down my torso, tracing the contours of my body. The sensation of the fur on my legs brushed against my fingertips, a reminder of my unique existence from skin to fur.

I realized I was more than just a goat and a human, but a distinct species.

They had a name for what I was. Was I truly a faun? The thought lingered in my mind, accompanied by why there were no others like me. I couldn't help but question why I was alone. If my species had a name?

"Hey?" Her hand landed on mine. I placed my hand on top of hers to connect her to me further. Her lips held a ghost of a smile when she looked up at me.

"You okay there? Did I say something to upset you?"

"F-f-aun?" I repeated slowly.

She nodded. "A faun. That is what your species is. Unless there is another name you call each other?"

I shook my head, strands of hair falling across my face.

"You don't know what you are?"

I shake my head again, a sigh escaping my lips. "No."

She bit her lip, but I didn't want her to feel more sorry for me than I did myself. I didn't care anymore.

I wasn't alone anymore. I had her.

Her delicate fingers gently glided through the velvety curls atop my head, their touch a tender caress against the smooth base of my sturdy horns. A shiver coursed through my body, like a gentle ripple in a tranquil lake, as my eyes fluttered and rolled to the back of my head, and I surrendered to the blissful sensation.

My shaft instantly hardened in my pouch, but I didn't care. When I opened my eyes, I knew she saw what she was doing to me, because she held in a laugh and brought up her other hand to repeat the motion on the other side of my head.

My hoof kicked against the cold, damp walls of the cave involuntarily, and a chill sent shivers cascading down my spine, causing my muscles to tense. I let out a long, eerie moan that echoed through the dark, musty air.

"That's my good little faun."

Yes, I am your good little faun. Please don't stop.

I groaned, but the sound of my pleasure broke the moment, making her gasp and step away. "Oh my, yes, well, um." Her face turned bright red, and she would no longer look at me.

"Lucy?" I tilted my head, and she pointed at my shaft.

Yeah, he has a mind of his own. Popping out of his pouch like that, but when he got big, there wasn't anywhere to put him.

"Can you put it back?" her voice shook.

Was she scared of it? Did she not think of it as impressive?

Compared to my body size, it was wide and would fill her hole nicely. Compared to a goat, I was massive. Theirs look like threads of grass.

"Lucy 'cared?"

Her face found mine, a look of panic washing over her face. "Cared? Scared? Do you mean scared?"

I swallowed and stayed in place, not wanting her to panic more.

"No, ah, no. Not scared. Uncomfortable, because your little faun is hanging out there. You should put it away." She kept pointing at it, then wiggled the same finger at me.

It wasn't little! How big did she want it to be?

I couldn't put it away now; it was awake. It was always hard now that she was here.

Since she'd rubbed my horns, it was only going to get worse.

"Here!" she exclaimed and ran to the back of the cave. She found a rag and pushed it out in front of her, making sure she didn't see my shaft. "You can wear it like a skirt."

A skirt?

Does my mate think I am a female?

She is not as smart as I thought.

Or is it because she thinks of my shaft as small and unworthy of her?

I let out a huff, took the rag from her, and stepped away. If it made her more comfortable, I would make this work, but I would not wear a skirt.

However, before I could make this cloth work, my shaft deflated enough to go back into my pouch.

Although, it was very uncomfortable.

I turned to show her the result, and she sighed. "Oh, thank the *gods*. That's what they say around here, right?" She rubbed her head. "You should probably put the skirt on, anyway. It might keep popping up in the middle of our conversation."

I gawked at her.

"And that's okay. It's completely normal for it to be so... hard and erect like that." She played with her fingers. "Completely normal and healthy. Now you know it is in working order, and you can do what you will with it! You have a healthy penis, that's fantastic!"

What's happening?

She clapped her hands together and turned around. "I think I need some fresh air. I'm just going to go outside and get some. Don't worry, I won't walk off the cliff. I probably should after this conversation. I just told a faun that he had a healthy working penis. Good thing he can't read my thoughts because I'm pretty sure it would be ten times worse."

I stood there, stunned, as I watched her stand at the mouth of the cave. Her hands were on her knees, and she was taking deep breaths.

Did she like my *penis* or not?

I waited for her to come back but stood ready in case she decided to jump off the cliff.

Lucy stood for a long time gazing out at the view. There was nothing but blue and green leaves spanning out against the forest. They were so thick you could hardly see the ground below.

Was she looking for them, the group that brought her here?

I hoped she wasn't, but I wasn't a fool. She wanted to get back to them, I was sure. Even if to make sure they were okay. They probably were. Ogres were stupid, and if the orcs led it away from the camp, there was little chance that the ogre would find them again if they were using the yellowcress. That ogre just happened to stumble upon them before from all the loud noises.

"Lucy?" My hooves clicked closer to the mouth of the cave. I had already started a fire and made dinner for her.

Because I was a good male, and I was doing well.

I had stolen some food from Calliope and her orc. I didn't think my mate would appreciate eating roots. I had bread that would last a few more days before I had to get more, and the meat I'd caught myself was fresh.

Though I'd grown increasingly self-sufficient, the art of baking—with its delicate balance of ingredients and timing—remained beyond my grasp.

Lucy hummed and turned to meet my gaze. I felt like it had been many moons since I'd seen her face when it hadn't been long at all.

"E-eat?"

My heart leaped when I could form the words. It was coming so much easier, just being in her presence.

Could it be the bond, with the goddess' will helping me?

With a bright smile, Lucy uncrossed her arms, the tension visibly leaving her shoulders. "Sorry, I didn't mean to have a panic attack." She took tentative steps toward me and reached out her hand toward mine.

She was touching me.

Please, penis, do not come out.

"This was a lot. More adventure than I have ever had in my life, actually, and I have been to many places in my lifetime."

I gave her adventure!

"And wow, these nails are sharp!"

She took my hand and flipped it over, her fingers trailing my palm.

"Not as rough as I thought. It is actually really soft. These nails though, wow, just fascinating. Not nails, more like talons. Can you shred meat with these?"

I can shred your clothes.

I nodded enthusiastically.

"There is so much I want to learn from you, Mr. Tumnus."

I let out a bleat and took my hand away, crossing my arms like I saw her do when she was uncomfortable.

"Right! Sorry, sorry!" She ran her fingers through her hair. "I need your name. Do you have a name? Can you say it?"

I ground my teeth and stuck my tongue out at her. She was still going to be calling me Mr. Tumnus in her head. I just knew it.

"Oh, come on." She tugged on my arm. "I really am sorry. I know you hate that name. Come on, be a good little faun, and please tell me your name. We can eat and then work on your speaking. I think our problem is you have a longer tongue. We can work on tongue placement, so we can have a better conversation. Please?"

She begged sweetly, and my shaft twitched in my pouch.

Down. Stay down in the pouch of loneliness.

I huffed in annoyance. I cannot say my name. The sound at the front always came out like a whistle. I did my best, with my tongue flailing about until all that could be heard was "imon."

She wiped my spit away from her eye. "Right, okay. *Imon,* then?"

I shook my head and stomped my foot.

"A sound before *Imon,* then?"

I nodded. "Lucy touch?" I held out my hand for her arm to lead her inside for her warm food, and she nodded. She sounded out more letters in front of *Imon,* and when she finally said my name, I nodded excitedly.

"Simon! That's your name!" She smiled, jumping up and down. I couldn't help but follow her movement when she wrapped her arms around me. I paused, taking in long whiffs of her hair.

Her body was warm, and I was melting into it.

"Simon, great. We have a name! Thought it might be more fantasy, like what the orcs have. I'm glad it's so normal. Not to say you are normal. Aren't you are just fascinating? Amazing!" She blushed and stepped away. "Now, I won't call you the other name anymore. Okay?"

I nodded and gave her as wide a smile as she gave me.

"Good." Her arms slumped at her sides. "Well, Simon. I know it's dark, and you made all this food, but I really do need to get going."

I tilted my head when she looked over at the table.

"Wow, you made this?"

It was basic food. Bread rolls, meat and fruit. I hadn't cut the fruit because I didn't want any pixies to smell it and come inside.

Not that I had seen any pixies in the Wood, but you never knew.

They were evil.

"I have to get back to camp. Make sure everyone is okay. People will look for me, and it isn't proper if I just stay up here. It isn't considerate. Perhaps you can take me back, and I can come back and visit tomorrow?"

I balled my hands into fists.

I thought we were getting somewhere. I thought she was more comfortable. She wanted to leave me. My mate did not want to be in my presence.

I shook my head and huffed loudly; louder than I had ever done before. I shook my head again, feeling the weight of my horns.

"No." I stomped my foot.

Lucy reared her head back, her eyebrow raised. "No? No, you won't take me back right now? Do we need to wait until morning?"

I stepped forward, still not touching her since I had not asked.

"No. Lucy, 'ere." I pointed to the floor of the cave.

She stood there with her mouth open until she glared at me. "Are you saying I can't leave?"

I straightened my back, crossed my arms, and nodded.

"Lucy mmm-ine." I bleated.

CHAPTER ELEVEN

Lucy

I PLACED MY TREMBLING hand on my pounding chest, feeling the rapid thump of my racing heart. My body tensed, and the sound of my heavy breaths echoed into the cave as I took three cautious steps back from Simon.

The sweet, innocent faun—whom I had no business finding attractive—with the curiosity of a child, just dared to look me in the eyes and say, *Mine*?!

My brain shut off, trying to reboot.

He had thoughts—complicated ones. He knew words yet had trouble speaking them because...? Well, I wasn't sure why. Simon understood everything I said, so why had he never had the chance to speak his mind?

Simon had no one else to talk to, but surely he would have at least tried to speak? He should speak and know how to move his tongue. If I was guessing correctly, he should at least be in his twenties, even early thirties, but even that estimate was moot because nothing in this realm aged.

This place was confusing.

Why couldn't he speak?

Simon stared at me with a smug look. He widened his stance, his hooves shining with the light source that filtered in. He thrust out his chest, showing off his lean, muscular body. You could see the deep v-line, that Adonis' Belt I'd read far too much about.

I wasn't a prude; I could appreciate the male body. I'd looked at the shifters before I came here. Dutton, for one. His body was nice, but it did nothing for me.

Yet, Simon, why did I feel more attracted to him than anyone I had come into contact with? That same question echoed in my head time and time again, but then that word registered again...

Mine.

He said I was his. The one word that was spoken often in this realm. It was when a mate claimed another, and this faun just told me I was his. He claimed me. Words that were not taken lightly around here.

Surely not. He must be mistaken. Yet, if Simon knew the words of the realm, then he knew what they meant.

He'd claimed me!

Me!

I drew a deep breath, calming my nerves. He could speak that word so well, the way he drew it out. It had a hint of a growl in it, a bleat at the beginning, but he said it.

The idea that soulmates were real, that a goddess paired couples together based on their souls, was a sweet notion but one that couldn't possibly be true. It had to be on body type or smell, or favorability to procreate. He wasn't claiming me because I was his soul mate.

Was he?

I wanted to believe it; the sweet, fictional satisfaction of someone claiming me, taking me, and making me theirs, but this would be by far the weirdest pairing, if I had ever seen one.

Human and orc, sure, okay, that worked. I haven't seen those couples in person yet. The idea was scary. The size difference, the personalities... there were big differences there.

A faun, the only faun that I had seen as yet, thought I was his mate?

Maybe he was mimicking what he had seen?

My pussy was crying at the thought that he wanted me because I was destined to be his.

Ovulating! I was ovulating, and that was what he'd smelled. I was in the middle of my cycle. He had heightened senses. He could tell my body was primed for birthing a child.

I knew it! It wasn't a soul thing; it was just... he was horny.

I was, too. In fact, I don't remember my body getting this hot over anyone staring at me like he did.

Desire swam in his eyes, dilated pupils, panting, grunting, a slight whine in his voice, the whole nine yards. That fanny pack wasn't hiding much. I was worried **it** was going to pop out at any moment, and yup, there it went.

Please don't wink at me.

Simon didn't move, letting it hang out of his front pocket. It was really... wide. Great, I was running out of adjectives. Girthy, yes, that was the word I was looking for.

Simon stepped closer to me, making my heart rate increase. My heart was going to flutter out of my chest at this rate. I continued to walk backwards until I hit the cave wall, and his hand landed on the wall at the side of my head.

He had the 'male lean' and had never even read a book in his life, I was sure. His breath was warm when he placed his nose closer to my neck. I turned my head so as not to breathe in his scent, which smelled too much like home to me. A home I'd never been to but wanted it to be.

He took light sniffs along my neck, barely touching the skin. My body prickled with goosebumps. "Lucy, touch," he said, then dropped his tongue out of his mouth and licked a spot on my shoulder.

My knees buckled, and I slid to the floor.

I was grinning wildly, and my hands slapped my cheeks. I couldn't believe he just did that.

Did he not know how incredibly sexy that was, what he just did?

I cleared my throat and went to stand. He tried to help me, but I pushed his hands so they stayed at the sides of his body and narrowed my eyes.

He only wanted me because my body was in its prime, not because he thought I was his mate.

I couldn't be anyone's mate. I was weird, not of this realm, and very much not cut out to take the enormous penis jutting out, staring at me like a one-eyed monster.

"Simon," my voice grew stern. "I am not yours." I put my hands on my hips. "I am a human and not of this realm. I cannot be your mate. You need to take me back to my camp so I can make sure everyone is okay."

Simon mimicked my stance. "No!"

He came closer, though not touching me. Sick as it was, I wanted him to touch me. I wanted him to grab me, but he didn't. His slightly furred lips tickled my ear, and he spoke the word that still took my breath away.

"Mine."

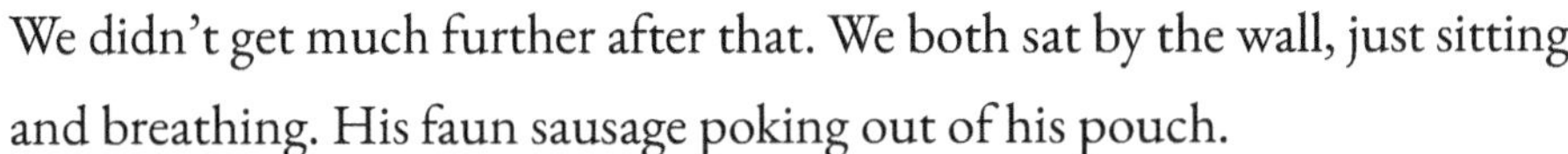

We didn't get much further after that. We both sat by the wall, just sitting and breathing. His faun sausage poking out of his pouch.

I didn't dare look at him as I started to argue with him again. I spoke to the wall, not into his eyes.

Simon threw a faun-fit as we argued, and he stomped around the cave. I was worried about males of this realm; they were aggressive. The ogres and shifters were, but I had never seen them hit a woman.

Simon, he was visibly angry. I kept asking to leave, but instead he offered me food, and his enormous bed for me to rest, while he sat at the front of the cave on a mound of fresh hay to give me space.

He didn't ask to sleep beside me, but I saw the longing look.

Why did I feel guilty?

Why was I being so difficult? Was it so hard to believe in a goddess and a fairy tale when I was already living in one?

I tried to remember any of the times my father had read fairy tales to me, but he never had. He was a single man, engrossed with his work, who just happened to have a daughter. He read research notes to put me to sleep because his voice was calm and soothing.

I lay against the pillow, drifting in and out of sleep throughout the night. Not for fear of Simon hurting me, but because of all the what-ifs. He was the first one who had made me feel—well, not broken. My body was awakened, but I was also leery.

What if I put my emotions into him, and he had a mate out there? His real one, not one who was ovulating?

I rolled my eyes when I saw the first light source appearing in the sky. Simon was already up and leaning over the cliff. He crouched down, one ear perked up, and then he took steps to back away.

This caught my interest immediately, and I got up to see why he was acting secretive. Voices from down below caught my attention, and I raced out of the cave.

Before I could scream, Simon whispered, "Lucy, touch," and kept my mouth covered so I wouldn't alert them.

"Lucy!" I heard Elmira's voice shout out into the Wood. "Lucy!"

I struggled in his hold, but Simon kept me there with him, yet did not drag me back to the cave.

"We should split up; two groups. Each take an orc," Dutton said from below. I stilled, hearing his voice. Other voices followed, and I realized that everyone from the group was safe.

I struggled again when I realized people were still looking for me, and I needed to get free. I grunted and pushed against Simon, but he was too strong. Everyone in this realm was too strong.

Slowly, he dragged me back to the cave when the voices vanished.

By the time I broke free, I knew it was useless to go back outside. They were gone, and I was left alone with Simon.

He panted, his chest rose and fell, but at least his junk wasn't hanging out.

"You can't keep me like this!" I flung my hands up in the air. "It's kidnapping! You could go to jail for doing that where I am from. You can't hold me against my will!"

"Lucy, mine!" He banged his chest.

My pussy fluttered at the tone of his voice, the ferocity and determination that he really thought I was his.

My brain had to win out, or I was going to jump his faun sausage.

At least I had an IUD.

Ugh, not helping yourself, Lucy.

Arguing against him would not work. I needed him to talk back. That was the only way to reason with him.

"Fine," I said simply as I folded my hands over my chest.

Simon's eyes turned into slits, and he walked around me.

"If I am going to stay here, you need to learn how to speak to me. This whole caveman talking won't do." I waved my hand in front of me.

Except in the bedroom. By all means, you can boss me there.

Oh, my gods, shut up, Slut Lucy.

"I need words, Simon. We need to have conversations. I can help you with that if you are willing. Then, we will talk and come to an arrangement. I am not yours to keep. You cannot keep a person."

Simon came closer, like he was a predator. Could he be a predator? He was a faun! Then, those fangs, that resembled a vampire's came into view when he smirked. He showed me his hand and sought permission before he pushed my hair back behind my ear.

"Lucy... like... meee."

I swallowed. "Well, look at that. You said a whole sentence," I whispered.

The backside of Simon's claw ran down my cheek, tickling my skin. "Do not make fun," he said utterly slowly. He was concentrating really hard; I could see how he was trying to move his tongue.

Yeah, you want that tongue moved somewhere else. Maybe between our legs?

Shut up, Slut Lucy.

"I s-smell you," he growled in his throat. "You want me, too."

He pressed his chest against mine, and I knew that his dick just slipped out of his fanny pack. It lay against my stomach, hot and twitching against me.

Abort, abort!

"Just because you smell me doesn't mean I want you. Just because I'm wet doesn't mean I'm ready."

Simon's eyes go wide. "-et?"

I reached up and pressed my fingers to his mouth. Moving his lips to help create the W sound. He watched my mouth and repeated.

"Wet," he said. "Lucy is wet 'or S-simon."

I cleared my throat. "It is a natural response from a woman when she is around someone who is attractive. That does not give consent."

Simon backed away, taking a long draw of the air between us. "I will mm-ake you want S-simon."

I thought my ovaries had just exploded.

The stuttering, the lisp, they didn't matter. He was dead serious. He was going to make me want him? Why was that hot?

Still, I held firm to the notion that I couldn't be his mate. I just couldn't handle the heartbreak if I really wasn't.

Chapter Twelve

Simon

My mate was playing hard to get.

I did not see that with Calliope when she found her mate. She threw herself at him and gave into him willingly.

I did not know what I needed to do to prove that she was mine. Did she not feel the same fire I felt when I touched her?

I knew her body wanted me. I could smell her more times than others. When I came closer to her, her aroma only grew. Her body trembled, and I felt pride rise within my chest when that sweet scent rose between her legs.

I tugged at my horn. She was wary of me because of what I was.

I have watched the orcs do games and tasks to prove their strength and worth, to show their ability to care for a female. I would do the same for her because I knew she was worth it.

I had already saved her from an ogre. I already showed I could protect her. Now, I would keep her fed and healthy, all while asking permission to touch her. She would come to me—I would make her want me until she could not stand it.

She ate little the night before, so as the light sources rose further into the sky, I stepped away from her even though it hurt me to do so. I watched her while I pulled fruit and bread from the bags to see if she would run again. The dried meat that I had hung and dried myself, I pulled from the rope where I prepared meals .

Lucy watched me intently and came closer.

"Eat," I said as I laid it out on the table. I didn't have cups or plates, but it was clean enough. I was used to eating grass, rotten food and even paper in my previous life, so sitting at a table was a step in the right direction.

It was still strange to me, preparing a table for her. This should be normal for a human or anyone with arms and legs. I instantly felt shame come over me, not having at least a plate to put her food on.

My mate looked over the wooden surface. She didn't think twice as she reached for one of my favorite fruits and took a plentiful bite. I watched the sweet juice run down her chin and licked my lips.

After she wiped her mouth with the back of her hand, she spoke, "How did you make the bread? You don't have an oven in here."

Heat burned my face when I shook my head.

"Simon, what's wrong? Did you take it from someone?"

I cleared my throat and nodded.

"Simon, we are going to use our words. I know you know them. Take your time, obviously, I can't go anywhere," she muttered. "I'm going to help you the best I can." My mate sat back in the chair and rubbed her forehead. "In fact, this all works out in my favor anyway, being up here with you."

My ears perked up, and I felt my tail wag behind me.

"This will be great to put down in my report. I'm here in the Wood to record species of plants and animals for research. You can be the first big project I write about." Her eyes lit up, but I remained skeptical.

I didn't want to be recorded as if I were an animal that lived here.

I huffed and put the loaf of bread next to the fruit she had put on her side of the table. Then, sat on the other side.

"What? Why did you get all huffy?" She tilted her head. "And start talking, even if it is a *yes* or *no*. You will get used to using your tongue."

I want to use my tongue in other ways, but you won't let me.

Instead, I was faced with the idea that my mate thought of me as an animal. I had to prove to her that despite my looks I was good enough to be her mate.

"I am not an animal," I drawled slowly. "I was animal. Not animal anymore."

I fidgeted in my seat when she said nothing back right away. She just stared.

"What do you mean you are not an animal *anymore?*"

"I am not an animal. I think." I pointed to my head. "I..." I wanted to say I didn't eat grass, but grass settled my stomach if I ate food that disagreed with me "I have dis-ires. W-ants. Not be lone-ly. I do not get hard for anyone else but you."

My mate let out a strangled cough. "For someone who doesn't talk, you talk awfully blunt."

I let out a bleating laugh. "If one is s-silent, it does not m-mean they are s-stupid."

"Why haven't you tried to speak with me before, then?" Lucy crossed her arms and scooted away from the table.

How did I tell her I had listened my whole life and never uttered a word? I was a goat. I did not have the ability or desire to. My tongue was short, but I knew I was different when I did not follow the herd. I had no way to communicate. Calliope was the only one who understood I was different until that potion fell onto my head.

"I just st-start-ed... pra-practice... practicing." I wiggled my lips, getting used to using the muscles.

"Why? Why practice now?"

"B-because of you."

My mate's face turned bright red, and I smiled in triumph. She wiggled in her seat after silence hung between us and then stood up.

"I don't know how to tell you this, but I really need to use the ladies' room." Her head darted side to side and then glanced over at the bed.

Ladies' room? I rubbed my chin, then realized what she was looking for. *She had to piss.*

"Cooome?" I bleated and slapped my hand over my mouth.

My mate smiled, and I groaned. I sounded like an idiot to her. I tried to be a good male, but I sounded stupid. She would never see me as more than just an animal.

"Hey, don't be ashamed." She ran toward me and hooked her arm in mine.

She was touching me all on her own. My heart skipped and my ears twitched.

When she realized what she did, she pulled away.

"I think it's cute. And I'm sorry about calling you an animal. It's just what I saw when I first met you. I didn't know you yet, and when you didn't talk, I worried—"

"Dat I was m-more animal than what I am."

She nodded and looked away from me in shame.

I couldn't blame her for thinking that. If the positions were reversed, however, I do not think I would think like her. My cock and the bond knew she was meant to be mine.

I just needed her to see that, instead of seeing me as something to record in her book.

I would break her. Just as her friend said. The bond would become stronger until it snapped and she would come to me.

I suppressed a groan in my throat. When she did sleep, all I could think about was rutting her in the bed I had made just for her.

I led her outside when I felt my shaft try to escape my pouch. I would not have her be upset with me. She may still think of me as an animal if it continued to come out.

But I could not help it around her.

We rounded the cave to a small path that passed between the cliff and the rock face. I motioned for her to follow behind me to the tall grasses she could use.

"Nope, not going over there." She shook her head quickly. "I don't have to go anymore."

I huffed out a breath. The path was wide enough for my hoof, and when I saw her bare feet, I realized that she was not equipped with good footing.

Humans were soft. From being around a human before, I knew they could get sick and hurt themselves easily. Why had I not noticed that she had no shoes?

My mate getting hurt in my care sent panic through my body.

"Will carry. Lucy touch?" I held out my hand, but she shook her head again.

"No, we will fall. How the heck did you get us up here? That path isn't wide enough for the both of us!"

She doubted me.

"N-not let my mate fall."

Something passed over her face. Was it longing? Did she want me to be her mate? When I'd blinked, the look was gone, and she bit her lip.

"How are you going to do it?"

"Lucy touch?" I reached my hand out, almost touching her. As soon as she motioned her head to the first nod, I swept her off her feet and took the few steps over the path.

She didn't scream, but she wrapped her arms around my neck. Within seconds, we were on the other side. When I put her feet to the soil, she let out a breath and kept her hands on my forearms to hold her steady.

"We can't do that again."

She would have to if she wanted shelter. This area was barren, only tall hay and a tree that grew on the other side of the cliff that swayed in the breeze. There wasn't much room to do anything here but stare up at the stars, but enough where she could relieve herself.

"Alright, turn around." She wiped her hands on her dress. "You can't watch; don't be pervy."

Pervy?

"I watch. Dang-er."

She scoffed. "It won't take me that long. You can't watch! And great job using your words. Have to say, you are doing better than I thought. Maybe you have been lying the whole time."

I frowned. Does she want me to talk or not!? I knew my speaking has improved, a lot better than I imagined, but when the motivation is a mate in my nest, who wouldn't want to speak.

Lucy moved away, her footsteps were muffled by the soft earth as she vanished into the thick brush.

I remember Calliope spoke to her orc about not watching her use the bathroom. I understood what the orc felt like now; I did not want to lose her.

"Faaaaast!" I yelled, turning away while I crossed my arms.

When I heard the stream finish, I turned and she squealed in surprise. I came up next to her, pulled my shaft out of my pouch, and urinated right where she had been.

"Ew, gross!" She stepped away. "What are you doing? Why are you urinating right where I was!?" She turned away to give me privacy.

Once finished, I turned and kicked dried grass behind me. "To cover your ss-scent. Dang-er."

"And what, you have alpha urine?"

A low, guttural growl rumbled in my chest, the vibrations traveling up into my face as my lip curled into a snarl. "I am not an alpha. I am a f-aun. I protect Lucy. No one will s-smell you but me."

I took my hand and rubbed it over my mouth to soothe the aching muscles. I would rather place them on her slit to massage her scent on my face.

I still had much work to do, but I was a stubborn goat.

"Interesting," she whispered under her breath. "So, would you urinate on another female's spot if she was ready to become pregnant?"

I blinked at her several times. What was she talking about?

"You know, if they were"-she tapped her finger to her lip-"in heat. Like how animals get when they are ready to have a cub or pup. Shifters and mammals, they go through heats, right? A prime time to get pregnant. Say there was another female with us. Would you pee on their pee-pee puddle, too?"

Where was she going with this?

I stepped up to her. Taking a long, deep breath of air, I could smell her arousal. She may say she did not like the idea of me covering her scent, but perhaps she was more animal than she realized.

"I ooonly protect what is mine. You are my femaale. I *urinate* to hide your scent. No others." I leaned into her ear, but not touching her. "Do you like that I protect you? Only you?"

Her lips, soft and inviting, parted slightly, revealing a glistening sheen that beckoned me closer. I could almost taste the sweetness in the air, as my eyes fixated on them with an insatiable hunger, and the sound of her panting breath filled the silence.

Then, an idea.

"Or, are you in a hu-man heeat, Lucy? Is thaat why you smell so good?"

A blush of pink spread across Lucy's face, giving her a rosy glow. I inhaled deeply, the crisp air filling my lungs, and in that moment, understanding dawned.

I stepped closer, not touching because I did not ask, but my breath fanned her cheek. "You want my s-scent?" Her whimper sent a shiver down my spine, and the muscles in my back tightened, like a bowstring. "To be protected from other males, I mark you with my scent."

Her body went rigid, and I backed away.

"Y-you," she whispered, her voice trembling with a mixture of fear and excitement. "You put a scent on me. That is what everyone was smelling the other morning."

A low growl rumbled in my throat, making her gasp in surprise.

"You **were** in my tent."

Chapter Thirteen

Lucy

"Did you touch me?" I hissed. "Did you touch me in... places?" Heat flooded my face, making my cheeks burn.

Simon's face fell.

"Plaaces?"

Did I really want to know? Part of me did, but the other didn't. Just because it would ruin how great that orgasm really was. My body was all for this; my mind wasn't. I couldn't entertain the idea that he'd touched me, otherwise, it would ruin what enjoyment I had.

Truthfully, I woke up with my hands between my thighs, knuckles deep inside of me. He wasn't there.

He didn't touch me there. It was a dream.

The scenting, though?

I took a deep breath and let it out slowly. "How do you scent-mark me, Simon?"

Simon shuffled from hoof to hoof. "Lucy touch?" He extended his hand, palm up, fingers slightly splayed.

This Consent King was going to take me out. I could feel myself getting hot in places I shouldn't.

Hoe Lucy needs to get a grip.

I nodded, and his fingers closed around my wrist, his touch surprisingly gentle as he guided my hand to the side of his neck. "It is strong there. Not covered with yellowcress root."

I swallowed and pulled my hand away. That was how he stayed hidden, and no one could smell him very well.

Simon had watched me sleep and scented me. He didn't touch me other than that, I concluded. He didn't know better. I couldn't have faulted him for any of that if he thought I was his mate, either.

That was just how things worked around here.

A brilliant burst of light danced across the vast expanse of the sky, illuminating the gray clouds that floated by. The crashing of thunder echoed in my ears, and I saw the downpour of rain in the distance. The dark, foreboding clouds loomed closer, casting an ominous shadow over the wood.

In one swoop, Simon scooped me up into his arms and trotted over to the side of the cliff where the thin path awaited. I buried my face in his chest, not daring to move so we wouldn't plummet to our death. In seconds, it was over, and he'd placed me back on the rockier terrain.

"B-big storm. Get inside."

Over the next several hours, Simon climbed up and down the cliff. The storm was settling in, and he said he was retrieving food and water. I didn't dare go outside. I only had one set of clothes, and sitting in a cave, soaking wet was not on the agenda.

Especially when, technically, one of us was already naked. We didn't need both of us running around with exposed privates. What if his body betrayed him; heck, what if mine betrayed me?

Why couldn't he just put the skirt on?

This whole "can't leave the cave, one bed, big storm, close proximity" trope was really working for him. My body was a tight wire, ready to snap.

Simon approached me while I sat on his bed, and he held out a plate full of grapes, cheese, and a roll of bread. Where was he getting this food? He obviously can't make cheese. Where were the cows?

My eyes blinked several times. He doesn't make milk, does he? I was not eating goat cheese he'd made himself, was I?

He's male, Lucy, what the heck?

"Where did you get the cheese?" I blurted, as he poured more water into a basin at the far end of the cave. Simon's ears perked up as the deafening thunder outside reverberated through the musty cave, causing the ground to shake beneath our feet.

I winced, and Simon came closer to me, sitting on the bed.

He was so close to me again, but instead of feeling offended, knowing that he wanted my body, I wasn't. I felt comfortable with him sitting there while the storm raged outside. The power of the storm was strong. You could hear the howl of the wind and the snapping of trees.

The tents were made to withstand a storm of this magnitude. Magic, or something or other, to keep them from being broken, but I was still glad I was in a cave. The fire was roaring, and for being a cave, it was cozy.

"Friend gave me food. I kept her until she found her mate."

I raised a brow. A she? So, he has spent time with other women?

Wow, way to be jealous.

"Friend? And did this friend not teach you boundaries?" I crossed my arms over my chest. "She didn't tell you not to touch or steal people?"

Simon tilted his head. "Her mate did that to her."

I pinched the bridge of my nose.

Of course he did. That was what this realm was all about.

Besides, you thought it was hot, anyway.

"But did you not talk to her?" How could he not talk to his friend, who was giving him all this food?

Simon shook his head, a frustrated sigh escaping his lips. "I didn't talk. Not the same now. I not her friend anymore." He lowered his head and stared at his hands.

I knew that having a mate could make males and females more possessive and territorial, but did you have to drop all your friends once you are mated? That seemed absurd, and it made me angry for him. Simon didn't have anyone, and now he was alone in this cave and had to kidnap someone to make a friend.

"If you were both friends, then you should remain friends," I argued. "Why would she not want to talk to you once she got a mate? That's just mean and cruel! Maybe she was never really your friend if she went off with some male."

Simon darted his head toward me. "No, she wants to be friends. Her m-male—"

"Is a possessive asshole? Not being able to see your friend because you have a mate is ridiculous, Simon. If you want, I can go talk to the jerk so you can have a friend."

A woman that you never talked to. She could be beautiful, lovely, and Simon used to spend all his time with her.

But...I did feel pretty smug that Simon only talked to me.

Simon's lip curled into a smile. "Lucy upset if I talked to her?"

I paused. Wait a minute. Would I be upset?

Simon admitted I was the only person he'd tried to talk to. Would I be jealous if he went and talked to his friend? I shouldn't be jealous. *I wasn't his mate.*

Yes, I would be jealous. Should I admit that?

I scratched the back of my neck. "We aren't mates—"

Simon's growl was a low, guttural sound, like the rumble of distant thunder.

"I think you should be able to have friends of the opposite sex. You must have had a friendly bond if you protected her."

"We protected each other." His shoulders fell limp. "She does not need me."

I scoffed. "Did she tell you this? Or did you think this all on your own?"

Simon twisted his mouth to the side, his furrowed brows creating deep creases on his forehead. I watched intently as his moist, pink tongue slipped from his lips and delicately licked the side of his mouth.

"And you really never spoke before me?"

Simon shook his head. He looked at me like I was something precious. Sure, my father gave me love and attention, and he was proud of me for getting this far in life, but no man had ever looked at me the way Simon did.

As Simon's piercing gold eyes locked with mine, I felt a rush of excitement cascade through my body. It was as if time stood still, and all I could hear was the thumping of my heart echoing in my ears.

Simon didn't just look at my body, he looked at me. When I rambled, when I questioned everything he did, he just listened. My body had come alive in his gaze. It was a gaze that spoke volumes, conveying admiration, desire, and a profound connection that left me breathless.

He was the only one I ever had sexual feelings for.

In that moment, I realized that no one before had ever truly seen me the way Simon did. His gaze was like a gentle caress, unraveling the layers of my soul and making me feel truly seen and cherished. Even if his courting style was... different.

I stood up from the bed, breaking the connection that became far too deep and too fast.

Simon was a puzzle. A puzzle I was going to figure out. Why he never spoke before me and who this female was. I needed to know it all.

Simon's shoulders slump in disappointment. He stood up from the spot on the bed and went to the pile of hay on the opposite side of the cave. The storm raged outside, the thunder shaking the cave below our feet.

"Sleep, Lucy." He curled up in the hay and closed his eyes.

I wanted to say he could sleep in the bed next to me, but his tiny snores could already be heard.

The confusion within my body, the fight with my mind and my heart were becoming too much to bear.

"Why do you fight it?"

The voice echoed in my head when I felt the heat of something warm on my chest. I reached up to feel what could cause the strange sensation until I felt those all too familiar curls.

As his tongue delicately traced intricate patterns around my breast, I gasped, overcome by the intense heat of his breath caressing the curves of my chest.

"Oh, wrong. This is wrong," I whispered.

It didn't feel wrong. How could something that felt so good be wrong?

Another hand crept up my side, grasping the other breast. I wanted to push it down between my legs, but the claws were all I could think about.

What if he scratched me? Just enough to let me feel the power of his hands?

I let out a moan, my legs widening for him to settle himself between them. I felt the heat of his stomach pressing against my core. My hips rolled, trying to gain the unfamiliar friction I needed.

Yes, I needed it. The dream that I was in, I needed it.

A barely audible "Please," escaped my lips. "Please, touch me."

His tongue flicked against my nipple. I opened my eyes and gasped when I saw those golden eyes stare back at me, hungrily.

"Lucy, touch." No question, a statement. His tongue snaked out between his lips and licked my nipple. He opened his mouth to engulf it all, sucking the entire breast into his mouth.

My pussy fluttered around nothing. I wanted something there—his tongue, maybe his dick.

Ugh, why hadn't I felt this before? Sex was going to be far better than I ever imagined it to be. All those years of ignoring and not being bothered with it, then Simon had lit the candle on fire, and I was going to become a sex addict.

Simon let go of my breast, his mouth trailing up my chest to my neck. He nuzzled against me, and my arms wrapped around him to hold him there.

It wasn't just the physical part that felt so good, but the care he was putting into my body. He touched me gently, then grabbed me harshly when I moaned for more. He was playing me like a fine fiddle. Simon knew exactly where I wanted it—even when I didn't know myself.

"My Lucy." His breath hitched when his mouth came to my shoulder. He peppered kisses, licks, and bites along my body.

"Please!" It was a cry of desperation. "Simon, touch me."

He didn't laugh to mock me or make me feel bad, instead, his head traveled lower. His licks became swirls of delight when he reached my navel and finally between my legs.

He pushed my legs open wide, and knowing this was a dream, I didn't even care. "Please lick me down there."

My boldness shocked me, but in this dream, I could do what I wanted, right? I mean, I didn't go to bed naked.

This was a dream.

He took in a long draw of my scent, and his nose moved back and forth, inhaling my arousal deep into his lungs. I could feel the warmth of his breath on my most intimate part as he prepared to take me in.

And with that promise, he parted my lips with his fingers, revealing the secret depths of me. He lowered his head, and I felt the gentle pressure of his mouth against me. The sensation was electric and had me relaxing into his mouth.

His tongue made slow, deliberate strokes, tasting every inch. He was thorough and precise, exploring every hidden crevice. As he went deeper, I felt an intense heat building within me, a desire so strong it was almost painful.

His hands cupped my hips, drawing me closer to his face. "Mmm," he hummed, his claws sinking into me.

I arched my back, pushing myself ever closer. My breath came in short pants as he sunk his long tongue deep inside me.

I whined, "Please, suck. Suck on it, please."

A guttural growl tore from his throat, his body stiffening and contorting into a tense, animalistic form. Snarling, he sucked in a breath and then began kneading my hips with a determined touch.

I cried out, feeling my orgasm hit me. It was impossibly stronger than two nights ago. This was euphoric and earth-shattering. I thought I had gone to the heavens and now was crashing back down to the soil.

I wanted more; I wanted to feel his—

"Lucy okay?" his voice came from a distance, but he was right there. "Lucy, are you okay?"

A warm hand wrapped around my arm, and I jolted, leaving this dream-like state behind and waking up in a dark cave. A lantern shone on the table, and Simon's face was only half-lit.

His face was wild, his eyes dark, and he was breathing incredibly hard as if he had run a mile. Simon hovered over me and lifted his hand from my arm. "Lucy, touch?" he questioned, and all I did was stare back at him.

I could feel his erection on the side of my hip. It was hot, and when I stared down, it was leaking precum, which glistened with the lantern's light.

My heart was in my throat, but the haze of the orgasm I just had in my dream was making me bold. I was still horny, and Simon was hovering over me like he was going to eat me.

I lifted my hands from my dress, the fabric clinging slightly to my thighs, which I had hiked up beneath the covers. My fingers were wet—no, soaked—and I realized he wasn't the one touching me in my dream; it was just me.

I stared into his wild eyes and traced his erection with my wet fingers, feeling the heat radiating from it. My voice, rough and husky from disuse, barely sounded out the words, "Simon, touch."

He seemed to hold his breath, while his eyes locked on mine as if searching for permission. Finally, he nodded slightly, his breath hitching. One hand gripped my hip, and the other pushed the dress away.

His lip turned into a snarl as he gently used his claws to pull down my white cotton underwear.

"My mate smells pretty."

Chapter Fourteen

Simon

I THOUGHT MY MATE was in distress when I heard her muffled cries on the bed.

I watched her blanket slowly slide away from her trembling body, revealing a glimpse of her vulnerability. The air filled heavily with her unique scent, which soon enveloped the cave.

Of course, my shaft was awake!

My mate's cries echoed through the cave, mingling with the low, haunting moans that had also escaped her lips. Her hand traveled down the curves of her body, delicately exploring beneath the fabric that concealed her slick.

My breath caught. *It wasn't fair; I wanted to be those fingers.*

I licked my lips and came close to her body. Just one lick, one lick would be okay.

I let out a muffled whine when her back arched off the bed. I wanted to suck on her breasts, suck on her nipple and nibble it between my teeth.

Why was the goddess punishing me? Why was my mate so close, yet so far away?

I'd promised I would not touch. I would not take her unless she begged me. But it was hard—too hard. I thought the day would never come, but here she was.

The command "Simon touch" hung heavily in the air; with those two words, my ruin was complete. I extended my hand and felt the softness of her body as she leaned into me. I prayed she was fully awake because she could never go back from this, and I could never go back to not touching her.

My hands trembled when I pulled down the white cloth. It was pristine white, and my mouth watered to think that what lay beneath was now mine.

I'd seen naked faes, fairies and shifters, but none of them held a candle to my mate. I'd never had the desire or the drive to be attracted to anyone else but her. This bond would end me.

As I turned my gaze towards her, my lip curled into a snarl, and my eyes fixated on her glistening lips, illuminated by the soft glow of the lanterns. In the background, the low rumble of thunder echoed through the air, creating a sense of foreboding as I inhaled deeply.

"My mate smells pretty." I lowered my head and rubbed against her heat. She cried out, and her hands reached for my horns.

She tugged on them with a firm grip, her thumbs massaging the base. The tension in my body intensified as my throbbing shaft grazed against the soft blankets.

I would release my seed if she continued to touch me.

I took a greedy lick at her slit. Her gasps filled the cave as I savored her taste, which ignited a fire within me that only she could quench. Every lick, every suck brought me closer to my desire to lose control and let the beast in me surface.

Then, when I sucked in the small nub at the top of her slit, she nearly flew off the bed. I smirked, taking more licks at this pleasure spot.

Her grip tightened on my horns, eliciting a low, guttural growl that vibrated through my very being. But I held back, kept my control, and focused on her sweet essence and the way her body responded to my touch.

I pushed forward, my tongue seeking the hidden treasure between her folds. Her cries grew louder and more insistent, urging me. I lapped at her with renewed vigor, savoring each moan and shudder she gave me until I thrust my tongue inside her.

"Simon! Please!"

My shaft grew impossibly hard, as my hips pushed against the bedding. "Simon, oh, gods, I'm going to come."

I didn't understand what she meant, but I continued at my pace; suck, lick, suck, then suddenly, she arched her back and screamed. Her arousal poured into my mouth. I greedily took her in, savoring the sweet taste.

I gripped my shaft and tugged on it several times until I moaned into her slit and spilled my seed along her thighs.

Yes, you will smell of nothing but me now.

I rubbed my cheek along her folds, taking up her scent.

My mate panted, her hands letting go of my horns.

"Gods, what just happened?" Her arm flopped over her stomach. "What did we just do?"

I meticulously cleaned my mate, savoring every bit of her essence with gentle licks. She became my preferred drink, and I wished for more chances to quench my thirst with her.

I hummed, licking the inside of her thighs one last time before crawling up her body. My shaft was already hard again, and I wondered if she would let me—

"Simon?" she gasped when she saw I was hovering over her.

Did she forget I was here? *That wouldn't do.*

I did not know the female body well, but I knew where to sink my cock.

"Lucy is mine," I whispered into her ear.

She swallowed. "Simon?" Her voice shook as I took my fingers, retracted my claws, and sunk them into her heat.

I gently caressed her most sensitive part, feeling the slick warmth of her arousal against my fingertips. With a possessive growl, I nipped her neck. As my heart pounded in my chest, the exhilarating sensation of owning her body consumed me.

I wanted my cock inside her, but as I delved deeper into her body, I quickly realized I would not fit her. I continued to push deeper, feeling my fingers slide smoothly inside her. Her body trembled beneath me as I slowly claimed it. Every inch of me was filled with a burning need to mark her, to make it clear to everyone that Lucy belonged to me.

Lucy's arms wrapped around my neck, as my cock rubbed up against her leg. Our scents intertwined, and my hips went into the motion of my fingers, while my body pressed against her, feeling her warmth.

She cried out as my finger thrusts grew more reckless, fueled by my endless desire to give her pleasure. Her breasts bounced wildly as I moved, each motion bringing me closer and closer to the edge of ecstasy.

"Mine," I growled into her neck as she screamed into my chest. My fangs itched to sink into her flesh, to leave a mark on her body. Her body sucked my fingers tightly until I fell onto her.

Lucy thrust her hands into my hair, taking long whiffs of my scent. My body trembled violently, but a low, comforting purr rumbled in my chest.

"How, what—" she began, but a deafening roar cut her off.

My ears perked up, but my body was still not over releasing so much seed. I put my fingers to my lips and motioned for her to stay quiet.

"Clothes," I whispered. I did my best to shove my shaft back into my pouch, and I trotted to the mouth of the cave. The rain was not coming down heavily any longer, but now just a trickle.

"I smell it. Hu-man." The deep crackling bass of a voice immediately made me snarl.

I ground my teeth in anger. It was the ogre, and he'd found us. He was at the base of the rock face and stared right up at me.

The yellowcress root could have washed away, and my mate's arousal must have triggered the monster. I bared my teeth and ran back inside. The ogre was large, and he could climb up the side of the cliff if he used his feet to kick into the stone.

The dimly lit cave trembled violently, sending plumes of dust swirling through the air. Deafening cracks echoed as jagged rocks cascaded down, crashing against the cave floor.

This home was supposed to be safe. Now, it was no longer good enough.

Fueled by a surge of rage, I bent over and grabbed a small boulder. With a grunt, I heaved it skyward, the weight straining my muscles. The rock plummeted downwards, hurtling towards its target with a resounding thud. The ogre's anguished cries echoed against the rock face. Enraged, the creature pounded its colossal fist against the rocky surface, creating thunderous booms.

"Come, we go." I motioned for my mate to come with me. I grabbed my emergency satchel with water and food, and gripped her hand.

My mate pulled me back. Worry danced across her face. "How did he—"

"Our s-cent. We go."

I felt my mate's heart pound in her chest when we got outside. A large hand was already grabbing onto the side of the cliff.

"How can he—" I put my hand over her mouth and swooped her up in my arms. There wasn't time to ask questions, but I knew my mate always had questions.

"Shh, keep you s-safe."

"I don't have on any underwear!" she hissed.

My smile widened, and Lucy rolled her eyes.

"Of course that would make you happy."

My mate squeezed my neck tight as I walked along the thin path where I'd taken her earlier to relieve herself. I trotted over to the side of the tall grasses and was met with a steeper, more difficult area to climb down.

But I would not tell her that.

"Simon, no," she gasped, her breath catching in her throat as she clutched me desperately.

Hmm, my mate was very smart.

The rocks were wet. I was carrying extra weight, but the ogre would not wait.

Another roar came from the cave, and my heart sank as I knew our home had been destroyed. I'd make another one more worthy of her, but now I must concentrate.

"Hold me, don't scream," I whispered, my lips brushing her forehead, feeling the warmth of her skin.

She scoffed. "Yeah, I'll do my best."

If my mate was not at risk, I'd stay back and fight the ogre and show her my abilities to keep her safe. Even the orcs had trouble bringing an ogre down, but they did not run as fast as I did. I prayed to the goddess that my mate did not think less of me for running from the ogre.

Snarls echoed across the cliffside when the ogre poked his head around where my cave once was. His heavy, hot breathing caused steam to tumble from his mouth as the rain did its best to extinguish the flames of his anger.

I gripped my mate tightly with one arm and used the other hand for balance. The rain made my grip weak, but my hooves were still steady amongst the sharp, jagged rocks.

The wind whipped around us as I leaped from one rock to another, each jump jarring my mate in my arms, eliciting a small whimper with every landing.

At least she was not screaming.

I smiled and shook my head. Making my leaps quicker until we landed on a nearby tree limb. She sighed in relief when I caught my breath. The thickness of the limbs on this side of the wood would be our way to escape.

The ogre's roars grew louder once he jumped from the cliff. The land shook, and we felt it in the trees. I hunched over and covered my mate with my body to keep her scent hidden as the ogre's frame came into view.

The rain muted his stench. It was usually vile and repulsive, but it gave me an idea that might save us.

With new determination, I hopped the last few tree branches to the soft ground. I stayed hidden in the thickest parts of the wood. He couldn't run; he was slow, but he was trailing us.

"Where are we going, what are we going to do?" she whispered against my neck, and I grunted in reply, "W-water." I didn't have time to concentrate on speaking; I needed her in the water, and fast.

The stream that I frequented was overflowing. It was perfect to dip both of our bodies under. I jumped in, not giving my mate a warning. She gasped when she came back to the surface.

"Fudge brownies! What are—"

I swiftly pressed my palm against her quivering lips, feeling the warmth and softness of her skin beneath my touch. As I held my breath, straining to hear, thunderous footsteps came closer, causing the ground to tremble.

"Out," I pulled her back up into my arms. The strength of the water and her dress were heavier, but with my muscular hind legs, I was able to push us out. As our soaked bodies dripped behind us, I went to one of the widest trees I could find.

The trunk itself was as wide as three orc cabins, and the plum-colored leaves shone with the trickling of rain. I grunted, slipping through the mud of the stream bank, my nose flaring in determination.

I quickly assessed the knots in the tree as I ran towards it.

Lucy's arms tightened around my neck, and I used both hands to grab hold of the knots. "You are like a freaking monkey with hooves!"

With a derisive snort, I continued my ascent, muscles burning. As we brushed against the leaves, they created a sheen of golden sparkles within the branches.

Once we had climbed high enough, far out of his vision and his ability to smell us, I sat her down beside me.

The rain was still a steady trickle, and with our bodies drenched, I hoped that had washed away most of our scent.

The ogre stomped toward the stream, the mud squished beneath his toes and splashed on his legs. The creature leaned back his head, his round, bald scalp reflected by the fireflies, and took in a deep breath. I held my mate impossibly tight and placed my hand over her mouth.

The ogre released a scoff, his nose sniffing and huffing, as he went in a direction away from us. I let my shoulders relax and let my hand drop away from Lucy's mouth.

Her eyes were wide with fear. Once she let go of me, she grabbed hold of a branch so tightly her knuckles became white.

"H-how did he find us?" She shivered against my body. "I thought ogres were pretty rare. Why does he keep popping up?"

He came after her because he had smelled her before when she was with her group. Once an ogre wants something, he will stop at nothing to get it.

I cupped my mate's chin and turned her face toward me. "I protect you."

"I need to get back with the others. They can all help," she said with no hesitation.

I huffed and let out a bleat. The bigger the group, the more likely the ogre would find her.

"No, dangerous. You safe here."

Her eyes narrowed. "I am not; we are not. There aren't enough of us, Simon. That thing could hurt you or me! Hurt someone else. Has anyone—not human—tried to talk to an ogre? It can talk. Surely not that stupid."

I pulled her into my arms to calm her shivering. She was cold and wet, and I needed to get her warm quickly. Humans get sick easier; I knew that.

"You cannot reason with ogres. Orcs have tried."

"But—"

I forced her nose into the crook of my neck. She took a deep breath and sighed.

"Promise you, you are safe." I rocked her back and forth. "I protect you."

A low growl rumbled in my chest as I ran my sharp claws through her hair. She leaned against me and sighed, finally giving in to me.

CHAPTER FIFTEEN

Simon

MY MATE DIDN'T FALL asleep until dawn.

The towering tree we had sought refuge in shielded us from the relentless downpour that had continued off and on through the night. Its gnarled branches, covered in lush foliage, had provided a sturdy haven for us.

The rustling of leaves in the wind had whispered a soothing melody, as the scent of damp earth mingled with the crisp freshness of rain. Nestled in the protective embrace of the tree, I felt a comforting sense of security.

It felt safe. It felt right being here with her.

My mate held onto me before she fell asleep. I knew it was because she was scared, but I couldn't help but feel a sense of pride that she knew I would protect her.

I wanted to stand up and bang on my chest.

Except my mind was on the ogre to celebrate for too long. They were persistent in hunting for what they wanted, and when I lusted after my mate, I had forgotten just how powerful her arousal was.

No longer. I would make sure her scent was no longer detectable when she hungered for me.

Because I would always give her what she wanted.

A small shudder ran through Lucy as she nestled under my arms. I didn't want to let her go after the encounter with the ogre. My body shielded her scent. The ogre would not know my smell, and he only wanted my mate.

Unfortunately, she was still wet from soaking in the deep stream, and I knew she would become sick if I did not get her dry.

Once the first hint of a light source entered the sky, her body relaxed, and she fell limp in my arms. I gently pressed my nose against her neck and encircled my hand around her throat, feeling the steady beat of her pulse beneath my thumb.

No one would touch her. Not those souls that brought her here and definitely not that wolf shifter, Dutton.

I grabbed several leaves nearby and laid them down in the wide area of the tree where I had held her. It cupped inwardly deep enough. I knew she wouldn't roll out of the tree. It would have been the perfect nesting area for us while she rested and I figured out what we should do next.

I pressed my lips gently to her forehead, feeling the warmth of her skin against my own. As I let go of her body, a slight shiver ran through her, causing a pang of concern to stir within me. I couldn't help but wonder if it was a longing for my touch or a sign of her falling ill.

I leaned in close, my trembling finger tracing the delicate contours of her face. As I brushed my finger against her flushed cheek, I could feel the warmth radiating off her skin, a stark reminder of the feverish nights

Calliope used to endure when she would become sick. A deep sigh escaped me, laced with frustration and impatience.

I could not let my mate get sick.

I reluctantly released her, inhaling her scent once more. With anticipation coursing through me, I cautiously ascended a sturdy, moss-covered branch, and my eyes diligently surveyed the canopy. And there it was, my desired prize, beckoning me from three trees away.

Agilely leaping across branches, I reached out and tightly grasped the giant leaf, its majestic hue a fusion of deep purple intertwined with delicate pink veins. With a vigorous tug, the leaf severed from the tree, causing a cascade of ethereal white downy cotton to erupt from beneath the leaf. It will serve as a good blanket, and I could peel the rest to make a nest around her.

I repeated the process until I had gathered enough of the white fluff that would work as her bedding. I raced back toward Lucy, who was groaning in her sleep.

I let out a nervous bleat and fell to my knees.

"Lucy?" I brushed her hair from her face.

She didn't wake, and I let my hands touch various parts of her body. She was warm and still wet.

I swallowed harshly, knowing what I was about to do. She would not like this. She thought being naked was improper, but I didn't mind her naked.

This was for her health, which was most important. I took my claw and undid the string that held her dress together. The fabric fell easily off her body.

I groaned when her breasts fell free. I should not look; I should take care of her, but my body refused to listen.

"Simon," she breathed, the sound barely audible above the rustling leaves, and my body froze.

I laid behind her in order to keep her warm. My arm reached around and cupped her breast. She eased back into me, and I felt my shaft erupting from my pouch.

"Lucy, mine."

She wiggled against me and used my body to heat her own. She sighed, and my body filled with pride that she wanted me close.

I fondled her breasts, kneading them beneath my palm. "Mmm, Simon." Her backside rubbed against me, and I let out a whine. As I took a deep inhale of her hair, I nuzzled deeper, taking my tongue and licking up the side of her neck.

Yes, she wanted me. This was okay.

She settled, her body knowing I was near, and she fell back into a deeper sleep. I was happy she was more comfortable with my touch and could sleep again. However, that gave me a problem I needed to take care of.

A sweet but sufferable problem.

My mate didn't say another word, and I continued to peel the rest of the clothes off her body. If she had hair on her legs like mine, I would have begged her just to go naked. Unfortunately, she was raised as a human, and I knew my dreams to always see her naked would never come true.

But what if others saw her naked?

I let out a snarl and rubbed my head on her shoulder.

No, no one would see her naked but me.

Once I had the dress off her body, I laid it on a nearby branch. She stirred slightly, mumbling incoherently as I placed the fluff around her body. My heart ached at the sight of her pale skin, goosebumps rising from the cold and the fever that threatened to take hold.

She nuzzled into the fabric, seeking solace even in her unconscious state.

Was it possible to be jealous of the fiber that kept her warm? My fur could do the same.

The nest where she now rested made her look like a goddess. I was nearly stunned with awe at how beautiful she was.

I had a mate.

My shaft fell out of my pouch when I saw her move her arm. One of her breasts was exposed, and my balls hung heavily inside my pouch with a need I must express.

She was sick. I had to find supplies, but my body yearned for hers, and I could not take care of her properly with my shaft blowing in the wind.

I cautiously moved backward, my hand tightly gripping a sturdy branch for support. As the breeze swept through the trees, I noticed how it caused the tip of her breast to stiffen, creating a tantalizing sight. The sight alone made my mouth water, craving the sensation of touching and tasting her once more. A deep groan escaped my lips as I instinctively wrapped my hand around my shaft, consumed by desire.

My seed leaked from the tip, and I rubbed my thumb over the bulbous head.

The gods would strike me down.

I gripped my shaft tightly, one hand at the base, the other rubbing the exposed form up and down. My mate had always been a sight to behold, but now she was something otherworldly, a vision of beauty laying limp and vulnerable in our makeshift nest. I couldn't help but let out a deep, guttural growl as I stared at her. The desire to claim her as mine, to protect her from all harm, consumed me.

It was the animalistic side of me. Thoughts of rutting her into the soft nest, slipping inside while she slept, painted beautiful pictures in my head.

I could not do that. I was not an animal.

I squeezed my eyes shut and took a deep breath, trying to regain control of myself. I was the protector of my mate, and she needed me strong. But my body had other ideas. My shaft throbbed insistently, threatening to spill my seed if I didn't take care of it soon.

Did she want to touch me?

The thought of her soft hands gripping my shaft, staring at me with lust, would be my undoing. I grunted while I stared at her and stroked myself. The veins in my shaft enlarged, my body went rigid, and the idea of having Lucy lick my shaft while I licked her brought a newfound vigor to my strokes.

With a hoarse cry, I came, spilling my seed beside the nest.

Exhausted but satisfied, I took a moment to breathe before turning my attention back to Lucy.

Kneeling beside her, I heard a soft sound coming from her and looked down to see her moving slightly beneath the cotton blanket. Instantly worried that she was cold or uncomfortable, I draped the extra cotton over her exposed breast to keep her warm and covered as much as possible.

"Lucy," I whispered softly to her, "my Lucy."

I licked her cheek, feeling her body tremble ever so slightly in response. It was enough to reassure me that she wanted me.

Stroking her hair away from her face, I watched over her intently as I planned to find what we needed to get through this illness. But first things first, we needed food: fresh berries, vegetables, roots, or anything edible nearby would do the trick for now.

I straightened my back. I could not afford to be weak when she needed me most. I carefully stepped over the branches that led down to the forest floor, keeping a vigilant eye out for danger. Time was of the essence. I would not have Lucy become sick because of my negligence.

I quickly raced back to the cave. I knew I had herbs that could help her.

Since being alone and no longer roaming meadows and lands outside of the Wood often, I had gathered many plants and roots and dried them in case I became ill. I couldn't depend on Calliope and her mate to take care of me. They had each other, and I was alone.

My preparation was a blessing. Now, she will see me as a fit male.

Upon returning to the cave, I found it was not as destroyed as I had imagined. The scent of my mate's arousal lingered on the blankets, which had caused the bed to be shredded to pieces. Large rocks and boulders still sat in the cave, but I could remove them. The corner still held my preparation area for food and the spot where I kept my herbs for healing.

I sighed in relief and grabbed a leather satchel and put as many herbs as I could inside. For sickness, sleep, taste for food, and the most important of all, the yellowcress to keep our scent suppressed to a minimum.

My seed would keep the ogre away for now, but if Lucy wanted my body, I would not deny her. I would make sure she was protected, and then she would see what a fit male I was and let me claim her.

I grabbed a kettle and cups, as much as I could carry, and slung the satchel over my back. I would need to make a fire at the base of the tree to prepare her a tea that would be absorbed easier into her body, to reduce the fever.

When I returned to our nest, tears of pride filled my eyes as Lucy stirred and mumbled in her sleep for me. She unconsciously shifted closer to my warmth when I approached. I carefully lifted her body, whispering her name, but she did not wake, and my brows furrowed.

Was she sicker than I realized? Panic engulfed me as I held the iron cup filled with the herb tea, that was now cool enough for her to drink. I tickled her lips with my finger so she would part them and tried to tip the liquid into her mouth. She sputtered, and it fell down her chin.

A grunt escaped my lips as I set the cup down; the sticky sweetness of the spilled herb was already clinging to her chin as I wiped it away. She wasn't swallowing.

I scratched my head and looked around for an answer, but I knew I would not receive one.

I sighed and cupped her face. There was one way I could get it into her mouth.

I took a sip and placed my thumb on her bottom lip to help part them. Her breath was warm when I pressed her lips to hers. She swallowed and let out a hum in contentment.

My shaft rose once again, and I cursed myself.

He came out at the wrong time, every time.

My lips lingered, even after the drink had left me. I picked up the cup and drank more, just to have an excuse to place more of the drink into her mouth.

My fingers threaded through her hair, pulling her closer to my body. Reluctantly, I let go of her lips and placed my forehead on hers.

"You will be my undoing."

Lucy settled into a deeper sleep—one that would soon be free from fever or pain—and I allowed myself to rest too, lying beside her under the protective canopy of our branches. The desire to claim my mate still throbbed within me, but I needed to get her well.

She would not have gotten sick if it weren't for me, but I would show her I could take care of her.

CHAPTER SIXTEEN

Lucy

I'M NAKED.

I was as naked as the day I was born, lying in an enormous ball of fluff.

I pushed the large blanket away, which had been a type of leaf with a massive amount of cotton underneath. It had been snow white and so soft that I would have sworn I was sleeping on clouds. Beneath me had been more of the cotton but no leaves. Whoever had made this bed had ripped the cotton from the leaf and laid it beneath me.

Simon.

But why was I naked?

Did he rip my clothes off?

I covered myself with the blanket leaf, making sure my breasts were no longer exposed.

Did it really matter right now? I rubbed my forehead and cursed myself.

I let him touch me before; of course he would think he could see me naked.

And when I mean touch, he licked me.

There.

Sweet Rosalin Franklin, what the hell was I thinking?

I pinched the bridge of my nose. What would my father think of me being with a faun? What would any respectable human think of this? I just entered this Bergarian Realm knowing full well shifters and other species existed. They had a human form. But there was nowhere in the texts of Bergarian about Simon.

He was an evolved goat/human hybrid who had no full human form.

Would our species even be compatible if we had children?

I gasped and covered my mouth. Why was I thinking about that? There was no relationship here. Simon was curious about my body, that was all.

Right?

I saw my dress hanging in the tree. It had been washed free of mud. Then, there was this bed he made for me in the tree. Would an animal go to such lengths just to see and touch my body?

He speaks, Lucy. He has thoughts and desires just like any complicated being. His speech is just limited because he's never tried to talk.

I nodded my head.

This is fine. Everything is fine.

I'd get to know him better, figure out more about his life and how he knew this other woman in the Wood, along with her mate. Perhaps I could get answers from them, too.

I took a quick look around the tree to make sure Simon wasn't near. I put my dress on, minus my underwear, because those were back in the cave. Crap, I went commando, and I was sure Simon loved every bit of that.

I leaned over the tall, sturdy branch, feeling the rough bark beneath my fingertips. From my elevated position, the panoramic view unfolded before me. It was a beautiful mix of jungle and forest vegetation.

The acrid scent of burning wood and ash filled my nostrils, making my eyes water. The smell was so strong it tickled my nostrils, bringing tears to my eyes and a slight cough. I squinted and saw the orange glow of a fire flickering just a few meters away. Its flames danced and crackled.

I thought about calling Simon, but I wasn't about to have him hold me and jump down the tree with those hooves.

Would I mind leaning up against him? Feeling his body on me.

Ugh, my clit was already tingling at that thought.

No, my body would not win this.

I gripped the branch, determined that I would conquer my fear of heights, and slung my leg over. This wasn't so bad. I had my hands on a limb. I could feel the thicker branch on the bottom with my feet.

"That's it," I whispered, the sound barely audible amidst the rustling leaves and chirping birds. Slowly and steadily, I carefully maneuvered my way down the rough, gnarled branches as I took my sweet time. With each step, the rough texture of the bark tickled my toes, a reminder of my shoeless state. Despite the inconvenience, I couldn't help but enjoy feeling nature.

"Besides, when humans walk barefoot, studies have shown an increase in red blood cells, suggesting improved immunity. Barefoot walking has also been linked to higher levels of antioxidants, less inflammation, and better sleep. You just need to embrace it, Lucy. Everything is going to be fine."

My foot slipped on a moss-covered branch, and I let out a loud squeal.

Kitty whiskers! I'm gonna die.

I closed my eyes and held on for dear life.

A loud bleat came from below, and I felt the tree shake.

"Oh, my god! Please don't let me fall!" I screamed.

Warm arms wrapped around my torso from behind me. "Lucy, I have you. Let go."

I kept my eyes closed and shook my head. "No way, nuh uh!"

Simon chuckled, his deep voice vibrating through me. "Trust me, Lucy. You won't fall. I won't let you."

"You sure about that? Because I'm just bad luck. I got kidnapped, chased by an ogre twice, and woke up in a tree, naked. Luck is not on my side."

Simon huffed. His warm breath ran down the front of my chest, and instantly, my breasts felt heavy, and my nipples hardened.

Seriously, the worst luck ever this week!

"Are you going to hang in the tree all day, then?" He snorted.

I bit my bottom lip, my nails piercing the moss-covered branches. "Yup."

Simon kept one arm wrapped around my waist and the other raised as he put it on top of mine, which held on tightly to the limb. "My mate will not hang in the tree like a rodent. You are too precious to drop. Besides, we are not that far from the ground," he said with the smoothest voice.

Had he been practicing while I slept? How long did I sleep?

"I'm not gonna open my eyes until we are down there."

Simon barked in laughter. "Of course."

I took a deep breath and slowly released my grip on the branch, feeling Simon's strong arms supporting me. He had carried me down the tree safely until my bare feet touched the soft grass below.

I fell to my knees and put my head on the forest floor. "Never again. My feet belong here. Sweet solace."

Simon stood beside me, his hooves coming into view.

Now who looks like an animal, Lucy?

I stood up quickly, knocking off the leaves and bits of dirt on my recently cleaned dress, ready to thank him for saving me yet again. Should I thank him though? He was my kidnapper.

It wasn't proper not to thank him, so I glanced up and opened my mouth to do just that. Instead, I screamed in terror.

There was blood dripping from his mouth. It was on his chest, his arms, and hands, and I checked my dress to see that blood had covered me as well.

He was a faun vampire!

As I screamed in terror, Simon's face contorted into a look of confusion and concern. "What's wrong?" he asked, his voice laced with worry. He stepped closer, but I held up my hands to stop him.

I pointed to his chest, my hand trembling as I did so. "Blood," I stuttered out.

For a moment, his eyes widened in shock before he looked down at himself and let out a deep sigh. "Oh, this," he said dismissively.

What did he mean, "Oh, this?!"

My heart raced as my mind tried to process what was happening. Blood? He was covered in blood? Was he sucking blood from an animal? Was it his own? Did someone attack him?

"Whose blood is it?" I demanded, my voice shaky. "Did you drink it?" Because it was all over his mouth.

Simon reached up and wiped some of the blood off his face with the back of his hand. "It's a root I have dug up. It leaks red," he explained calmly. "I was about to wash it in the stream because I did not think you would want to eat it when it leaks."

Not blood. And I believed him. Although he kidnapped me, he had not lied to me. "You are not hurt at all?" I asked, concern filling my voice.

Simon smiled, his fangs glinting in the light sources glow. "Are you worried for me? For my safety?"

I turned my head as I narrowed my eyes. "Of course, I wouldn't want you hurt." I put both hands on my hips.

"You care for me!" He jumped and galloped around me. "You accept me as your mate!"

I held out my hands for him to slow down. How in the heck did he get that from me just trying to make sure he was alright?

"Easy, Simon. I don't..."

He nodded his head excitedly, ready for me to speak.

Crap. I didn't want to break his little heart. I also didn't want him to think we were mates and we would be together forever. There would be a point where the group would find me and take me back. I had my father to still look after and a mission to finish.

My heart constricted in my chest at the idea of not seeing him again. He had grown on me, and in a twisted way, I really cared for him. He was sweeter, kinder, and more innocent than other men I'd seen or met.

And the orgasm. I mean, who could forget that?

"Simon, you don't know we are mates. Mates are—"

"You are my mate!" He stomped his hoof. "I will prove more to you. I have worked on my tongue." He continued to blab about speaking and exercising his tongue.

My traitorous body thought of other things he could do with it.

He took in a long whiff and smirked. "Your body knows. Soon, you will know, too." He huffed and stomped off to the stream.

I watched as he trotted away, a mix of confusion and desire flowing through me. What was happening? My thoughts were scattered, trying to keep up with the revelation that I might be his mate and the inexplicable connection I felt towards him.

I took a moment for myself to sort out my feelings and gather my thoughts. Those few minutes alone made me realize that I hated the idea of being alone, in a forest with an ogre after me. I walked over to the stream where Simon had gone, and as I approached, I noticed something odd. The water seemed to shimmer slightly, creating a strange play of colors in the shallow pools of the stream.

I let out a heavy sigh, feeling a twinge of disappointment. I longed for the comforting weight of my trusty notebook in my hands, the pages ready to be filled with my observations. It *was* the reason I was here.

I settled myself on the massive rock, with its rough surface pressing against my skin. The roots that Simon had been digging for were thick and gnarled, sprawled across the rock beside me. As I examined them closely, I noticed tiny droplets of red, like delicate jewels glimmered in the light. These must have been the roots that Simon had described earlier.

My body instantly recognized that he was approaching, the hair on my neck stood on end. My body was a dang traitor for him.

I turned around and saw that he had washed his toned body from the red dye that had come from the roots. He was wet, the light sources glistening on his muscular chest and his lean torso.

Um, yum?

Why did everyone in this realm have to be so attractive? Especially him?

Simon pulled out a book from behind his back and lifted it toward me. "What is this?" I asked, my curiosity piqued when I flipped through the pages. They were empty.

"You had a book that you wrote in when you were with your group. I don't know where it went, but I have this empty one." He nodded toward it. The cover was thick leather, decorated with intricate designs. "I want you happy. Will this book make you happy?"

I let out a puff of air. "It does make me happy, Simon."

He made me happy. To be honest with myself, I didn't think I'd ever been this... free. For the first time in my life, I've gotten my hands truly dirty, enjoyed desires I'd never felt, and had a connection that went far beyond anything I have ever encountered.

I needed to drop the social standards I had learned and stop shunning the unknown. I had this feeling inside me that I was not sure of, but it was telling me to embrace whatever Simon and I had.

Could I do that?

What if I wasn't his mate? I'd be so disappointed, but what if I never felt sexual desires again? This could be my only chance, just to have him for a little while.

Was this worth the heartbreak?

Simon beamed and sat beside me. He held up the roots that he had washed and offered me one.

I couldn't get any more immersive than this, traveling around a forest with a faun who no one knew existed.

I took the root from his hand and sniffed. It smelled like cinnamon and sugar. He urged me to take a bite, and I tentatively bit down on it. An eruption of flavor burst on my tongue.

It tasted like a churro.

"What's this called?"

Simon shrugged his shoulders. "I don't know. Orcs don't eat it. They don't know about it because it is in the ground. I could smell how sweet it was myself." He sat up straight. "My nose is better than an orc's."

I stifled a laugh and took another bite. I opened the notebook, saw a pencil on the side, ready for me to use, and began to draw the roots, giving details on its taste and smell. I also put a brief note beside it that only a faun could sniff out the sweet-tasting roots.

Chapter Seventeen

Lucy

As soon as I finished sketching out the roots, I took another bite. I was surprised by how sweet it tasted coming straight from the ground. I expected it to be something bitter and more earthy in taste.

Can I say earthy?

Bergarian-y?

I put the notebook down and saw Simon washing more roots. My interest piqued, and I leaned over his shoulder. "Where did you get them?"

Simon sat back on his legs; his hands rubbed down his soft thighs. An imagery flashed in my mind: my hands running through the soft fur as I dug my nails into the muscle. My insides fluttered.

Would he make whimpering sounds like he did the last time we touched?

Did he want to touch me again after that? I could be too much trouble now that we had that stupid ogre after us.

"The roots?" He broke me out of my thoughts.

I nodded eagerly. "Where do you get them? What plant do you look for, and where do you dig them up?"

Simon eyed me and tilted his head. "Why do you need to know? Whenever you want them, I'll get them for you. You don't have to search for food. It is my job to provide for you."

He puffed out his chest to appear larger. Instead of looking big and tough, it made my emotional wall drop for him. He was so innocent and was trying so hard.

"No, silly. I want to know how I can find them so I can write it down in this book." I pointed to the book sitting by itself on the rock. "You see, the whole point of me being here is to gather information about the Wood and send it back to the Cerulean Moon Kingdom. There aren't that many people who know about the Monktona Wood, and most fear what is inside of it. Especially when there are nothing but ogres and orcs inside. I'm trying to give everyone an insight of what it's like inside."

Simon tilted his head and chewed the remaining root in his mouth. His thoughtful face was utterly adorable, and I wanted to squish his face together and say, "Who's a cute wittle faun?"

But I wouldn't. I didn't want him to think I was being condescending. He was just—Simon.

"You did not come to the Wood to find a mate, then?"

I frowned. "I'm a human. While humans have found mates in Bergarian, I don't think I would have one. I came from Earth with no ties to anyone. We just answered an ad on the internet looking for a scientist and somehow we were selected, as if it were fate." I rubbed my lips together. "I came for a job, not because I was hunting for a forever partner. Honestly…" I paused as I tried to find the right words.

"I've never found anyone attractive to me. Who would fit my tastes? It's hard for me to have a relationship with anyone because I don't have… those special desires."

Simon's mouth was parted like a goat ready to be fed.

Alright, I can't beat around the bush with this. He needs bluntness.

"Sexual desires. Sex!"

He continued to stare at me.

"What we did earlier! You, on top of me. Touching each other!" I covered my face. "I've never wanted to before."

He gave me a toothy grin.

Ah, Skittles!

"And why would a goddess give me a mate anyway if I don't have those feelings to do that?"

Of course, Simon's excitement deflated.

My thoughts made my stomach churn. I would like to have a mate, but I couldn't wrap my head around the thought that I could have one. I didn't know what to look for, and I didn't get to ask the queen those questions because I was too busy and excited to see shifters, fae, vampires, and the other lot.

Simon turned away and shoved the roots into his satchel. "Don't you want to find someone? Not be alone? We do not have to touch if you do not want to." He looked hopeful as he stared at me.

My lips tilted downward. I wanted to touch *him.*

"I sought no one before. It wouldn't be fair to them. It's natural for beings to seek contact, physical contact. Besides, I'm not alone. I have my father." I picked at my red-stained dress. "We can care for each other."

Simon shook his head. "Not the same."

He was right, it wasn't. I had never seen my father with a significant other since I was a child. My father believed he would never find the right woman for him, one that shared the same interests in science, enjoyed reading and exploring unknown places.

"It's not. But he is my father," I stated. "What about you?" I decided to change the direction of this conversation. I was feeling way too vulnerable. "Do you remember your parents? If you don't want to talk about it, you don't have to." I placed my hand on top of his. He stared at it longingly and put his other hand on top of mine.

"I do not know them. I do not remember a lot of things." His face went red, and he avoided my gaze.

More questions surfaced, but seeing how the light died from Simon's features, I realized I should leave it alone. I didn't want to see him sad, not after everything he had done for me. I'm pretty sure I slept a day or so because he had set up a base camp here around the fire.

Yet, I still wondered. I needed to know more about Simon, this faun that had me chomping at the bit, wanting to understand him and his sweet ways.

"I don't know my mother," I muttered under my breath.

Simon's head popped up, and his gaze met mine.

"I don't. I have never met her, but I know of her." Was I really ready to tell him my story? It was a part of me I never shared with anyone. Everyone believed that my father had a relationship with a woman, and she gave me up to him. Or that she died, which was partly the truth.

"My father was on a conference trip in South Africa. It's a place, back on Earth," I added. Simon scooted closer to me and squeezed my hand tighter. "He wasn't planning on leaving the hotel where the conference was being held, but since he was already in a new country he had never visited, he decided to go explore when he didn't have a meeting."

I smiled and remembered when he first told me about my history. It made me realize what a kindhearted man he was. A little eccentric at times but a wonderful man, nonetheless.

"My father…" my voice croaked, "was walking through the Port Elizabeth streets just after dark. He was warned not to go out after dark, being a tourist and all, but my father,"-I chuckled-"isn't one to take heed of any warning."

Simon scooted closer to me again, and I saw the warmth brimming in my eyes. "He heard a scream. A blood-curdling scream and ran straight toward it. When he got to an alleyway a few blocks down, he saw two thugs roughing up a woman. He charged right away; he didn't care about his safety. When they saw my father, they ran, but the woman they had assaulted had been stabbed."

Simon's ears pulled back, and his arms wrapped around me. It felt good to be hugged. The only person I allowed to hug me was my father, but this was surprising. It was just like the night the ogre scared me.

I'm so screwed.

"Anyway, she was pregnant. Heavily. My father took her to the hospital, but they couldn't save her. Her heart stopped beating, but they managed to save the poor baby inside her."

Simon whimpered and pulled me into his lap. I didn't stiffen, instead I laughed as I got up close and personal with his face. He had such soft hair on his cheeks. His nose was slitted, different from mine, eyes big and wide, but I could read his emotions like an open book.

"My father asked what was going to happen to me. They found out who the woman was, but she had no contacts. Judging by her clothes, she was poor and homeless. They told my father I would be just another child amongst others in a broken system. Being an orphan on Earth isn't a good thing, Simon. It's hard to find parents to love you. I'm sure there are others that have a great life, but the odds weren't in my favor."

Simon put his nose into my neck and took a deep breath. I tried not to laugh as his whiskers brushed my cheek.

"Dad adopted me then and there. Well, he said he would take me. It took months to get the paperwork right, but from the very beginning, he's always been my father."

"He is a good male." Simon threaded his fingers through mine. "Without him, I would not have you."

I felt a rush of emotions as Simon held me close; his sincerity warmed my heart in a way I never thought possible. His simple words meant more to me than he would ever realize. My father was a good *male*. Selfless, caring, and kind.

Would my father mind if I began to care for a faun who had those same qualities? A person other than my species?

Father had kept me away from men for so long, that I had developed a strange fear of other men and had never had much connection with men anyway. Now that I had met Simon, it was different. Simon wasn't a man—or animal. He was a lot more than I gave him credit for.

As I gazed into Simon's eyes, I saw a reflection of my own feelings mirrored back at me. It was a strange sensation, realizing how much we both had a physical and, dare I say, spiritual connection? I never thought of myself as spiritual. It was just the facts, but I couldn't deny this. Despite our differences, we had forged a connection that ran deeper than I could have ever imagined.

With a soft smile playing on my lips, I leaned in and pressed a gentle kiss to Simon's cheek, feeling his warm fur beneath my lips. In that moment, surrounded by the crackling fire behind us and the soothing sounds of the birds chirping, I knew I was in over my head.

I was falling for him.

And I knew I wouldn't be able to stop.

Simon's back tensed up; his face flushed with a deep shade of crimson as I gently pulled my lips away from his warm, flushed cheek.

I tried to hide my smile, but Simon grew flustered and let out a long bleat.

Simon's embarrassment made me laugh harder, the sound echoing through the quiet forest around us. I tried to compose myself, but every time I looked at Simon's adorable red face, another peal of laughter bubbled up.

Finally, when I caught my breath, I reached out and gently touched Simon's cheek. His fur was soft beneath my fingertips, and I felt a surge of affection for this gentle faun who had stolen my heart.

I hope you or your goddess won't break it.

"Sorry, I didn't mean to do that." He cleared his throat and coughed. "Here, I will show you how to obtain the root." He took me off his lap, and I saw that his shaft had popped out of his pouch.

In the daylight, it looked impossibly larger, and since I had decided to embrace whatever connection Simon and I had, I couldn't rip my eyes away until he turned his body to hide it.

This is for science, I told myself. Yes, for science.

One could enjoy the fruits of a well-endowed faun before he found his real mate.

"For science!" I squeaked, and Simon turned, his body looking every bit delectable with water trailing down his muscular body.

I covered my mouth and stood. "Yes, for science. I need to know how to retrieve it."

Simon kept his problem hidden and nodded. "Come this way, I'll show you."

CHAPTER EIGHTEEN

Simon

SHE GRACEFULLY BENT OVER, her body lowering towards the dark pit that I had dug. The rich scent of damp mud filled the air, mingling with the faint aroma of the tantalizing roots I had discovered. As she hovered above, the sound of her gentle breaths mixed with the rustling of leaves near her. Her plump ass was up in the air, and I tried my best not to look.

She's my mate, I can look.

These desires make me want to rut her into the soil.

Yet I wanted her to like me and trust me, so I could lick at her slit again.

I'd dreamt about the paradise between her legs for days, sinking my tongue deep and lapping up her arousal. Since she was so sickly, I kept my hands to myself after the first time I'd massaged her soft breasts.

That does not mean I did not release my seed all over the nest.

The herbs made her better; **I** made her better. She acted like she was only in a deep sleep.

I hope to be rewarded for my dedication to her.

Because I wanted her.

"This is just fascinating! You can't smell the roots above the ground. Not even until you've cut them. Except for you, of course."

My chest swelled with pride.

I had given her my ax. Her tiny claws would not break the root. I knew many humans had shorter claws that did nothing to protect them. No wonder Calliope's mate was always so protective.

In my previous form, I did not understand.

My thoughts and speech had grown more complicated since knowing my mate. The spell that made me who I was, has now made me grow. Or maybe it was her. She had helped me evolve. I was able to talk better with a little practice, whereas before it was very difficult to try.

"You can really smell it under all this dirt?" My mate rose from the hole. Her hands were covered in the red liquid. It looked like blood. No wonder she was so upset earlier, but the scent alone made her smell that much sweeter when it was on her skin.

"Yes, the scent is stronger when you break the root and it leaks," I replied.

"Hmm, bleed might be a better word." She tapped her finger on her mouth. It left a trail down her chin. She also had smudges on her cheek. I licked my lips. Would she be angry if I just licked it clean?

"How do you prepare it?" She tilted her head and held onto the bundle she had in her hand. Her arm was soaked, her clothing even more so. When I washed her clothes earlier, it was difficult to get rid of the stain. I used most of my cleaning rocks to get rid of it.

Now, there was no hope for her clothing.

Good thing I made her some.

I smiled, excited that her clothes were ruined now.

"I wash the root in the stream. Most of these roots are only found near water."

"Hmm." She set the root down and looked down at her fingers. "Is it the root or the substance coming from it that tastes good? I know when we eat it, some of it is still left inside of it." She held up her hand and licked between her fingers where the red liquid trickled down her wrist. I stared in awe, watching her while her tongue circled her finger until she stuck it into her mouth.

My shaft, which *had* calmed down, poked outside of my pouch. The taste entranced her too much to take notice, and I wasn't about to push my shaft back inside while she had not noticed. My body inched toward her to take in her scent along with the sweet treat.

I panted, towering over her. I felt like a predator for the first time in my life. I had always been the prey. People slaughtered my kind, and yet here I was, above her, watching her eat a delicious substance from her hand.

Did she know I was strong? Or did she find me weak, like one of those goats I used to be?

My throat felt dry while I watched her lick more juice off her finger. She picked up more of the root. "Mmm, it's in the liquid and in the root. I think this tastes better than those desserts at the palace—don't tell Queen Clara that, though." She giggled and closed her eyes.

My body vibrated at her innocence. She did not know how much I wanted to do to her. Was it the animal in me or the mate bond? My body wanted her, and in such a short time, I was ready to have her all to myself forever.

I inched toward her and slowly grabbed her wrist. Would she do that for me? Lick and suck my shaft while the moans left her lips?

Her eyes fluttered open, a look of confusion on her face. I licked the back of her hand, and she let out an audible gasp when I continued to lick that sweet, sticky substance from her wrist.

My fangs scraped against her skin, and she shivered as her eyes widened. I couldn't tell if it was from shock or desire. Her breath came in soft, steady pants. My shaft inched further out of the pouch at the way her body responded to me.

If she responded just by the touch of my hands and my tongue, what would she do when other parts of me touched her?

I licked between her fingers, tasting the salty skin beneath the 'blood-stained' liquid. She moaned softly, a noise that set my blood on fire. I wanted to taste more of her, to explore every inch of her body with my lips and tongue.

"Simon," she whispered. "What are you doing?" Her voice was shaky, unsure.

I met her eyes, holding her gaze as I slowly pulled away. I didn't have words to form. I was unsure what to say. What was I doing exactly?

I continued to lick through her fingers, and her breasts pressed against her dress. I swore I could see the tips of them peek through the material, and I let out a hard breath of air between them.

"Your taste... I can't stop." I swallowed one of her fingers into my mouth, twirling my tongue around it. I licked down her palm to her wrist.

Before I could nip at her wrist, her hands flew up and cupped the scruff of my face as she pulled me to hers. Her lips found mine with urgency, and her tongue darted between my lips.

What was she doing?

I parted them, and her tongue entered my mouth.

So warm, so wet... everything I ever dreamed kissing would be.

Her hands gripped the back of my neck, pulling me closer as our kiss deepened. I could taste the lingering sweetness from the juice of the root on her tongue.

I wrapped my arms around her and made her straddle my waist. She grunted in response, situating her pussy next to my shaft.

Shit! This dress. Her clothing was the only thing keeping my shaft from her slit.

With a quiet growl, I broke the kiss, and my eyes locked onto hers. "Lucy," I rasped hoarsely, my voice barely above a whisper.

She smiled, a devious grin spreading across her face. "Simon," she answered back just as quietly. Her eyes darkened to a level of desire that I never knew I would see from a female.

She wanted this just as much as I did.

Thank the goddess!

I leaned in again, and our lips met once more in urgency. This time, it was different. She had hunger, the same as mine.

My fingers grazed the roots beside me, still bleeding the red, sweet liquid. I broke the kiss and held up my fingers, and she leaned forward, taking them into her mouth.

I imagined it was my thick shaft, and I let out a whimper, bucking my hips against her.

I was going to expel my seed, just watching her lick my fingers.

Once she finished, she grabbed the back of my head, tightening her grip on my hair. She pulled me forward and controlled the kiss. As our tongues dueled within our mouths, her fingers continued to play with the hair at the back of my neck, sending shivers down my spine. I wrapped my arms around her waist, pulling her even closer to me, and rubbed myself into her heat.

"Gods, Simon, what's happening? It feels so—"

I rolled over and pushed her into the soft moss. My mouth left hers while I licked down her neck. There were traces of the sweet liquid from the roots, but that wasn't what I wanted anymore. I just wanted *her* taste.

I emitted a low, guttural grunt, the sound reverberating in my throat. My tongue glided down her chest, the taste of her skin lingering on my taste buds. My rough claws tugged at the fabric of her stained dress.

Lucy's breath hitched as I continued downward, her heart pounded against my ears. I traced the curve of her chest with my tongue, savoring the taste of her skin as she moaned my name.

She wants this.

She wants me.

My claws cut through the fabric as if it were parchment and left a trail of shreds on the forest floor.

Her breasts came into view. They were soft, so full.

I took one into my mouth, teasing the nipple with my teeth before suckling gently. She moaned in pleasure, her hands reaching up to grab my horns.

Her thumbs rubbed at the base, and I let out a bleat. I paused, full of embarrassment, my face heating at how I let out such a primitive sound.

Lucy panted and sat up. Her hand reached out and pulled at the back of my hair. "I don't care, Simon. I enjoy hearing you."

My mouth parted as she pushed me up off her body. She got on top of me with her legs spread, and her heat sat on my shaft. I swallowed heavily, feeling the wetness of her arousal.

She had lifted her dress, so she could feel me.

Her heat was all around me. It was on my shaft and in my nose.

This all felt like a dream.

"I like your sounds," Lucy whispered against my lips. "I like them a lot," I whimpered, my eyes closed when her forehead met mine. "Every sound, do you hear me?"

She moved her wet slit across my girth. My hands gripped her waist as I helped move her.

"I like my little faun losing all of his control."

What was she doing? Why was she so commanding? Were all females like this?

I like it—so much!

Her wetness coated me. She slid effortlessly along my shaft.

She leaned down, her lips brushing against mine, and whispered, "You want this, don't you?"

I nodded, my mind hazy with excitement and desire. I wanted her and needed her more than I had ever needed anything in my life.

She smiled, a wicked glint in her eyes as she adjusted herself over me. I felt the warmth of her folds wrapped around the tip of my shaft, and I groaned at the sensation of being possessed by her completely.

"Say it," she hissed, her eyes locked on mine as she continued to ground her wetness on me. "Say it or I'll stop."

Excitement ran through my body as I choked out the words. "I want you. So much."

Her smile widened as she finally moved in earnest, her hips sliding against me in a steady rhythm. Her breath was shallow and uneven, but she maintained control over the situation.

This female was not disgusted with me.

My hands gripped her waist tightly as she ground against me. My claws just barely scratching her skin with each thrust.

This felt so good. Why had we not done this earlier?

I let out a rough grunt.

"That's it," Lucy hissed again, her breath hot against my ear. "Let me hear you."

I did as she asked, giving in to the primal urges. My bleats turned into growls and grunts as my seed covered my stomach.

Lucy cried out as her fingers dug into my chest. I used her arousal and my seed to move her up and down my shaft. Her breasts bounced in front of me, and I leaned up to suck one into my mouth.

"Simon!"

I snarled and bit into her breast. My fangs sank into her. Her body shuddered against me when she let out a pleasurable cry.

"Yes," she moaned.

I didn't let go. I let my fangs stay latched to her flesh until her head rolled back. My fangs released, and my mouth popped after licking the peak of her breast.

I felt her slit contract against me. I wanted to sink into her. I was ready. I was still hard, ready to slip inside. I whimpered against her neck when she leaned forward, her whole body rested against mine.

My fingers dug into her skin while I held her on top of me. I wanted her scent surrounding me, to enjoy and relish in the moment.

The horrible thought of the ogre coming back because of her scent snapped me out of my senses.

"I must clean you."

I wished it was with my tongue, but time was crucial.

"Quickly, my mate, we must."

My mate groaned, her head leaning on my shoulder. I pushed up from the ground, using the strength of my legs to take her to the stream. I stumbled but kept her in my arms as we hit the stream. I took her waist deep, and luckily, the water was warm during the afternoon with the light sources beaming on it.

I dunked us to our necks. She gasped and wrapped her arms around me, her head lulling to the side.

"Wooo, everything is spinning," she giggled.

I raised an eyebrow and helped her wash her hands.

She must be happy with what we had done. I knew I was. We were much closer to mating, and I could not wait to complete our bond.

I continued to pour water on her skin, rubbing her breasts, neck and face. She moaned, pushing her breasts into me. I bit my cheek. I must wash her. I could not let the ogre come back.

"Simon," she swayed. "We should do more."

My ears perked up, and I stared at her.

More?

"I can go again. What about you? Do fauns have refractory periods?" She fluttered her lashes.

I tilted my head to the side. "What is a re-fractory period?"

She giggled again and reached into my pouch. I let out a bleat, stumbling back into the stream when she gripped my shaft.

"Simon, what a big dick you have!"

"Dick?"

"Yeah, your cock, your faun sausage, that big hunk of meat." She rubbed her hand up my shaft. "Ahh, no refractory period. I bet you could go several times." She squeezed her hand around my shaft, and I let out a long moan. "We are going to have so much fun, my little faun."

I felt my cheeks burn up. This was not my Lucy. Where was my Lucy? She would never grab my shaft like this. *It isn't proper,* she would say.

Was it the roots? Did she taste too much?

I cleared my throat and pulled her hand away from my shaft.

"Yeah, we shouldn't do it in the water, should we? I need to see all of it."

My ears twirled, and I looked away.

I pulled her around my waist, and she squealed. "My clothes are all wet. Are you going to take them off of me now?" She tried to wink, but both of her eyes closed.

Is this a mating ritual for humans?

I hit the beach and set her down, then shook the water off.

"You look just like a little goat when you do that!" she said happily, but it made me stand up straight.

"No, not a goat." I looked at her skeptically and shook my head.

"Hokay, sorry. You are the cutest wittle faun ever!" She stood and pressed both of her hands to my cheeks. She squished my face with her hands, puckering my lips. She leaned in and placed a quick peck on my mouth.

Goddess, I broke her.

Dear Goddess, I really broke her.

"What in the Moon Fairy's name is going on?" A large orc pushed through the foliage. He bent under a limb, and when he stood, he had a big toothy grin on his face. "Lucy! I found you!"

Sugha.

My body went rigid when he spoke. Every inch of my muscles tensed and coiled like a spring. As I stumbled and fell face-first into the dirt, I could see the particles of soil and grass being kicked up by my impact.

I let out a huff, angry that my body had betrayed me. I didn't stay frozen, just for a few seconds. *I was getting better.* I pushed myself up and shook my head.

"Miss Lucy, what did you find here?" His face fell. "And why are your tits exposed?"

I bared my fangs and stepped in front of Lucy to hide her from the orc. I crouched into an attack stance, ready to jump to defend her if I needed to. He would not touch or look at her.

"My boobies are out! Heavens me, I thought there was a draft."

I looked behind me, and I saw her palming them. Instantly, my shaft was trying to poke out of my pouch, and I slapped my hand on my forehead.

Sugha raised his eyebrow, and his mouth hung open. "Uh, Lucy, are you alright? You don't sound okay, and who is this fellow?" Sugha pointed at me, and I growled out again.

"Mine!" I snarled and pushed her back.

Sugha crossed his arms and laughed. "Well, this is certainly a turn of events."

"Simon, Sugha is a friendly orc and—"

Sugha unfolded his arms. "Wait, Simon? Calliope's Simon?"

Hair stood up on my neck when I felt Lucy's fingers dig into my shoulders, and

a snarl ripped through her teeth. "What do you mean, Calliope's Simon?"

CHAPTER NINETEEN

Simon

As my mate's breasts pressed against my back. The scent filtered through my nose. Her body's involuntary response to me. Her arms enveloped my stomach, creating a comforting embrace that I had craved.

"Who is Calliope?" she growled.

My ears perked up at her voice. She sounded... possessive. Possessive of me!

Sugha smirked. "What is going on? I have stepped into another realm." He rubbed his hand across his forehead. "I didn't know humans could growl like that."

"I said—" Lucy snarled.

I whirled around and wrapped my arms around my mate, cutting off her words. She huffed when I put her face up to my neck, and she took in a deep breath.

"No one to concern yourself with," I whispered to her. "You are my mate and no one else."

Lucy let out a deep sigh and nestled even closer to my neck, her soft breath brushing against my skin.

Please, faun sausage, do not fall out of my pouch.

Sugha approached, and I jerked my head towards him.

"You can speak? Last I heard, you were unable, and you haven't even visited—"

I growled and bared my teeth again. This male spoke too much, and he was purposefully upsetting my mate.

"Silence! Don't say her name."

Sugha's eyebrows furrowed, and he shook his head. "You know Calliope has been upset you haven't been around. You could at least—"

A loud snore came from my arms. I sighed and hoisted my mate into my arms.

I knew Calliope would be upset that I had not visited. I, at least, let it be known that I was around every few days or so. I did not go near her, though. She didn't need me, not anymore. She had her mate.

"I know I have not visited Calliope, but I have found my mate." Lucy snuggled deeper into my neck again. "Calliope has a mate of her own, and he detests me."

Sugha frowned and shook his head. "He doesn't detest you. It's Valpar. Besides, Valpar would do anything to make Calliope happy. That means letting you near their home."

I grunted as I stepped away from him. Valpar did not like me there when I was more of an animal, and he would not like me now- especially now.

He liked no male near Calliope, but I would not cause her distress or make her choose between the two of us.

She would choose him, anyhow.

"He said he would eat me."

Sugha's eyebrows rose, and he let out a bark of laughter. "Valpar doesn't even eat goat. He prefers a redder meat. Besides, he would never eat his female's pet."

I scowled and let out a bleat. "Heeey, I was not a pet. I was her companion, and I watched over her!"

Sugha eyed me, taking my form up and down. "Calliope is just worried, and now I am worried for Lucy. The search party is looking for her, and she needs to return. Since you say she is your female, you can come with us."

I growled. "I will go nowhere with you or those useless wolves. They have failed to protect her. I fed, sheltered, and healed her when she was sick. The goddess gave her to me and no one else! She will never leave here!"

The fear that she could leave me gripped me like a vice. I had been so caught up in our paradise that I forgot about the outside world. The search party, the ogre, they could all take her away and push me aside. What if they thought of me as an animal, a monster, and hunted me? Punished me for taking her?

They were poor excuses for males. I saved her when they couldn't.

"Her father knows she is missing. You cannot hide her here." Sugha sat down on a boulder near the stream. "He's worried, and the king and queen are traveling with him. You do know the king of the Cerulean Moon Kingdom, right? He's brutal, a worthy opponent to even an orc. He gave Lucy's father his word he would bring her back. You do not want to be hunted by him."

I turned my head and sniffed into my mate's hair. I wouldn't give her up; I refused. If she knew her father was coming to find her, would she leave me? I did not want others to know where I was or what I was. I was alone, and I would not have people see me as an animal. I did not want to feel that pain in my chest.

Only Lucy saw me as, well, me.

I wouldn't give her up.

I stomped my hoof. "It's dangerous. The ogre is hunting her. The ogre must be gone before my female can see her father, and only him."

Would her father reject me? Tell me I was not a good enough male? Tell her to leave?

"And I must be with her."

Sugha sighed heavily and settled his bag on his thigh. He shifted through the contents and pulled out a bag. "This has yellow cress in it. Hide her scent."

"I already have that." My face turned a deep shade of red.

"You need more; I can smell her. If I can smell her, so can an ogre." Sugha snickered and threw it toward me. "How about you tell me what's going on with her? I don't know Lucy well, but I know she would not act the way she did, showing her tits and all."

"Breasts!" I barked. "She calls them breasts; it isn't proper to call them anything else!"

Sugha rolled his eyes. "Now that sounds like her. What did you do, anyway? Is she drunk?"

My mate snored again, and I placed my hand on her head to keep it steady. "No, she didn't start doing it until I bit her—"

Sugah stood to his feet, and the weapon on his back shook behind him. "You bit her? Like shifters and fae do? Does that mean you are mated? I do not smell the bond?" He came closer and took a sniff. Instinctively, I backed away.

"Don't smell her!" I petted her hair. "I bit her, but I don't know how to bond her—yet. I will figure it out soon." It felt right that I should bite and rut her. I did not have the confidence to do so. Not when she didn't insert my dick inside her.

Sugha rubbed his hand down his face. "I hear females like to be bitten. I cannot wait to experience it myself." He licked his lips and stared off into the distance. "Yes, I have many things I want to try after getting hold of a Karma Sutra book from Queen Melina. There were notes in it that I found most fun."

I'm sorry, what?

I continued to back away, giving the orc some space. He was the strange one, and I did not want my mate near him at all. I'd seen her laugh with him, and I would not have her laugh at his jokes any longer.

Mine.

"Lucy acted strange after you bit her? I am wondering if it could be a partial bond. Not that I am an expert or anything, but you being so different from everyone else, who knows what it means."

I tilted my head.

"You see, shifters and fae bite and fuck to seal their bond. Orcs, we brand our mates."

I shivered in disgust. I saw too much of that the day when Calliope was claimed by her male. I had actually seen far too much before that day as well, but it was so terrifying I couldn't look away.

Like when Calliope's male crushed a pixie with his bare hand—you just can't look away.

I internally gagged.

"How-how will I know what to do to claim my female, then?" I rubbed my hand up and down Lucy's back. She let out a snort and wrapped her arms around my neck.

Sugha shook his head. "I do not know, especially because of your predicament. I've never seen a creature like you, especially after that potion spilled onto your goat form. You are a brand new species." The orc rubbed his chin thoughtfully. "Are you sure she is your fated? Or did you just pick her?"

I growled out again, and my female's head perked up. "I said he's mine!" Lucy yelled.

I patted Lucy's back and shoved her head back into my neck. She took a deep breath and promptly fell back asleep with a snore.

I did not have to explain myself to this orc. He doesn't have a mate himself yet. He would not know how it felt to know that a female or male was his.

I narrowed my eyes at the orc, and he raised his hands in surrender. "Alright, she's yours, then. It isn't fair. Why can't I have mine?" He kicked the dirt with his bare feet. "Anyway, bonds, you need to find that witch that keeps helping all the human females. Her name is uh… Starla. Yeah, Starla. Ellie talks to her all the time, my brother Thorn's mate. Calliope has been visited by her as well, perhaps you should go—"

"I will see Ellie," I quickly added. I didn't want Lucy to see Calliope, not yet, especially if Lucy was being so… jealous. Which already had me hardening at the idea.

I only cared for Calliope as a friend and nothing more. I worried Lucy might do something unpredictable, especially with how she was acting now.

Once my mate was better, maybe they could be friends? My ears twirled with excitement.

But then that meant I had to talk to Calliope.

What if she didn't like my voice? What if she got angry that I didn't learn to speak to her first?

Sugha cleared his throat. "If that is the case, then go see Ellie. I assume you know the way since you wandered these woods and have stolen meat from me and my brothers."

My mouth dropped.

Sugha let out a playful laugh and came forward. "We all knew of your struggle. You must not take things seriously. We always make extra. Calliope made sure that we made more than we needed, just in case. She sees you as not only her friend but her brother. Now that you are half-human, that makes more sense."

I did not know what to say. Calliope thought of me as her brother? Me?

"You think too much. She is fine. Valpar keeps her busy. Just know Valpar will not hurt you, especially when you look half-human. Now go on, I'll tell the others Lucy is fine and make sure we camp near the entrance of the Wood. We need to keep her father safe."

I nodded in thanks and stepped away.

"Ah, and Simon. Fated mates are made for each other. Do not let her be afraid of you entering her. Give her a bit of stretch, make her come—"

"Staaaahp!" I bleated out. "What is wrong with you?"

"I'm trying to help. As I watched from the foliage, it seemed your mate was dominating you. Females like dominance too, or so I've read."

I huffed. "She enjoyed doing things to me. I will let her do what she wants."

"Hmm, I guess it could go both ways, then." Sugha turned his back and walked back into the brush. "Give her a good release, for me, when you shove your cock inside her!"

I roared and stomped my feet several times toward him.

He chuckled until I no longer heard his footsteps stomping away from us.

That orc is strange.

Chapter Twenty

Lucy

Holy freaking dino nuggets.

My eyes were still closed, but I felt every bit of Simon's skin around me. We'd been walking awhile, from my guess, because my face was plastered to his chest, and he had got a good steady rhythm walking through the wood.

He was moving fast, but he was hardly out of breath.

Dang, I needed to work out.

But what the heck was wrong with me? I felt so drunk. I'd only drunk once in my life, on my twenty-first birthday, alone in my tent. I was determined to know what it was like to have a drink, and I stole my father's whisky.

I didn't have a lot of friends sure, but Father gave me a great birthday. We celebrated with the small community we were staying with. Peru was a beautiful area, but I was determined to have at least a bit of alcohol.

The whisky was so foul. I kept thinking it would taste better after every sip, but that wasn't the case. I got drunk because it was my first time, and had a huge hangover the next day. The llamas were not kind, and I heard them screaming while they were being sheared that following morning.

Never again.

Simon's bite, though? I have no hangover. Instead, I feel remnants of the buzz from the night before.

It was a drug I could get used to.

I wondered if I could just ask Simon to bite me each night before bed. He could also work that nice tongue of his and get me off. Maybe even impale me on his cock a few times.

Oh, I hope we do that next.

I wiggled in Simon's hold, and he paused his steps. I stared up at him, and he stared right back. His head tilted to the side, and his ears did that cute whirl thing.

Was he waiting for me to speak?

"Em, hey." I wiggled my fingers toward him like an idiot.

His nostrils flared, and I squeezed my thighs together.

Just looking at him made my hormones go crazy. I think that bite might have made me crave him more because all these physical responses were insane. I'd never read or heard anything like this. Perhaps our bodies were just chemically attuned to one another.

That orgasm earlier was just mind-blowing. They kept getting better and better. If all my orgasms were like that, he could bite me all he wanted. Orgasmic biting, yes please!

I giggled.

"Lucy, are you alright?" Simon asked hesitantly while he lowered us to the ground to sit. "Are you feeling better?"

Was I feeling better? I didn't know how to answer that. I felt like my body needed to be stuffed with your cock, Mister Faun, sir. Yet, I couldn't tell you that because I didn't want to seem like a crazy woman.

Did it really matter? It was Simon, and I felt safe talking to him, which was all against my better judgment. He was a red flag. A red flag that I liked.

"Yes, I'm fine. I'm not... giddy like I was earlier, thank the gods." But then I remembered. "Wait, who is Calliope?" I blurted.

I didn't forget my actions earlier. They all came running back to me, and I slapped my hand over my mouth. I showed my breasts to Sugha.

He'd seen my boobs!

Simon groaned, and he rolled his head back. "I feared you would want to know her."

And just like that, I forgot about flashing the goods. I scoffed. Of course, I would want to know who Calliope was.

"Are you sure you are alright? You acted strange earlier." He settled me on his lap, and I didn't fight sitting there with him. I wanted to be close, but then I realized something was very, very different.

I wasn't in my dress. Instead, I wore a bikini top that wrapped around my neck and back. My lower half was a short skirt, all made from a soft leather hide. Not only was I clothed, but now Simon had a cloth wrapped around his waist.

Great! Now we were Tarzan and Jane.

"Do I even want to ask about the clothes?" I pulled at the top. I wasn't even mad. He'd seen me naked. I ground against his dick; I mean, what else had this male not seen?

My *butthole*, but I'm not gonna think about that.

Simon pulled me impossibly closer. "Your clothes were soiled. I made this for you, do you like it?" He leaned closer, assessing my face.

I blinked several times, and I pinched the fabric between my thumb and index finger. He did a great job. It was thick enough so no one would see when I was, ahem, cold. Albeit risqué from what I would normally wear, but this was the Monktona Wood.

"Yes, it fits nicely." That's it, Lucy, immerse yourself in his culture. Go with the flow. "Now, who is Calliope?"

I was not a jealous person. The only time I got jealous was when people were in relationships, and I had wished I had such a connection with someone. I had it right now—until he found his mate. He was also allowed to have relationships with other people.

Simon shuffled me in his lap, his mouth twisting. He grunted a few times until I put both hands on his shoulders. "If you have had relations with another woman, I need to know. I'm not mad."

Because, diseases! I'd rubbed my vagina all over this faun's log.

"Relations?" He questioned.

"Sex stuff. Things we did earlier, but more." My eyes widened to give him emphasis.

His face turned a bright red, and he looked away. "You are the first I have touched."

I relaxed and took a deep breath to calm myself. "Good, that's good."

Simon's head snapped up and snarled. "Has another male touched you? I will kill them."

Oh, cute, fluffy Simon had a mean face.

Crap, a tear just ran down my leg.

I shook my head violently. "No, no, not in any way!" I waved my hands in front of him. "I have never had these feelings before, these wants. You make me want to... uhm."

Simon's nose flared again, and his hand slipped up under the cloth skirt. When I rubbed my legs together, I realized I wasn't wearing underwear.

Great, gonna be chafing something fierce if I'm damp all the time.

"You want me now?" He purred against my neck, his warm lips tickled against the back of my ear. "Because we can take a break from our journey, and I can sate you."

Where did he learn to talk like this? In fact, as the days went on with me by his side, the easier it had become for him to communicate.

As his warm, wet tongue delicately caressed my earlobe, my brain scrambled. The sound of his gentle sucking made my nipples pucker. While the soft touch of his roaming hands sent shivers down my body, he asked, "Lucy, can I touch?"

I didn't point out he was already touching, but his grip on my breast stopped my words of reply. I whimpered against him, pushing myself further into his body.

"Your scent is strong." His hand dove between my legs, cupping my mound.

My eyes rolled back in my head while I parted my legs for him. I panted, trying to think of anything else but his body so close to mine, so much more skin contact than when I wore that dress—it was too much.

I tried to break from his hold, but he held onto me tighter. Not that I complained. I really didn't want him to let go. "Calliope... who is she to you, then?" I breathed.

Simon's hand reached up under my skirt, his fingers touched everywhere but where I wanted most.

"I was not always in this form," he rasped and suckled on my neck. "Not the half-man, half-beast."

I rested my head back onto his shoulder, feeling the soft brush of his fingertips against my skin as they delicately explored the curves of my body. The huffs of his breath pushed my hair across my cheek.

"What do you mean?" I released a deep, throaty moan as he slid two fingers inside me. With a subtle twist, he caressed my insides, causing a wave of tingling sensations to ripple through my body.

"You know there is magic here." His fingers thrust into my body, and I let out a cry.

I couldn't stop him. My body wanted this. I couldn't get enough of him. My pussy wept for him.

"Y-yes," I choked.

Simon thrust into me again. "Calliope saw I differed from the animals that lived within the palace pastures, saw I was alone." I gasped as his thrusts grew faster. "She rescued me and called me her friend."

Simon inserted another finger. I felt the sting of his fingers stretching me wide. It was a good pain, one that came with pleasure while his thumb rubbed against my clit. I reached up and pulled on his horn. He growled into my ear.

"From then on, I wanted to protect her. I couldn't think much, not like I can now, but I knew I owed her my life." Simon gripped my breast and pressed his erection into my backside.

I let out a long moan, and my hips bucked against his hand. "I'm so close."

Then Simon took his fingers away. I cried out when he turned my body so I was straddling him. "I've got you, female."

Simon's cock had fully emerged from his pouch. As I observed, my eyes drank in the sight of it. Its impressive size was visually striking, as it appeared long and astonishingly girthy.

Where was my notebook when I needed it?

A pearl of liquid streamed down his veiny shaft, and I licked my lips.

Simon huffed and shoved his fingers back inside in one swift thrust. My forehead fell on his shoulders, and I deterred my attention to his dick.

I grabbed hold of his shaft beneath me and squeezed.

"Nnhn!" he huffed, and my hair whipped around my head. "I need to tell you."

I gently caressed the smooth texture of his skin, feeling the warmth radiating from his body. Soft moans escaped his lips. With each stroke, a slick sensation coated my fingertips, allowing me to glide the liquid up and down the length of his shaft.

Romance novels, don't fail me now.

"Ugh, Lucy."

"Tell me." I pressed my lips against his. I slung my head back. We were both panting, our hot breaths fanning our faces.

Simon pressed his hand to my lower back, holding me still until my body seized as I came, and a bright white light exploded behind my eyes. "Simon!"

"Yes," he breathed, "let me have it."

My body collapsed on his, his cock was still thick in my hand, but I couldn't let go.

As I relaxed in his arms, my eyes closed, and then he blurted, "I-was-a-goat-when-Calliope-found-me."

My eyes popped open, and I leaned back to stare into his eyes. There was shame written all over his face, then fear. He'd got me to relax and then dropped the biggest bomb I have ever heard.

The question was, did I care?

He was a goat?!

"What?"

"I tried to save Calliope. There was a potion; a pixie tried to rid her of the spell that the fae king had put on her, to keep her life happy. I wanted to save her from the pain it would release. I jumped in the way to block it. It got on me, and I passed out. I woke up and was—this." He waved his hand down the length of his body.

Ten long seconds passed by. My hand still gripped his dick, as my head needed time to reboot.

Magic. It was what floated around in this realm. I tried to understand it, but even the witches at the palace said that magic was not always understandable. It grew; it evolved. Potions, spells, curses, hexes - they all sounded the same to me, and in my lifetime, I knew I would never understand.

"What kind of potion?" I whispered.

Simon gripped my thighs, his claws digging into my skin. "It was supposed to release curses."

With that one line, I knew that Simon was never meant to be a goat.

Call it my gut intuition, but I knew it. I didn't care if he lived his life as a goat; I cared about who he was now.

A potion that relieved curses? That meant he was a faun *before* he was a goat. Did he not understand that?

"What do you mean 'supposed to'?" I ran my hand up his shaft to relax his thoughts.

Hoe Lucy is here.

"Calliope was rid of her memory curse, but it turned me into a faun! It works differently on an animal."

I giggled and ran my finger down his cheek. "Simon, I think you were always a faun."

"I remember nothing else but being a goat—an animal."

"Just because you were an animal does not mean it wouldn't have the same effect on you."

I didn't understand how he couldn't remember his life before he was a goat, but I knew that walking and talking wasn't a new concept to him. He was learning way too fast.

His mouth opened to argue, but I leaned forward and did something so outrageous; I licked the head of his cock. Simon's body shuddered beneath me when I held a firm grasp at the base.

"Fuck," he breathed loudly and put his hand on my head. "Fuck, I can't…"

I couldn't fit the whole length inside my mouth. Instead, I concentrated on my tongue and swirled around the head. His claws scratched down my scalp and dug his fingers into my hair. His hips bucked him into my mouth.

Oh, this was so much better than reading and imagining it in my head.

Simon growled. "Suck me harder, mate." I hummed into his cock, and he shouted a beastly snarl as the hot jets of his come slid down my throat.

I'd never tasted come, but I thought it would be salty and bitter. His was not. It tasted like the roots we had eaten earlier.

Like a damn good churro.

I definitely needed to write this down.

"Female," he snarled and pulled me up by my hair. His hand, like a vice, tightly encircled my throat, constricting my airflow. I could feel the heat of his breath on my skin as he brought me closer, his lips crashing against mine with a feral intensity. His rough hands roamed my body, tugging at my clothing with an urgent hunger. "I want to sink my cock so deep inside you that you will not know your life before me."

He pinned me to the ground with both my wrists with one hand. His cock was swollen and dripping from the cock head.

He wasn't gonna fit.

But he could try if he wanted... Hoe Lucy would not complain. I was soaked. I was pretty sure the ogre would find us soon with all the scents, but that was future Lucy's problem.

I wanted—no, needed—him to be inside me.

The red, angry head parted my folds and entered, but as he pushed forward, the girth below the head expanded.

Too much, too thick.

My fingers dug into his biceps. "I can't, no more."

Panic set in. I was a freaking virgin. No dildo had his girth. There was just no way this was going to happen. "I can't, I can't." I shook my head, but still my legs wrapped around his waist, wanting to invite him in.

His free hand stroked my forehead. "Shh, just the tip."

Famous. Last. Words.

Simon pushed and pulled the head of his cock in and out of my pussy. My clit pulsed, feeling the brush of the thick head. With my clit already swollen and over-stimulated, I crashed around him. He picked up the pace and used his hand to rub the lower half of his cock.

Simon's forehead met mine, and with a guttural snarl, he pulled his cock from me and I felt thick ropes of his come fall on my stomach.

He rubbed his nose against mine. His lips grazed my cheek and lips, and he said, "We will make it fit. This I promise you." All while he smeared his come around my stomach.

At least he kept his word - just the tip.

Chapter Twenty-One

Simon

She knows my secret.

My mate took it better than I had hoped. I expected her to be disgusted and reject me. Seducing her and bringing her pleasure would be my weapon when I needed to tell her something important.

She was more compliant and more understanding when she knew I could make her feel good.

Despite not knowing how to pleasure a female in the beginning, she had made it easy with the sounds she made. I liked how she directed my horns where she wanted me. I needed direction in the beginning, but I knew her body now.

We walked silently through the Wood, and I could feel its subtle power around me, buzzing for me to reach out and touch her. I wanted to be closer, and I knew she wanted me too, but she was holding herself back. Like my touch would eventually break her.

That was what I was hoping.

My mate wouldn't let me hold her in my arms and carry her. She wanted to wander while we walked and take in the sights of the forest.

I think she was worried about our earlier interaction. My shaft is quite large, and she is small. That was a minor thing to overcome. I had seen an orc's, and if they could place their cocks inside their mates, then I was sure I could bury myself in Lucy.

Right now, I worried for her feet. They were not tough like my hooves. Her feet were soft, and with the twigs, branches and leaves, she could hurt easily.

Humans were fragile.

I watched my mate intently while she wrote in her book. Knowing she used something I gave her brought me pride. I provided for her. I took care of her and made her happy.

Technically, it was Calliope's, but she gave it to me one day, hoping that I would try to write.

My fingers were not that good yet. I could thread knots, tie ropes but doing something as intricate as writing, that was far beyond what I needed to learn while living in the Wood.

My mate stepped on a piece of soft, velvety purple moss, its vibrant color contrasting against the earthy tones of the surrounding lands. The mosses spread across the lands, even finding their way into the depths of the Wood.

As my mate gingerly placed her weight on it, a gentle crunch resonated beneath her foot, accompanied by a burst of tiny lights. Intrigued by the enchanting display, she knelt down, pressing her palm onto the moss. More of the tiny stars erupted from its surface, shooting upwards towards her face, filling her eyes with wonder and causing them to widen in awe.

Her pencil moved frantically in the notebook while I stopped and checked our surroundings. After making my mate's arousal bloom so much, I had to take the yellowcress and sprinkle it over the both of us.

Even with the root, I could smell myself on her skin where I rubbed my seed onto her belly.

When she knelt and took a closer inspection of the moss, she lifted her backside into the air. My shaft stiffened in my pouch, and I cursed myself and looked away. There was something about her being on her knees, her ass in the air. It was my animalistic side, wanting to take over and rut her from behind.

My cock did not fit.

She was my mate. It was supposed to fit inside her. Why would her body not accept me? Was I too large?

I grunted in disappointment, and Lucy stood to brush off the clothing I'd made for her. The book already had pages and pages filled since I had given it to her.

She smiled, put her notebook under her arm, and reached for me. Her giddiness made me smile when she gripped my hand.

I stared at the fingers she just intertwined with mine. Lucy nodded her head in the direction we were going. "Come on."

My heart fluttered, and my ears waved back and forth. I could hold her hand while we walked. It was better than before, feeling so far apart, but now?

Lucy swung our hands back and forth. "Have you never held hands?"

My thumb grazed over her knuckles. "No, never. You are the first."

She beamed at me. "My father was the first to hold mine, but he doesn't count because he was my father. I guess you would be my first, too."

I would be her first for everything, that was for sure. First to stick my fingers inside her and soon, my shaft. I knew her taste when no one else did. I knew she was mine in every way.

But why did I not fit inside her?

I hoped this witch could help because I was lost. I didn't have all the answers and now, new questions had risen.

Lucy said I was a faun, to begin with, not a goat. I didn't see how that was possible. I only remembered being a lowly animal. Yet, I differed from anyone in the herds that I had lived in.

I didn't find desire in mating; I did not rut. I didn't know how many times farmers tried to catch me and dispose of me because I was not doing my duty. I had no desire for those females.

Could I have always been a faun? What happened to me to become all animal?

Lucy squeezed my hand and tugged on it. "Hey you, watcha thinking? I asked you a question?"

My eyebrows raised, and I cleared my throat. "Just about where I came from. If I *was* a faun."

Lucy nodded. "I've been thinking that, too. I really believe you were a faun, before. It makes sense."

I tilted my head to the side.

"You speak well, Simon. Like you have done it before. You have learned quickly how to use your hands and walk on two legs. That isn't an easy feat."

"The bond—"

Lucy stopped and stood in front of me. "No, no bond. You have done these things before me, Simon. You're smart, and walking and talking, they're like riding a bicycle. Once you start doing it again, it comes naturally."

I did not know what a bicycle was, but it didn't matter. I huffed and pulled her closer to me. I wanted her touch, her body close to me.

"With how long everyone in Bergarian lives; technically living immortally until fatally wounded, I think you are old."

I scoffed. "I am not old. I feel young."

It was Lucy's turn to roll her eyes. "All the orcs are old, King Kane is old, yet they look no older than thirty. Every creature here is ageless, besides the humans."

"The elder orcs have aged," I countered.

"Except them, I'm still trying to figure that out. There are always exceptions in science. Anyway. I know what you are. There are stories about you on Earth. The majority may not be true, but your presence is known there. I think"—she tapped her lip—"you, or at least your kind, have lived on Earth before."

My mouth dropped. "You think there are more of me?" I squeezed her hand. "I am not alone?"

Lucy shook her head confidently. "Nope, and I bet there are more. The way the religion here relies heavily on the human versions of Greek Gods, I bet there are other creatures and species from Greek Lore. Minotaur's, centaurs, Medusa, Pegasus. Gods, could you imagine?" She stood up on her toes and leaned into me. "All those creatures might be here in the Wood! Or better yet, in someone's farm." Her face paled. "They could get eaten!" She squealed and pulled on my arm. "We have to save them."

She pulled on my arm again, almost yanking it from my body. I whirled her around until she slammed into my chest. "There were no others like me." Calliope stated she met no other animals like me."

Lucy pressed her forehead to my chest. "We should still look, just in case, after we meet up with the witch. Could you imagine meeting a Minotaur?" Her eyes sparkled.

"I do not know what a Minotaur is, but you cannot meet them," I growled.

Lucy pouted. "Why not? It's part of my job. I need to draw them and take scientific no—"

"Have you drawn me?" I interrupted. "Have you drawn what I look like?"

Lucy bit down on her bottom lip. "Mm-maybe. Part of you, um."

When we walked through the Wood, I knew she was drawing and taking her notes. What she wrote, I wasn't sure.

"Let me see." I pulled her away and tried to grab the book from under her arm.

She squealed. "No! Don't!" She put it behind her back, but since I was taller, I could reach it. I pulled it away from her and hopped away.

"You have drawn me. I must see."

Lucy cried out. "No, you big meanie! Give it back!"

I chuckled and trotted away from her, climbing the nearest tree using only my hooves.

"What are you doing? Come down here, you cheater!"

"I cannot help that your feet are not as skillful as mine."

I flipped the pages of the notebook. She had already filled it with pictures in our short time walking. The roots, the white fluff from where she slept; it was all there. Then I stopped at one page and my eyes widened. It wasn't a picture of just me—it was one part of me.

My cock.

She drew my cock!

"Hey, give that back!" Lucy shouted as she ran towards the tree. Her determination to retrieve her notebook was both endearing and amusing. I couldn't help but smirk at her persistence, then I quickly flipped the page to hide my... private parts from her view.

She could have the real thing—if she wanted.

"Simon!" she snapped. "That has educational stuff in there."

Educational? It has my cock inside it.

I flipped back to the page with my body and sat on the limb. I let myself dangle just above her fingertips.

"Simon!"

"What do these words mean?" My claw ran down the page. "What did you write?"

Lucy put her hands on her hips and stared. "Why do you want to know?" her face blushed.

I smirked, amused at what she could have written. I wish I knew how to read, but obviously, I didn't have the capability. "Tell me what it says, and I'll give it back."

I'd just steal it back from her later.

Lucy wrung her hands together. "Ah, stuff. Just stuff we did, what happened. A description of what it looks like."

I gave her a fanged smile. "And what does my cock look like, my mate?"

Lucy's face turned a beautiful shade of red. I wanted to lick the apples of her cheeks. "Just that it's big!"

I snorted and gazed down at the drawing. She had captured every detail, and that must have impressed her.

Except I am too large.

I flipped the notebook closed and jumped down from the limb. She scowled and ripped it out of my hands.

"This is private!" she snapped and held the book to her chest.

I walked closer to her, and she backed away from me until she hit a tree behind her. I put my hand beside her head, closing her in. Her scent surrounded me. Her body trembled, not out of fear, but... because she liked this. She liked it when I pushed her and played with her.

"Tell me, Lucy. Do you like my cock so much you had to draw it?" My nose flared, and I rubbed my face against her cheek. "You want me inside you, don't you?"

Her arousal perfumed. I prayed to the goddess that the yellowcress root held, and that ogre didn't come stomping around.

"Tell me," I whispered.

"S-simon, I—"

"Call me your mate." I pressed myself against her. "Tell me."

Lucy shook her head and held the notebook tighter around her chest. "I can't say that."

"Why?" I growled. "Have I not proven myself?"

Lucy's mouth dropped. "N-no. I am just saying mates would be able to fit, wouldn't they? You are just so big, and I... I... I don't think we are compatible in that way. Your real mate—"

My cock fell out of its pouch, and I pressed it against her. "You think this is made for someone else?" I growled. "It only does this for you." I gripped my shaft and held it tight. "Only you."

Lucy swallowed and let out a slow, steady breath. "I just worry that... someone better is meant to be your mate. You don't know how to claim a mate. As Sugha said, different species claim their mates in different ways. What if you are wrong about knowing I'm yours? I am not even sure how to tell if someone is my mate—I'm human."

I wrapped my hand around her wrist and placed her hand on my chest. "Do you feel this? It beats for you. It wants you. Why can you not believe that? Don't think like this." I pulled the notebook out of her hand and threw it on the ground. "Think with this." I placed my hand between her breasts.

I tried to hide my disappointment when she still did not call me her mate. I leaned forward and licked her from her shoulder to her cheek.

She sighed and wrapped her arms around me.

I prayed to the goddess that the witch we sought would help her see reason.

CHAPTER TWENTY-TWO

Lucy

I'm too attached. Far too attached.

I wanted to tell him he was my mate, but my mind wouldn't let go of one important thing. I'd never connected with anyone; he was the first. If I had given in and told him he was mine, my whole heart would believe it. There would be no going back for me. I'd never connect with another person.

If this whole mate thing is true and not some biological response, I needed to know how I would feel it. How would I truly know? I needed to talk to another human. What did they feel?

That was why I had tried not to touch Simon while we walked through the forest. I tried to take in the scenes around me, gather the information that I could, and keep my mind off of him. Of course, it led me back to drawing his dick in my notebook and he was damn proud of that.

Not to mention he was cute as hell but had a dominating streak I adored.

I wanted to give in so badly, and he nearly took me earlier. What was I thinking, trying to have sex with him? He was too big, and that meant only one thing.

We weren't mates.

Once I spoke to Ellie, a human who had found love in an orc who was her mate, I thought I would feel better about all of this. Simon would have to see reason and then take me back to the party where my father still waits.

I had a sliver of hope we were meant to be together, but my mind wouldn't let this go. When people got married, it was because they had similar interests, they got along, they wanted the same things, and even those sometimes failed.

Mates, those partnerships didn't fail, from what I gathered. All because a goddess said you were meant to be? It was hard for me to process.

The light sources had faded just above the trees. Darkness had fallen, and there was a chill in the air. Simon noticed, and with one swoop of his arms, and had me wrapped in one of those leaves that had the bright white cotton attached from the large sack he had been carrying.

Like a soft Lucy burrito.

I'd protested, saying I was a big girl and I could handle walking with the blanket, but he came up with an excuse I couldn't ignore. "My female will not be getting sick again. The goddess will punish me, and you may never accept our bond."

Cue the swoon.

I was going to eat all of this up and remember it until I passed from this Bergarian plane if he wasn't truly mine.

In the last leg of our journey, our eyes were greeted by the mesmerizing sight of a vibrant fire dancing amidst the dense foliage. The deafening crackling of the flames echoed through the air, while the tantalizing aroma of sizzling meat wafted towards us, igniting a hunger that rumbled deep within my stomach. Desperately, I tried to conceal the growls, lest they betray my voracious appetite.

There was a log cabin sitting peacefully at the center of the clearing, its moss-covered roof blending in with the surrounding trees and vegetation. Meat hung around the porch, for later consumption, swaying in the gentle breeze. Someone had stretched furs on wooden frames to dry slowly in the warmth from the light sources. Vibrant flowers of all colors bloomed around the cabin, adding a pop of color to the otherwise earthy tones of the woods. It gave it a lady's touch.

It looked like a peaceful paradise in the middle of the Wood.

When I gazed over at the fire, a large hulking orc stood by it, throwing more logs into the flames. Someone had erected a spit with a wild boar turning and roasting on it. Laughter reached our ears, along with the playful screams of a child. Immediately, I nudged Simon to put me down so we could go greet them but he held me tighter and pulled us away.

"What's wrong? Isn't this Ellie and Thorn? The ones we can ask about the witch?"

Simon's facial features hardened. "I've never spoken with them. I don't know how Thorn will react when we enter his territory," Simon muttered under his breath.

Orcs were very selective about who entered their domain. I was surprised we hadn't been noticed already for how territorial they could be.

"I can announce us. Surely he won't mind another human."

Simon backed away from the clearing. "We should wait until dawn."

I huffed and crossed my arms. That meat smelled too good, and waiting until dawn when I wanted answers was not happening. So, I yelled, "Hey! I'm a human! I mean no harm!"

Simon slammed his hand over my mouth and growled. "You don't startle an orc, Lucy."

Immediately, Thorn stopped what he was doing and grabbed a giant club. Ellie held their child tighter. The tiny orc gazed in our direction, and I could see the pretty green face filled with rage.

Maybe it wasn't such a good idea.

Thorn stomped over. His feet made the ground tremble. I grabbed a limb to keep Simon from running away, and within seconds, a towering orc appeared, looming over us.

I could see the similarities between Sugha and Thorn. The nose for one, and how his tusks were pointed. There was a difference, though, and that was the large frown on his face, while Sugha always smiled.

Thorn took in a large breath. His nose flared as he towered over us. "I can't smell you and didn't hear you approach. Who the—"

"I'm Lucy!" I interrupted. "Sugha is your brother, correct?"

Simon let out a low, rumbling growl. With a gentle touch, he carefully set me back on the ground. Taking a defensive posture, he positioned himself in front of me, his strong presence radiating a sense of protection. "Back away from my female."

Oh, that was hot!

Thorn's expression softened and backed up. "You're Valpar's female's pet."

Simon let out a bleat of annoyance. "I am not—"

"He is no pet," I said and put my hand on Simon's shoulder. "He was her companion; now he is a faun. I'm going to have to ask you to not call him a pet again."

Thorn narrowed his eyes and crossed his arms. "You're female is foolish."

I scoffed and matched his stance. Simon reached behind and grabbed my arm, squeezing it gently.

"I wouldn't have brought my female here unless I needed to," Simon said and blocked me from Thorn's gaze. "But I need help from a witch. Your female might know where she is."

Thorn rolled his eyes. "And why would we give you that—"

"Honeybuns!" Ellie called out. Thorn rolled his eyes and let out an exasperated sigh. "Would you move and let them come in? My gods! Don't act like there is a stick up your butt."

Simon relaxed his stance and snorted. "Honeybuns?"

I giggled along with him, and we both got a glare that could curdle milk. Thorn grunted and jerked his head toward the fire for us to follow.

He kept his eyes on us with his club at his side. It was the size of a whole tree limb, but it looked sturdy, considering he'd probably used it to bash so many things with it. There was no sign of rot, just tiny gashes of scars where brute force had been applied.

Thorn lifted the club, and my eyes followed. He took it in with both hands, bouncing it like a baseball player would do before he came to bat. "This is from the dragon scale tree."

My eyes widened when he spoke. It was no longer accusing and harsh. "They are nearly impossible to destroy. I was lucky this branch had fallen at its own will. The gods gave it to me."

The woman by the fire leaned her head back and sighed dramatically. "Are you talking about your big stick again?"

Thorn growled playfully—if that were a thing for an orc. His lip tilted up, and he gazed at her as if she was the one who brought up the light sources each day.

"Female, I'll talk about my weapon for anyone willing to listen. This female seemed interested."

I perked my head up and chirped, "Yes, I am interested in the stick. I'm interested in learning all about Monktona Wood. It's my job. I'm Lucy, by the way."

Ellie snorted a laugh. "I'm sure Thorn will love to tell you all about his stick. His is a little lumpy, though. I'm Ellie."

I stuck out my hand and went running toward her. "It's so great to meet you. I'm the new research scientist that—"

Thorn snarled and stomped in front of me. I heard Simon grunt, his hooves making a pounding noise on the soil. Before I knew what was happening, Simon had lowered his head and charged into Thorn with his horns.

Thorn grunted and stumbled backward. His eyes lit up, and he rubbed his stomach, staring down at Simon.

"Get away!" Simon bleated and ground his hooves into the dirt. He was ready to try and fight an orc who was at least a foot taller than him. Simon was also a slimmer build, but that didn't take away from the fact that he was strong, too.

"Thorn!" Ellie yelled. "Get your cakey butt over here. Lucy isn't going to hurt me or our child!"

"I will protect my miresa and my orcling, do not deny me that honor." He balled his hands up into fists, but he turned and stomped over to the fire. He stood beside Ellie, still cuddling the mini version of Thorn.

I saw Simon, still filled with anger. He stomped his hoof and appeared that he was ready to charge again. I grabbed his hand to pull him back.

Seriously, males of this realm were something else. It was hot, don't get me wrong, but it was kind of ridiculous.

"Simon," I hissed. "Calm down, you are making Thorn grumpy."

"Thorn is always grumpy," Ellie smiled. "Comes with the whole 'mated to an orc' thing. Besides Sugha though, I think he is the only happy orc I've ever met."

Simon's face softened, and he squeezed my hand. "That is why we are here. He said you know of a witch that helped get you two together. I'm hoping to speak with her."

"We both have questions," I sighed. "And I want to know everything between you two and this cute little mister you have right here." I bent over and smiled wildly at the little green orc baby.

"This is Kiah. He's our son." Thorn stood up, thrusting his chest out with pride. "Our firstborn, and there will be many more to come."

Ellie shuddered. "Let me get over this one first. I still feel like my hips are just getting back to normal."

The not-so-small baby babbled and blew a spit bubble.

Simon did not have a poker face. His face was full of horror looking at their orcling. I thought it was cute, in that orc baby kind of way.

"Aren't you adorable!" I tickled the enormous feet.

Kiah let out a loud scream of happiness, and Simon screamed back, his tongue flopping out of his mouth.

We all looked at Simon as he covered his mouth in embarrassment. The baby giggled and screamed again, and Simon opened his mouth and bleated again, also. He didn't seem able to control his reaction.

Aw, I wanted to squish his face.

The baby or Simon's face, I wasn't sure.

"Right, so do you both understand where Simon came from?" I asked.

Ellie didn't laugh at Simon. In fact, no one said a word about his actions. Instead, she patted her child on the head. "Of course, he was once Calliope's companion, now turned faun. Gossip travels fast. We've been helping feed him when we can."

Simon's shoulders dropped. "You knew I was taking your food? I'm sorry. When I had just become what I am now, I—"

Thorn grunted and turned the spit on the fire. "Yes, we never heard or saw you coming. You impressed me. It has made me more aware of my surroundings, that anything can get into my land. The only way we knew it was you was because you always left flowers. Ellie appreciates them. Glad to see you talk now. We thought you were just stupid."

"Hey!" Ellie and I both screamed at the same time.

Simon slapped his hand to his face, utterly frustrated. "I need the witch! I want to seal the bond!"

Ellie gasped and covered the tiny green thing in her lap's ears. "You are mates? That's wonderful!"

"Wait, wait, wait!" I said and stepped closer to the fire. "We don't know that for sure. That is why we need to speak to this witch, Starla. Is that her name, Simon?"

Simon snarled and stepped towards me. He wrapped his arm around my waist and tugged on the back of my hair, exposing my neck. "You are my mate."

My body instantly complied.

"Your scent tells me so." His nostrils flared, and I was happy he was wearing a cloth to hide his shaft because I could definitely feel it on my stomach. We did not need the baby to see that.

Ellie fanned herself. "That's so hot. Remember when you used to do stuff like that, hot cakes?"

Thorn groaned. "We have an orcling. I will not subject Kiah to those private encounters."

"Only when he's sleeping. Which is rare. Do you see, Lucy? I have bags under my eyes. Between Kiah and Thorn, I can't keep up. It's the boobs, I tell you. They both want them."

I didn't pay much attention to Ellie, it was on Simon who held me against his torso and gazed into my eyes.

"I see the uncertainty in your eyes, Lucy, but I hold true to what I said. You are mine, and if the gods don't believe it to be so—I will keep you, anyway."

Insert dramatic sigh here.

Chapter Twenty-Three

Simon

I looked like a fool standing here.

My mate sat down next to Ellie, and I watched as a gentle breeze rustled through her hair. She reached out and began playing with the tiny monster sitting on Ellie's lap. His vibrant green hue caught the setting light sources, which appeared to make him glow. Ellie commented on the orcling's tiny tusks and his braided hair. The thing took after his father's likeness.

Only parents could love such a thing, but my Lucy was being nice when she sat next to it. Surely, she didn't think that thing was... cute.

She thought of me as cute; was she lying?

Thorn and Ellie chatted with Lucy. Her hunger for knowledge was evident. Ellie, being of the same species, understood Lucy and was helpful in explaining Thorn and her dynamic.

Thorn essentially kidnapped Ellie as well, and Lucy scratched her head in thought. This Wood was known for kidnapping, and I wouldn't be surprised if it always remained that way.

Females needed to know when their males wanted them, and they would do anything to protect them.

The tiny green orc's crying cut their conversation short. Thorn scooped up the child, held him in his giant arms, and stomped back to the cabin.

I wanted to have that—one day. I wanted a family of my own, a child, and a home. We would never be alone because we would have each other.

"We have a tent you both can use. I'm afraid we can't invite you in," Ellie said, brushing off her dress as she stood. "Orcs can't have fun sleepovers."

Lucy nodded and stood with her. I pulled her into my arms, happy to have her again. "I will find shelter, that is my duty as her male."

Lucy rolled her eyes. "Simon, let's take the tent. We don't need to sleep in a tree again."

I grumbled and nipped at her neck. Her knees buckled beneath me, and I held her up. "I will find shelter. I am your—"

Thorn huffed and threw a bundle across from the fire. "Take the tent. Otherwise, my Ellie will curse me the rest of the night, and I need to empty my sack."

Lucy gasped, and I shouted out a bark of laughter. "I would like to do the same."

"Oh my gods, Simon!" Lucy playfully slapped me on the shoulder.

Thorn shook his head. "Just unwrap it. It will have everything you need. It's one of Osirus' tents."

Ah, I have spent time in many of Osirus' tents. I knew with Lucy's curious mind, she would find it most entertaining. Just this once, would I allow taking a tent from the orc so my mate can experience it.

She wanted to experience all things.

Perhaps more of my cock.

"Thank you for your kindness. I will repay you for all you have done for me." I clenched my jaw at my idiocy of the past. My time getting to know my new body and how to survive out in the Wood was unfortunate, but I would repay all the orcs I had stolen from.

"Simon," Ellie consoled. "You do not need to repay us. I can't imagine how you felt being alone like that, in a new body and getting to know your new surroundings. I wish, as well as Calliope, that you would have asked for more."

I turned my head away, my face filled with heat. I didn't need pity. I was a male, and just like the orcs, I had some sense of pride.

Lucy wrapped her arm around mine. Instantly, my body calmed, but the embarrassment was still there. Lucy must think of me as a fool for stealing food.

Ellie, Thorn, and the orcling went inside their cabin. The fire was still lit, and in time, it would be nothing but warm embers. I untied the sack, ready to unleash a new moment for Lucy to experience. I have spent no time in the Cerulean Moon Kingdom, but I know the magic of the Golden Light was bright due to King Osirus.

Once I unrolled the tent, it unfurled with a satisfying rustle; the fabric billowed out and caught the light source's fading light. It wasn't abnormally large, but it provided enough space for Lucy to walk through without having to stoop. As I hammered the stakes into the ground, the metallic clang echoed, and my excitement grew. Lucy's curiosity was piqued once the stakes were secure, as a soft glow from inside the tent seeped through the fabric, casting a warm and inviting light outside.

I stepped in front of her, bending at the hips and opened the flap to invite her in. I was ready to see the sense of wonderment on her face. "Come inside."

Lucy tentatively stepped inside, and a gasp left her lips. My dick twitched from her innocent noise. I had heard once before when I had part of my cock inside her. I already wanted to do it again.

"This is, wow! It's like out of a book."

She gazed around the tent, taking in the mesmerizing sight of the ornate pillows and blankets arranged meticulously in the middle of the spacious interior. It smelled of the faint scent of musky wood, mingling with the earthy aroma of the furs that now adorned the walls. The furs of other creatures in the Wood replaced the absence of the tapestries that usually hung inside. It appeared that this was now a tent decorated for an orc instead of royalty, which usually these tents were made for.

Lucy strode in, her fingers touching every piece of fabric she could. The tulle that hung from the top of the tent, the silk pillows, even the furniture that was erected. One would not believe all this could come to be in just a small, bundled sack.

"How is this possible?" She let out a soft, melodic chuckle and gracefully lowered herself onto the plush bedding area. As I gazed at her, she appeared even more captivating; her beauty was overwhelming. It was a surreal moment, as if I couldn't believe that she, in all her stunning glory, belonged to me.

"Magic," I simply stated.

She let out a deep sigh, as her body sank into the soft cushions. The room was dimly lit, casting a warm, golden glow on her figure. As she leaned back, her arms supporting her, and her breast pushed out. My eyes were drawn to her, mesmerized by the way her breasts gently pushed against the clothing I had made for her. A nervous anticipation washed over me, causing my mouth to dry. I licked my lips.

"Of course it's magic." She ran her hand through her hair. "Everything is about magic here. If there isn't an explanation, it's blamed on magic."

My brow furrowed, and I stepped closer to her and kneeled just below the platform so I could look up at her.

Like a servant for a goddess.

"I'm sorry, it's just... I grew up in a human world where people didn't believe in magic. I didn't even believe in Santa, the Tooth Fairy or the Easter Bunny. I knew they weren't real because my father told me at a young age that magic wasn't real. Coming here now, seeing that it is, just broke all of my belief system. It's a blow."

I tilted my head, reached up and placed a lock of hair behind her ear. I let my fingers linger on her neck, and she instinctively leaned into my touch.

She is breaking.

"I cannot imagine going from never believing in magic or gods. I see magic every day, so I've always believed. Even when I was an animal. Was it sad not to believe in the things you speak of? I have never heard of Santa, or a Tooth Fairy?" I questioned.

The corners of her lips twitched. "I know that they weren't really real. They are entities that humans made up. It was to bring spirit into the holidays, to a world that didn't believe in magic."

"And now that you see it's real? Do you believe it?" I don't know why I needed to hear that she did. It was sitting right there in front of her face, but if she *was* actually believing in the magic, she could believe in the gods, too. Believe that there is such a bond.

Lucy's lower lip quivered, and at that moment, my heart pounded with fear. Reacting swiftly, I gathered her fragile form into my embrace, feeling the weight of her against my chest. As I held her close, her scent entered my nose, mingling with the aroma of her teardrops. I could hear her soft whimpers, accompanied by tears cascading down her flushed cheeks. With tender care, I cradled her delicate head in my hands, using my fingertips to wipe away the salty trails that marred her beautiful face.

"Please don't cry, Lucy. It hurts me."

She sniffed and shook her head.

"I thought you would like the tent. That is why I did not fight it. Let us stay elsewhere. I will take you where this won't upset you." I made to stand, but she grabbed my arm, halting me.

"No, no. Simon, I'm so sorry. You must think I'm crazy. I just—"

"Shh, shh, I do not. You are the smartest human I have ever met."

Lucy giggled and tilted her head back. "How many humans have you met?"

I twisted my lips. "You are the third, but I still stand by what I said. You are also the smartest of all the realm. You know how things work, you read and write. You care for the Wood and do not destroy it. You keep nature how it is and do not destroy it to find out the inner workings."

When I watched her while she studied the Wood—before I took her—she was always careful, delicate. The orcs took care of the forest, but the shifters did not give as much care. The Wood is thick with vegetation. They use their claws to clear away trees and limbs to make room for their traveling packs. Lucy would take the path less traveled but not break nature. She was even more careful than I.

"You are the smartest I know. It may not mean much from me, since I do not speak with many, but you are the best."

Lucy's face turned a bright shade of red. "Thank you, but even with shifters, orcs and the like, I have a hard time believing in magic."

I took her wrist and placed it on my heart. "The only magic you need to feel is my bond with you. I am not good with words, but my feelings for you are true."

Lucy's tears, I assumed of frustration, flowed again. "I'm scared you will find your real—"

"Enough," I growled and tangled my fingers in her hair. "I may not know a lot of things, but I know we are meant to be. You feel it, you just deny it."

"I don't often feel powerful emotions such as this, and don't want to get hurt. I don't want my heart to break."

"And it won't, as long as you are with me." She nibbled on her bottom lip. "And I'll have you know, I will not let you go—ever! "If this witch says we are not meant to be, I'll tell her to fuck off, and I'll take you anyway."

Lucy blinked back in surprise. "You cussed, and you—you just said you would make me yours, permanently? Simon, a bond is sacred, you should—"

I pushed her down into the mattress and pinned her arms at her side. "Do not tell me what I will and will not do. You are my mate in every sense. I know it, so there is no reason to be upset over this."

"I-it's just—"

I pressed my lips to hers. It was the only way I could get her to see reason. She was mine, bond or not, but I knew there was a bond. It was infuriating that she didn't see that—didn't feel it.

I ran my hand up her leg, and she moaned and groaned when I removed it. "See, you crave me as much as I do you. Now, stop this nonsense of overthinking. Believe in the magic and the goddess' will."

She huffed when I released her and continued to lay there, unmoving. "We will get our answers soon, and you will see."

CHAPTER TWENTY-FOUR

Lucy

A BLINDING, RADIANT LIGHT danced and flickered before my tightly shut eyelids. Startled, I blinked repeatedly, my eyes straining to catch a glimpse of the source. It backed away, revealing the blue wisp floating gracefully in the air. It tapped my nose, leaving a faint tickling sensation, before gracefully twirling away as I stirred. Struggling to lift my head, I strained against the tightness enveloping my body.

Simon's face was buried in my neck, with locks of my hair in his mouth. It appeared he was chewing my hair, but as I pulled it from his lips, he hummed and tiny snores filled the tent. I tried to hold back my smile while I peeled myself from him.

He was out for the count after a hot make-out session—saying it was to help me forget my worries. His cock was sitting outside his pouch, hard and already at attention. I leaned forward to get a better look, but the whisp came over and pulled at my hair.

I waved it away like a fly and snorted. "What do you want, little trouble-maker?" If the light had shoulders, I bet it would slump when it dipped lower. Instead, it floated lower and whirled about the room and left the tent.

The last time I saw a whisp, I had naughty dreams of Simon, got scent-marked and chased by an ogre. Did I want to go down that path?

If these whisps were tiny directions to your fate, I should follow, right? I looked down at Simon's sleeping form. He was curled around the pillow I was using and took a long pull of my scent.

Curiosity getting the better of me, I grabbed the lantern by the opening of the tent. The fire was low but exuded a great amount of light. The one small flame could light up meters in front of me.

The whisp waited outside, and I put one hand on my hip. "Alright now, you are supposed to show me my fate, right?"

The whisp didn't answer, of course, and instead spun in a big circle and dashed through the clearing where the cabin and our tent stood and waited at the edge of the tree line.

I bit my lip and gazed back at the tent before I made the ultimate decision to follow.

I mean, why the hell not?

For science!

Instead of walking, I eagerly darted after it, my heart pounding with anticipation. The whisp danced through the air, its faint glow illuminating the surrounding darkness. With each leap, it gracefully bounced up and down from tree limb to tree limb, creating a mesmerizing spectacle.

As I followed the whisp, my footsteps were hushed, barely making a sound on the forest floor. I was led down a narrow path, barely visible, but recently walked. The branches had been cleared aside, revealing the way forward, and the soft soil beneath my feet gave way gently with each step.

As I ventured deeper into the enchanted forest, the aroma of damp earth and the sweet scent of blooming flowers filled the air, creating a sensory symphony.

It was so clean, so fresh. A far cry from any place I had been to on Earth.

I trampled on the purple moss, and tiny lights burst into existence, shimmering like stars beneath my feet, and their ethereal glow enchanting the forest further.

I laughed when the light stopped just ahead of me. It wiggled back and forth in front of the thick brush, as if ready for me to catch it. Holding my lantern, I ran forward and as I jumped to grab it, the whisp disappeared. I fell through the bushes, and I was standing in front of a hot spring.

Of course it was hot, but the air was crisp and cool, with a gentle breeze brushing against my skin. I could see the steam gracefully dancing above the water, creating a mystical aura. Carefully placing the lantern on a smooth rock, I ventured closer to the hot spring. The shimmering water glistened under the moon's soft glow, beckoning me with its alluring charm.

I stepped closer, and the surface of the water rippled as if in response to my presence.

"Magic," I muttered to myself, "or it could be just a frog that hopped into the spring." I shook my head and stared at the beautiful bioluminescent plants in the pool. When I lifted my head to get a better sense of my surroundings, a woman was patiently waiting on a rock high above and waved at me.

I gasped and stepped back. Her head was tilted to the side, her elbow resting on her bent knee as she sat. She was donned in leather pants, an arrow braced on her arm, her bow sitting on her back. On top of her head was an organic, decorative headpiece that could be mistaken for tiny horns with vines wrapped around it.

Was she a fairy of some kind? A fae?

The woman smiled. While she looked youthful, her eyes were old and appeared to be full of wisdom. "At least you remain curious, perhaps it won't be so difficult for you to see."

I stepped back, ready to run. I wasn't about to get caught up in a trap. Those whisps were crazy, and I wasn't about to get hunted down again.

"Easy there," the woman said and held up her hands. She sat up straight on the rock. "Not going to hurt you. I don't hunt your kind."

Hunt my kind?

She slid off the rock, which was sat beside a trickling waterfall. She must have approached when I was gazing into the pond. The splashing of water hid her footsteps. I never noticed her before.

She was the female version of Peter freaking Pan.

"I haven't been around a human in quite some time, I forget how skittish you all are. With no weapons on you, no claws or speed, I guess it is to be understandable." She put her hands on her hips, and I saw the definition of her body. She was slim but muscular. She could take me out if she wanted.

I'm gonna die.

"You are always full of questions. Why are you so quiet now?" She tilted her chin up.

"I-I—" I couldn't form words. I had forgotten how to talk. Now I felt like Simon.

She gracefully jumped from rock to rock. It was slow motion as she did until she got to the rock nearest to me. She sat down with a quiet 'Hmph' and crossed her legs. "Now, what is this about not believing in a bond or magic? You're the first human to question it since coming to a place like this."

She leaned over the spring and drew her finger into the water. Tiny little fish that shouldn't be able to survive the heat of the spring nibbled on her flesh.

I bit my bottom lip. She was right. I was being callous about all of it. Physics, chemistry, biology– all from Earth– didn't make sense here. They had their own sets of rules to go by.

I found it maddening yet exciting all at the same time.

When I first took the job, I was told to record, and put names to, the different species of plants and animals. I could study their behavior, write it all down and eventually have a book just on the Monktona Wood. Along with doing that, I've asked, why and how? That wasn't part of this job, but I wanted to know.

I was having trouble letting go and letting the world around me live. I wasn't letting myself live.

I bowed my head and looked at my fingers like they were the most interesting things in the world. She was so beautiful it hurt. "I'm a scientist; I'm supposed to ask the tough questions. I'm not from here, none of it makes sense. I didn't study religion or believe in anything other than science."

The woman hummed and nodded when I gazed up at her. "You don't need to believe in anything."

"Uh, but there is magic, for all the unexplainable things that are happening around me, in this world. The witches, the wisps, the bonds—Simon says it's magic. "

"It is magic," she stated. "No need to believe when it's actually there. Magic is the tool used to put things in motion by someone who can wield it." She paused again and opened up her hand. Tiny lights came together, creating a tiny fox in her hand. It moved, rolled and ran, but all stayed in the exact same spot on her palm.

"You don't have to believe in magic, Lucy. Magic is real; it was real on Earth. It is very much a part of even a human's everyday life. Magic isn't science, and science isn't magic, but one and the same. It is the air we breathe."

I opened my mouth to argue, but she continued. "How does a caterpillar come to be a butterfly?" The fox shifted, and a caterpillar appeared in her hand. "Just because humans have a fascination with categorizing, dissecting, and breaking things apart to see how they work, shouldn't mean you should forget the magic that made it come to be." She scoffed.

I watched the caterpillar wrap itself into a cocoon.

"Humans want knowledge because they think it is power, but the power is just how things are and one's ability to enjoy what is. I have never understood why humans waste so much of their tiny lifespans to categorize and make up rules. When those rules are not met, they all get so grumpy. You, however, are the first I have seen that has not destroyed the nature around you to understand it. For this, I thank you."

My body relaxed as she continued to explain. I didn't believe in dissecting things to know about them. I usually watched. My father and I both practiced that.

The cocoon soon broke open, and a butterfly appeared. I went and sat by her on the rock, and the butterfly that sat in her hand took flight and landed on my knee.

"Why does the platypus have the mouth of a duck, the feet of an otter, tail of a beaver and lay eggs for their young?" She raised her hand, and the butterfly came flying back to her. "And one of my favorites, how about the first intake of breath of a child once they are born? Isn't that magic?"

My eyebrow furrowed, and I lowered my head.

The woman straightened up, and the butterfly landed on one of her horns. "And what about a bumblebee?" she said excitedly. "They are so fat.

By the law of human physics they shouldn't even be able to fly!" She giggled and slapped her leg. "Really, though, they are actually Earth realm pixies in disguise. By magic, of course, because we can't have humans freaking out about tiny little people. Humans already steal enough honey as it is."

My mouth gaped open. "They are pixies?"

Dear gods, I hope I didn't accidentally kill one.

The woman nodded. "You see, the Earth Realm has its own magic and the unexplainable. As a scientist of this realm, you just have to accept it as it is. There isn't an answer to everything. In any realm, the magic, the norms, and life are different."

I let out a large gasp. "There are other realms?"

The woman tilted her head and narrowed her eyes. "You are getting off track. But yes, there are. The Underworld, the Celestial Kingdom—Poseidon's Realm doesn't really count, it floats between Earth and the Celestial. Depends where he wants to go."

My mouth gaped. "Are there more?"

The woman shook her head, but I guessed there was another by the way her lips tilted at the edge of her mouth.

"What is the other?" My eyes widened.

"Curious you are, and I will tell you for your sake of your curiosity and respect for nature, but you are never to go there. It is wild and untamed; dark magic runs rampant, and if that comes here..." She pressed her lips together in a thin line. "It would destroy all the realms."

I nodded enthusiastically. I wanted to know all the things.

"When you enter Bergarian, it is instructed you to stay on the path from Earth to Bergarian. You are not to fall off that path, otherwise you would be lost in a sea of darkness. Beyond that darkness is a realm called The Moving Province."

My eyes widened, and I clutched my skirt. I wished I had my notebook.

The woman hummed and leaned back on a rock. "And that is all I can say about that."

With that great new information to write later, I let out an enormous sigh. What she said made sense about magic. What made even more sense was the Earth had magic as well. Except I, and so many others, were too blind to see it and take it in for what it was.

"What about the gods?" I added. "What of them?"

The woman smirked and nudged me. "That is a bit strange, isn't it?" She tapped her finger on her nose. "The same gods that are in the Earth Realm are here, too. Do you think there is a connection?"

I rolled my eyes. "You're mocking me."

"Am I just?" She fiddled with the guard on her arm. "I just told you there was an Underworld and a Celestial Kingdom, and you believed me so easily, yet you still ask about the gods? You aren't that dense."

My shoulders slumped. Did I already believe it?

"And the bond? The Moon Goddess, soulmates, are they real?"

The woman shrugged her shoulders, and the tiny lights that were once a butterfly turned into a crescent moon. "I don't know, are they?"

Rustling from the bushes gave me pause, and I jerked my head to see Simon breathing heavily. "Lucy, I've hunted for you! Why did you not answer my voice?" His body was full of sweat, dirt, and grime. I stood up, away from the woman, and walked toward Simon.

"I'm sorry, I got distracted, but here, let me introduce you to—" I turned, and when I looked back, the woman was no longer there.

CHAPTER TWENTY-FIVE

Simon

Lucy turned and threw her hands up in the air. "She was right here, I swear it! There was a woman; she had horns and a bow with some arrows on her back!" My mate grunted and stomped her foot. "I'm not crazy!"

She certainly well looked crazy.

I stepped forward and put my hand on her shoulder while her back was turned. She jumped and placed her hand over her heart when she faced me. "I swear there was—"

I kissed her, my furred upper lip tingling with the smoothness of her skin. "I believe you. I never said I didn't." Of course, there would be something—someone there. I wouldn't be surprised if it was a goddess. I've heard the orcs being visited by the Moon Goddess before.

As our bodies pressed together, a wave of relaxation washed over her, causing her muscles to loosen. Her weight eased against mine, her body molding perfectly into the contours of my own. I let my fingertips glide along the smooth expanse of her sides, relishing in her warm, bare skin.

I made the best clothing.

I gripped the back of her head and tugged Lucy by her hair. "What did she say?" I whispered into her lips.

If it was a goddess or a witch, I needed to know if they were helpful in my endeavor to take this female and make her mine.

Lucy licked her lips, tasting me upon them. "That I have always been around magic, even on Earth. Bumblebees... bumblebees are pixies! They aren't just some unresolved scientific phenomenon." She let out a manic laugh. "It's everywhere. It's this place, it's even you."

I did not know what she spoke of, about these bumblebees. All I knew was that she believed in the things she could not explain.

Good, because I was tired of waiting.

I pressed my lips to hers once more, feeling her heat. Her moans mingled with our breathless gasps, and the scent of her desire lingered around me. Her nails scraped down my back, sending shivers of pleasure coursing through my body.

As our kisses grew more heated, a primal desire surged through me, driving me to claim her completely. I parted her lips with my own, deepening the kiss with a hunger that matched the wild beating of my heart.

I felt her hands tangle in my hair, pulling me closer as she arched against me, igniting a fire that blazed out of control.

"Take off your clothes," I rasped.

She blinked up at me in surprise, frozen with hungered eyes.

"I said to take them off, or I will rip them off for you," I rasped.

If she had started to believe in the ways of this world, she would soon understand my desires for her as well. There was nothing stronger than a bond. Lucy felt it, I knew it. Now, I needed to guide her, so she knew my intentions without holding anything back. Even myself.

Lucy shuddered in my hold as her hand reached for one side of her top. It was painstakingly slow, but I waited patiently as it was pulled to the side.

"Lucy," I growled in warning. "You do not know how much I want you."

She swallowed. "I think I have an idea." She stared down at my pouch, where my shaft poked out. It pulsed as my seed leaked from the head.

"No! You do not know how much I want to make you mine. Keep you, forever."

"F-forever?!" She let out a high-pitched squeak, her eyes widening as she slowly backed up, her feet entering the warm spring. "I haven't even talked to my father about all of this." The sound of this confession was met with a soft chuckle that escaped my throat.

I stalked toward her, and my hooves pounded the soil as I did. "He has no choice, and it is no longer yours. This bond is between two people, not him. Once I make you mine, you will live as long as I live. Our souls and our bodies cannot live without the other."

Her chest rose and fell quickly.

"I said, take. It. Off!"

She hesitated for just a moment longer, then swiftly removed her top, the fabric sliding off her body with a soft rustling sound. The spring's clear waters shimmered under the moonlight, casting a gentle glow on her bare skin.

My eyes, captivated by her beauty, grew darker with lust, a low growl escaping my lips. Her breasts, perfectly shaped, seemed to invite my touch and the sight of her hardened nipples awakened a primal desire within me, urging me to taste their sweetness.

My ears twirled in excitement.

It worked. She actually did it.

This female just needed a firm hand.

I smiled predatorily as I advanced toward her, my movements slow and deliberate. My hands reached for her waist, pulling her closer to me so she could feel my shaft against her stomach. My lips met hers once again, this time more fervently than before. I tasted the salty sweat from her heated body, and my fingers trailed against the skirt I had made for her.

With one swipe of my claw, I untied it from her hip and slung it away from the pool.

My fingers traced delicate patterns on her skin, causing small bumps to rise along the way. With the steam of the water rising around us, I trailed my finger up her inner thigh. She closed her eyes, her head leaning into my chest when my fingers touched her slit.

"What other words do you use for this?" I rubbed the tiny nub that caused her to buck against my fingers.

Lucy moaned, her face rubbing against my chest. Her scent surrounded me, bringing desires I should not have right now. Rutting her into the dirt, her pretty face dirty and taking my large shaft where it would not fit.

"A clit," her breath hitched. "And down here..." She grabbed my wrist and pushed me lower. "It's a vagina, or a pussy, a cunt—"

Mmm, cunt. I liked this word.

I slipped two fingers inside her cunt and slowly backed her further into the pool. These pools had healing properties. I learned it accidentally when I had scratches up and down my body from learning to walk. The warm water soothed them, as well as my aching body from using parts of me I was not used to.

This would be the perfect time to stretch her.

I guided her backward until her back hit a large rock. She hissed, feeling the rough surface. My fingers did not leave her. I stroked the inside of her cunt with my fingers until she was a panting mess.

"You are going to take my cock this time."

Her eyes widened. "I don't think I can, Simon you are—"

I grabbed her wrist with my other hand and made her wrap her hand around it. I grunted, feeling the warmth of her hand on my shaft. Goddess, I wanted her so much it hurt.

"I am large, but you are meant to be mine. You didn't want to let me in before, not truly."

Her lips parted. "I wanted to let you in... ahhh!"

My thumb grazed her clit. I rubbed it in slow circles as I pumped my fingers in and out of her. "You closed your body off to me. You wouldn't let me—"

"Fuck!" she cried out, her hand squeezing my shaft.

I groaned and wiggled my third finger inside her.

"No, Simon, please!" she begged, her voice shaking. "I can't take it all!" But her hips gravitated toward my thrusts.

Her words only fueled my desire. I knew she was mine and would not stop until I claimed her completely. She wanted me to take her, to hold her captive in my arms.

I wiggled a fourth finger inside, harder and felt her tight walls grip my hand. Her moans woke the wildlife, making birds fly away from the spring.

Mm, I liked this.

"You are mine," I growled, thrusting deeper. "You will take every inch of what I give you, won't you?"

She whimpered underneath me, her body trembling as I dominated her cunt. My thumb continued to tease her clit, her hips bucking against my hand. The surrounding water splashed with our movements.

"Ahhh! Simon, yes!" she moaned, her orgasm crashing over her. Her muscles clenched my hand, and hers stroked my shaft.

I groaned, feeling the tension built up inside me, released. My seed leaked into the pool. She looked so beautiful, and my body had given way too soon.

"You're ready for my cock, if you accept me." I traced my nose up her neck to behind her ear. I let out a contented purring noise that I didn't know I could make.

My mate never released her hold on me. My seed floated away into the waters. She hummed and pressed her fingers into my pouch.

"What's in there?"

I chuckled and pulled my fingers out of her slick and licked them with my tongue. The waters did nothing to dilute the taste. "Why don't you put your hand inside and find out?"

I had to give into her curiosity. If this was what she needed to do to fully accept me, then this was what we would do.

Her cheeks were still tinged pink from her release, but that did not stop her as she dipped her hand inside the horizontal pouch that kept my cock inside.

I groaned and pressed my hand to the rock to hold myself upright.

I let out a long, frustrated groan.

"It really is a pouch," she hummed lazily. "And my gods," she stiffened when she held my seed sack.

I smirked. It was full, so heavy, even after my latest release. I was ready to release every bit into her.

"Simon—how?"

I nibbled on the side of her neck, and her body relaxed again in my arms.

"Why ask questions when you can feel?" I licked down her neck and onto her shoulder.

She leaned her neck to the side and bared it to me.

I felt fire light up behind my eyes as I stared at the clean spot on her neck. I wanted to mark it. I wanted to mark her all over so everyone knew she was mine.

Utterly mine.

I pressed my mouth to her shoulder, nipping and sucking. She groaned, and her hand went up to squeeze my shaft again, and my body shuddered against her.

"Yes, I want to feel. Please touch me," she begged.

Mmm, begging.

"I will take you; what's rightfully mine." I pressed my body against her. I pulled us above the water so could let my cock rub up against her stomach. I was leaking seed all over her, scenting her with it.

My mate leaned her head back. "No, not for science," she muttered to herself, and I pulled away.

I furrowed my brows and parted my lips. Did she not want me?

She grabbed my hand and put it to her breast. "I want it, for me. For us."

My heart thundered in my chest, and I pressed a heated kiss to her lips. I hungrily parted her lips and sank my tongue inside.

Yes, yes, I would take her now.

I lowered my head to suck at her hardened nipple. She groaned in frustration and pulled on my horn.

"No, inside me. Please put it inside me."

I refused. I wanted her to feel good, to drown in ecstasy, and there was one way I could do it.

I took the soft skin into my mouth, biting around her breast. She didn't scream, instead she cradled my head as I sank deeper into her flesh. I groaned, flicking the nipple with my tongue.

"Please," she cried. "Don't make me beg."

I removed my mouth, licking away the blood that dripped down her skin. "I like it when you beg for me."

Her head shot up from leaning on the stone, and her eyes narrowed.

"I have begged for you too much, it is only fair." I pulled her toward me and had her wrap her legs around my waist. I waded deeper to keep her cunt in the warm, healing waters.

The head of my cock probed her entrance, and her body stiffened.

"Relax, my mate, I will take care of you. You will take me well."

Four of my fingers did not match my girth. *Eh, close enough.*

I pushed forward, and her tight walls gripped me so tight I saw the heavens. "Aggnhh."

She whimpered, and I felt her fingers claw at my back as I slowly sank deeper into her.

"That's it," I whispered hoarsely. "Take me, take all of me. I know what my mate needs." We stared into each other's eyes.

"A good dicking, apparently!" she said.

I inched forward, and I felt my cock extending her lower stomach. Her eyes were wide with fear and confusion, but there was also pleasure in them.

A blush stained her cheeks as she nodded, urging me on with her gaze. And then she spoke, her voice barely above a whisper, "Please..."

With that word, I thrust forward, filling her. I had buried every inch of myself within her. She cried out in pain and pleasure, arching her back as she clutched at my shoulders. Her soft moans filled the air around us as I assaulted her cunt.

I tightly grasped onto her hips, feeling the softness of her skin against my fingertips as I thrust deep inside her with a rhythmic motion. She pleaded for more, her voice filled with a desperate longing as the thick veins of my cock rubbed against her clit.

"Tight, so tight. Milk my seed," I growled. I imagined each thrust branding her on the inside.

She was mine.

"You take my cock so well, human." I felt fur sprouting on my back, sending a shiver of excitement down my spine. My arms prickled and fur exploded down my arms and stood on end. Thick muscle bulged, my fingers lengthened as I dug into her hips.

My body stiffened. I wasn't turning back into a goat, was I?

But no. That wasn't the case.

I still had my thoughts, my mind and my desires. I was still the same. This was something different, and I would look into it later when my cock wasn't so deep inside my mate.

I snarled and felt my body rise; it felt stronger, more beastly. I heaved in deep breaths as I continued to push in and out of her. I didn't care what was happening to me, as long as she felt pleasure.

"More," my mate whimpered. She stared up at me, her eyes filled with lust. "Oh gods, your eyes, they're red. You're big, all over." Her hands squeezed my bulging arms.

I huffed, my warm breath breathing across her face.

"Oh, fuck it! Fuck me harder!"

Her cunt squeezed around me before she let out a hoarse scream.

I looked down at her, my eyes locked with hers, and I could see the raw desire in her gaze. She wanted this, needed this, and I was more than happy to oblige.

I thrust harder and deeper, feeling her walls tremble around me as she called out my name. My fur continued to grow, my body changing in response to the intensity of the mating heat coursing through us. The frenzy built inside me, and I knew it would not be long before we both reached our climax.

She gripped my hips tightly, her nails digging into my skin, leaving small marks that only served to drive me further into a frenzy. Her cries filled the air, each one a symphony of pleasure and pain.

"Yes," she panted. "Yes, like that. I'm going to come again!"

With each word, each moan, each gasp for breath, I felt myself about to spill. I have pleased my mate. It was my turn.

"Simon!" she cried out my name again, and her voice rose in pitch as her orgasm neared. "I'm going to... oh gods, yes!"

I felt her muscles tighten around me once more, and I knew it was time to give her what she so desperately craved. With one last thrust, my cock pulsed, and I emptied my seed and coated her womb.

I hissed and pushed my cock deeper if that were possible. My legs shook in the spring, but I held her tightly against the smooth stone. Her head fell to my shoulder, and the rest of her body became limp.

That was incredible. I nuzzled against the side of her face, taking her in. I pray to the goddess she cared...

"I think I love you."

My hazed eyes blinked several times.

I knew this word; I knew what it meant. I'd heard Calliope tell her parents and her mate. It was a powerful word.

I wrapped my arms around her back and fell back into the spring. Unfortunately, some of my seed would wash off, but my cock was still buried deep inside her.

While my mate would feel delirious from my bite, I was the one who was feeling an added high. My mate truly cared for me.

My fingers threaded through her hair, and my body tightened around her.

"You care?" My voice was deeper than any other time I had spoken.

Lucy rose from my chest, her lips parted. "Simon, your voice..."

My cock was hard again, and I bucked into her pussy.

"Ahh, again?" she whined and dug her nails into my chest.

Yes, again. I needed her. I needed more.

I moved toward the bank of the spring. Once we reached the edge, I pulled us out of the water and flipped her over, putting her on all fours.

"Yes, I need you."

I shoved my cock deeper inside her, her pussy met with no resistance how slick she was.

Lucy's head slung back and pushed herself back onto my shaft, meeting me thrust for thrust.

"Simon, are you okay? Not that I'm complaining—"

I gripped her hips and pushed myself in and out of her body. My cock was an angry red. Lucy cried out moans of pleasure, and I snarled when she threw her head back and let out a scream.

"Yes, female, eat my cock. Soon, I will have all your holes." Fire burned inside me, I could not get enough of her. My thirst was not quenched, my desire was not sated. I needed all of her and to become one with her.

She lowered her body so it was just her backside in the air. Her face was in the dirt, begging me for more.

I would give my mate **more**!

Chapter Twenty-Six

Lucy

I was getting railed, literally.

Simon was making guttural, animalistic grunts and growls that echoed into the forest. The sound was raw and primal, surely sending shivers down the spine of anyone who might hear it. His eyes burned with an intense, fiery red, which pierced through the darkness. The air was heavy with the scent of musk, as if his very presence exuded a wild, untamed energy.

Gone was the sweet, almost innocent faun. He was on a damn mission. *And I, hoe Lucy, was here for it.*

As cliche as it sounded, Simon knew me. He knew me better than I thought I knew myself. One look, and he understood I had opened myself not only to this world, but to him, too. I was at the edge of the cliff, and I took the jump.

To take all of him. Not just for science.

He knew I was his the moment he met me. Did I? I never believed in love at first sight. I needed more; that was me, and Simon didn't give up. He didn't give up on us when I would have, right from the beginning.

And in such little time, he claimed me.

I'd known him for only a few days, and yet I wanted to spend my life with him.

Part of it was the mating bond that everyone in this realm talked about.

I didn't know if I fought it. I think I knew it was there when I felt the sexual connection with him, but I didn't fall in love with him right away. The bond only pushed me toward him. What I did next was all by my will alone.

I'll have to write down my feelings in order of appearance later, because I think I broke him when I told him I loved him.

I freaking loved the faun.

He thrust into me again, and the sound of our bodies slapping echoed into the forest. A strained whimper escaped my lips, the feeling of his forceful grip on my waist intensified. Surprisingly, his cock now fit perfectly inside me, a sensation that left me puzzled as to why it hadn't before.

Maybe subconsciously, I didn't want to let him before, and my body just closed off because I hadn't accepted everything?

Why are we thinking about this now, Lucy? You are getting your vagina pulverized!

I let out a long moan as another orgasm rushed over me. I could no longer stay on my knees. I let them slide down into the mud, but Simon wasn't done with me. He pulled my hips up and continued his ravenous assault.

Oh, I needed a break. He needed to hurry up and come again.

"Please, please fill me up."

Simon paused for a mere moment, his deep growl reverberating through the dense forest. I could feel the weight of his tired body as it pressed against my back, the heat of his breath cascading against the nape of my neck, carrying the musky scent of his arousal.

I was completely boneless, my body was spent. I lost count of how many times I orgasmed. I think Simon was trying to make up for all the years I hadn't had one.

Well, I think he made up for it.

Simon's heavy body surrounded me, putting a pressure on my body that made me feel utterly safe. It didn't matter if I was face down on the moss-covered ground, it never felt so right.

Simon roared, his hips slammed into my backside, and hot come filled me.

I was almost half asleep when Simon lifted from my body. He grunted and rolled me onto my back. His hand cupped my cheek, and I saw the full change of his face.

Red eyes stared back at me. His cock was hard again, leaking on my thighs and stomach. I licked my lips involuntarily, and he let out a grunt of satisfaction.

Was I ready to go again? Because he certainly was.

Take that, Mr. Tumnus.

He leaned forward, his tongue licking my cheek, when I felt it.

Vibrations on the ground. I wasn't the only one who noticed. Simon perked up his head, his ears standing on end, and he snarled.

"What is it?" I whispered.

Simon didn't answer. His nose flared, and he huffed several times. He was still in this beast mode he had turned into. You would think his dick would have gone down, but that wasn't the case.

"Ogre," he finally said. "It heard and smelled us."

I knew he meant to say that the ogre smelled *me*. I didn't think the ogre would care much for dick. Ogres wanted humans.

I opened my mouth to ask what to do next, but Simon picked me up and took me back to the spring. "What are you doing?" I hissed and wrapped my arms around him. He took me deeper into the spring to the point where we were swimming. I could swim by myself just fine, but he wasn't letting me go.

As we ventured through the narrow gaps between jagged rocks, their rough edges scraped against my skin. The mesmerizing sight of bioluminescent fish dancing in the water surrounded me, their vibrant colors illuminating the dark abyss. The sound of water lapped against the rocks from Simon's jerky movement. He put me down, then turned to leave me. I was quickly brought back to the present.

"Stay," he grunted.

"Wait!" I reached out and pulled on his arm. When he came back to me, his brow was furrowed and his mouth drooped. His teeth even looked longer and there was a wild look in his eyes. "Simon, stay here, we can hide."

"I will not, I will kill—"

Branches broke, limbs fell from the trees and a large grunting ogre stepped out of the forest. He was taller than some of the trees, and he took his hand and brushed them away from him like they were tiny plants.

"Hu-man." He took in a long draw of breath.

My body was hidden well between the rocks, but I ducked lower so he wouldn't be able to see me.

Simon snarled and climbed up the rock as he stood tall and proud, his cock still hanging out of his pouch.

Why was that so hot?

Yet dangerous. The ogre was huge, and it generally took several orcs to take one of these things down!

The ogre let out a throaty laugh as he looked at Simon. Simon was standing tall, his fur bristled and his teeth were bared. The ogre's eyes narrowed, and he growled in response.

The ogre tilted his head, the mucus from his nose dripping down into his mouth. "You were with the female. I smell her." Simon didn't speak, but his hands balled into fists. "You no match for me, little monster." The ogre's voice boomed, causing the trees to tremble. "I'll crush your head with my fingers and find the female!"

Simon snarled again, his anger rising. He turned to me, his eyes fierce and full of determination. "Stay there," he hissed.

Simon leapt off the wet rock, jumping to the next one with such agility. He had no weapons except for his claws and hooves. My heart flew into my throat. This was insane. He was freaking insane!

The ogre let out a booming laugh, obviously amused by Simon's bravery. "Little monster, you cannot defeat me!" He raised his massive fist and swung it towards Simon, who dodged it with a swift leap.

Simon was agile and fast, while the ogre had slower movements. Each swing of the ogre's arm, Simon was able to dodge. I didn't know if Simon could survive a hit, but he never backed down, though. He darted between the ogre's legs to try and find a weak spot. I bit my lip, watching in horror as the battle unfolded.

The ogre continued to taunt Simon, whose laughter echoed through the forest. "Give her to me, you dirty goat!" he roared as he swung his massive arm again. This time, Simon dodged it just in time and landed behind one of the thick tree trunks along the tree line.

For a brief moment, I thought he was safe. But the ogre wasn't deterred. He smashed the tree where Simon hid. With the tree gone, I poked my head over the rock and saw that Simon wasn't there.

He wasn't anywhere.

The ogre chuckled and whipped his head around him. "Gone already? Pitiful," he sniffed, the mucus sucking back up into his nose. "A worthless creature—"

Simon roared, jumping down from one of the tallest trees. I gasped, watching him fall. The ogre looked up, not ready for the assault. Simon landed on the ogre's face, his long claws diving into one of his eyes.

The ogre roared, the ground and trees trembling. A dark, green liquid oozed from his eye and face.

Ew, is that its blood?

I held back a gag and did my best to hide my body so I wouldn't be seen.

As the struggle continued, I could see Simon's determination in his eyes, his resolve was unwavering. The forest echoed with the sounds of battle: the crunch of breaking branches, the muffled yells of frustration from the ogre, and Simon's fierce growls.

Suddenly, Simon leaped from the ogre's face and onto one of the long branches above us. He used his muscular arms and made himself into a catapult. He pushed back on the limb and let go with a swift motion. He propelled himself towards the ogre. The branch had been pushed back so hard it slammed into the ogre's face.

The ogre roared again, clutching at his now-blinded eye and stumbling backward from the hit. He was knocked off balance and fell to his knees.

Seizing this opportunity, Simon jumped onto the ogre's back and began clawing at him viciously. With each swipe of his claws, blood dripped from the ogre's back like a waterfall. The ogre bellowed in pain and fury but was powerless against Simon's quick, relentless assault.

It was a train wreck that I couldn't look away from.

The ogre thrashed and got up. Simon was making weird noises, but I didn't know what they meant. Was he hurt? Was he exerting himself too much?

I couldn't sit here and wait. I was going to be the dumb heroine in my story and get him to stop. This ogre was too big and powerful, and Simon's claws would not be able to hit any vital organs.

I swam to the side of the pool and raced out. The ogre was throwing his arms around like Simon was a fly. One hit, and Simon was going to get knocked out. "Simon!" I screamed, taking steps away from them.

I wasn't completely stupid.

Simon's back was to me, but his head perked up when he heard me. I could see the rippling muscles beneath the fur that had grown on his back. When his head turned, his face was feral. Long fangs, red eyes, nose flaring.

Chills ran down my spine as I watched just how scary he was. My cute little Simon was -terrifying.

In a hot way? I guess reading monster romances paid off.

He huffed and let his claws scratch down the ogre's face one more time before he jumped off its body. Simon galloped toward me and picked me up, throwing me over his shoulder like the first time we met.

Ahh, the memories.

"Female, I said to stay."

Em, excuse me? Female?

I slapped Simon's furred back and growled at him myself. "You are not the boss of me." *Just the boss of my pussy.* "Simon, you could have gotten hurt!"

Simon let out an unintelligible sound and sprinted us off through the woods. I felt the limbs slapping my butt and let out squeaks of discomfort. Simon paused, then put me into his arms like I was his bride, and ran off again.

His jawline was set and his eyes wild. Droplets of dark, green blood were spattered on his face. This was not Simon. Not at all.

We arrived back at Thorn and Ellie's home in record time. Thorn was ready to meet us; he had his club and a more scornful look on his face than before. "Where is it?" He huffed. "Tell me now so I can destroy it."

"It's down," I spoke quickly as I tried to cover my breasts. "It's blind in one eye, wounded near the hot spring."

Thorn nodded, his eyes narrowing as he shot a piercing glare at Simon. Thorn stood tall, he squared his shoulders, and tested the weight of his club in his hand. With a surge of determination, he launched himself forward. His footsteps echoed in the distance and his voice resonated through the air as he called out, the sound carried to us by the wind. "Her scent will be covered here, do not leave the confines of my territory."

Simon gripped my body, anger raging through him. I didn't know Simon could be so emotional like this. It was all a completely new side.

Another reminder that I barely knew him, but it was extremely hot at the same time.

He was protecting me in his own way.

Simon charged to the tent, not bothering to move the flaps away. He put me on the bed as gently as he could and huffed when he grabbed a blanket and wrapped it around my body.

His breath was heaving, his chest rising and falling rapidly. His claws ran through his hair, sweat dripping at his temples.

Yup, I was pretty turned on.

Simon's nose flared. He jerked his head toward me with a lustful glare. I shivered under his scrutiny when he narrowed his eyes and clenched his fists.

"Female, you could have been wounded, hurt. Why did you—"

"Simon, you aren't acting right!"

Neither was his body. His cock was hanging out of his pouch… still!

"You are crazy and horny—crazy-horny—and going off and fighting an ogre that is three times your height. You need help to defeat that thing!"

Simon bared his teeth.

Yup, more turned on.

"And your body!" I waved my hand up and down his body and bulging cock. I meant muscles. "Something is wrong!"

I tapped my cheek, and my eyes widened in realization. Heat, well rut, for males. Goats go through a rut and can act absolutely insane.

Simon was going through his rut, and most likely, his first one.

"I will protect what is mine, and I will go back and destroy the threat." He turned his back to me. "Stay in the tent. When I return, I will claim you in every way. I'll bite every part of you and sink my cock in every hole until the bond takes place."

Well, cover me in root juices.

When Simon turned, Ellie was standing on the other side of the tent. Her baby was on her hip, babbling and chewing on a dragon scale branch. Ellie pulled up a straw-like device to her mouth and blew. The tiny toothpick that flew out of it shot Simon in the chest.

Simon snarled and pulled out the toothpick. He nudged Ellie to the side so he could step past her, and just two seconds later, I heard a thump outside.

I raced to the tent flap and saw Simon lying face-first on the ground.

Oh, I hope he didn't hurt his dick. That would be painful to bruise.

But wait. "What did you do to my mate?" I squealed at Ellie.

CHAPTER TWENTY-SEVEN

Lucy

"Aw, you called him your mate!"

Kiah clapped his hands and blew a bubble with his lips.

I readjusted the blanket around me, tucking it in around my body so I could use my hands to check on Simon. I kneeled on the ground and shook his shoulder. He was still warm, breathing, and let out a huff into the dirt.

"What did you do?" I asked again, irritated.

Was she going to sit there and coo over the fact that I said he was my mate?

"Ah, well, I had to put him out before he hurt himself. Thorn said it would be for the best." She tapped the straw-like dart gun on her chin. "And I have to agree with him. Simon has the best intentions, but ogres are dangerous."

I carefully rolled Simon over, my hands grazing his smooth skin as I searched for any signs of bumps or bruises. The faint scent of the ogre's blood and dirt was there. Relief washed over me as I realized Simon was unharmed, his skin clean and untouched by injury. The lingering residue of the ogre's presence clung to him.

"What did you hit him with?" I rubbed my fingers where the dart hit. It was as tiny as a pinprick, barely noticeable.

"It's a dart that can knock out an ogre for a day. It works well, so the orcs can catch and decapitate them without much fuss. Clean and easy to clean up, you know? With Simon, he will be out for a few days."

My mind raced before I went into full panic mode. Just hours ago, she told me their story. This must be the same poison that Thorn accidentally exposed her to when he captured her and then nursed her back to health. Ellie would have died if Thorn hadn't massaged the special oil into her skin to revive her muscles. What about Simon?

I gritted my teeth and stood in front of her. Who cared if she had an orcling in her arms! "You don't know that! Simon is so much smaller than an ogre! This could kill him!"

Ellie shook her head vehemently. "No, it can kill a human, not a person with special healing abilities from this realm. Remember, things here heal quickly. They have faster immune systems. Scratches heal in a few hours rather than days. Simon will be fine. Trust me."

My mouth hung open in dismay as I turned to Simon.

"I can withstand the poison now that I am mated to Thorn. I *accidentally* pricked my finger when I was pregnant because I couldn't sleep. That was the best rest I have had in ages." Ellie eyed the dart longingly in her hand. I grabbed it from her and held it away.

"No, you don't. I need help with this."

Ellie chuckled and raised Kiah back up on her hip. "Fine, party pooper. Let's get him inside the tent."

Ellie continued to explain her reasoning for why she darted Simon. He was acting crazy, not how an average male would act. When I told her I believed he was in a rut, she *'awwwed'* in understanding.

He was protecting me in the only way he knew how. Simon wanted the threat destroyed and if I let it continue, he may have succeeded, but I couldn't stomach watching him destroy the ogre piece by piece.

Ellie unceremoniously dropped Simon's hand once we got him on the bed. She was stronger than I was. The arm she pulled seemed like a pillow behind her while I was huffing and puffing.

Again, I needed to work out.

"Might want to cover that." Ellie snickered. "His dick is quite prominent, large even for a faun, isn't it?"

I blushed furiously and covered it with a blanket. Not that it did anything to hide just how big of a problem it was. It was leaking and twitching. I groaned and slapped my forehead in distress.

"And what an interesting pouch he has." Ellie leaned over to try and examine his covered bulge .

Even when Simon was drugged, the thing was all set to go.

I quickly covered the rest of his body with a blanket. "He *is* rutting, as I said. At least that is what I have concluded. He's showing the basic signs of what animals do when they need to expel their seed, and it appears your drug will not subdue it."

Ellie hummed in agreement. "Told you that dart won't keep him out for long. I'd say he has a few days, though, since I gave him an ogre dose. It will give your vajayjay a rest, at least."

I turned away, covering my mouth with my hand.

"Yeah, smelled both of you a mile away." Ellie looked at my shoulder. "No mark yet?"

I sighed and shook my head. That was the whole reason why we needed Starla.

Ellie carefully lowered Kiah onto the soft, plush blankets spread across the blanketed floor. As she did, I glimpsed his bright, curious eyes, taking in the colorful surroundings. Kiah's tiny hands grasped the blanket, and he brought it to his mouth.

"I'd have him go for your shoulder or a neck bite." Ellie pointed toward me. "That is how most of the realm does it. Only the orcs don't, but I think that is because of their tusks. Could you imagine being bitten by those?" Ellie shuddered.

It made sense, but didn't I want to find out for sure? Simon said when he got back, he was going to bite me everywhere, and I believed he would. The bite on my boob was something else. When he hit the right spot, what would I feel then?

Was it an experiment I was willing to try? My body immediately said yes.

Kiah, who was playing on the floor, grunted and stared up at me. His beady, little yellow eyes were judging me. I just knew it.

He couldn't read my dirty thoughts, could he?

"I need to speak to Starla," I muttered.

Ellie shook her head. "Sorry, there just isn't a way to contact her, and she only specializes in orc matings, since they are so different."

I tilted my head and stared at her in question.

"She's part of a witch collective that helps orcs to get their mate because they are obviously not the traditional soul to become mated with."

I pointed to Simon, rather than his dick, which was sticking up under the sheet. "What about that? How is that traditional?"

"All guys get hard-ons," Ellie scoffed. "If Starla hasn't seen you yet, it's because she thinks you have it under control or you are smart enough to figure it out for yourself. I mean, it took me a few times because I was pretty broken after my relationship before Thorn happened." Ellie picked up Kiah and held him to her chest. "That all changed rather quickly once I believed Thorn would never leave me."

"Because of the bond?" I asked.

Ellie smiled. "The bond helped, but I fell for him because I wanted to. I still have a choice in the matter. I wish I fell for him sooner and let go of all my doubts and past issues, but I am happy with the outcome."

I understood exactly what she said. Ellie had a whole month before she bonded to Thorn, yet here I was after a week and ready to do it myself.

I was not completely hopeless, I guess.

Ellie departed, leaving me with a sleeping Simon. I didn't know the effects the poison would have on him, but before Ellie left, she said she used to be very conscious when it appeared she was sleeping. Simon could be wide awake at this moment, and I wouldn't know.

I cleaned him up the best I could with what I had, using the clean water and rags that I would refill from the buckets in the room. I carefully washed him from head to toe, trying to be as gentle as possible. Despite his condition, he looked peaceful in his sleep, and I didn't want to disrupt that. The water felt warm against my skin, and I couldn't help but think how strange it was that I was taking care of a faun in this manner.

As I cleaned him, I noticed a subtle change in his breathing. It seemed to deepen and slow down, as if he were responding to my touch. It made me smile knowing that even in this state, he was still aware where I was.

This faun was nuts.

As I got closer to his groin, I lifted the sheet off of it and stared at it. I mean, who wouldn't stare at it? It was a thick thing of beauty.

Can a dick be pretty?

It was the only one I had ever wanted.

I washed around him, wiping away the dirt and grime. Once satisfied, I went to replace the sheet but saw his dick twitch. Not once, but several times.

I gazed back at his sleeping face. No signs of distress. He looked sound asleep.

Except his dick was wide awake. All big, throbbing and with precum leaking out of it.

Poor thing must be hurting.

I licked my lips and made sure the tent flap was shut. I kneeled between his spread legs and lowered my head to it.

I wasn't considering doing what I was thinking, right?

Hoe Lucy was back.

What if he was in pain, having his dick sitting upright and hard for so long? On Earth, they said that if your erection lasted more than four hours, you should go to the hospital. That's at least what I heard dad talking to some other man about.

And... blue balls? Was that a thing?

But we weren't on Earth, Lucy. We were in a magical realm. Surely you can leave his dick alone for one second for him to get better.

Then, it twitched again.

Impulsive thoughts won this round.

I grabbed the base of his cock, not thinking of the consequences. I hadn't had time to ask for consent to touch him while sleeping, but I felt that since he had seen me naked asleep and actually freaking undressed me, this would be fine.

Yeah, I'm gonna go with that.

I was just trying to help him out; this was for him, not me.

I swirled my tongue around the cock's head, and Simon's breathing picked up.

It wasn't long before I felt his body tense, the rhythm of his breath hitching as I continued my ministrations. His cock twitched again, and I couldn't help but smile at the sight of it.

"Simon," I whispered, unsure if he was conscious or still asleep. "Are you awake?"

A low groan was his only response, but it was enough to let me know he was aware of what was happening. My heart raced with a mix of excitement.

This was so—*naughty.*

My jaw could only open so wide, but I felt the muscles in my mouth relax. His come was warm, tasting of the root we had earlier. I took him deeper into my mouth, relishing the way his hips involuntarily bucked slightly into my mouth.

Simon's groan came from the back of his throat as I continued to pleasure him, and I couldn't help but feel a sense of power knowing I was the one bringing him this much pleasure, even while his paralysis held him.

I hummed as more come leaked from the head. I dipped my hand into his pouch and held onto the large sack. It was drawn up against his body as he tensed, and I felt his come explode into my mouth.

I slurped around his cock, cleaning him up. I didn't know come could taste this good, but I was here for it. "Mmm, Simon." I wiped the come away from my mouth and noticed dick didn't rise immediately afterward like it had been doing.

Perhaps the poison will keep him limp for a while.

I nestled myself in the softness of the bed next to him, drawing the warm covers snugly around our bodies. As I exhaled deeply, the sound of my contentment mingled with the rhythmic beat of his heart, resonating against my cheek.

"Good night, Simon. Sleep well."

Chapter Twenty-Eight

Simon

I HAD LOST ALL concept of time.

I did not know when it was day or night or how long I had slept. My body was heavy, and not just my limbs but my heart, too.

I was in a vulnerable state where I could not protect my mate. The ogre still lived, and I had been incapacitated by a human female! I promised myself I would never harm a female, and I wouldn't. I would, however, harm the orc since he didn't seem to have a handle on her.

How dare she!

I would head butt him right in his large sack so he could no longer procreate.

It would be a gift to the Monktona Wood if no more of those green orclings inhabited it.

As soon as I felt tension in my body, I tried to lift my arm, but it still did not move. It was frustrating, to say the least. I let out a grunt of annoyance, and instantly, my mate was by my side, her arm over my chest.

"You okay, sleeping beauty?"

Excuse me?

At some point, she relieved my shaft. I wasn't able to take care of her, and I knew I would need to repay her for such a deed. Laying here, not giving her pleasure, hurt me more than feeling this undeniable need to rut her.

I felt it in my blood. It was a flood, raging behind my ears. I've tried my best to be calm, but I had no ability to make my shaft... still.

I had no control even before the poisoning incident.

"Simon, you're, uh, having a problem again?"

I felt the heat rise to my cheeks. I could not hide from her.

"Goddess, I'm so sorry, Simon. Going through a rut, and you can't do anything about it. Your extra fur is all damp. Are you suffering?"

A rut? Was that what this was? I thought it was my need to bond with her, not a rut. Then again, wouldn't it be the same? My soul wanted her, and my body. Wasn't it all relativity the same at this point?

I felt her warm grasp around my shaft, and I involuntarily groaned. When she tried to suck my cock inside her mouth last time, I could not hold back my release. It was downright embarrassing how quickly I expelled my seed.

"Simon, are you in pain?" Her lips brushed my ear.

I thought I was getting some of my movement back, but not enough to tell her I wanted. She could do whatever she wanted.

Suck my cock again, my sweet mate.

Her thumb twirled around my cockhead and my hips bucked.

"Ellie was right, the poison didn't hit you as hard as I thought it would."

Ellie? Curse her. I would have my shaft buried deeper into my mate right now if it wasn't for her.

Lucy giggled. "I wonder if orgasms heal you faster?"

Orgasms? Does she mean my release?

"I really want to do something else, something we haven't tried, on land anyway."

My heart stopped when I felt her straddle my thighs. Her hands held my cock firmly.

I was going to break her if she took me like this.

"I talked to Ellie over dinner; she said that orcs have magic come."

If I could snarl, I would. I did not need my female hearing about magic orc seed. The only *seed* she would get would be mine.

"She said it had properties that can soften the muscles and change the inside of a woman so they can take their partner. I'm thinking that yours might do that, too." Her thumb went over my cock head, and I heard her pop it into her mouth.

Sweet Moon Goddess.

"I think the reason I couldn't accept you in the beginning was because of my self-doubt, lack of belief. I think if we do it this time... it will work." Her voice had gone raspy. I could smell her arousal heavy within the tent.

She rose on her knees and rubbed her clit along my veiny shaft.

"I don't know why, but I've never been this turned on before. Staying in this tent with you just makes it worse. It's like your... smell has changed. I want to rub myself all over you."

I smiled inwardly. My scent was calling to her. She wanted me, my cock.

"So, hoe Lucy is here, and why the hell not? I'm sure you'd like it too. And we are mates, so it's fine," she told herself, I think more than me.

Yes, yes, female.

Lucy grabbed my shaft. It was wet, and I felt the distinctive tug as she positioned the head at her entrance. I felt the heat of her gaze on me. My cock slipped inside, and by the gods, it was tight.

With a deep breath, Lucy sank down onto me, inch by inch, her walls gripping me tightly, causing my heart to pound in response. A soft moan escaped her lips as she fully impaled herself on my throbbing shaft.

She was wet, hot, slick. With the combination of her pussy strangling, I think I might die.

"Oh, god," she whispered. "You feel so good inside me."

Her words fueled me, my body strained, and finally I could feel my fingers wiggling.

Lucy's hips moved wildly, each thrust taking us both closer to the edge. The air was filled with our gasps and moans, punctuated by her frantic movements. It was as if she was in her own heat, taking what she wanted.

I tried as much as I could, but I couldn't get my body to move. All I could do was endure her assault on my body, letting her use me without helping her.

I felt my shaft thicken each time I pressed inside her. I wanted to caress her stomach and feel the seed filing her womb.

My body tensed, waiting for when we would both reach our release.

She leaned forward, her hands gripping my shoulders as she rode me harder and faster. Her breath came in short gasps, each one driving her closer to her pleasure. "I'm going to come," she panted. "I can feel it building-"

And then, with a shout of pure ecstasy, she released. Her body convulsed, and I dug my claws into the blankets.

As Lucy cried out and shivered in the aftermath of her orgasm, I felt my seed unload into her. With a deep growl, I jerked my hips upward into her one last time, releasing my seed deep within her core. The sensation was overwhelming; it was as if my very soul had been consumed by the heat of her pussy.

I was utterly tired and spent. I don't remember being this tired except for when I turned into what I was now.

Lucy let me stay inside her and leaned against my chest. She was completely naked, and I enjoyed feeling the warmth and the softness of her skin. Her breath tickled the hair on my chest, and instead of fighting to wrap my arms around her, she wrapped hers around mine.

"I'm sorry if that crossed a line, but that was—wow."

I couldn't agree more. If she wanted to use my body without me doing anything, I would let her. I would even tie myself to the roots of the forest floor so she could experience this again.

Because I didn't mind it one bit.

Lucy

It'd been three days. I'd taken care of Simon more times than I could count. It would just get hard, the head of it would turn red, and I couldn't leave him in pain.

Blue balls *was* totally a thing.

He should be on the mend, but he still snored at times. I had planned on giving him a sponge bath later this afternoon if he hadn't woken up by then.

Yeah, we both liked those sponge baths.

As I stepped outside, a gentle breeze brushed against my face, carrying with it the scent of pine trees and wildflowers. The air felt crisp and invigorating, a vast contrast to the stifling, polluted air of Earth.

Here, in this vast expanse of untouched nature, the sweet chorus of birds and animals filled the air, harmonizing with the rustling leaves. The absence of buzzing insects was a relief, a welcome change from the constant annoyance of their relentless itchy bites on Earth. In this serene wilderness, they seemed to respect the balance of nature, knowing that humans were mere visitors and not a food source.

I stretched, raising my arms up high. I was wearing the clothing Simon made me. Thorn had retrieved it from the spring when he went to get rid of the ogre.

I felt it was my duty to wear them and not what Ellie had presented to me later. I felt like I was going against a faun code.

Unfortunately, when Thorn went to check on the ogre, he was no longer there and Thorn said he was not about to chase it through the Wood because he had his family to take care of. Not that I would argue with that. I didn't want his family to come into danger because of me.

It was our own fault that the ogre appeared at the spring; our scent had brought the ogre. It was far too close to Thorn and Ellie's cabin.

Thorn had spread an extra dosing of the yellow cress around his territory and more around Simon's and my tent. Thorn grunted as he did so, holding his nose until the scent of our prior activities went away.

Talk about me turning six different shades of red. He knew I was doing something because, obviously, Simon was passed out. Thorn gave no judgment, but Ellie was over there cackling, elbowing me, and asking how it felt to ride a lifeless body beneath me.

I gave her an honest answer: that it was great having power over Simon while he slept. Red flag for me? Sure, but Simon kidnapped me and saw me naked.

Payback!

"Do you think he will wake up today?" I asked, as I helped Ellie clean some dishes from lunch by the fire. Thorn had set up a washing basin outside and put coals underneath so Kiah could take a bath.

He was the happiest baby I had ever seen, screaming and roaring just like any other orc.

Ellie shrugged her shoulders. "Good question, it's almost been a few days. What do you think, Sugar Tits?"

Thorn's head leaned back, and groaned. "Not in front of a guest, Ellie."

Ellie winked at me and threw another toy into the giant tub for Kiah.

"Any time, I'd say. In fact, I bet he is lying there waiting for you to fuck him while he sleeps."

I gasped.

Thorn chuckled and shook his head. "You said he's been moving his arms? Has he spoken at all?" Thorn asked.

"Nope, but he had a hard time speaking when he was first learning, and that was only a week and a half ago. I wouldn't expect him to get his voice back so quickly."

Thorn straightened his posture, the crisp scent of pine filling his nostrils as he inhaled deeply. His forehead creased in concentration as he ventured through the clearing on the other side, the soft crunch of leaves beneath his feet echoing in the stillness.

"What is it?" I asked, standing.

Ellie grabbed a towel and pulled Kiah out of the tub. "Smells like wolves. Shifters. They don't often come this far into the Wood."

I jogged over to Thorn. If they were wolves, they would have to be from my group.

"What do you want?" Thorn roared. His posture was intimidating toward the shifters that stood on the other side as they shivered, which I presumed was from fear. I recognized them instantly and jumped in front of the massive orc.

"Hey, guys!"

Dutton looked away from Thorn's imposing stance and let out a sigh of relief. "Oh, thank the goddess you are here." He ran his hand through his hair. "We have been looking everywhere for you."

I blinked several times and looked up at Thorn. "What do you mean? Sugha was supposed to tell you I was okay?"

Dutton shook his head. The other wolf was shaking, looking like he was about to pee himself, staring up at Thorn.

So much for the best warriors of the kingdom.

"No, it's not that." Dutton coughed. "It's your father, he's here, he was waiting to see you, but—"

Dutton and the wolf stared at each other.

"But what?" I stepped into the trees, grabbed his arm, and pulled him toward me.

"Your father fell into a deep sleep, and we can't wake him up." Dutton choked on his words.

I stood frozen, my mouth hanging open. "What do you mean, he fell asleep? I need more information," I demanded.

I could not get upset, not yet. He may have had too much bourbon. He could have just been exhausted. That was a lot of traveling coming here, and now being in the Wood and all, it could have been overwhelming.

"He went to sleep one night and then didn't get up!" Dutton explained. "It's been two days. Humans don't sleep that long, do they?"

I took a deep breath, trying to keep the panic out of my voice. "Is he pale? Hot to the touch? Is he sweating? I need more, Dutton," my voice rose.

Dutton stuttered and stepped back, not from Thorn, but from me. My hand voluntarily moved toward Dutton, and I couldn't stop.

"No fever, no sweating, his skin looks fine, in fact, it is different..." Dutton paused and rubbed his hand up and down his arm. "Texture! Yes, that's it. Texture."

Different texture? What the hell does that mean?

"See for yourself. We don't know what's wrong. Everyone is afraid to touch him because they think—"

"Think what?" I growled. "What are they thinking, just leaving an old man in a tent by himself? Has anyone attended to him, or checked on him? Looked for scrapes from a plant, a bite from an animal, anything?"

Dutton swallowed. "No, they haven't, Miss Lucy. Please don't be angry."

I blew air between my teeth, letting Dutton see my frustration. He gulped and grabbed hold of his companion by the shoulder.

I stomped my foot. "We must leave now. Shift to a wolf, and you take me."

Thorn pulled me back by the shoulder. "You trust these wolves?"

Dutton and his companion looked hopeful, nodding their heads like little puppies.

I gave them a narrow look. "No, I don't. Anyone just leaving an old man alone in a tent for days makes me have trust issues, but what choice do I have?"

Thorn stood up to his full height. "I believe waiting for Simon to wake up is for the best. I will not take my female near a bunch of psychotic dogs."

"Hey!" Dutton defended. "We are trying to make this right, and you weren't easy to find."

Thorn huffed and leaned over, his hot breath fanning Dutton's cheek. "Good. Keep it that way."

I pushed Dutton away from Thorn and snapped my fingers in front of him. "Shift, let's go. Time is a-wasting. Hope your mate doesn't mind me being on your back."

Dutton's lips turned into a smile. "What mate?"

"Fucking shift!"

CHAPTER TWENTY-NINE

Lucy

As Dutton raced through the Wood, the wind flew through my hair and tickled my nose as it whipped back and forth. The air's cool touch brought relief to my warm face, a welcome reprieve from thoughts rolling through my head. Amidst the curious world I should enjoy flying by, heaviness lingered, as if the weight of guilt was suffocating every enjoyment.

I left Simon back in the tent.

I hoped he would understand. The poison was leaving his body. He wasn't under any duress. Just the random twitch, making his claws pierce the sheets. Even his facial expressions had come back.

As I gripped Dutton's fur to keep myself from falling off his muscular back, I told myself he would be fine. I'd fed him through these past days. It was a porridge Ellie showed me how to make, though I was sure Simon hated it from the cough he would often give. He was nourished, safe, and warm back there because of me. He would wake soon. But a whole new world of guilt filled me.

I hadn't thought about my father hardly at all. While I knew Sugha would put him at ease telling my father I was safe, I didn't think about what my father's reaction could be.

Did Sugha tell him I was mated to a faun? Was that why he was sick? Sick of just the thought of me being with someone other than a human when he didn't like human males much, anyway?

Father wanted men to treat me right. He wasn't doing it to be completely overbearing. I didn't have a desire to be with anyone else or even date, so his reasoning, his protection to keep me safe, was his way of showing love.

Was it healthy? Eh, probably not, but it didn't bother me since I didn't have any sexual desires for anyone anyway.

With Simon, though? What was father going to say about that? He kept me away from humans, and now I was going to bring home a faun!

Simon wasn't even a shifter who could shift from human to animal, but a person who was both.

This would have been so much easier to deal with if I had dated before coming here. Ease father into the idea that I could date. I was thirty years old. It was just that the first person I found attractive was a faun, and we hadn't even dated. We just jumped right into... well, being together. Not just physically, but intimately.

All because of a bond that brought us together. A bond that we didn't know how to seal, and it was making me a nervous wreck to be away from Simon. My stomach was full of bricks, and it got heavier the further away I went from him.

Gods, I hope he didn't wake up while I was gone.

Then again, I'd never been one for much luck.

I pushed the thought away and tried to concentrate on Dutton's movements. One warrior was tailing us, making sure there weren't any signs of the ogre lurking in the trees.

We were going so fast, I didn't think the ogre could catch us, but one stepping out in front of us could.

As we ran, for what felt like hours, we came to the clearing at the front of the Wood.

Towering trees and the crumbling of the wall surrounded the clearing on the other side.

The light sources filtered through the leaves, casting dappled shadows on the ground. Someone had neatly arranged carts filled with supplies and flanked by tents, tables, and chairs in the middle of the clearing, with a large, crackling bonfire at its center. The crew, who had accompanied me on my journey before Simon took me, were all gathered here, and their faces lit up with bright smiles as they lifted their heads to greet me.

"Lucy, you're back!" Elmira ran toward me when I dismounted Dutton.

I dusted off my hands and braced myself for the big hug. "Sorry about riding Dutton on the way here, I know that is usually a no-no."

Elmira waved her hand in dismissal. "Who cares, he isn't my mate."

The shifter beside us, who had shifted in the forest just a minute ago, chuckled. "Yeah, you rode him. Long and hard and—"

Elmira punched the naked shifter in the shoulder, and he hobbled off laughing.

Dutton's shifting caused his bones to crack, the sound echoing through the clearing, while a faint rustling accompanied his fur being pulled back into his body. The sight of his transformation made me gag. I would never get used to that.

I am glad I did not get mated to a shifter.

Dutton gave a dashing smile toward Elmira. "Sure about me not being your mate, sweetheart? I'm tired of your games." He cupped his groin and gave it a shake. "My teeth are aching to take a bite of that subtle ass."

Elmira snorted and threw her head back. "After the expedition is over, I told you. Then, maybe I'll bite you."

Dutton held his hand up to his chest, puppy dog eyes at play and all. "You wound me. It is I who should claim you first."

I groaned and stepped away from the conversation. Now wasn't the time to figure out their weird relationship. It was for me to check on my father.

I rubbed my forehead and headed for the biggest tent. Since it lacked royal decorations, I knew it wasn't Kane and Clara's tent. I hadn't even seen them in the area. If I was under no duress, they may have returned to the castle because their presence wasn't needed.

As I approached the tent, I could feel the curious eyes of the others watching me in curiosity before pushing open the flap. Inside, I saw a double bed cot, neatly made, resting on the dirt floor of the tent. A desk stood on one side, cluttered with papers and writing tools. On the other side, my father's suitcase sat open, his belongings neatly arranged as if he were planning to stay here for a long time.

I kneeled down and picked up the blanket that was covering his head. From the outline of the blanket, he was curled up on his side and a loud snore broke the silence.

"Father?" I leaned over and pulled the blanket away from his face. I was not expecting to see what I did.

It didn't look like my father at all. It was a younger man, head full of chestnut brown hair with a lush goatee on his face. When I pulled the blanket down further, I found he was naked from the waist up. A tattoo of a hand covered his heart. I covered him back up quickly, and the smell of bourbon and cigars hit me. The wave of nostalgia fluttered around me at the familiar scent, and I was left speechless.

He smelled like Father.

But what was on his chest?

"Father?" I touched his shoulder and shook him. I wasn't about to leave until I had answers, and if he hadn't woken up for anyone else, surely he would do it for me.

Because I was his daughter, and I demanded it.

"Father!" I shouted and shook him again. He snorted, grunted, and laid on his back. His eyes flew open, and he sat up straight.

He blinked a few times, his bleary eyes trying to focus on my face. When recognition finally dawned upon him, his eyes widened in surprise, and he scrambled to sit up properly, pulling the blanket around him self-consciously.

"Lucy!" he mumbled, his voice rough from sleep. "What are you doing here?"

I crossed my arms over my chest, trying to maintain an air of authority despite the shock and confusion swirling inside of me. "I could ask you the same question, Father," I said coolly. "What is going on? And what is with this?" I twirled my finger around his face. "You look so young." I breathed. "Did you drink a potion, get some magic face cream?"

Father chuckled and rubbed his hands up and down his face. "It was a special cream, alright." His chuckle turned into a full-blown laugh, and I stepped back from him.

Goddess, had he succumbed to some sort of Wood fever?

"I think you might be sick." I patted his shoulder. "Let me get some tea for you or something."

I turned my back and walked toward the entrance of the tent as Father stopped laughing. "Wait, wait, come back." He waved his hand over. "I know my skin is different. Everything is different, but for good reason."

I eyed him warily and came closer to him. He waved me closer, and I sat on my knees next to him. "You were out for days. Everyone was so worried. They came and found me and—"

Father huffed and grabbed both of my hands in his. "Lucy, everything is fine." He patted my hand. "Everything is more than fine."

That's what people say when they become sick with a disease, then the next day they are dead or dying. I'd witnessed it myself, and so had Father.

I opened my mouth to argue, and he cut me off again. "I have a mate, Lucy!"

My jaw dropped, leaving me speechless.

He got a mate... at his age? Well, he didn't look his age anymore. He looked as young as me.

"I... I... what?" I asked breathlessly. "You have a mate? Where is she?"

Father chuckled and let go of my hands. He stood up, showing off his old man pants of tan and yellow plaid that he always loved.

When I saw his back, beautiful designs completely covered it.

"Are you sick? Did you sell your soul to Hades?!" My mind was reeling with a different hypothesis of what could make his body look like that.

Father laughed again, a full belly laugh I hadn't heard since I was a child. He kneeled next to me and brushed his thumb over my cheek.

"This is how my mate marked me. This is his signature, his hand over my heart, and the brand of his coven on my back."

My brain shut off. Not because he was mated to a guy, but because a coven could mean two things.

Vampire or warlock. Vampires bit and drank their mate's blood to complete the mate bond, so that only left the former.

I think I was more surprised with this than I was with Simon being my mate. My dad was mated!

"Well, where is he?" I demanded. "He left you alone, asleep for days!"

Father shook his head and stood up. "He visits me in the night. There is still hatred for their kind. My mate is very private. We have been seeing each other since I began my travels here."

That wasn't very long ago, a little over a week.

"You guys sealed the deal after only a week and a half?" I blurted. "You didn't calculate anything, just went in blind and mated with him? He could be evil!"

Father's brows narrowed. "And that is why he is private. A lot of warlocks have had poor reputations here since the war. Witches seem to get leniency. Rune visited me in the evenings, every single one. We stayed up all night, and I would work little during the day. When Sugha sent a message that you had found your mate, I knew you would be in excellent hands after experiencing this bond everyone raves about."

My shoulders slumped. What the hell just happened?

"And you are official now?" I waved my hand up and down his torso. It wasn't flabby, overweight, or even old and wrinkly. He was a lean, buff guy now. "The bonding made you into this?"

Father nodded. "Yes, it appears so. I used to look like this before you, you know." He winked. "I woke up a few hours ago and wrote down my findings for future reference. It's normal here to change, to become younger and healthier. I checked through the text just to be sure, but what I went through is completely normal. Rune even said I would change, though I hardly believed it." Father sighed dreamily.

"I will live like an immortal. Until fatally wounded or poisoned. You die when your mate dies because a soul cannot live without the other." Father picked up his notebook and began to write.

"They said you slept for days."

Father picked up his pencil in thought. "Yes, I was out for a few days after I was bonded. Again, completely normal. It takes time for his supernatural genetics to latch onto my DNA. It is to make me more like him, so our bodies are more compatible. Humans are the perfect specimens; we are a blank canvas. I will soon gain his power as well. Learn to wield it, use it just like him."

Mind. Blown.

"It's absolutely fascinating," Father continued. "I cannot wait to explore it further."

I cleared my throat and tucked a strand of hair behind my ear. "It was the same with the human females who had bonded with their mates. They became stronger and could hear and smell better. They don't turn green though, they don't turn into orc females."

"Interesting," he said and wrote it down. "They are not green in the slightest?"

I shook my head. "No, but they give birth to full-blooded orclings. They don't look human at all."

Father tapped his pencil to his lips. "I would, very much, like to know how they procreate because of the size difference."

"Magic come," I muttered.

Father raised his head from the book and hummed. "What was that?"

I shook my head. I was not going to talk about magic come with my father. That was my hard limit.

Yet, riding your sleeping mate was not a limit.

I groaned and put my head between my knees. I was going to be sick. What had this world done to me?

Father stepped over to me and kneeled. His hand rubbed over my back until he felt the soft leather of the outfit I wore. "This is wonderful. Did your mate make you this? Does he feel you should wear what he offers you?"

"Father, I—"

Father cleared his throat and sat beside me. He closed the book with a loud thump and played with his beard. "I'm sorry, that was out of line. I will not make my daughter into a study. I want you to be happy, Lucy. That was my one wish when we came here, that you would find someone worthy of you. I was hoping for a prince or a warrior of some kind. Living in these woods, with so many dangerous creatures, was not ideal."

I raised an eyebrow at him.

"For safety purposes," he corrected. "But I believe the goddess knows what she is doing."

My eyes widened. A man who craved nothing but scientific proof for everything, never believed in any religion, a higher power or life after death, is now contemplating that the gods were real. No, correction! He believes they *are* real.

Father hung his head. "I have done you a disservice, Lucy. For that, I am sorry. This place, the bond I have found, are all unexplainable, but I know it to be true."

Chapter Thirty

Simon

I STRAIGHTENED MY POSTURE, feeling a surge of newfound determination coursing through me. I had finally regained full control over my body since the moment of poisoning. Inhaling deeply, I tried to sniff out my mate's scent lingering in the air. My nose twitched and flared.

My mate wasn't here. She hadn't been here in some time, either. The air was absent of her scent, and I hadn't heard from her in some time.

I moved my legs, kicking the stiffness away until I stood on both hooves.

"She was foolish. She should have waited," Thorn said from outside. He stomped closer toward the tent. "He's still out. What kind of male is he if he's been out for three days?"

My ears perked up, and I narrowed my eyes.

I was a half of his size. How dare he? And what does he mean by she should have waited?

I burst out of the shelter, my hooves skidding on the damp moss, threatening to send me tumbling. The sound of Thorn's knife scraping against the wooden brick filled the silence as I locked eyes with him. Ellie stood by his side, her hand resting on his shoulder, a concerned expression etched on her face.

"Simon, you're up," Ellie said and stepped around Thorn. "Lucy will be so happy to see you—"

"Where is she?" I snapped.

Ellie's gaze lowered to my pouch, and Thorn stood up to hide his mate. "Can you put that fucking thing away? I don't need my female seeing your tiny shaft."

I growled. "If it is so tiny, then why do you care if she sees it? I bet it is larger than yours!"

Thorn's growl reverberated in the air. The ground trembled under his heavy footsteps as he stomped towards me. With a forceful toss, he hurled the block of wood away, and it landed in the fire. The glint of the knife reflected from the light source and its sharpness threateningly pointed in my direction.

"Faun, you dare to challenge me," he seethed, the intensity of his voice sending chills down my spine. "It is best that your female left. You don't know how to hold your tongue."

The extra fur on my back stood up. I bent my knees and lowered my head, my horns tingling, ready to run and plow into his assets.

"That's enough!" Ellie shouted. "This is ridiculous! Simon, Lucy left!"

I straightened up and rounded Thorn. His body followed me as I got closer to his female. Out of respect for his mate, I tucked my shaft back into my pouch as best as I could without damaging it. I still felt an undeniable need to *rut* my mate, a sensation that had not left me even while I slept.

I was grateful Lucy understood my pain. If not, I feared my shaft would have fallen off in the days I slept.

I stood in front of Ellie with my claws buried in the fur at my sides.

"Wolf shifters took her. She rode on the back of one. They said her father was sick, and she went with them." Ellie tilted her head to where Lucy was last seen.

Thorn scoffed and growled toward his mate. He was saying things I couldn't make out because I was too busy forming a plan.

To find what was mine.

"You shouldn't have told him. Make him figure it out on his own. He led an ogre near our home, his body is weak, he couldn't even—"

I pulled out my shaft while Thorn was scolding his mate, who merely rolled her eyes without care. I aimed it right toward his enormous foot and released a long stream of piss.

Thorn lifted his foot, his face full of shock, and when he was about to speak, I lowered my head and head-butted him in the gut. He roared as he fell on his backside, and I darted away, running straight toward where Lucy had gone.

Ellie's laughter was loud enough to be heard through the Wood as I charged through the brush of the branches.

Thorn roared in frustration, screaming for me never to return and that I was never welcome back.

I had no reason to come back. His mate had poisoned me. He called me small and said I was not worthy of my mate. They were both more trouble than they were worth.

It was difficult to find Lucy's scent. It had dwindled within the Wood. But then, I felt the Wood surround me once again, guiding me to where I must go. The trees bent, and the leaves fluttered, pointing to where I must follow.

It didn't take me long to find her, with the brush of a branch pushing me in one direction, I darted down a path less taken and found her scent once again.

I was not angry that she left me. I understood it was important to take care of family. Calliope taught me how important it was. She took care of me like one of her own; rescued me when I needed it.

My mate was smart and knew I would wake, and that I would come to find her.

And I would find her.

It is, though, unwise to travel with wolves. The ogre was still afoot, and a few wolves would not have been enough to save her. They couldn't even beat an orc two at a time. What made her believe they would save her from an ogre?

My hooves flew across the soil, and birds flew from the branches. I nearly hit them with my horns since they were not paying attention to their surroundings. They barely heard me before I made my presence known.

The fur that had sprouted on my back days ago was still present, from the rut, as Lucy called it, which fueled me further. I'd slept for days. My body was well rested. I hoped Lucy had taken care of her father enough so he could get better on his own, because it was my turn.

I needed her *now!*

The forest thinned out as I ran, with the trees giving way to a small clearing. In the center, I saw her—Lucy—standing with the wolf shifters. They all had her surrounded, along with a tall figure in the middle. Long green hair and tan clothing hovering right above my mate. The dappled light sources' filtering through the leaves above created a magical look to the area.

One wolf in particular was standing close to my female. Too close for my liking.

With my stealth and speed, no one saw me barrel out of the woods because they were all foolish. They were not waiting for an ogre to strike.

Without hesitation, I charged forward with my horns lowered as I barreled into the wolf nearest to my mate. He flew through the air and landed with a thud, momentarily stunned.

"What the fuck!" The shifter clutched his stomach.

The other wolves backed away, leaving my mate and two males standing next to her.

I huffed, my chest heaving, and shoved my horns toward them to back away.

Lucy's eyes widened in surprise as she saw me coming to her rescue. "Simon! Stop!"

But I didn't stop. I turned and picked her up, feeling the weight of her body against my chest, and the warmth of her presence seeping into my skin. As I lifted her, her scent filled my lungs. With a swift motion, I threw her over my shoulder, hearing her gasp.

The male with vibrant green hair, his robes adorned with intricate black swirls, held a pulsating green ball of light in his hand. As he stood there, a faint hum emanated from the ball, creating a mesmerizing glow. Beside him, another man with a stubbled face reached out and firmly grasped his wrist. "It's alright," he reassured him, his voice carrying a gentle tone amidst the yelling of the wolves in the background.

I bared my teeth, feeling my adrenaline surge as I locked eyes with them both. The sharp scent of anger filled the air as I slowly backed away, but the piercing sound of crackling from the ball of light echoed from the warlock's hand. Despite my retreat, the vibrant green-haired male stood firm, and his unwavering gaze increased the tension in the air.

Suddenly, a soil-shattering explosion rocked the ground next to me, causing a cloud of dirt to billow into the air, stinging my eyes and filling my nostrils with the heavy smell of burned dirt. The deafening sound of the blast echoed through my ears, leaving them ringing in its aftermath. The sheer terror of the moment made my cursed body tense up, my muscles freezing. In the chaos, I fell, my body crashing onto the ground. As I fell, I twisted my body to shield my mate from bearing the full impact of the fall.

Lucy screamed, but she was protected.

"Rune, stop! It's alright!" Lucy stood in front of me, putting out her hands.

I could soon stand, and I quickly jumped in front of Lucy to protect her.

This Rune rolled his hands, and another ball of light appeared. He pulled it back, ready to wield it at me again, and Lucy scrambled passed and stood in front of me.

The warlock hesitated, his glowing ball of light wavering as Lucy bravely stood between us.

"Please, don't hurt him. He was just trying to protect me. He's my mate!" Lucy pleaded, her voice filled with desperation.

I growled as I bent my knees and lowered my head, ready to charge.

Rune's gaze softened as he looked at Lucy, then at me. He slowly lowered his hand, the ball of light dissipating into thin air. The tension in the clearing eased as the other wolf shifters backed away cautiously.

"I apologize for the misunderstanding," Rune spoke, his voice calm yet authoritative.

Lucy turned back to me, concern etched on her face. I shook off the dirt and leaves that clung to my fur, eyeing Rune warily as he approached us.

"On behalf of Lucy's father, please let me thank you for protecting her," Rune said, his green eyes meeting mine. "You are a formidable guardian, and I can see the bond between you and Lucy is strong. He has spoken highly of her and hoped of her safety."

A male stood next to Rune with his arm now gripped tight around his arm. He nodded quickly and swallowed. "Yes, yes. Thank you. What he said, certainly."

I grunted in acknowledgment, but still on edge but willing to listen.

"Simon," Lucy tugged on my arm. "This is my father, James Watts." She nodded to the male with the beard on his face. "And this warlock is... well, his mate, Rune." Lucy let out a huff of unbelievable laughter.

My eyebrows rose, and my eyes bounced from both of them. When they approached, my arms wrapped around Lucy as I pulled her back.

While they perhaps were her fathers now... I wasn't about to let them get close again. They had taken her away from me once, and I wasn't about to have them do it again. She was unclaimed, and I have not had my time with her. It wasn't enough.

Lucy went to her father so willingly, and he wasn't even sick. Did she not want me anymore? Was her father being sick a lie? Would she rather go to her father than me?

My anger rose, and I huffed warm air through my nostrils as I picked her up and threw her over my shoulder again.

"Simon!" Lucy squealed and banged her fists against my back. "What in the gods' names are you doing!?"

Lucy's father barked out in laughter. "I see ruts are the same in all animalistic species."

Rune smirked and agreed with a knowing nod. "Agreed. Even with these new species that grace the realm, it appears no matter the origin of animal they will all present a rutting instinct. I suggest you assure your daughter of our blessing so she doesn't worry about you or herself."

Blessing? My mate did not need her father's blessing. I would take her anyhow.

I turned and saw the wolf shifters all staring back at me. Most of them were wide-eyed, staring at me with wonder, but they were the least of my worries. I could outrun them on my two legs easily, even when they were on four. I knew these woods better than any of them.

"Have fun, Lucy. Let the bond take over!" James said as the Wood parted for us.

Lucy huffed in annoyance and crossed her arms. "This is the most embarrassing thing I have ever been through!" she shouted.

The wolves snickered behind us, and I jogged faster away from the group.

CHAPTER THIRTY-ONE

Lucy

A FEW MOMENTS EARLIER...

My father squeezed both my hands in his. We were sitting on the soft bedding. That I now realized that he and his mate had most likely tossed around on.

I held back the bile in my throat.

"Will you ever forgive me?" My father pleaded. He looked up at me with those sparkling eyes. How could I ever say no to him? The man who rescued me from the foster care system. Saved me from growing up alone and, instead, opened my eyes to worlds of adventure and a hunger for learning.

"Father, of course." I wrapped my arms around him, and he squeezed me tight. "I just can't believe you fell for someone so quickly, but I'm so happy for you—so happy."

He chuckled and released me. "Like I said, when you know, you know. I guess I've been searching in the wrong places all my life. I never ventured into the opposite sex. Because that was frowned upon during my upbringing, I never explored it. Once Rune spotted me and revealed himself, my body and my heart hadn't felt that alive—well, ever."

I held back the grimace about his body coming alive, but his heart? It was sweet, to say the least. "I can't wait to meet him. Does he only meet you at night?"

Rune should overcome his shyness and fear now that they've mated. The shifters shouldn't hold hostility against the warlocks, anyway.

As if he read my mind, a voice spoke in the corner. "No longer," a velvety, quiet voice said. A man emerged from the darker corner of the tent, and his green shoulder-length hair swayed with each step. As he drew nearer, his darker skin complexion shimmered under the candlelight, adding depth to his presence.

The tanned robes he wore were adorned with intricate, dark-colored runes that danced along the edges as they moved closer. He smelled of mint and a spark of ozone, like lightning ready to strike. With a gentle sway, the robes gracefully followed his every movement. Finally, he reached us, his warm smile casting a comforting glow that embraced us in its radiance.

Father stood up and, like an excited teenager, jumped in his arms and wrapped his arms and legs around the tall warlock.

I covered my mouth to hold in the laugh, but Rune's smile spread further, and he cupped the back of my father's head. "I've missed you, James. I'm sorry I was away. I was here every night while you slept."

My father nuzzled into his neck, mumbling comforting words I couldn't hear, while I sat awkwardly waiting. But I could see they were sharing a moment, a bond that Simon and I shared.

Rune put my father down and cleared his throat. "Proper introductions should be in order," my father said. Rune straightened his back and rolled his shoulders. He appeared more proper now, so I stood and held out my hand to shake, but he pulled me into a bone-crushing hug.

"Thank you for filling James' life with joy, Lucy. I hope you can accept me into your family as well now."

Well, just make my heart melt like chocolate.

I sniffled and nodded with no words able to leave my mouth. I patted his back awkwardly and pulled away. "I'm glad to see my father happy. I'm happy when he is. I hope we can spend more time together, but I'm sure, as with most bonded couples I have seen, you'll like to have time together in the early days."

"Yes, most bonded couples usually disappear for the first couple of years," Rune said and grabbed my father's hand. My eyes widened, but I knew this to be true. Years are just specks of time to the Bergarians.

"I see your mate has not yet marked you." Rune nodded to my body, nowhere in particular.

I cleared my throat. "Well, once I accepted that this magic was real, that a bond was real for me—" my voice trailed off. "We needed a witch, the one they called Starla. She has helped the orcs deal with their bonding, and I had hoped she could help Simon and I."

Rune tapped his thumb on his thigh in thought. "With your and your father's intelligence, I'm sure you could figure that out on your own."

I scoffed. "Simon said he would just keep biting me until he figured it out."

Rune and Father made a face.

"I guess if you are into that sort of thing," Rune said, waving his hand dismissively.

"I'm not sure if she is. I kept her away from boys most of her life; my fault again, but I didn't find anyone worthy of her. I was overprotective."

Rune put his hand on Father's shoulder. "As you should have been. I would have thrown a bolt of electricity up anyone's arse, who dared to touch her."

I smirked while they talked about me. I liked Rune more and more, and eventually, I wouldn't mind calling him Dad or some sort of parental name in the future. I mean, we were all going to be living for quite some time.

Which brought a new question: how old was Rune?

"Old," Rune said without missing a beat.

Did he just...?

"Read your mind? Yes. And James will, too, once he gets a handle on his powers, in twenty years or so. I didn't do it on purpose. You are just very loud." Rune tugged on his earlobe. "Which is understandable. You have a lot of feelings you have never felt before. Once you are bonded, no longer fully human, you will keep me out better."

I pursed my lips and looked away, embarrassed. It was true, but it wasn't my father's fault I had all these mixed feelings. I'd never connected with another male emotionally or physically.

Father stepped from side to side, squeezing Rune's hand.

"It wasn't completely your fault, Father. I didn't have those desires to be with someone until Simon. I wanted a special connection, one with electricity, desire, curiosity. A normal human man wouldn't entice me, I don't think. Then again, you never know if you had allowed me to date. Would I have taken the chance? I can't say that for sure. Am I happy with how the things turned out? Absolutely. I feel like I saved myself for the right male, my heart feels full. I feel this is where I am supposed to be. In a place where I can explore, understand a male that invites curiosity, understands my quirks and gives me an opportunity to explore.

I think I have been more afraid and, dare I say, ashamed because Simon is just well—"

"Very different and not human." My father said, grabbing my hand. He stroked the top of it lovingly, like he did when I was a child before he would put me to sleep by reading those horrible research journals. "My sweet Lucy, how is he any different from the shifters? Take the king of the Cerulean Moon Kingdom. He turns into a beast and even speaks in his animalistic form!" My father threw his hand in the air. "He gives consent, has complicated thoughts, and is able to speak for himself."

I let out a breath and stepped away. "Yes, I know this. I have thought of this before."

"You have chosen him already then," Rune said. "His scent on you confirms it."

I groaned. "But of course." I turned back to both of them. "Seeing both of you has made it the last piece I needed. Both of you are happy. I can be happy now. I just don't know how to solidify it. Shifters have intercourse and bite into the shoulders, warlocks with magic, orcs with their uh." I swallowed. "Brands. What of Simon and I?"

Rune turned and sat on the chair by Father's desk. He leaned on it with his elbow and rested his cheek against his fist. "Fauns are close to human and animal. I'd say they are the closest to shifters you could get. I think it would be logical to try the shoulder first. What do you feel when you are intimate with him?"

Father's face paled, and turned away.

I felt sick, too. This wasn't something I was willing to talk about in front of both men.

"Come now, James. This is our daughter. We must figure out how to help her claim her happiness as well."

James shook his head. "You're right. It's just hard when you have raised her from a newborn. I don't want to think of my daughter being—deflowered."

"Too late," I whispered, but unfortunately, my father heard.

He hissed through his teeth. "Is that what that smell is? The fresh grass and flowers?" Father sat on Rune's lap, with his head leaning on Rune's chest. Rune laughed and wrapped his arms around him.

They were going to be perfect together, and I was glad to see Father with so much more animation than I had ever seen him have before.

"We will figure it out on our own," I said. "I guess if the gods haven't willed us to know yet, we are to figure it out." I shrugged my shoulders. "I am still a little miffed. We don't know Simon's origins. I mean, no one in Bergarian has heard of Simon's species, while on Earth, we have heard tales of fauns from Greek Myths."

Rune nodded as he listened. "I have spent time on Earth as well. I have heard of the tales. There are many mythical creatures that I have not heard of in this realm such as minotaurs, krakens, and a tale of Medusa. Now that we've found Simon here, I wonder if more unknown people are among us."

I put my thumb into my mouth and began biting the nail. This is what I was afraid of all along. "You don't think the Bergarian people have accidentally killed creatures under a spell and didn't know, do you?" My hand went over my chest. Simon didn't think it to be true, he was just a goat then.

Rune rubbed his chin thoughtfully. "I don't know. It breaks my heart to think that was the case. Surely, the gods wouldn't allow this to happen."

"In Greek mythology, though told by humans, they could be vengeful, even hurtful."

Father nodded in agreement.

Rune pursed his lips and let out a breath. "It is true, and that statement I cannot contest with. However, it is best you keep your voice down, you do not know who may be listening. Many gods are on the humans' side. They even come down from their Celestial Heavens to give advice to unsuspecting, unbelieving humans who need a good dose of clarity."

My mouth dropped, and my face heated.

How the heck did he know? Was he?

Rune winked at me.

"Old warlocks know a thing or two."

Father sighed. "I didn't know I had such a thing for older men."

I guess I had a thing for older fauns too.

Rune slapped his hand on his thigh. "Where is the faun, anyway? Two unbonded creatures being away from each other this long, especially an animalistic one, would drive them crazy."

I rolled my eyes and rubbed my hands down my face. "Yes, there is a story to that. I best tell you, it's quite a long one. Father, you might want to cover your ears for part of it."

Rune chuckled and played with my father's hair. "Yes, then afterward, I suppose I must meet the rest of the shifters outside. They know of my presence, and they have surrounded the tent but haven't entered. I'm glad to see they have some common sense."

Chapter Thirty-Two

Simon

THE TREES FOLDED AWAY from me, enabling me more speed. I reached our tree, where I'd first tended her before, much quicker than the half day it should have.

Lucy had wrapped her arms around my neck. She no longer struggled. Instead, her slick coated my arm and it took every ounce of restraint to keep running and not stop to lick between her legs for a snack.

"How did we get to this part of the forest so fast? Lucy asked as her head swung around trying to gather her surroundings. The trees moved in such a way that they didn't bump into her head. I was grateful because she was not being graceful in the slightest. I had tripped several times myself in the excitement, and after the second time of almost falling, the roots had moved on their own for me.

I would not stop to find out why we appeared here so quickly. My cock was throbbing, and my seed was leaking all over the wood. I was no better than an orc.

Those green, misshapen monsters.

"Simon, slow down, or you will be tired before we get there."

I huffed and let out a bleat. My face heated, and I grunted to sound more male.

"Don't be shy," she said and caressed my face as I slowed down. "I like it when you make those animal noises. It gets me turned on."

I swallowed and stopped at the base of our tree. I could see the fluff at the top. I hoped no animal had made rest there, otherwise there would be blood to spill.

Lucy wrapped her arms tightly around me, her fingers digging into my back, as we prepared to leap from branch to branch. The air was filled with the sound of leaves rustling from our movements, blending with the distant chirping of birds. I could feel Lucy's soft skirt brushing against my skin, sending shivers down my spine.

She was warm, so very warm.

I grabbed some of the plumpness of her flesh and held on, using the other hand to balance myself. She hummed, licking the juncture between my shoulder and the column of my neck.

She would be my undoing.

When we reached the top where the bed was made, I saw it was clean and free of any other scents. I dove for the middle, knowing that my skills were good, and we buried ourselves into the clouds that even the gods would be envious of.

Lucy moaned. My hands roamed up her body, feeling the softness of her skin under my touch. Her hands clung to my back, fingers running through the thick fur that had gathered there. She pulled me closer as she arched her body to meet mine. I kissed her passionately, feeling the fire that ignited between us growing stronger with each passing moment.

As I viciously tore at the delicate fabric of the clothes I had crafted for her, the sharp sound of my claws shredding against the material filled the air. The sight of the torn pieces strewn about, like petals from a ravaged flower, gave a twisted satisfaction. The scent of the torn fibers mingled with the scent of her slickness, creating a blend that hung heavily around me.

I reveled in the tactile sensation of the fabric yielding to my force, my fingertips tingling with the destruction. With every rip, the anticipation of seeing her exposed flesh consumed me, an intoxicating desire that pulsed through my veins. She was my captive, my mate, bound by the invisible chains of my possession and our bond.

The knowledge that her essence would forever carry my scent and her soul would be eternally entwined with mine fueled my insatiable hunger.

No male would touch her, no male would ever be able to scent her.

Mine.

My hands slid down her sides tracing the curve of her body before reaching her hip. With a swift movement I cut a slit down the side, allowing the garment to fall into the soft bedding unnoticed. Lucy gasped as she felt the cool air on her skin, but I knew it was nothing compared to my lips that trailed down her neck. Her fingers dug into my body when she felt the contact of my skin on hers.

I felt her tremble beneath me when I sucked on her nipples. "Simon, I'm ready. Just hurry and fuck me!"

My cock throbbed as it rubbed up against her leg. My seed trailed up her inner thigh while I hovered over her. She looked like a goddess with her hay-colored hair spread against the pure white.

Her dusky nipples were tight and painted a beautiful contrast. I leaned down and licked them again.

"Simon, stop teasing!"

I let out a huff. "You have had all the fun with me; it's my turn."

I let my hand roam down her stomach and felt the top of her slit. I ran my hand over the small patch of hair. It was damp, smelling sweet, and my cock pressed against it. I leaned my head back and let my cock pulse against her entrance.

I knew she was ready for me. Without hesitation, I let the warmth and wetness engulf the tip. With a deep breath, I pushed inside, feeling her walls clutching at me, eager to accept me fully.

"Oh, Gods," Lucy moaned beneath me, her voice shaking with desire as we moved together in perfect harmony. Her arms locked around my neck once more, pulling me deeper into her embrace.

"How do you accept me so well without the waters?" I went slowly, taking my time so I could feel every part of her.

"Magic come," she breathed, moving her hips along with my shaft.

Magic come? Sounded interesting to talk about—*later.*

I thrust deeper, my eyes locked with hers as we shared this moment of raw passion. She met me gaze for gaze, showing no fear or shame but only desire and love that burned bright like a thousand light sources. It was in that moment that I knew I could never get enough of her, and that I would crave her touch for all eternity.

I could feel my sack inside its pouch swaying. My movements becoming erratic. I pulled out my shaft, and Lucy cried out.

"Shh, I will take care of my mate." I rolled her over and put her on all fours. This seemed right, it felt like the perfect position. I shoved my cock inside her in one swift motion. Her head fell back for me to catch her by the hair.

"My female, my mate!" I snarled and let out a half roar, half bleat.

Lucy pushed back, making her own gasps and moans.

"Does Lucy feel good? Does Lucy want more of her faun?"

Sweat beaded up on her back, pooling down her spine and settling on the two dimples on her lower back. I paused and drew circles between them and brought the liquid to my lips.

"Simon, please. I need to come," she begged and looked back at me. "I thought you wanted to make me feel good."

"I do, but you left me." Lucy raised a tired brow. "Squeeze my cock with your tight cunt. Show me how much you want it."

Lucy's mouth dropped but quickly curved into a smile. "You talk so dirty for a sweet faun."

"This faun isn't sweet. My cock is going to break off holding in this much restraint, now squeeze it!"

Lucy laughed and flexed her pussy around me. I shuddered and thrust my hips into her again. She screamed, and I felt a rush of her slick coating around me.

"Yes," I crooned at her. "Yes, give me more of it."

I laid her on her side so I could see the perfect view of her breasts and grabbed the sensitive meat of her backside. I hit it hard, watching the flesh turn a beautiful pink.

Lucy yelped and turned to me with wild eyes. "Do you like a little pain, along with my shaft inside you?"

She bit her lip. "Are you trying to punish me for having sex with you while you slept?"

I slowed my hips and leaned forward, pushing my cock further into her body. One wrong move, and I would spill my seed, which would not be a bad thing as I had much to give her.

"No, I appreciated your endeavors. This was for running away from me when there was an ogre hungry for you. Those wolves can do nothing for you. Only I can protect you, you know this."

She hummed and bared her neck to me.

My teeth ached to sink into her flesh there. More so than her breast. It called to me.

I leaned closer, my nose grazing her neck, teasing myself and her.

"Simon," she whispered. Each time she breathed, my name was its own song. I didn't think she realized how badly I wanted her to be completely mine. Her lack of connection to me pained my soul.

"Bite me." She nuzzled her cheek against mine, which was buried next to her.

I let out a puff of warm air across her heated skin. "Is that what you want?"

She nodded quickly and shifted her body slightly. Her pussy clamped around me, and my sack tightened, ready to spill.

"Then say it," I whispered. "Say it out loud. Tell me how much you want me. Enough for the forest to hear."

I felt her muscles contract in her neck. My tongue licked down the column, my fangs descended, and I felt them tingle in anticipation to mark her around her shoulder so all would see.

My hips moved slowly, teasing her clit as it split her wide. My finger brushed her swollen clit, one wet swipe and she came undone around me.

"Simon, please."

"You know what to say," I growled.

"I want you to claim me! Please, please claim me, make me yours."

I groaned, and my teeth gently poked her skin. "Louder! Let the Wood hear you."

"Claim me, Simon! I want you to claim me! Shove that big cock into my tight little pussy."

My ears stood straight up.

Okay.

I thrust my throbbing cock inside her. The branches of the tree waved as I continued my assault, twisting around us in my peripheral. My teeth continued to scratch and graze her skin, teasing her.

"I said it. Why aren't you—"

"Patience. I'm waiting for the right moment when we both fall apart. When we both screamed silently into the Wood."

The branches, adorned with vibrant green leaves, gracefully intertwined above our heads, enclosing us in a natural sanctuary. When a gentle breeze swept through the foliage, the leaves rustled and whispered, their delicate sound blending with our hushed voices, as if only the trees themselves were privy to our bonding.

Lucy's breathing became heavier, her heart beating faster against my chest. I could feel it through our entwined bodies. Her eyes were wide and filled with desire, as she realized what we were about to do. Her body stiffened, her breath hitched, and her walls constricted around me. I felt the surge of her release enveloping me, pulling me closer to my own breaking point. My fangs ached, and my hips thrust harder, faster. I wanted to claim her completely, mark her as mine in every sense possible.

"Please," Lucy pleaded, "I can't take much more."

Her words send a jolt of pure desire coursing through me. In that moment, the Wood seemed to hold its breath in anticipation of what was to come. And then it happened, we both reached the point of ecstasy, our screams silenced by the murmurs of the forest around us.

As I thrust deeper and harder into my mate, I finally found the moment I'd been waiting for. With a roar that echoed through the space that now surrounded us, I sank my fangs deep into her shoulder.

"Yes, yes!" she cried out, her voice hoarse from her pleasure. "I'm yours, Simon."

In response, I thrust harder into her, each movement causing another wave of pleasure to wash over us both. My cock twitched and pulsed inside her while ropes of my seed spilled into her. She wrapped her arms around me, pulling me closer as we became one with each other.

I pulled my teeth from her skin, licking the blood away and watched the bleeding stop instantly. "I claimed you," I growled, my voice barely audible over our ragged breaths. "You are mine, Lucy, and only mine."

Lucy moaned, her hands gripped my back as I continued pounding into her body.

"Simon," Lucy whispered, her voice barely audible above the sounds of the surrounding forest. "I feel it coming again…"

With that, I pushed deeper into her, feeling the walls of her pussy tighten around me again. My cock throbbed and pumped out another stream of hot seed deep inside her, filling her completely. Before I could bite her again, she lifted her head up and sank her teeth into my shoulder. My eyes widened. This wasn't expected. The mix of pain and pleasure sent me over the edge again, and I let out a roar that echoed through the trees.

As we collapsed onto the soft, white cloud, entangled in each other's arms and covered in sweat, blood and arousal, I knew that we were both irrevocably changed by this experience. We had claimed each other in ways that could not be undone.

CHAPTER THIRTY-THREE

Simon

THE NEXT FEW DAYS did not involve rutting and fucking, as the orcs would say. My mate described it as lovemaking. We touched each other intimately, savored each other's bodies. I kissed her in any place I wanted as she submitted to me, and I submitted to her, letting her explore me and sate her curiosity, letting her touch places even though I was afraid to explore.

She touched inside my pouch where it was most sensitive. In places, it instantly made me release my seed. Before, I would have felt embarrassed. Instead, I felt pride because my mate would beam with satisfaction, at making me feel good. She would lick up my release and again tend to me, the same as I would do to her when I explored her body.

She was a whole new female. I couldn't understand how she had come so far in such a short amount of time. She went from not accepting me fully, just fulfilling her body's reaction to me, to fully giving me her soul and her heart, and I couldn't be more excited.

I felt her within my soul as soon as I had bitten her. Body and spirit, we were perfectly matched. It was as if a binding had wrapped around us, to seal us in this world and within the next if we ever left this plane. It was fragile, but it was there. Once she surprised me, and had bitten me, the binding was stronger, turning that tiny thread into a rope that could never be broken.

Once she had bitten me, my body relaxed, and the fur on my back sunk inward. I was no longer the savage beast that had to sink my cock inside her to claim her. I was sated, but that didn't mean I was done with her.

I craved her more than ever.

I craved her body, her mind, even her smile. The way she grabbed my horns so I could lick her pussy, the taste of my seed and her arousal mixed into a perfect mixture.

As those early/first few days went on, I noticed differences between my mate and my friend Calliope. Calliope slept a lot during her transformation when her soul was sealed. Lucy did not sleep long. She would awake within hours, pull my cock from my pouch and wake me with her mouth on my shaft.

Lucy also sprouted horns, which were similar to mine and curved around her head. They were much smaller, but they were beautiful, and I swelled with pride that she looked like me—that we matched.

She did not grow hooves; she still had her toes. She did not have the hind legs of a goat, and I was happy about that. I loved Lucy how she was, but the horns, they warmed my soul. It made me feel not alone.

I never questioned why she possessed horns while the orc females lacked their male companions' physical attributes. I was a faun; I differed from the shifters and orcs. That was the only reasoning I could give.

As we rested in each other's arms and the days passed, I had flashes of dreams or memories that I had never seen before: of creatures like me, of fauns in meadows and in forests, which didn't look like the Wood at all. They were a lot plainer with evergreens—green leaved trees—berry covered bushes, and streams with small fish.

I saw very few females of my kind, but there was one who would approach me often. She would lower her body since she was much taller than me and reach out her hand to guide me to follow her. A warmth bloomed in my chest that made me realize this female was a mother figure, the way she would pet between my horns and nuzzle my nose with hers.

As I held my mate and let my fingertips soothe her skin from the rough ways I took her, the mother figure would appear in my mind. I didn't will her to be there; she would just appear in my mind. Her smile was bright, and we were both happy. At times, a male would take her hand, put me on his shoulder, and we would run through a meadow with other fauns just like us.

I had a family!

I wasn't the only creature like me!

I wasn't ready to share with Lucy about this fresh memory, yet. I didn't know what to think of it. Was it wishful thinking? Did I create this family on my own? Was it real?

I waited each hour to see another memory unfold. I wanted more answers about who these other fauns were. Was it really my life? Or simply what I wanted?

I watched myself as a young faun laughing, screaming and bleating for the hand-carved toy my father had made. The father held it up high, and I jumped, higher and higher. I finally used my head and used the rock beside me to jump off to get higher. I grabbed the toy that was out of reach and screamed in excitement.

When I landed on the ground, I froze. My mother ran toward me and gasped in fake sympathy when I giggled. Father shook his head and picked me up while I hugged the wooden toy tightly.

I felt warm inside. It really was me.

I had parents.

As the days went on, more memories surfaced.

I knew their faces by heart. My mother had hair like mine, while I had fetlocks—hooves with thick, overgrown hair—like my father. I remembered their voices and their touch.

While I enjoyed the time with my mate, I was also gifted answers to my past.

My mate didn't know any of this. She was blissfully unaware. I never gave her any reason to believe she was not getting the attention she deserved, because I gave her all the attention she wanted when she wanted it, even when she appeared to be sated.

My mind knew to wander when my mate was sleeping or in a hazed state, because I would wander back into a world where there were more of my kind, but the longer I was there, the darker it became.

I sensed the heavy, worried looks on my parents' faces as the memories wore on. The fauns migrated deeper into the forest instead of prancing and dancing within the meadows like they usually did.

My father appeared to be a leader of some kind, urging many to follow him into the thick forest.

Humans in the distance had gathered, pointing in our direction. What looked like curiosity to a child was actually ill intent. My mother scooped me up into her arms while my father herded the rest inside the forest. The humans ran toward us with torches while the herd took off into the forest. The forest shielded us, branches sealing/hiding the opening and hiding us within.

I clung to my mother and felt the fear inside me. My heart thundered, and my mother petted my back, whispering that everything would be alright. The fire from the torches dimmed within the forest. It held the humans back, but for how long?

My father's hand wrapped around my mother's shoulder. He looked back into the darkness, and his warm breath seeped down into my hair. I heard him shout to the rest of the herd, bringing us into the small clearing in the forest.

There weren't many of us, just a small herd, but when we gathered, there was a male with striking red hair that floated with the air, as if he was under the seas.

I clung to my mother, watching him. He wasn't a human, that I knew. There was a striking power to him I couldn't describe. I felt safe here, as did everyone else, but I couldn't understand why.

There was a rustle in the woods to my left, and my mother held me tighter, though I squirmed. I wanted to be let down to see what it was. I was a curious kid, and sitting for too long was torturous.

"No," I whispered to myself. This was wrong, so wrong.

I watched as my mother put me down, and I walked toward the bushes, then a hand clamped over my mouth.

Someone dragged me into the forest despite my bleating and crying. I could see my parents walking forward, not looking out for me. Tears pricked my tiny eyes as I watched them go toward the red-headed male.

They left me!

Even in this memory, I felt my body heave out a shaky breath. My mate, who was asleep in my arms, held me tighter, and I held onto her as tears leaked down my cheeks.

They were under a mesmerizing spell. They had to be because they didn't look back. None of them did, and went into a light so bright it blinded me until they were gone. Something dragged me through the forest, away from the clearing.

I let out a whine and shook my head to clear away the memory. I didn't want to look anymore, didn't want to remember.

Lucy gasped, and her arms wrapped around me. Immediately, one of her hands went into my hair and stroked between my horns, just like I saw my mother do.

I grunted, trying to hold back the tears. A male should not be this weak in front of their mate. I was to be strong and fearless. I was to protect her and—

"Simon," Lucy whispered and continued to pet my hair. "It's okay, I'm right here."

I bit the inside of my cheek and nuzzled into her neck. The mark on her shoulder was right there, a reminder that she was mine, that she would always be mine, and she would go nowhere else. We were together forever.

Were my parents together? Had they died?

What happened to them?

Lucy didn't ask questions as she ran her fingers through my hair. My chest made a rumbling noise, and Lucy let out a hum-like laugh.

"You sound like an enormous cat. It's like purring, but not quite right."

I sniffed and kept my nose buried into her shoulder. I was on top of her, keeping my face away. I didn't want her to see me distressed, but I knew she could feel me. I could feel her emotions as well. She was worried, but there was understanding mixed with her emotions. It was strange to feel what she felt. I couldn't understand it.

"I know why you are upset, Simon." She took her fingers and ran them along my scalp. "This whole time, I've been seeing what you see."

I held onto her tighter, not willing to move. I was afraid but also curious as to how she knew.

"It's like watching a movie reel. It's strange. I see you as a little thing, a tiny little faun, and two very proud parents."

I let out a huff into her hair, and my hands roamed up her naked back.

"They were so proud of you. Especially when they put that cute little flower crown on your head. It had those pretty thick branches on it. Your dad had one, too. Do you think your dad was the king of the fauns?"

I shook my head and closed my eyes tighter. Too afraid to speak.

"It looked like it. And you are the little prince of the forest. I think that is why the Wood here listens to you. How it bows to you and moves away so you can run. Look how fast you move through it."

I let out a whine.

Lucy kissed my forehead, then her hand ran up and down my cheek. "You were taken, do you realize that, right? It was for a reason, though it wasn't to punish you or your parents."

I sniffed and dared to pull my head up, no longer hiding from her.

Her thumbs came up and wiped under my eyes. She rubbed her nose with mine and placed a gentle kiss on my nose. "I'm not an expert with the fates," her voice cracked. "I'm not an expert in bonds, soul mates, or the like. I know little about this land; how you really became a goat, how you became friends with Calliope, but I know one thing." She placed a kiss on my lips.

She opened her mouth, rubbing her tongue against me. Both of us had tears rolling down our faces by the time we stopped. "I know this." She placed her forehead against mine again. "Fate brought us together. If you had gone with your parents, I wouldn't have met you. We wouldn't be together. I'm glad you are here with me. I would be so, so lost without you, Simon. You are the missing piece I never knew I was missing."

I let out a whine and buried my face in her breasts.

"And I am so sorry you haven't had your family and have been so alone. We will find them one day. I promise." My mate laid her cheek on my horns and stroked my cheek with her thumb.

I cleared my throat. "But I am happy," I said. "I am happy the way things turned out. I have my mate, and I would do it all again. Be taken from my family, become a goat, just so I could have you, Lucy. I wanted what my parents had even, as a young kid. And you gave that to me."

Lucy held my head tighter to her breasts and let out a long sob. "I love you, Simon. So much."

My ears pricked up, and I raised my head to meet her eye-to-eye. "And I love you, Lucy." Then, I rubbed my nose with hers.

CHAPTER THIRTY-FOUR

Lucy

I FELT SELFISH. TOO worried about acceptance from my father and if I was doing the right thing to be with Simon. Simon believed in me from the very start, put his worries away to capture me, and forget the missing memories that haunted him.

I had my memories.

My earliest was when I was five, and Father had taken me to some remote island. We were on a beach, and I got to play in the sand on a day off. We built sandcastles, made moats and collected seashells all day. By the end of the day, I was exhausted. As the stars came out, I fell fast asleep by the fire, with the waves crashing against the shoreline and the heat of the fire warming me.

Simon's last memory was of how his parents left him with an unknown attacker who dragged him away. His parents were in a hypnotic state. He had to know that. They would never have willingly left him. The person who took them had to be a god. He was beautiful, just like the woman with the stunning horned crown at the hot spring.

She was a goddess. I just wasn't sure of which one. The god that led those fauns away took them in the blink of an eye while I watched from a distance. I knew Simon was being dragged away, but I kept my eye on the god as he waved them toward him.

Floating red hair and beard, a sea-foam colored robe with soft linen pants. His feet were bare, and he held a trident in his hand. Poseidon was one of the major gods I learned about in high school.

But why would Poseidon be leading the fauns away? He was the god of the sea, and fauns were land dwellers.

I ran my fingers through Simon's hair. He wasn't dreaming; he was in a deep sleep. I knew it was deep because I couldn't see or feel anything. He had slept little the past several days. He had tried to brush off all his memories and tended to me instead of discussing what he had seen.

I wanted him to bring up all these memories on his own. I didn't want to pry, but when those memories got too dark, I couldn't help it.

I should have stepped in sooner.

I nuzzled my face into his forehead, my fingers stroking his cheek. I didn't know how many more of his memories would come back to him, or why they were coming back now, but I would be there for him just like he was there for me during my time of doubt.

I saw food being set inside our little bungalow, as I like to call it, by the door again when my stomach growled. It was in a neat little woven basket similar to the tree that had woven itself into a beautiful home for us. In fact, the tree had grown larger while we slept. The soft bedding looked smaller compared to what it was when we first filled the space.

We had two windows that let the light in. In both windows, baskets hung outside, that grew huge blossoms which brought a clean-smelling fragrance inside. The floor was no longer sunken in but now flat, easier for me to walk on.

We still didn't stray from the bedding, too cozy to move and too dedicated to our nest.

Yes, a nest. That was the best way to call it.

I disentangled myself from Simon's arms. He groaned, reaching for me, so I brushed his face with my palm and placed a kiss right above his forehead, in between his horns. "I'm just getting the food by the door."

Yes, the place had a door now, complete with wooden hinges. I didn't know if Simon was conjuring something in his head to create a home for us or the forest was doing it on its own, but I would not ask questions.

It was nice not asking questions and just letting things be. I was calm and just accepting of my fate.

The only question I had was why Poseidon took all the fauns. Fauns that appeared to be on Earth because the foliage around them was definitely from Earth. That was how humans came up with the stories of fauns, because they had, in fact, been on Earth.

Also, the minotaurs, centaurs... all of those creatures, had Poseidon taken them, too? Because humans were after them all?

I gritted my teeth at the thought. Humans could be terrible beings.

I picked up the basket just outside the door. Everything was brought to us. Even water. Giant leaves wrapped and fused together, corked with... I don't even want to know what with.

A thick mushroom?

Don't question it, Lucy.

I brought it closer to the bed. In it were fruit and vegetables, including Simon's favorite roots, all recently washed. Leaves for hygiene to brush one's teeth and other assortments of good-smelling flowers for our home. While I loved the fresh food, I was really hungry for some meat.

And not just Simon's sausage.

I gently brushed my fingers across Simon's soft, warm cheek, feeling the smoothness beneath my touch. "Hey, let's get you to eat something. You feeling any better?" I kneeled down and peppered kisses along his jawline. He smiled and buried himself further into the clouds.

Simon wrapped his arms around my waist, and his face went between my legs.

"I know what I want to eat," he growled playfully.

I begrudgingly tried to push him away. "No, no! Simon, we cannot right now!" I grabbed him by the horns, but he pushed me down anyway. While I felt I had more strength in me, better to match his, I gave up quickly, submitting to him as I felt his tongue part my folds.

"Simon," I breathed. "We can't stay in this nest forever."

Simon hummed and pressed kisses to the top of my mound. He went higher, kissing my stomach until he reached my breasts. "I do not see why not. No one is in charge here to tell me what to do."

I raised an eyebrow. "Really? Do I need to put you in your place, then?"

Simon put both his hands beside my head. His eyes glanced over my petite new horns. His eyes twinkled when he saw them. While I didn't have the lower half that matched, I saw how much my new horns pleased him. I liked them, too, I especially liked it when he used them to push my mouth further onto his dick.

I shivered, remembering how he gripped my hair tightly when I slightly gagged.

Simon lowered his head, ready to place a kiss on my lips, when there was a knock on the door. Both of us made a face of confusion, as though asking ourselves if there really was a knock.

We had lost track of how many days we had spent here, only going out to bathe and relieve ourselves, but we expected no one to come here. Especially since we had just mated.

Whoever was at the door, knocked again, and Simon snarled. I felt a fresh wave of his scent descend on me. My body heated, feeling the heat of his over me. His scent would turn me on in an instant, but any sort of jealousy and he would scent me as well, making me crave him and only him.

"Don't do that," I slapped his chest. "We are going to stink up the room!" I hissed.

More than it already was?

Simon huffed. "Stay here, bury yourself into the nest. I'll tell them to leave."

"Can you smell who it is?" I asked and shuffled around to find my ripped clothes somewhere in our bungalow. The branches rearranged above me. I braced myself for a limb to fall, but a vine brought down a white dress. I pulled it from the vine and inspected it. The fabric was soft, thick but still breathable. It reminded me of the nest that we sleep in.

The vine hovered in front of me as if waiting for me to say something. "Ah, thank you?" I told it and petted the vine on top like it was a dog. It shaped itself into a heart and rolled back up into the top of the thick branches that covered the top of our tree house for a roof.

Weird.

I put the dress on, and Simon turned around with his hand on the door. "Why are you dressed? Take it off!"

I opened my mouth and threw out my hands. "Just because I have horns," I pointed to my head, "doesn't mean I get to go naked. I got nothing to cover my boobs and my lady parts!"

Simon pouted, and someone banged on the door again.

"Go on, answer it!" I shooed at him.

Simon growled and cracked the door an inch, then a little more, and more, until it was fully open. "There is no one there." He stomped his hoof and slammed the door.

I tilted my head, went to the nearest window and stuck out my head. Simon followed me and pulled me back.

"They could still be outside. Stay here." He huffed and led me back to the nest. But when we turned, we saw someone already standing within our home, standing next to our bed .

The woman wore a wrinkled pair of grey joggers and a large pink t-shirt. She wore her hair in lopsided pigtails. One side of her eye makeup was done, while the other was smeared, either from crying or rubbing her eye, as if she had forgotten she'd even applied makeup. "Oh, I fucked up," she muttered to herself.

Instead of feeling afraid, I was utterly confused.

Simon grabbed my hand and pulled me behind him.

The woman chewed on the piece of gum in her mouth for a moment longer and blew out a large bubble, popping it when it got too large.

"Listen, please, please, please, do not tell my boss about this. I just got this job. I literally just got it three weeks ago, and I already screwed it up!" The woman got on her knees and had her palms planted together in a pleading manner. Simon backed me up, and the vines from the top of the bungalow lifted her up to standing.

Simon's body relaxed and brought me to his side.

"She's a witch. A not very good one," he whispered to me.

"How can you tell?" I asked.

"Smell that?"

I sniffed the air. It was familiar, ozone, like lightning during a storm. Similar to Rune. I nodded at Simon in understanding.

"Again, I'm so sorry." The witch pulled on her pigtails to release the rubber bands and ran her fingers through her hair. "I've got some mad ADHD. This is my first job outside the coven. And with the goddess, no less. I can't believe she thought I would be good with this, giving me such an important job with so many more qualified witches. She put me in charge of all the fauns. Me! Look at me! I haven't even gotten dressed today!" She snapped her fingers, and her sloppy clothes vanished.

She now wore dark jeans and a cute, hot pink blazer. Her bright blonde hair was in a bun, and her dark-rimmed glasses sat on top of her head. A notebook was in her hand, and she looked like the perfect... receptionist?

Simon and I both stared at her in confusion, and she tilted her head back at us.

"Is this okay? Should I change into something different? Maybe less formal? Oh, he's naked, and you are half naked, should I be—" She moved to snap her fingers, and I jumped forward to grab her hand.

"Nope, nooo. You are just fine. You look great." I patted her hand and looked back at Simon, who was too stunned to speak.

I rolled my lips together and tried to make sense of it all. "What do you mean, job and your boss? The Moon Goddess? A job like Starla, perhaps?"

The witch nodded excitedly.

She cleared her throat and tapped the clipboard with her fingers before she flipped a few pages over and read out loud. "Hello. My name is Sable, and I am a member of the Witches Monster Bonding Guild, hired by the most benevolent, the Moon Goddess. I am here to help you on your journey to become bonded."

Sable looked at us both, and her shoulders dropped. "But you have already done that without me." She frowned.

Simon crossed his arms and puffed out his chest.

I rolled my eyes and put my hand on her back. "That's okay, you are just learning."

It would have saved us from bothering the orcs, having Simon get drugged, me riding out a lot of his rut while he was asleep, getting kidnapped in front of my dad and his new mate, but hey—no biggie.

"It's alright. Is there anything else you can help us with besides telling us how to bond?" I asked patiently. Simon pulled me back, his nose buried into the fresh mark on my shoulder.

Sable sighed heavily and looked down at the notes in her notebook. "Well, I could tell you more about your past, but you should be getting more of your memories back, if you had any memory loss."

Simon huffed in annoyance, his warm breath traveling down into my dress.

"I can answer questions like why Poseidon took all the fauns and why you were accidentally left," Sable suggested hopefully.

Simon's ears picked up, and he let out a long bleat of excitement. "Yes!"

Chapter Thirty-Five

Simon

SHE KNEW ABOUT MY parents, my family.

Overcome with frustration, I wanted to shake her until she told me everything, but I refrained. I knew I was more than an animal now, and I couldn't just jump at the chance to harm her. I was more than just a wild beast.

Lucy gently caressed her hand up and down my arm, her touch providing a comforting sensation. Then she stopped and gripped my arm and conveyed a sense of urgency, as if she was trying to anchor me in place. I could feel the tension coursing through my body, causing my muscles to tighten. The weight of my body pressed down on the tips of my hooves, grounding me to the spot. Meanwhile, Sable's vigilant gaze added an air of caution to the scene, her eyes fixed on me.

"Why don't we sit? Outside, maybe?" She adjusted the glasses on her head and walked to the door. Her gait was more confident than it was before.

Lucy nudged me but didn't step away. I would have fallen over if she had. "You got this," she whispered, linking her arm with mine. "Every step of the way."

I let out a trembling breath, the sound escaping my quivering lips, as my hooves clicked rhythmically against the rough texture of the freshly laid wooden floors.

Since when did we have a treehouse?

Once outside, Sable seated herself on a nearby rock. She crossed her legs the best she could and tried to look regal.

I sat on a nearby patch of moss where I was most comfortable and pulled my mate between my legs. I buried my nose into her hair, huffing and puffing through it until I reached her mark. She shivered and wrapped her arms around mine that were placed already around her waist.

Sable cleared her throat and flipped through her notebook to halfway through. "What would you like to know first? You have already bonded, so obviously we can skip that part. Your souls are linked. You can feel each other's emotions, you're paired together in this life and the next," she explained what we already knew.

Lucy hummed as I licked the bite mark on her skin. "And I can see his memories, too," Lucy added. "He stopped remembering right when they dragged him into the forest."

Sable hummed and bit on the end of her pen. "Yes, the Moon Goddess is aware. She will halt a memory and will continue it when the owner is ready."

I huffed and shook my head. "I don't want to see it." I pressed my horns to the back of my mate's head. "Can you just tell me instead? I don't want to relive it."

Sable wobbled her head back and forth. "That can be arranged."

I squeezed Lucy, fear enveloping me, but curiosity was winning. "Yes," Lucy said for me.

Sable sighed. "There was a witch hired by humans. They wanted to steal Simon so they would have power over the herd since Simon was the prince. They wanted your father, Field, to help them with their crops. The witch agreed, only if you were not harmed."

I lifted my head from Lucy's back to stare back at Sable. She frowned and rested her head on her hand.

"When the witch saw she had taken you just as Poseidon had taken all the fauns, she felt extremely guilty. She planned on helping the humans so far to help them with the growing season. She didn't want to keep a young faun away from their family for long. Just enough to get coin to get her back to Bergarian.

"Unfortunately, with Poseidon taking all the fauns, including Field, the wielder of the forest, there was no way for the bargain to be completed. With your father gone, the forest had no one to listen to and serve. The branches and limbs gave way, allowing the humans into the forest. They were coming for the witch and her promise. If they came, they would find you, extort you. Since they knew of the witch's plan, they would keep you with them as their slave. Humans didn't understand magic, and with their emotions at an all-time high, they would have tried to make you wield the forest.

"Being so young, the forest had not yet recognized you as its commander, you see. The witch feared for your life."

I ground my teeth and looked away.

Either way, the witch should not have taken me from my family.

"The witch did what she could at that moment. She used all the magic she could from her body, draining herself of everything she had, and turned you into what you spent most of your life as: a goat. She had little magic left after such a spell. It would have replenished in time to turn you back into your faun form, but...

Lucy laced her fingers with mine and squeezed.

"She had to deplete all her magic to defend herself and you from their outrage of the humans, for not fulfilling her promise. She was beaten and left for dead but kept you safe from all harm. And you stayed, Simon. You stayed with her until she was well enough to stand."

Lucy rubbed her thumb over my fingers.

"With you being so young, you lost a lot of your memories when you were turned into a goat. You didn't understand right from wrong or what even had happened to you. But you are loyal, and your true character has shone through your trials, Simon."

I huffed, still annoyed.

"The witch, still hurt, took you to the portal to Bergarian. You would be safe there, and hopefully, she would find a way to change you back. Magic wasn't the same back then as it is now. Magic grows, and it took a lot of planning to change things back to the way things were, back then. She wasn't able to complete the full journey to the coven of witches in the Bergarian Realm. She did, thankfully, make it to Bergarian where you have been safe."

Sable shrugged her shoulders sheepishly. "I am sorry it was because of a witch. I swear we aren't all like that though, just like not all humans are selfish, evil, and want to pillage everything. Sorry," she said to Lucy.

Lucy shrugged her shoulders as well. "No offence taken."

Lucy's shoulders dropped. I felt her sadness through our bond. I wrapped my arms around to comfort her this time and nuzzled my nose into her neck. "It's alright," I said. "I don't remember all that time I was alone. Time had no meaning to me when I was an animal."

I lived my days blissfully unaware, until Calliope. I ate, drank, slept, and played. I didn't have many friendships. I knew I was different, saw animals as idiots, enjoyed my extravagant nests to sleep in, and once I met Calliope, she was a new friend that understood me. Then Lucy—the one I always knew was meant to be mine was my new light source to follow.

"You know. Technically, a few weeks ago, I was supposed to go find you, Simon," Sable said, drawing circles in her notebook, "on Poseidon's orders, and bring you back to the herd."

"No!" Lucy shouted and wrapped her arms around my neck. "You can't take him!"

I snarled and pulled Lucy away from the witch.

Sable snorted and threw her head back in laughter. "Relax!" Sable held her hand out. "The Moon Goddess told Poseidon no way! That Simon's mate was too close, and it would ruin everything. Poseidon had no choice but to let you stay." Sable grinned and clapped her hands. "Poseidon wasn't overly thrilled. You being his creation and all. He was ready to reunite you with all the fauns."

I tilted my head, not sure what to feel. Did I want to see the rest of the herd? More than I wanted my mate? The answer was difficult.

In my cherished memories, my parents radiated pure joy as they twirled gracefully amidst the vibrant wildflowers in the light source-drenched meadow. The melodic symphony of rustling leaves and chirping birds served as the soundtrack to their love-filled dances in the enchanting forest. Their love for one another was real, a tender bond that overflowed with affection and tenderness.

I gazed down at Lucy, her eyes full of questions. She didn't have any judgment as she touched my face. "You can want to see them," she said. "I've always wanted to see my birth mother."

I shook my head. "I would rather have you in my arms, right now," I said. "I will see them again. I feel it here." I touched my chest. "Won't I?" I asked Sable.

Sable bit her lip nervously. "Yes, you will see them again."

Lucy and I looked at each other.

Sable let out a breath. "It will be a long while. Poseidon is very protective of his creatures. Especially after the incidents that happened on Earth."

"More incidents? More with other creatures, you mean? Humans hunting and trying to use them?" Lucy asked.

I didn't let go of Lucy, too scared my world would take her away from me.

Sable stood from the rock and walked closer to the stream. The clean water created a melody that drowned out the noises I could hear from my memories of the humans screaming across the meadow. I could hear their cries to catch the fauns, to capture us and take what they wanted.

I shook my head, not wanting to listen anymore.

"While all realms have their problems," Sable began. "Humans fear the unknown. What they fear, they destroy or take to use for themselves." Her eyebrows furrowed, and her cheeks pinkened. "And on Earth, humans were persecuted for a long while by the supernatural kind before it was outlawed during the dark ages."

"What—" Lucy began.

Sable held up her hand. "No history lesson on that. The gods have forbidden me to speak of that history. They are trying to be seen in a better light." She let out a shaky breath. "Now that humans are becoming stable, we don't need to kick up the dust on Earth. Humans are open to magic.

We have shifters, witches and others living amongst humans. Monsters on Earth are a possibility for the future now. We have orcs here now in Bergarian; things are progressing."

I stood, holding Lucy in my arms. "Were orcs living on Earth?" I asked.

Sable shook her head. "No, orcs have always lived here. The only way humans know about orcs was from when the shifters went to live on Earth, and humans heard of orcs as horrible, nasty creatures from thousands of years ago. You know how legends twist among themselves."

Lucy wiggled for me to put her down. "And these monsters, fauns, minotaurs, all these Greek gods and creatures, was it Poseidon who created them?"

Sable eyed me. "Most. Ares had some help to create wolf shifters, specifically with the Moon Goddess. Other gods had requests to create other creatures, supernaturals, monsters for purposes that I don't understand, with Poseidon's help." She clamped her mouth shut as if she had said too much.

"So, everything is wrong about history. Everything we have learned is."

"Wrong. Yes, it's wrong. Most of the things humans and the supernaturals believe are wrong. Now, we really must stop talking about all this before I say something I shouldn't." Sable sat back down on the rock and wiped away the sweat forming on her forehead.

"Kitty whiskers," Lucy whispered.

"I think I am done with all this." I scratched the base of my horns and wiped my hand down my face. "I suggest you do not do this to the next faun."

Sable frowned and wrote in her notebook. "Sorry, I didn't mean to just info-drop everything, but you asked."

Lucy jabbed me in the stomach, and I stepped backward. Her strength matched my own now, and I rubbed my side. "Do not be so rude, Simon.

It isn't proper. She just gave us a lot of information here. Sable, he didn't mean it. It's just, well, it's a lot. Emotionally. He can't see his family. Do they know Simon is okay, at least? Is his family okay? Where exactly are they?"

Sable turned her back to us and crossed her arms. "I don't know. Is that too much information?"

I huffed and stomped my foot. "That is information I need to know!"

Sable snickered. "I need to hear a *please*."

I lowered my head and scuffed my hoof on the ground. The vines lowered from the trees and picked up Sable under her arms. She screamed as the vines held her steady for me. I didn't ask them to do it, they just did it on their own.

Lucy jumped in front of me and held out her arms. "Don't you dare! I don't care if you are a prince of the whole Wood, you do not headbutt Sable."

I stood up. "Just a little?" I held my finger and thumb close together. "It would make me feel better."

She shook her head. "Absolutely not. I know you have been through a lot today, and if you are good, I'll make you feel better." She gave an exaggerated wink, which I knew as *pleasure time*. "But you cannot do this."

I sighed, and the vines let Sable go. She pulled down her blazer and adjusted her glasses.

"Glad to know you have adjusted into your princely role." Sable glared at Simon and sat down. "And to answer your question, your parents do not know you are missing."

I frowned. "They don't?"

Sable shook her head solemnly. "Poseidon knew you were missing, and he didn't want them to be upset. He wiped everyone's memories of the missing prince. Poseidon will return their memories of the missing prince once the fauns are placed here in the Wood. You are the test run for the fauns. You are to get the Wood ready for their return."

That seemed to snap me out of the depression that had built inside of me. At least my parents were not suffering; they hadn't missed me. I hadn't missed them until recently. Knowing that I would be in charge of preparing for their return brought a new set of goals for me.

"We lived in the trees?" As I posed the question, I observed the flickering recollections that danced before me like vibrant bursts of light. The imagery was far superior to the dim confines of the cave, where the chill in the air could make it arduous for my companion to ascend the rugged terrain.

Sable gracefully flipped through the pages of her worn notebook, and the sound of paper rustling filled the air. She delicately turned it around, revealing a collection of sketches. As my eyes scanned the pages, I could see intricate drawings of charming little homes similar to the one the Wood had made for us. The sight of these bungalow-like dwellings, as Lucy had called them, brought back memories of one I lived in with my family. They were nestled amidst towering trees. I imagined the limbs of the trees stretching high above, their branches out of reach for the average human, but perfect for a nimble faun to jump from knot, limb or bark in the trees.

Would Lucy be able to climb?

Lucy looked down at her feet. While she didn't have hooves, she didn't flinch when she walked with her bare feet over tiny rocks and branches.

"I bet I can climb that now." Lucy looked up at the tree. "Doesn't seem so scary anymore." She elbowed my side.

I dug deeper into our bond, and it was true, she didn't seem afraid.

"The bond," Sable said, as if she could read my mind. "And as time goes on, it will get stronger, more confident."

I ran my hand over my horns. My past and future life's mystery had been mostly answered.

CHAPTER THIRTY-SIX

Lucy

We were both info-dumped.

Simon's emotions were all over the place through the bond, and rightfully so.

He wasn't alone. He had a family, even a herd. Unfortunately, he was left behind, but he has me now.

Simon didn't appear to be too upset over it once he found out that they didn't know he was missing. The promise that Simon would meet them one day gave him excitement for a reunion later.

How would that dynamic work out?

I had mixed feelings about it. I would support Simon through his feelings. Bringing his family here in the Wood when it was time for him to meet his birth parents.

Sable couldn't give us much more information other than his mother's name was Meadow. He smiled at that, loving how his parents' names matched so perfectly: Field and Meadow.

Other questions we wanted to know, more like I wanted to know, were like why the orcs were left in Bergarian while others were taken back to Poseidon's palace. That wasn't Sable's area of expertise, and wasn't her information to give. Neither were the ogres that had terrorized the Wood. We may never know, and that was just how things were.

Gods told you what they willed, what they deemed appropriate and the lesser beings had no say.

As for the fauns, Sable told us as much as we needed to know for now. In the future, the fauns would return, and Simon would be the overseer or king. Though fauns never really saw Simon's father as a king, he was a leader, but in today's terms, he was one.

Simon shuffled his hooves and looked everywhere but at Sable when she told us how important it was that we established ourselves in the Wood and understood the plants, the wildlife, the streams and everything within it.

Simon would be the protector, showing the fauns the way of the land, how to live in this new territory, since it was so different from what it was on Earth.

Simon stared off into the distance, his jaw tight. Sable finally handed him the notebook that she had been clutching so tightly since the beginning of our meeting. She seemed reluctant to let it go.

Simon took it and flipped it back and forth.

"You'll help him. I know you will," she whispered to me. "Again, sorry about messing up earlier. And just remember, take your time. It will be a long while before the fauns come back. Many, many years." She scratched her head and mumbled a few more things under her breath; words of confidence, 'sorry' and 'call if you need anything' were muffled, and then she *poofed* into a large billow of pink sparkly smoke.

It didn't affect Simon when Sable made a mess of the forest floor. His mind was elsewhere as he stared at the clean stream flowing through. I grabbed the notebook that hung at Simon's side, and he let it go willingly.

When I opened the book that Sable had been reading, it held tons of hand-drawn pictures, diagrams, and history of the fauns. What I found interesting was that everything was written in Latin.

Thank the gods Father taught me how to read Latin.

When Simon looked down at it, he scoffed. "I can't even read. I don't think I was old enough yet when I was taken." He frowned and looked away. "How can I help my herd if I can't read?"

I rubbed my hand down his back and pulled at his waist. "First of all, I don't think fauns did much reading. I saw them taking care of each other, living, playing, running, playing music in your memories." I rubbed my face against his neck. "Your father led with his heart, and you will do the same." Simon sighed and wrapped his arms around me. "If you want, though, I will teach you everything I know. But I'm teaching you English because we don't need to accidentally conjure some sort of magic with this Latin."

Simon's eyes went large. "No, don't want to do that." He bit his lip, his shoulders deflating. "I don't know how we will ever be ready for them. How am I to know all the Wood?"

I gave him a small smile. "Patience, my good little faun. I think it will go by quicker than you think. We have the orcs to help. You've got me," I winked, "and this book." I held it up. "I bet we can find substitutes for favorite foods and get some tools made. It will be great."

Simon didn't look 100 percent convinced.

I would make it work though, so help me, I'll figure out how to summon that god out of our damn stream to make my mate happy.

The next several days, Simon processed all the information thrown at him. It was my turn to console him. Well, I don't know if console was the word for it because all he wanted to do was continue the honeymoon phase. Which meant more touching and, well, rutting.

After spending time in our nest, I would read to him from the notebook. We would look together at the pictures of what his herd's homes looked like in the past. A lot of it was instructions for chairs, wood carvings of toys and making tools. The bungalows in the trees that I liked to call bungalows, were actually called thatchets.

I enjoyed reading out loud, and Simon was already learning the words quickly as I read the words in English, instead of the way it was read in Latin.

I was so proud of him as he asked questions, wanting to learn more. I even grabbed my notebooks which were given to us by the Wood. Even the original one when I first began my journey into the wood. Then the extra notebook, the one that Simon had gifted me with the picture of his—sausage.

Once Simon was able to write his name correctly, he signed his name on that one approvingly. He even wanted to hang it up on the wall of our thatchet!.

I told him no, because once we had company in our home, I didn't need everyone looking at what was mine.

Luckily, Simon already understood a lot of the Wood. He'd also lived in the trees with Calliope before living in a cave. He had adjustments he wanted to make to the thatchet and drew plans of a rudimentary elevator, so I wouldn't have to climb.

Which, I could climb perfectly now, but he still saw me as a fragile human.

I finished brushing Simon's long hair while he continued to draw his plans for this elaborate elevator, along with swinging bridges from tree to tree. I separated the hair and began braiding. "Everything is going to be fine," I whispered and grabbed the leather tie as I finished. I rubbed my cheek against his, letting my scent cover him.

It was another new feature we found out about myself. I could let go of a scent. It came out right behind my ear, just like Simon. He loved it when I scented him; it made him forget what he was doing so he could scent me in return.

I stepped away, leaving him cold from my touch. He jerked his head away from his work, threw his pencil down, and stalked toward me.

"You know that, right?" I asked playfully.

Simon turned me around, and we fell into the giant pile of cotton, which was now covered in layers of blankets to resemble a bed. I had sewn one large blanket for the bottom to be a sheet to cover the cotton and the top blanket to cover us for easier cleaning. The perfect equivalent to a duvet.

Simon pressed his torso against my back and hummed, his hot breath skimming over my horns, sending a shiver down my spine. "I could relax better if you wouldn't wear so many clothes all the time." His scent surrounded me as I took a deep breath to calm myself.

I scoffed and shook my head. "I don't have fur like you do. I get cold. It isn't—"

"Proper," he mocked. "I know. Can you at least show your stomach more? I can make your clothes and not rely on the Wood to provide for you all the time. I don't tell them what to do, they just do things they think I need. I can do things for myself."

The thatchet shook like it was offended.

I held back a smile. "If it would make you happy, King of the Wood."

Simon scoffed. "Don't call me that. The only thing I am king of is this cunt of yours." Simon lifted my dress off me and tossed it across the room. Then he trailed his fingers down my naked stomach to my pussy and two thick digits sunk into me. I gasped, and my hips bucked up toward him. Simon tutted. "No, you don't get to come. You get to feel my fingers inside you the rest of the night."

I growled and pushed my butt into his cock, which was already out of his pouch.

"It won't work on me. I can control my animalistic urges now that I am a king of this cunt."

This faun!

"Since you are king, does that make me queen?" I rubbed my butt against him, and I felt his come leaking between my cheeks.

Simon groaned, and I felt his Adam's apple bob in his throat. "I will not let you win. You sit there like a good female and sleep."

I stuck out my lip and pouted. I didn't think I would actually crave sex this much in my life, but when you were with the right person, it just goes out the window.

The bed was empty the next morning. Along with my vagina.

Disappointing.

It was a first to wake up alone because Simon was my personal pussy-licking alarm. When I crawled out of the fluffy cloud bed, I quickly put on my dress, minus the underwear and found a few bags that Simon had brought down from the cave yesterday.

He had slowly brought several items from his old home to here. I decided late in the night, while he was snoring, his little goat lips flapping away in my ear and his fingers sunk into my weeping vagina, that he was going to visit a special person today.

I shoved several dresses inside our bag, along with a notebook, just in case I found anything interesting to jot down. And let's face it, there always was. I padded over to the door and swung it open to find Simon just on the other side, with a surprised look on his face. He held a wooden tray filled with freshly grilled meat.

I immediately dropped the bag and squealed, "Yasss! I needed some meat!"

Simon's mouth hung open. "Was my meat not enough?" He reached down and grabbed his pouch.

Alright, I need to talk more about the proper time to use slang words.

"Simon, yes, your meat is enough. I'm talking about to digest, to put in my stomach. Although, you did not give me any meat last night, because you thought punishing me for calling you King of the Wood warranted it."

Simon smirked and winked.

What have I created?

Simon shut the door and saw the discarded bag on the floor. "Are you going somewhere?" All the mischievousness on his face faded, and a scowl replaced it.

I took a hunk of the meat that was delicately soaked in a fruit marinade and swallowed it in one gulp. "*I* am going nowhere; *we* are going somewhere." I licked my fingers. "I'm sorry. Have you eaten any?"

Simon huffed and guided me to a chair he'd made the other day. "I tried out several pieces and gave you the best. I made a sauce using ground-up roots and fruit."

I hummed and ate more. "As much as I enjoyed eating raw fruits and veggies, I was craving protein. This is great."

Simon pulled up a chair and spread his legs so he was surrounding me. I pulled apart the tender meat and placed some into his mouth. He closed his mouth around my fingers, sucking off the juices, then chewed.

And now I'm gonna get all wet.

"Yes, I was feeling weak. Being a goat, I could eat anything. While in this body, I crave more meat and fish. Does that have protein?" He pointed to the meat.

I nodded. "Yes, fish, beans and nuts have protein, too. It's important for the body. Especially with all these muscles you have." I reached out and gave his arms a squeeze. He flexed automatically, and I giggled.

Simon cleared his throat. "What is with the bag, Lucy? Where do you want to go? Are you not happy here? Is our home not good enough?" Simon's voice went higher and higher as he kept speaking.

I shook my head, put the tray on my lap, and grabbed his hands. "Simon, stop! What's wrong?"

Simon took a deep breath and sighed. "Just want you happy."

I chuckled. "Simon, I'm super happy." I twirled a piece of his hair away from his face. "I'm the happiest I've ever been. In fact, I want to make you happy for once. You are always doing nice things for me. I want to do something nice for you."

Simon tilted his head in confusion. "You are my mate. You are my nice thing."

I bit the inside of my cheek to stop from smiling, but the blush on my face was too red to not give away how utterly adored I felt.

"Simon, I think it's time we go meet the person who made all this possible."

Simon raised an eyebrow, and his ears twirled.

"I think it's time to go see Calliope."

Chapter Thirty-Seven

Simon

I had Lucy, that's all I needed right now.

I didn't want to complicate my life any more than it already was.

Calliope had always stayed in the back of my mind through all of this. My mate was the most important. Now that I had her, I wanted to spend all my time with her and the future we would build.

Calliope would be fine without me. She would forget the time we spent and fill it with her mate.

With enough time, their bond would strengthen, and her memories of me would fade. Besides, I knew when I wasn't wanted, especially after my transformation. Valpar made that clear. I was a competition for her time.

I understood that now. I didn't want a male around my female, either. Lucy didn't find Thorn attractive, or Sugha. She stayed with me in the tent even when I was asleep and took advantage of me when I could not move.

I nodded to myself. Yes, she found me far more attractive than those orcs.

When I changed, I was uncomfortable around Calliope. I wasn't the same, not the same companion as I once was. I had thoughts and insecurities that grew by the day. I understood they needed their time.

What about my mate? What would she feel if Calliope wanted to hug me? Calliope was a hugger.

I felt nothing but friendship with Calliope, but my mate may not see it that way, or would she?

Maybe Calliope might hit me. I left her for many moons and did not show her I was well. She may think of me as dead.

However, Lucy would not budge despite much insistence that we should stay. She was determined to go and before I knew it, we were already on our way, trudging through the Wood, feeling like I was off to my death.

"Simon, why are you so glum?" Lucy ran and jumped on my back. Lucy had been running circles around me. Her energy was plentiful, and her feet were hard yet soft to the touch. She didn't wince at the branches or roots beneath her feet. Instead, her movements were graceful, like a true faun dancing within trees.

"I am not sad, I worry. What if Calliope is angry with me?"

Lucy released her grip around my neck and slid down my back. She jumped in front of my path and made me stop. "You think she would hold a grudge for not seeing her?"

"I haven't seen her in so long. Even less since I found you. You conquered my thoughts, heart, and body." I wiggled my eyebrows and pulled her toward me. "She did the same with her mate when he came into her life, but—"

"Simon," Lucy whispered and used her fingers to tickle under my chin. "I know little about her, but she kept you safe, was your best friend, and wondered where you were, as Sugha said." She lifted a brow and tilted her head toward me. "Yes, I saw that memory where he told you that."

My face heated.

"She will be very understanding, if not excited."

I swallowed the lump in my throat and nodded. Calliope was a kind soul, but I could not help but be nervous. What will she say when she realizes I can speak?

Lucy pulled me along as the Wood opened up a path for us. She swung our hands together as if she had no care in the world.

I brushed off all the worry and watched my mate in the new clothing I prepared for her for this journey. The short skirt and the top showcased her stomach and back. Yes, everything would be fine, everything would work out.

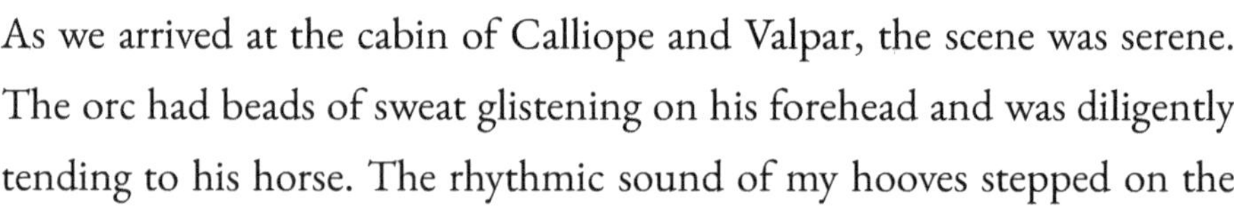

As we arrived at the cabin of Calliope and Valpar, the scene was serene. The orc had beads of sweat glistening on his forehead and was diligently tending to his horse. The rhythmic sound of my hooves stepped on the dead foliage.

The sharp scent of hay and leather wafted towards us, mingling with the earthy smell of the surrounding woods. Meanwhile, Calliope lay sprawled on a soft blanket, soaking up the light sources' light.

"I cannot do this." I gripped my mate and pulled her back into the Wood. The leaves and trees covered us, and the yellowcress masked our scent. Even with my scent covering her, I would not allow her to be smelled by any ogre. Somehow, the Wood knew that too because the thick woodsy scent covered us more.

"Simon, come on. She's so adorable. I love her hair, it's so pink and bright. Do they have salons around here? Or is it natural?"

Lucy poked her head out of the leaves to get a better look, but I pushed her head down to keep her out of sight.

"If I recall, it's from a fruit she ate. Now, would you stay down and let me just—calm myself before we announce ourselves?"

Lucy snickered, and I felt her hand go into my pouch.

"You want me to calm you down?"

Goddess above!

"Mate, what are you doing?"

"Giving you the post-nut calmness you need. Now, be a good little faun and try to keep quiet."

Her small hand wrapped around my semi-hard shaft.

"Always ready for me, aren't you?" She stuck out her tongue and dipped it into the slit. She hummed quietly as she worked it around the tip. I closed my eyes and tried to focus on calming my racing heart, but Lucy's playful antics made it impossible to concentrate.

"Lucy, we can't do this here," I hissed through clenched teeth, trying to push her head away. But she was relentless, her fingers finding their way deeper inside my pouch, holding and stroking my sack.

"Just a little fun before we face Calliope and Valpar," Lucy whispered mischievously, her warm breath sending shivers down my spine.

I knew I should stop her, but a part of me yearned to give in to the pleasure she was offering.

She grabbed my hand and put it on her horns. "Use me, mate."

I whimpered. I loved it when she called me Mate. It made it more real, made me fucking feral.

I also liked the word *fuck*, too.

As I thrust forcefully into her mouth, the sound of our heavy breathing filled the air. I observed her eyes welling with tears, glistening as they streamed down her face. The intense sensation of my cock sliding deeper into her mouth heightened my pleasure.

"You wanted this," I whispered.

I observed her delicate movements as she gracefully lifted her skirt, revealing a glimpse of her soft, velvety skin. The sound of a gentle rustle filled my ears as she slid her fingers in between her pink folds. The scent of her arousal perfumed around us.

My mouth watered to lick up her slick. I didn't want to let any of it go to waste.

"I shouldn't let you touch yourself, but since our time is short..."

She hummed around me, causing my sack to contract. Since I did not fill my mate's cunt this morning, this was going to happen embarrassingly fast. I watched as my thick, veined cock disappeared into her mouth over and over again.

I picked up the pace, hearing her cunt make a wet noise with her fingers. "I want you to come. Can you come for me?"

My mate sighed and hollowed out her cheeks, pulling the seed from my cock. I strained to keep my sounds at bay as I released my load and threaded my fingers through her hair.

"What a good little mate, so perfect." I breathed out.

Lucy gave a tentative lick and rose, when suddenly the bushes shook in front of us, and a big smile and pink hair came into view.

"Simon! What a big dick you have! Holy cheeseburger!"

Lucy stood up, standing in front of me to hide me as I put everything back into my pouch. I waited for the inevitable, my mate's jealousy to unleash.

I saw my mate's wrath when I had bitten her many days ago. She didn't like the idea that I was even friends with Calliope.

I waited for the standoff to end, ready to grab Lucy so she didn't hurt Calliope.

"Oh my gods, it's so nice to finally meet you!" Lucy jumped toward Calliope. I reached out to grab Lucy, but Calliope pulled Lucy into a hug as well.

"You must be Lucy! His mate! I'm so excited you are here! The Wood is all excited. It's been the new popular gossip since me and Valpar got together. Let me tell you, he's so glad people aren't talking about us so much.

Valpar stopped just behind Calliope and stared down at me. "Thrilled," he deadpanned. "Stop sucking dick on my territory and come eat."

Lucy's mouth hung open, and she turned redder than her favorite candied roots.

Calliope only laughed and tugged Lucy's arm. "Isn't Valpar the funniest? Come on, I'll show you around. I'm so happy for both of you. So excited to have my best friend find a lady friend. And just so you know, he never had a goat lady friend," she whispered in her ear. "In fact, he never had a goat rut. I had wondered if he had anything wrong with his pee pee, but couldn't find a goat doctor to check it."

"Calliope!" I groaned and slapped my face.

Calliope turned toward me, and her face softened. "You didn't just learn how to come into your mate's mouth, but learned how to talk, too? Hope it wasn't all in that order, though, because that would be awkward."

Lucy giggled and pushed Calliope towards me.

Calliope took several tentative steps, as I did. Once we were close, it was my turn to look down at her. There were so many memories I had of her looking down at me with a smile on her face, telling me about her days, what bothered her, and how much she wanted to fit in. Now, she had a mate, as well as I.

We both grew up in our own way.

"Why didn't you stay and hang around with me?" She played with her fingers like she always did when she was nervous.

I grabbed her hand and held it in mine. "Because you had Valpar, your mate. You didn't need me anymore."

Calliope looked back at Lucy, who tried to give us privacy, but her curiosity was too great.

"I could have taught you to speak," Calliope whispered. "I could have helped." She frowned.

I leaned forward and tilted up her head. She gave me a sad smile. "I don't care if you look like this now. I'd always loved you, Simon. You're my best friend."

I breathed in a heavy sigh and wrapped her in a tight embrace.

"I know I can be a bit of a lost cause sometimes," I muttered. "You needed me as Simon the goat. Not Simon the faun." Calliope twisted her lips and pouted. "If I was a faun when you met your mate, I would have come between you both. I would never want that. But now..." I held my hand out to Lucy. "Now I have a mate, too, and it won't bother Valpar so much."

Valpar grunted.

"Like I said, not as much."

Calliope laughed.

"I have learned a lot about myself, and trust me, without you, I wouldn't be where I am now. But I have also grown. A lot. My growth also led me to become who I was meant to be.

Calliope pulled back slightly, looking deep into my eyes. "I can see that. You're different, Simon, in a good way. And I'm proud and so, so happy for you." She glanced over at Lucy, who offered her a warm smile in return. "And in case you are wondering, I'm not mad you left. Once Sugha told me what was going on and that you'd found a mate, I've been planning a party!"

Lucy's and my face dropped. "What?" we asked at the same time.

"Yup! A big ole party. Everyone is showing up tomorrow. I sent word to the entire tribe once I found out you were coming. Uncle Osirus won't be showing up, but I heard Queen Clara and the big, bad wolf are coming. I can't wait to see him."

"You are staying away from him!" Valpar barked over the roaring fire. "That beast is insane! I've seen him fight!"

Calliope waved her hand in dismissal. "I'm gonna ask him to shift and see if he will fight some testosterone-driven orcs. That's my gift to Lucy and her scientific studies."

Lucy clapped excitedly. "That would be really insightful."

Valpar and I groaned.

While Calliope and Lucy were becoming better friends than I expected, I didn't think I was prepared for all the trouble they may get into.

CHAPTER THIRTY-EIGHT

Lucy

Valpar and Calliope's cabin, which resembled Thorn and Ellie's, was nestled amidst the lush greenery. The sight of it evoked a sense of simplicity, but the charm was all Calliope's doing. The flowers that surrounded the cabin burst with a color that matched Calliope's hair. The cabin's exterior boasted beautiful vines that strung out to poles adorned with vibrant garments, belonging to a woman, obviously. They swayed softly in the wind.

There, on the porch, were two matching rocking chairs, one larger for the big hulking orc and one smaller to match Calliope's petite frame.

We didn't go to the porch though. That would be too close to their home. Instead, we stayed by the fire, where someone had shaved down the logs into benches to create a flat seating surface.

Calliope snuggled up to Valpar and looked like she should be a fairy rather than a human. It meshed well with Valpar, who was far grumpier than Thorn ever appeared to be. Valpar's face seemed softened though, when he looked at her, his hand always on her lower back, her thigh or hand.

She found him equally enthralling. While I was a little jealous that Simon knew her before me, I knew it was platonic. I owed everything to Calliope. Simon could still be wandering around Bergarian with a random herd of goats or eaten by wild animals. She saw Simon was different and took him under the fake-fairy wing she used to wear and made him the friend that she really needed.

Simon was mine, and he let me know that with each brush of his thumb over my hand. I knew he didn't have romantic feelings for Calliope. Simon feared I would jump up and hurt Calliope because I was a jealous maniac in the beginning. I felt the uneasiness through the bond. It was quickly squashed when we finally met.

I wasn't an overbearing freak like these males. As long as she didn't go wandering in his pouch, we would be just fine.

Only I got to wander in his pouch.

Soon after pleasantries, we all sat around the fire at last and had to give the entire story of how Simon and I met. Calliope was completely enamored by our story, grabbing Valpar's thigh as he threw jealous glances at us because Calliope was paying attention to us, and not him.

Valpar shifted Calliope, so she was on his lap, but still she listened with her full attention on us. Valpar grumbled and complained, taking in large whiffs of her scent while she oohed and ahhed over our short courting.

Simon was hesitant at first to speak about how we first met. I had to explain to Calliope how touchy-feely Simon was. I wasn't afraid, telling Calliope how curious Simon was about my body. Calliope laughed so hard she cried, which of course made Valpar upset and told me not to make his mate cry again.

Orcs were weird. Need to write that down later.

Calliope demanded to know more, every detail. I patted my finger against my lip and told her one tidbit he left out, and that he demanded to pee where I liked to pee.

Calliope snorted and waved her hand like it was no big deal.

Apparently, that was normal.

While eating dinner, the light sources set, the nightlife had taken up the Wood, and we finally finished our story. Calliope was completely spent from the excitement of the day. Valpar had her cradled in his chest like she was a small child and rubbed his cheek against the top of her head.

The goddess we had mentioned in our story, Calliope decided, was Artemis. I wasn't very familiar with the gods, but the way Calliope explained it, she was the Goddess of the Hunt, wilderness, and wild animals to name a few. It would make sense she would appear in the Wood and speak to me in a place as magical as this.

I touched the horns on my head. Did she have anything to do with my horns? The acceptance of magic, this world, the Wood? Was this her gift?

I silently laughed to myself. It all fit. It would make sense.

Valpar, who grunted, groaned and made comments not meant for anyone's ears but his own, was stunned into silence when we spoke of Poseidon. He scratched his chin and rubbed his soft stomach several times in thought. Valpar appeared stumped and was no doubt wondering where the orc species all fell into this. Calliope already had a devious plan to talk to Starla, the witch who was in charge of all the orcs, to find out exactly why the orcs weren't taken back with Poseidon and were left here.

My theory, which I expressed to them clearly, was because of the war that was here just over ten years ago. The gods knew that there would be a war against an evil darkness. I mean, they were gods. They had to have an idea of the future. The fate of Bergarian was in the orcs' hands as they were immune to magic.

That settled Valpar, until he then realized all of Poseidon's creations could be released into the Wood.

"Wonderful, now I will have to kill everyone to stay off my land," he grumbled quietly.

Calliope slapped his chest in dismay.

"Monsters are friends, not enemies," she repeated.

We didn't know if someone would send these creatures, monsters, or whatever we wanted to call them, here. Some could be released on Earth. There were plenty of places to hide there. The oceans, jungles, and deserts remained largely unexplored. Each world was a massive place.

Then, there was also the other realm, which I was not to speak of.

"I'm sure everything will work out...for the good." I tried to add, but Valpar growled and stood on the other side of the fire.

Calliope let out a large yawn and raised her arms over her head, one arm lazily going around Valpar's neck. "I think Valpar has had enough social interaction today. He's gonna have a lot tomorrow with the party, so I best tuck him in bed, if you know what I mean." She closed both her eyes at once several times.

"Is there something in her eye?" I whispered to Simon.

"No, that is how she winks."

Oh.

"We have a guest room, you can follow us." She waved for us to walk behind them, but Valpar let out a low warning growl.

Simon grabbed my hand and pulled me toward the Wood that was already parting for us to enter.

"Thank you for your kindness, Calliope, but we will take rest away from you and your male's home."

Calliope pouted. "Valpar, you are being rude. We built that bedroom for Simon, and now you won't let him in. He's a king of the forest, and you aren't showing any hospitality. I'm not sucking your cock tonight."

I choked on my spit as I tried not to laugh. Simon shook his head, his light hair swaying in the gentle breeze, and tugged at my arm, urging me towards the depths of the forest. As we approached, the woods came alive with a symphony of chirping crickets and rustling leaves, their sounds merging with the distant hooting of an owl.

The air was thick with the sweet scent of wildflowers, mingling with the earthy aroma of damp soil. A soft, cool breeze brushed against my skin, while the sight of the woods were illuminated by the twinkling glow of luminous flowers. I touched one to see it bloom beneath my fingertips.

I could hear Calliope arguing as we walked further and further away, until a loud crack echoed across the clearing. "Owie! That was not a fun spanking!"

Simon and I both bleated in laughter, his ears went straight up and my laughter continued.

I did not just do that.

"Simon, I can laugh like you now!" I laughed and bleated while he pulled me through the trees. The Wood continued to contort, and suddenly steps created by vines and branches appeared before us. I stopped laughing and became highly interested in what was happening.

Simon lifted an eyebrow, confused just as I was. The Wood was creating all this on its own, making what Simon and I needed. At this point, he didn't have to make tools, the surrounding nature would provide for him.

Secretly, I think he liked it, but he still huffed when we climbed the steps, and he guided me to a mini home in the trees with a different bed in front of us. It was made of blankets and an actual mattress.

"I don't think the Wood made that." I kneeled down and touched it. "Where did—?"

Simon sniffed several times. "It has a faint scent of Calliope and their cabin; the Wood must have stolen the bed from their guest bedroom."

Ahh, that was meant for Simon if he had stayed instead of wandering off when he first turned into a faun.

Daw, that was sweet of the forest.

This was going to be the guest house when we came to visit.

I rubbed my hand up and down the side of the mini bungalow; I mean thatchet. "Aw, forest, you are so sweet to Simon." I rubbed my hand up and down the threaded vine walls.

Simon crossed his arms, his eyes wild with jealousy. "The trees undermine me. I can take care of you on my own. I have taken care of myself all these moons, had a safe haven in the cave and created you a nest." He stomped his foot several times on the wooden floor and sauntered closer to me.

I smiled and stared up at him.

He acted like such a toddler sometimes.

His eyes grew dark, and he balled his hands up into fists by his side. "And fucked you the way you liked it."

And now I'm wet.

"Why don't you tell the tree that?" I hooked my thumb at the door frame. "If you wanna take care of me, just tell it."

The tree groaned as though the wind had swayed it, but I very well knew it was the forest whining in protest. I leaned closer to put my ear to the wood.

"Uh, huh. Right, yes, I understand." I pretended like I was listening to a secret.

Simon crept closer, his hooves hesitantly stopped in front of me. "Did it say something to you?"

"Yes, of course." I rolled my eyes mockingly. "They are complaining that you are being ungrateful and…"

He leaned forward and placed his ear onto the wood, so we were nose to nose.

When he settled, I jumped forward and pecked him on the lips.

Simon's eyes widened as he grabbed me and hauled me over his shoulder, throwing me onto the mattress. I bounced several times, and Simon pinned both of my arms over my head and peppered kisses all over my face.

"You are a lying female." His playful kisses turned into sensual ones and traveled down my jaw and on my neck.

I squirmed beneath him when he kept one hand on my wrists while the other traveled down my body to cup my breast. "I shouldn't let you come."

I gasped and shook my head. "Don't be a meanie."

"I've gotten you addicted, haven't I?" He smirked. "Good., That was my plan all along."

I gasped mockingly. "You're so cheeky for a faun. Where was this outgoing personality of yours just a few hours ago?"

The realization must have dawned on him, and he sighed, his body collapsing on mine. He curled up, still holding onto my boob, and wrapped his entire body around me.

"Calliope is going to do something stupid tomorrow."

I snorted and used my sharpened nails to scratch his back. He moaned delightedly as I groomed him with my nails and nuzzled my face into his hair.

"It's a party. What is so wrong about parties?"

Simon nuzzled my top to the side, revealing my bare skin. As he palmed my naked breast, I could feel the warmth of his hand against me. Simon closed his eyes, intensifying the intimacy of the moment.

"You don't know Calliope and the ways of the fae. You've spent most of your time with shifters. Fae are different, and Calliope's upbringing was primarily among the fae. They like parties and even if this is supposed to be small, it will be wild. I remembered those." Simon buried himself deeper into my chest until he was practically sucking at my breast.

Kitty whiskers.

I rubbed my legs together, trying to ease the ache.

"How did she even know we were coming?" I gripped Simon's head tighter as he sucked.

"Orcs are quiet," he mumbled. "I'm sure we were being spied on. I wasn't paying attention because I was too busy staring at your backside for most of the journey."

Before I could laugh, Simon was on top of me and sinking inside my greedy pussy.

Goddess, how did he always know when I needed him?

He was so thick; he was always thick. My legs automatically wrapped around him, but instead of keeping me on my back, he pulled me up while he sat on his knees. "Use those muscular legs and bounce on my cock."

Simon needed this, I felt the tension through the bond. He worried about our future, and tomorrow. He had grown up from being a goat, to faun, prince, bonded, to king in a matter of weeks. I sank down to his shaft, feeling him stretch me wide. This had to be the deepest I've ever felt him.

It was like my clit was being stretched and pulled. I felt every vein of his dick as I moved myself up and down on his hard length. "Simon, gods, why are you always so big."

Simon's firm grip on my hips propelled me forward, the urgency clear in his touch. The rhythmic thud of my skin hitting against his fur thighs were reasonably quiet despite the pounding. I could feel my heart pounding in my chest, my breath coming in quick, shallow gasps. The scent of exertion hung in the air, mingling with the faint aroma of sweat. As we moved, the bounce of my small breasts matched the rapid pace.

"This slit has always been intended for me. It holds me tight and doesn't want to let me go, does it?" He grunted, his nostrils flared as my scent surrounded us. "You crave me like I crave you, don't you? You always have."

As I continued to ride him, my body responding to his every touch, every word, every thrust and I felt the familiar heat building within me. Simon's hands left my hips, only to grip my waist tighter as he lifted me and slammed me back down onto his member. My moans filled the room, echoing off the walls as we lost ourselves.

"Gods!" I gasped, feeling the climax build within me, so close that I could taste it. And then it was there, consuming me completely as wave after wave of pleasure washed over me.

Simon groaned as he felt my pussy clench around him; it was like a vice gripping him tightly. With a last thrust, he joined me in ecstasy, roaring out his release as he filled me with his seed.

"I'm going to destroy this pussy tomorrow." He snarled and gripped my thighs tighter. "I'm going to show them all how feral I can really be, better than any of those ugly orcs."

In my haze, I panted and tried to understand what he meant. I lifted my head to gaze into his lust-filled gaze. "W-what do you mean?"

Simon brushed away a piece of hair from my face and wrapped it around my horn.

"I am going to show them, as they watch the silhouette of me fucking this sweet pussy through a veil, how to really take care of a female."

CHAPTER THIRTY-NINE

Lucy

IT WAS STILL DARK out when I felt a tug on my big toe. I groaned and pulled it back and slung it over Simon's hip. He nuzzled deeper into my hair. A sudden cramp hit me in my stomach. I groaned, nestling myself further into the warmth of Simon's embrace.

Oh, yes, let me soak up all of your warmth.

There was another tug at my ankle. I jerked my head up in surprise and stared up at the bright, blue-eyed Calliope with three French braids on one side of her head.

She was like a warrior Pinkie Pie from My Little Ponies.

"Wakey, wakey! Time to get up!" She whispered and put her finger to her lips to silence herself rather than me. "We're late, let's get going."

Simon's grip tightened, his lips latched onto my neck and suckled. I groaned and laid my head back onto the pillows, ignoring Calliope promptly.

What was that woman thinking, waking me up in the middle of the night?

I felt myself drifting back off to sleep when I felt something tickle my arm. I went to grab it and flick it away because I thought it was a stray leaf, but I pulled Calliope's hair instead. She yelped, fell on my back and jostled me.

Simon grunted, his hands roaming hastily because I had moved. His mouth moved down my body and latched onto my naked breast.

Well, kitty tits.

"Calliope!" I hissed. "What the heck are you doing?"

Calliope stood up and brushed herself off. She put her hands on her hips and stared down at me like I was the one who caused the fuss. "Come on, you need to get out of here before Simon sees you. It's bad luck to see the bride before the wedding."

I stared at her like she'd lost her mind.

What was she talking about?

"We are bonded, there doesn't need to be a wedding, Calliope. Do they even do weddings here?"

Calliope's eyes rolled in the darkness so far back, I swore I saw the whiteness of her eyes. "Your father demanded he wanted to walk his daughter down the aisle. I made it happen." She stomped her foot on the mattress. "Queen Clara even brought the fabric, and your father number two," she held up two fingers, "said he was going to be the officiator. So up you get!" She leaned over and put her finger between my nipple and Simon's mouth, breaking the suction from his lips to detach him from my breast without ripping my nipple off.

At first, I was stunned. It was a much better option than what I was going to have to deal with, by ripping my suctioned tit out of his mouth.

"That's cute. He's a teat sucker. I'll teach you more tricks about that later. Now come on!"

There was no privacy in this place, was there?

She manhandled my boob, and I just let her.

I sighed and gave Simon a pillow. I saturated the pillow with my scent so he wouldn't move for at least an hour.

Calliope led me outside, which was completely different than how we left it yesterday. It was bright, nearly noon, when I stepped out. My eyes were blinded as I put my arm up to block the light sources. She grabbed my arm to lead me through the clearing that was now set up full of hanging flowers, chairs, tables, and a massive tent.

My father and his mate stood outside the beautifully decorated tent, adorned with vibrant flowers and winding vines. The air was filled with the sweet scent of blossoms, as colorful petals danced in the gentle breeze.

The sound of cheerful laughter and lively music emanated from somewhere to my right. Calliope waved, and I saw several orcs who were banging drums, playing string instruments and slapping each other when one decided not to pay attention.

The atmosphere was festive, a huge difference from what it was just the night before.

The intricate floral arrangements on tables created a sense of a romantic party that was really happening. My heart felt like it was going to explode the closer I came to my father and really took in the sight of him and Rune.

Father looked absolutely giddy, wearing a tan suit, with dark swirls to meet the same aesthetic of his mate. Seeing me, he ran, wrapped his arms around my shoulders, swung me around until my feet left the ground, and then set me firmly down.

"I've waited for this day, Lucy."

I tilted my head and raised my eyebrow. "You sure about that? I thought you wanted me single forever?"

Father slapped my shoulder. "Of course not. Just needed the right man. The goddess chooses right, so now I can rest in peace and do what I have always wanted to do. Walk my daughter down the aisle." His eyes became misty, and I pulled him in for a hug.

"I didn't know it meant that much to you." I rubbed my hand up and down his back affectionately. "I've never thought that much about having a wedding." Mainly because I never thought I'd ever find someone to care about so much.

Father sniffed. "I've always dreamed of it. Giving you away is such an honor. I know someone else has claimed you, but I still cherish the opportunity to participate in this tradition."

Rune stepped closer and handed Father a handkerchief. "I hope you are alright with this, Lucy. If you don't want a ceremony, we don't have to do it at all."

Father nodded. "Of course, of course. We don't have to do anything. This is your day, or not your day. I should have asked." Father's face turned a pretty pink, and Rune bit his lip as he admired his mate.

"But what about you two?" I swung my finger back at the both of them. "You both are mated. Don't you want a ceremony?"

They both shook their heads. "We want our daughter to have a day," Rune said as it was his turn for his face to turn red. "I want to be a part of it. It is more human tradition and with you both being human before..."

My lip curled into a smile. While I've thought little about having a wedding, it was really sweet, even sweeter that Father wanted one so badly.

Calliope danced on her tiptoes. "Please, please!" she begged. "I wanna have a party. I've never seen a wedding!"

Valpar stomped from behind her and put his hand on her shoulder. "I already put up the fucking flowers, and she doesn't want it anymore?"

I snorted and shook my head. "We are having the wedding." Not in the least bit worried about Valpar's outburst. Calliope screamed and jumped up and down like it was her party and quickly pulled me into the tent.

A sudden cramp hit me again as we entered. I found the closest chair, and I sat down, rubbing my stomach. Luckily, it was with a table full of sweets laid before me, so I grabbed the first block of chocolate I saw and stuffed it into my mouth.

That's the good stuff.

I grabbed another and another, filling myself with sweet chocolate, and another cramp hit. I stopped chewing, groaned, leaned my head back on the decorative chair, and pushed my legs together.

The realization of what was happening hit me. The wedding was going to be a disaster at the end of it.

Especially after what Simon said what would happen after the party.

"What is it?" My father rushed to my side. He was on the other side of the tent as he spoke to Rune about what sort of dress he thought I might like. Rune had been flipping through pages of an old sorcery book, holding up the white material on a nearby table and running his fingers through it.

"I think I might be starting something." I groaned and ran my hand over my stomach.

Of course! I would have my period.

Father and I were always open about my menstruation cycles. We were scientists, and he was not the least bit scared to talk about it. He told me about the birds and the bees, how women menstruated and how it was perfectly natural.

Calliope's head perked up, and horror struck her face the moment I said "menstruation."

At least she knew that word.

"No, no, no!" Calliope ran over and slapped her hands on the treat table.

"This cannot happen. You cannot have your period right now! Tonight is the ceremony where we all get to see you consummate your union. We can't have your blood scent around; it might, bring out the ogres," she hissed.

Father stood up to his full height, which wasn't very tall, and stared down Calliope. "Excuse me? Everyone gets to see her do what?"

I didn't see Father angry often. Just the time when Dutton hit on me and the few times when I got sick on Earth and he didn't think the doctors did enough to speed up my recovery.

Father's anger was rising at an alarming rate.

At least I didn't have to worry about his blood pressure anymore.

"Father, it's fine—" I went to reach for his hand, but he pulled it away.

"No, it isn't!" he snapped. "There will be no consummating in front of anyone. My daughter will do no such thing!"

Calliope tilted her head and pouted. Valpar, who stood outside of the tent, stormed in. "Who is yelling? Are you speaking to my female?" Valpar stood in front of Calliope, who was oblivious to being yelled at.

"It's behind a tent, silly. We just see the silhouette of them doing the deed," she said it like it was no big deal. She placed her middle finger and thumb together to create a hole with one hand and stuck her index finger through it with the other.

I snorted and threw my head back in laughter, only to have my father dart his head back at me as he narrowed his eyes.

I groaned and wrapped my arms around my stomach, then snatched another piece of chocolate. My head started to hurt, and my body was just generally feeling weak.

I couldn't handle this, not right now.

Rune, being the peacemaker, stepped forward and put a hand on Father's shoulder. "Just remember that customs here differ from your world." Rune turned his attention to Calliope. "Thank you for wanting to include Lucy. Right now, we have other things to attend to. Will you arrange to have some feminine products brought to the tent?" Calliope nodded eagerly, and Valpar's normally deep green face went very lime green.

Valpar rushed out and left us all with just our tiny family, and I leaned on the table.

A woman on her period, during her wedding day, in a white dress.

Could it get worse?

"Yes, it can get worse." Rune chuckled and kneeled down before me.

"It's creepy when you do that," I said, laying my hand on top of his, which was caressing my knee.

"I have a way to rid you of your mensuration, but it will be one hour of absolute torture, and it will dislodge the IUD you have in place. Not that it will help you any longer now that you are part faun."

Did I want to know how he knew I had an IUD in place?

Internally, I shook my head. *Nope, no, I didn't.*

"What will I do for contraception after?"

Father poked his head in front of Rune. "You don't want to give me grandbaby fauns yet?"

Goats in pajamas!

CHAPTER FORTY

Simon

As a sudden twinge twisted in my stomach, I let out a frustrated huff, the sound echoing in the quiet room. I mustered all my strength to push myself up, feeling the strain in my arms as I braced against the softness of the disheveled blankets and pillows.

They were thrown together in a chaotic heap, obstructing my view. Her stale scent filled the air. I furrowed my brow and shook my head, hoping to clear the fog that clouded my mind, while my fingertips grazed the wrinkled sheets, searching for any sign of my missing mate.

Sometimes, she liked to curl up into a tiny ball and hide beneath the clouds of our nest at home. Was she under the tremendous mountain of blankets?

"Lucy?" my voice came out low and gruff from my deep sleep. She liked my voice when I first woke and when I planted my lips between her thighs. Memories of her moans and whispers filled my mind, the sound of her pleasure echoing in my ears. The touch of her hands, gripping onto my hair and my horns, sent shivers down my spine as I recalled the intimate moments we shared just hours ago.

She enjoyed it when I spoke between her thighs and talked dirty to her. How she held onto my horns and rode my face.

I couldn't think of anything else more pleasing to do right now than that. I grunted when I felt another twinge of pain in my stomach. It became stronger as the seconds rode by while I pulled the blankets off the bed.

Where was she?

I snarled when I sniffed and tried to pick up her scent.

Stale.

She wasn't here!

I did not like to forbid my mate. In fact, I'd never forbid her to do anything, but if she continued to make a habit of leaving when I slept, I would have to do something about it.

I jumped to my hooves, then stumbled over when I felt another jarring pain in my gut.

Had I been poisoned by last night's meal?

I pushed open the creaking wooden door, and the blinding brightness of the light source's rays pierced through my squinting eyes, momentarily disorienting me. Ignoring the rough texture of the woven vine steps, I leaped from the towering height of the tree, a rush of wind brushing against my face. As I landed, my hooves thudded against the soft soil, sending vibrations through my body.

With a quickened pace, I sprinted towards the open clearing ahead. The once-empty space with a lone cabin was now teeming with life, filled with the cacophony of voices and the scent of bustling activity. Orcs and shifters mingled amidst the scattered tables and tents, creating a chaotic scene.

What in the Moon Goddess' name is going on?

Fuck, the celebration.

"There you are!" Calliope trotted over, wearing one of her fae-inspired outfits. It was far too short, and her chest was very exposed. I cleared my throat to look away, but she shoved me in the shoulder to pay attention to her.

"Lucy is getting ready in the tent. You slept nearly all day. That sleeping dust came in handy."

I narrowed my eyes at her. "What? You did what?"

Why were all these females poisoning me?

Calliope put her hands behind her back. "Sleeping dust. Rune, her daddy number two," she held up two fingers, "gave it to me so you wouldn't go meddling. You can't see the bride before the wedding ceremony. It's a human tradition. It's bad luck to see her or her dress before the big ceremony," she said perkily.

Goddess above!

"Is drugging them a part of the ceremony, too?" I growled. I had never been angry with Calliope, but there was a first time for everything.

Was Calliope always like this? Or did I only remember the good parts of her?

Calliope shook her head. "Nope, but I know males of this realm, and they get all grabby hands and 'she's mine. I can't stay away from her for more than five minutes.'" She rolled her eyes exasperatedly.

"You like it when your orc does it." I stomped my hoof. "Lucy likes it, too."

She shrugged. "Yeah, but I'm bringing dreams to life for her dads. They are such sweet—"

I doubled over and wrapped my hands around my stomach. It wasn't completely unbearable, but it was a pain I was not used to.

Calliope's little mouth went into an *O* shape, and her fingers danced along her chin. "I forgot about that. That is going to cause a problem."

I stood back up to my full height and took a sniff, suddenly smelling something metallic. My ears stood up straight, and my heart pounded in my chest when I felt panic through the bond.

"Lucy," I growled.

My hooves moved on their own accord and I felt myself being drawn to the tent. Calliope grabbed my arm and tried to pull me back. "Simon, she's okay. She's having her period. You know when women menstruate. Remember when I would have mine?"

I stopped in my tracks and looked down at her. I hated it when she got those dreadful times of the month. There were days she would stay in bed, hurting. I remember letting Calliope cuddle me, being the warmth she needed to ease her pain.

Why was I not helping my mate?

"I need to see her. She's having trouble." I stomped toward the tent again, and a firm hand gripped my arm.

Valpar grunted and pulled me to the side. I bleated in annoyance, and my hooves dragged into the dirt. "Let go!" My claws tried to break the orc's skin, but it was impenetrable, and he rumbled in displeasure.

"Simon, she's going to be fine." Calliope tried to pacify me, but I felt Lucy's pain run through me again. "Rune gave her some medicine to speed up her period, so she won't have it tonight during the party. That way, you guys can get down and dirty without the mess."

I roared, my teeth bared, as I furiously scratched Valpar's large hand that tightly gripped my arm.

"Blood will not deter me from claiming my female."

Calliope stopped in her tracks. "Oh, that's kinky. You into bloody sex?"

Valpar groaned and pushed me against the tree. Another orc who stood behind it grabbed a rope and they tied it around. "Let me go!" I snarled.

The only thing I wanted to do was comfort my female, to be near her. I could ease her pain and forget about this stupid tradition of this ceremony.

Orcs and shifters, who were setting up tables, glanced over but didn't give a second look. How dare they? Did they not know who I was?

I was part of this Wood, that they lived in. I could rip them all apart.

Valpar clapped his hands, removing the invisible dust from his hands. "Come on, Simon, it's a human tradition. She really is fine. It's a normal biological response in her body. Rune even gave her some ground up shit that will help her. The ceremony will be soon, and you will see how beautiful she looks in a gown." Calliope gazed wistfully up at Valpar.

I snorted, hocked up a wad of spit, and spat it into Valpar's face. "I've seen my mate bare. I don't need to see her in clothing," I seethed. "Let me go, or I will go to her, regardless."

Valpar jutted out his jaw and wiped away my spit. He stepped forward to hit me, but Calliope gripped his arm and shook her head.

Calliope's gaze softened and stepped toward me. Valpar put his hand on her shoulder. "No, leave him like this. I enjoy seeing him struggle. I heard what you did to Thorn, pissing on his foot, and now fucking spitting in my face..." his eyes narrowed.

My vision turned red.

"Consider it payback. Come, Calliope. We will let him go in a few minutes when it's his turn to get ready."

Calliope made a face like she ate something sour. "I had him tied up so he wouldn't ruin the dress reveal, not because of payback. I don't like that. Plus, he looks pretty upset, not knowing if Lucy is okay. I don't think I like this anymore. I don't want my friend mad." She pouted.

Valpar took a step back, his eyes fixated on Calliope as they stood face to face. The air crackled with tension as their voices merged in the argument. The sight of Valpar's furrowed brow and clenched fists revealed his frustration, while Calliope's crossed arms and furrowed brows mirrored her defiance. He never raised his voice to her, but Calliope was wearing him down.

A gentle breeze brushed against my skin, carrying with it the sickening metallic scent of blood. The putrid stench filled my nostrils, making my stomach churn. Anger surged through me like a raging inferno, intensifying the heat that prickled my skin.

I extended my senses, reaching deeper into the bond that connected me to my mate, searching for solace. But instead, another wave of twisted pain reverberated through my being, causing a sickening sensation to coil in the pit of my stomach.

She was hurting, in pain, and I was not with her.

This ceremony they spoke of, I didn't care. I saw her yesterday, saw her many times beneath me, above me, and I have seen her from behind. What makes today any different?

I let out a low, menacing growl, feeling the coarse fur on my back stand on end, prickling against my skin. The sound of my snarl echoed through the still air. As I strained against the tight bonds that confined me to the tree, the scent of damp moss and soil filled my nostrils, mingling with the metallic tang of fear that I had.

With each desperate struggle, the rough bark scraped against my sharpened claws. The bark moved beneath me, letting my arms move along with it. The Wood guided me to my escape.

I lifted my hand, my claws slicing through the rope as if it were parchment, and freedom sent a rush of relief through my body.

Valpar watched with surprise as I charged past him. He took one step toward me, and while the orcs held impressive strength and impossible armor of skin, I was much faster.

I heard a whimper in the tent as I approached. "It's alright, Lucy. I think you are at the tail end of it," a male's voice said.

I entered the tent with a snarl, the flaps rustling loudly. The air was thick with the smell of damp earth and musty fabric. As I stepped inside, my breaths were deep and labored, filling the silence with a heavy panting sound. My eyes, wide and intense, darted from side to side, searching for my Lucy.

My mate was lying on the couch, dirty towels in a basket on one side and James and Rune on the other.

"Get away from her," my voice was deep, unrecognizable. I didn't care if they were her family. She was mine to take care of.

The shorter one with impressive facial hair opened his mouth, but the green-haired warlock put his hand on his shoulder and had him step away. My mate whimpered; her hand clutched to her stomach. I kneeled before her, my hand going to her torso. It was warm to the touch, and instantly, instead of feeling the pain in the bond, I felt arousal.

Yes, I am impressive when I make an entrance.

As Lucy's eyes slowly fluttered open, I could feel the sense of relief washing over me like a warm wave.

"They kept me from you," I muttered and glared at the males to the right of me.

Lucy chuckled and ran her fingers down my cheek. "Bad luck to see the bride before the wedding."

I shook my head. "You are my mate. I am to take care of you. If human practice is not to see each other, then I don't want it. There is no luck, only fate."

Lucy sniffed and held out her arms. I wrapped my arms around her and glared at the two males who looked guilty beside us.

Lucy's father scratched the back of his neck. "It was just a tradition. I didn't know it would upset you so much, and yes, I should have spoken to you about it. My fault, all around my fault. Things happened rather quickly." James sighed. "I'm terribly sorry for mucking things up. Lucy has done nothing but talk about you all day. I'm surprised you have stayed away from her this long."

I grunted. "I would have come sooner. Someone planted sleeping dust on me." I stood up to my full height, holding my mate in my arms. She nestled her head in the crook of my neck.

Rune smirked and wrapped his arm around James' waist. "Animals are possessive. I was trying to save everyone some trouble. But you feel refreshed now, don't you?"

Lucy pinched the bridge of her nose. "Everyone out."

Both her fathers stared at her in shock.

"Out!" She shooed them with a hand sweeping motion, and Rune made the first move. He pushed James out of the tent, who looked longingly back at her, but finally left.

"Sorry about them. They are excited. Only child and all. Father had a picturesque dream of walking me down an aisle, and I was letting him get away with it. I didn't know you were drugged. I'm so sorry."

I nuzzled my nose into my mate's shoulder and took in a long draw of her scent. "You were in pain, without me. I never want that to happen again," I stammered into her skin. "I will be there for every time you...menstruate."

I pulled away from her shoulder, and she bit her lip. "Few guys would be willing to do that."

"I don't know if you have noticed, but I am not a guy. I am a male, a faun, and I will take care of what is mine."

She tried not to smile, and her fingers tickled along my jawline. "What about my fathers? Would you have stayed away if they had asked you to? For this ceremony and not see the bride before the wedding?"

I sat down on the shortened bed and wrapped my arms around her. "In the words of an orc, 'Fuck no!'"

She giggled and pressed her lips to mine. "Then, do you want to see it?" She fluttered her lashes at me.

I tilted my head in confusion. "See what?"

"The dress. Not a dress, but The Dress. Rune has worked on it all day. The fabric came from Queen Clara. It's supposed to sparkle when the light sources are setting just right. If you don't care about luck or anything, it's right over there." She pointed to a blanket that had covered a silhouette of a body with no head.

"How important is it to you that I wait?" I asked, and brought my attention back to her. "I will be honest. What I want is for you to be happy. I do not care what clothes you wear, you could walk to me naked to our nest every night, and I would be the happiest male for the rest of our eternity together."

Lucy's eyes moistened, and she leaned her forehead against mine. "Why do you always have the right thing to say?"

I licked my lips. "I don't know. Should I write a book for others?"

She barked out a laugh and planted a kiss on my lips.

"I will wait to see you, in this dress, so I may experience everyone else in their excitement. But I will only leave you alone for five minutes. It is enough for you to get dressed and meet me where you are supposed to," I relented.

Lucy nodded in agreement. "I think that is a lovely compromise."

My hand ran over her stomach. "And how are you now?"

Lucy sighed. "It's over. Rune did this one one-hour period thing. I won't ever do that again. I still think my uterus is falling out of my vagina."

What was a ut-erus?

Lucy shook her head. "I wanted to make sure tonight was extra special for you, being our *wedding night* and all." She wiggled her eyebrows.

I frowned. "If you think a little blood would have scared me, you are mistaken."

Lucy's eyes widened. "You would have still... done the deed with me being on my lady time?"

I looked deep into her eyes, and my nose brushed with hers. "Nothing could keep me away from your precious cunt, my sweet mate."

She pushed me away and laughed. "Holy blood sausage, Simon!"

CHAPTER FORTY-ONE

Simon

ELMIRA, A SHIFTER AND one of Lucy's companions from when she first entered the Wood, brushed and braided my mate's hair for the upcoming ceremony. She had a bite mark on her shoulder, and the scent of that idiot wolf, Dutton, entangled with hers.

Their courting game was over, and Elmira said it was everything she ever dreamed of in claiming her mate. She was a powerful female, and she still made her male work for it.

I was grateful I did not have to chase Lucy for so long and that she was more compliant than this shifter. I did not have the patience to run after my mate throughout the forest. I wanted a female who wanted to stand beside me, not run from me.

The queen had also entered the tent. I briefly remembered her in my time as an animal. I knew of her as an honest, benevolent queen and had a calming aura around her wherever she went. It even calmed Kane, the fiercest of all the shifters.

Kane was a large male. He took up the whole tent when he stepped inside. Markings and piercings covered him, and he scowled. Not that there was anything wrong with his appearance—he was just intimidating. If he ever went near my mate, I would not hesitate to defend her, but I would also never provoke him.

I could easily see his strength rival that of an orc. I would like to see what the outcome would be. There was a rumor he wouldn't fight an orc because of their standing in the war and his gratefulness towards them.

"Lucy," Clara broke the silence. "Now that you are a queen, you don't have to do any more research about the Wood. We can find someone else." Clara assured her as she sat in the chair next to her.

Lucy turned and brushed the shifter's hand away. "Are you kidding? I'm still doing it! I live here now. I have a forest that can even grow more rapidly before my eyes. It would be beneficial if I continued with my research. Please!" Lucy stood up and grabbed Clara's hand. "Please, let me continue."

Clara smiled brightly. "Only if you want to. If it gets too much, you let me know." Her head turned toward me. "For you, too, Simon. We know that you have a lot to prepare for in the upcoming years. We want you both not to feel too overwhelmed. Please let us know if you need any resources. Clothing, building materials, food cravings." She winked. "We will send everything you need. Osirus has sent word as well. Once the fauns arrive, we will segregate Monktona Wood into its own kingdom when you are ready."

Kane chuckled. "Yeah, the orcs are gonna love that."

Clara slapped him in the stomach.

I let out a shuddering breath, at which Lucy grabbed my hand and said for me, "That is a long way down the road. But thank you, we appreciate everything."

My arms wrapped around her waist. The soft white robe she wore covering her naked body, was too much. I wanted to grab her, take her to the nest and not worry about this ceremony.

It was important to her father, and now, we were supposedly important figures because one day, we would be 'souls that others looked up to'.

From a goat to a faun to a king?

The start of a kingdom?

I let out a huff, and Lucy pressed both of her hands to my face and squeezed. "You are going to be great. I can feel you stressing. We have many years to practice this stuff, okay, little faun?" she whispered.

I felt myself grow hard in my pouch and placed both my hands in front of me so it wouldn't peek out. I didn't need to have everyone staring at it if I was to be a leader one day.

"Okay, everyone out!" Calliope pranced inside the tent and grabbed my hand. "The bride needs to put on the dress, and I need to put all the flowers in the groom's hair!"

I groaned and followed Calliope out of the tent. I looked one last time at my mate, who smiled and waved before I left her for the final time.

Never again did I want to be separated from her.

I stood at the front of a restless crowd, as I shifted from hoof to hoof. The scent of anticipation and a mixture of food and excitement filled the air.

To one side, I saw the regal figures of the king and queen, along with the rest of the shifters. A deep scowl etched the king's face, his brows furrowed menacingly. His eyebrow ring sparkled in the setting light sources. I found it difficult to tell if he was looking at me or if that was just his usual expression. I found it impossible to tear my eyes away from him, as his piercing stare seemed capable of obliterating me in an instant.

The queen's sharp gaze caught his attention, causing her to grip his arm tightly. Her face contorted into a frown, and in response, his features softened. With a gentle nudge, his nose nuzzled against her shoulder, seeming to bring a sense of calmness to his body.

I swallowed heavily, feeling the dryness in my throat, and looked over to the other side of the crowd. The sight before me was overwhelming, a vast sea of orcs, their towering figures filling the space.

The air was thick with their presence, a distinct musky smell mixing with the scent of sweat and mead. Gods, they drank a lot.

Amidst the crowd, Thorn sat beside Ellie, the monster baby nestled on her lap. Thorn's arms were crossed tightly, his glare piercing through me like a dagger. I could hear the faint murmur of voices and shuffling footsteps blending together into a low hum.

In a bold gesture, Thorn raises two fingers, pointing them directly at his eyes before directing them towards me, intensifying the palpable hostility. My heart pounded in my chest, and I instinctively stomped my hoof back on the small platform, which vibrated beneath me.

Valpar, sitting beside him, banged him on the head with his fist and shook his head. "Leave the fucker alone."

Thorn grunted in annoyance, and I stuck my tongue out at him.

His lip curled up into a snarl.

Valpar smiled and tried to cover up his laughter.

While Valpar and I did not get along much, he knew how much his mate and I meant to each other. How much I was a friend to her for the years she was alone. He would do nothing to intentionally harm me. If he did, I would suspect it would be a brotherly sort of harm.

I grimaced.

As I turned my gaze towards the chair adjacent to him, my eyes registered the absence of Sugha's presence. A perplexed expression furrowed my brow briefly, but I swiftly dismissed it as music filled my ears.

Rune stood up straight beside me, his once-tan robes darkened to a richer brown to match the bark of trees around us. The crowd, that was standing in the back due to the lack of chairs, parted. I waited to see if my mate was on the other side.

It wasn't my mate who appeared first, instead it was Calliope. She wore a wispy flowered dress, carried a basket in her hand, and she threw flower petals down the aisle. Valpar stood and watched her, a possessive growl resonating over the crowd.

Calliope ignored him and continued to throw petals all over the ground, dusting the walkway for my mate. Once she finished, she hopped into Valpar's lap, and he quickly wrapped her up in his arms, a heated conversation beginning with how he didn't like everyone watching what was his dancing down the aisle.

My lip twitched into a smile; the music restarted, and I noticed my Lucy was standing at the far end of the crowd. My breath caught in my throat when I took in her form.

My mate gracefully held an enormous bouquet of vibrant wildflowers that matched the colorful blossoms woven through my intricately braided hair. As I gazed at her, I noticed every detail: the way her dress flowed with the gentle breeze, the light material covering her breasts, and the way it hugged her soft body. It glowed softly when the light sources hit the material, making her shine brighter than anyone around her.

Her father stood proudly by her side, their eyes locked on each other for a moment as he patted her arm that was linked with his, only for her to look back at me. While a sea of curious eyes wandered, the crowd's whispers were like the breeze. Amidst the gathering, her gaze found mine, drawing me in with its intensity, as if we were the only two souls in the world.

Flower petals fell from the trees, dancing around her and her father. She was a sight to behold, her hair done up similar to mine, a braid down her back and most of all, a flower crown around her horns. I couldn't stop taking her in, not sure where to focus first. She was far too good for a soul like me.

I was a faun who didn't have the strongest looking body, didn't have the fiercest growl, a male that was still finding himself—yet she still looked at me.

As she made her way towards me, with the soft petals of the wildflowers brushing against her flowing dress, I felt a surge of emotions welling up inside me. The love in her eyes was like a beacon, guiding me through the darkness that had clouded my heart for so long.

Thorn's scowl faded into the background as all my attention was drawn to her radiant smile. It was as if the world had dissolved, leaving only the two of us standing in a clearing surrounded by tall trees, and the music of the shifters weaving a melody that spoke to my soul.

When she finally reached me, her hand outstretched, I took it in mine, feeling the warmth of her touch seep into my very being. The weight of all the future burdens seemed to lift off my shoulders as I gazed into her eyes, so full of understanding and acceptance.

Without a word, she placed a gentle kiss on my lips, a promise of all the love and happiness that awaited us in this new chapter of our lives. And in that moment, surrounded by our friends and family, I knew that no matter what challenges may come our way, as long as we stood together, we could overcome anything.

Lucy's father was supposed to stand down, sit with the rest of the crowd, but he stood there with Rune. Rune read off vows, spoke of eternal love, the Moon Goddess, and whatever else he'd prepared.

None of that mattered to me. All of my thoughts and my vision were on her.

The one thing I heard was to kiss my mate.

Thank fuck!

As I pulled her close and placed my lips on hers, it was like being bonded all over again.

Her fingers tangled in my hair. I felt my shaft trying to escape my pouch. Perhaps it was wise to wear a large decorative cloth that matched the material of my mate, so I could concentrate on feeling her and touching her.

As my tongue grazed her lips, a roar broke through the woods. The music stopped, and both of our heads darted to the noise. Everyone rose from their seats as the orcs grabbed their weapons and raised them above their heads.

Lucy sniffed and grabbed my forearms. "That smells like a—"

As the deafening roar reverberated through the dense forest, the towering ogre emerged, his massive form casting a sinister shadow. The soil trembled beneath his heavy footsteps, causing leaves to rustle and birds to scatter in a frenzy. With a menacing swing, he wielded a colossal log. His thunderous roar echoed, sending droplets of his saliva soaring into the air, glistening under the dappled light.

The orcs all roared in reply. The shifters were bursting out of their clothing, ready to run toward the threat.

Kane's mouth moved into a predatory smile. "Now, this is a party!" He shifted, breaking out of his dress clothes, ripping them from his body. Clara darted away from him and gathered Ellie and Calliope, who stood in shock.

"Come on, let's get you all out of the way. Lucy!" She called after my mate and I pushed her in their direction.

"Go, you will be safe." I jumped off the platform, ready to go help the others.

Lucy grabbed hold of my arm, reluctant to let me go.

The tent that had been set up for our consummation was crushed by the enormous foot of the ogre. The orcs cried out in annoyance.

Lucy's father groaned in a fake, mocking tone. "Oh, no." He put both hands on his face. "That's terrible. I guess we can't do that part of the tradition, huh, Rune?"

Rune quirked his lip as they continued to watch the chaos.

We all heard a war cry that sounded familiar as we saw Sugha jump from a tree and land on top of the ogre's head. "I got it! I got it!" He wrapped a net around the ogre's face and turned the ogre's head, which seemed to be steering the beast in another direction, away from the party. "Orgamo! This way! You're too slow!"

I jumped back onto the platform. I would go after the ogre, but there was such a large crowd around the ogre, they may not need my help after all.

I held onto Lucy tighter as I watched a male of similar in size and look to Sugha follow after him with a spear. He kept whacking the beast with a blunt end of the spear to lead it back into the forest.

Kane leaped over chairs, his claws lengthening. "Can't wait to carve my claws into that!"

Lucy let out a burst of laughter. "This is insane!"

The once elegant, woodsy party turned into chaos, with the deafening howls of wolves piercing through the air as they darted in all directions, and the heavy thuds of the ogre's footsteps reverberating through the forest.

Kane, driven by sheer determination, leaped onto the ogre's back. The tough, armor-like skin of the ogre was nearly impenetrable, even with Kane's claws.

The ogre retaliated, forcefully tossing him aside, causing Kane to soar through the sky, the wind rushing past his face as he ascended higher and higher. Finally, he crashed onto the rooftop of Valpar and Calliope's cabin, where he landed with a groan.

"What the fuck! Kill that damn fucker! I'm gonna hang his fucking teeth as a chandelier in my house, damn it!" Valpar roared.

With a thunderous surge of power, the ogre's muscles rippled and veins bulged, his towering figure a fearsome sight. He bellowed a deafening roar, and the birds scattered from their perches in the trees. The stench of his rage filled the surroundings with a mixture of sweat and primal fury.

As his body moved jaggedly, the ground trembled beneath his immense weight. With a single twist of his hips, the ogre flung the approaching creatures away like rag dolls, their desperate cries echoing in the distance.

The ogre stomped, running through the branches. We all watched in confusion as the ogre fled at an alarming rate.

Shifters that had not been thrown off took after the ogre. The elder who looked similar to Sugha pulled himself up from the ground. "I'm not letting him get away. Let's go, orcling."

Sugha threw his head back and laughed, slapped the male on the shoulder, and they sprinted off. "Ah, to feel young again. Do you think we can cut his shaft off, do something fun with it?" Sugha shook his head with a smile.

Kane jumped from the cabin roof top and landed on his feet. He was about to sprint off when Clara called after him. "Leave it, Kane! The orcs and the shifters will take care of it!" Clara crossed her arms.

Kane whined, stared off into the forest and then back to Clara. She raised an eyebrow. He huffed and walked back toward us.

"Wow, she has magical powers." Lucy nudged. "Do I have that effect on you?"

I cleared my throat. Of course, she did. "With practice, I'm sure you will."

CHAPTER FORTY-TWO

Lucy

AFTER OUR UNINVITED GUEST had successfully ruined the after-party, Clara nudged me with her elbow, her touch sending a warm tingle down my side. Our uninvited guest had knocked over the tables filled with flowers, ruining them; they also smeared the burnt food in the dirt and spilled the orc mead from the barrels.

"What a waste," Kane muttered as he walked by the growing puddle.

Stringed violins screeched while two lone wolves tried to regain some sort of ambiance for the once-romantic ceremony, but the screams of laughter and howls in the distance of chasing after the ogre stomping through the Wood killed it. It was too hard to bring any of the party back.

Not that I minded. Simon and I were the introverts of the group, and we were happy to bring the party to a close.

"I should hunt after the ogre; he is after you. It is my duty as your mate to—"

Clara tutted and put her arm out to stop Simon from leaving the platform. Her mischievous wink added a spark of unease.

"Don't worry. There are enough wolves and orcs after that blasted thing. Sugha and Eman have been searching for that ogre for days. You would deny him such a prize?"

Simon and I looked at each other. I could tell he wasn't happy. He wanted to run, do some sort of alpha crap and prove himself. I hugged his arm closer to my chest, letting him feel the softness there.

That's it. Use your curves to seduce him to stay right here with you.

Simon's face softened.

Hell yeah, I'm just that good.

Clara bit her lip and held in a laugh. "You both will still get your sweet honeymoon. Your father and I had a *back-up* plan because he was going to destroy your consummation tent, anyway." She snickered. "I don't think he was ready for you to experience the Monktona Wood culture yet."

A sigh of relief for me, but a disgruntled grunt from Simon had me choking out a laugh.

Did he really want to show the orcs how well he pleased me?

Those who stayed behind from the ogre chase were cleaning up Valpar's territory. Calliope was trying to urge Valpar to follow where we were going, but he had his arms wrapped around her, whispering something in her ear that made her stop in her tracks. Her face blushed and she wiggled in his arms, but she didn't dare say anything after that.

Dutton and Elmira gave us a giant wave as we got closer to the forest line. "Go get some!" Dutton screamed at the top of his lungs.

"She already did, you perverted asshole!" Elmira replied and gave him a firm slap on his butt.

Simon and I walked hand in hand while Clara, Kane, and my fathers led the way through the Wood as the light sources were setting. Once we arrived, we came to an area with a large waterfall, bioluminescent birds skimmed the water and dazzling lights from the flowers that hung from the trees.

Just like everything else about the Wood, it was magical.

"I really need to make a map," I muttered to myself.

My father turned to me and brushed a tendril of hair behind my ear. "Thank you for letting me walk you down the aisle. It was one of the last human traditions I wanted to do. It will be a memory I will always keep." He pulled me into his arms. I had to lean down to give him a proper hug. Tears sprung to my eyes, and I did my best not to sob when he let go.

Rune stood there awkwardly, putting his arm around my father. "When everyone is ready, we would like to visit more often, or you can visit us."

I nodded and without reading the area around me, I bounded forward and gave Rune an extra big hug. I couldn't call him dad, or papa, or other cringy words for another parent—yet. I wanted that someday, but more time, more patience to get to know him was in order.

"Thank you. Thank you for finding my father and making him so happy." I rubbed my cheek against his, and he let out a sigh of relief.

"Thank you for letting me have him." He chuckled and pulled away. "And before I forget, there is a basket from Calliope in the back of the cave." He cleared his throat and nodded to Simon. "Good luck."

Simon tilted his head in confusion.

We all said our goodbyes, as awkward as it still was.

I mean, we were going in there... to do it.

And they knew...

Simon grabbed me by the hand and whipped me around in front of him. He pulled me up into his arms, and I squealed in excitement. "What are you doing?" I wrapped my arms around his neck, my dress dragging behind us.

"Your father said I must carry you to bed." He scrunched his nose. "I told him I was very capable of making sure you would not leave it as well. He did not appreciate my boldness."

I choked on my spit and laughed while he took us behind the gleaming waterfall that fell into the clearest pool. The pool was crystal clear, reflecting the colors of the night sky and surrounding vegetation. Small bubbles rose to the surface, creating a shimmering effect as they burst.

When we ducked behind the falls, I expected it to be dark, empty of anything but maybe a bed or a nest, but I was sorely mistaken, just like any expectation I had in this realm. But this exceeded anything that I could imagine.

The vines of flowers hanging from the cave ceiling were a vibrant blue, their petals shimmering with a mystical glow. The mushrooms on the cave walls emitted a soft, bioluminescent light in shades of yellow, pink, and orange, creating a gentle and magical aura.

The air inside was thick with a sweet fragrance. It reminded me of a flower garden in full bloom, the flowers smelled delicate and sweet, like a combination of jasmine and honey. With the rush of the waterfall behind us, the scent of earth and dampness mingled with the floral notes, creating a calming and enchanting atmosphere.

How was I to jump my mate when I felt like a gooey mess?

Good thing Rune rubbed some magic 'no baby making salve' on my stomach that would last me at least a few months.

Father would be pissed about that later.

Simon's nose traced up my neck, his warm breath trailing down to the mark on my shoulder, and a spark of arousal hit me quickly between my legs.

Okay, never mind.

I let out a whimper of need as my thighs rubbed together to get some friction. Simon would have none of it as he kneeled on the mattress filled with blankets and pillows. The vines that hung over us had beautiful hanging moss that tickled his horns.

His nose flared, and my dress, which was slightly loose around my chest, tightened as my breasts felt heavy with the urge for him to hold them.

With Simon, it always felt like it was the first time. The way his dick would stretch me so wide, the thick veins on his shaft that would rub my clit. I couldn't get enough of him.

And I needed him. Right. Now!

I felt my pussy dampen in an instant. Simon's nose flared again, and a low growl reverberated in his chest. "Your pussy is so needy for me, isn't it?"

I scoffed and shook my head. "No. I'm actually pretty tired." I raised my hands above my head. "I think I'm going to just go to sleep." I pursed my lips together to keep from laughing.

Simon's ears twirled, and he narrowed his eyes. "I can smell your want and feel it in the bond, don't you lie to me." He lifted up his lip, showing off a sharp fang.

Oh yes, bite me, faun daddy.

I placed my hand on my chest and wiggled for him to let me down. "I would never do such a thing." I twirled my finger around his bare chest. He was so chiseled, especially since we had bonded. I had wondered if it was because of the bond. Shifters become stronger physically..

I pulled some flowers from my hair and let small braids dangle around my face. I smiled at him, cupped his face, and pressed a sweet kiss to his lips. "Thanks for doing the ceremony. It meant a lot to my father, Rune and to me too."

Simon returned the kiss, sweetly at first. Then it turned hungry, desperate.

"It was my pleasure. However, you have lied to me." He raised his furry brow.

I bit my lip and let my finger run down his torso. Goosebumps erupted across his skin. "Like I said, I would never." I faked a yawn and put my hand to my mouth. "Here, help me undress. I think I'd like to go to sleep now." I turned and put my hands behind my head to try to untie the wrapped dress.

Instead of feeling Simon tackle me to the sheets, I felt something slither around my wrists. When I lifted my arms, I saw green, thick vines wrapped around my wrists and waist. I yelped in surprise and was turned to face Simon. His eyes had turned dark and were full of lust and desire.

"Like I said, I don't like it when my mate lies to me. I will punish mates who are dishonest."

My breath hitched, and I swore I felt a tear run down my leg.

New kink - unlocked.

I felt the vines wrap around each ankle. I watched as they slithered up my leg, up to my knees.

"Are you controlling them?" I gasped when I watched Simon slowly untie the tiny bows of my dress.

"I'm figuring it out," he mumbled below my ear and gave it a tentative lick.

My nipples tightened when my dress fell.

"I feel kind of weird that the vines are watching…"

Simon chuckled darkly, his deep laughter resonating in the dimly lit room. I could feel the rough texture of his hands as they slowly traced a tantalizing path up my body, sending shivers down my spine. "It's nature. They are used to this sort of thing."

His touch left a trail of warmth on my skin, igniting a longing that consumed me. Then he grabbed a vine with a thick bloom. He ran it across my breast. He circled my nipple, tickling me.

I panted as he let the bud explore every inch of me. From behind my ear, my neck, the curve of my hip to my stomach. I yearned for his touch to venture further, to caress my breasts and explore the depths between my thighs. I imagined it was his tongue. Goddess, I wanted him.

I whimpered. "Simon, please?"

Simon licked between my breasts. "You said you were too tired. Are you changing your mind?"

I tightened my jaw and nodded, conceding far too quickly.

Simon's lips curled into a smirk as he watched the vines wrap around my body for a better grip, and spread my arms and legs apart. Their sinewy movements weaved and tightened like snakes. I could see the mischievous glint in his eyes as he circled around me, his gaze taking in every inch of my exposed body.

"It's a shame because I'm not sure if I am in the mood anymore."

Okay, not fair at all!

I groaned and leaned my head forward.

The vine beneath my breast loosened and dragged itself over my skin. My body was over-stimulated. It was aching, wanting more. The vine curled around my breast and dug into my skin. Its movement was quick and unexpected when it pulled away, then whipped itself against my nipple. I gasped, my pussy weeping at the sting.

Simon flicked his tongue over the tiny red strike that was left behind, humming into my nipple. He backed away, observing the work of his vines.

The long, tentacle-like arms extended, poised for another strike.

My pussy tightened around nothing.

I was ready for it to happen again.

Simon walked back in front of me, a grin on his face.

Bondage and whipping, oh my goddess.

Simon's face turned serious, his knuckles rubbing across my face. "I should have asked first, is this—"

"Yes, yes!" I nearly creamed myself when the vines tightened around my waist. "Please, more."

Simon laughed. "What a greedy pussy you have!" The vines pulled me down into the slightly raised bed and pulled my legs apart as far as they would go. Simon's nostrils flared while he crawled toward me.

"You're drenched." His nose went straight between my legs as he took a deep whiff of my scent. "I can see straight through this lace. Did you wear it for me?"

I wiggled beneath him, unable to grab his horns and pull him deeper into my cunt.

I nodded, and his hand went down and slapped my pussy lightly. I moaned. My legs tried to come together to rub my needy clit.

Simon tilted his head. "You like this? Me punishing you?" His breath came in heavy pants.

The vines held me firm, preventing me from closing my legs. Simon looked down at me, his eyes glinting with excitement. "You want me to punish you, don't you?"

I whimpered, unable to deny it. "Yes, please, punish me. I shouldn't have lied." I tried to hold back my grin.

He smirked, and the vines tightened around me, pulling me even closer to the edge of the bed where Simon kneeled. "Ask your king for punishment."

Oh, we are playing the king card? Yes, I'll be the king's dirty, slutty queen.

I snorted, and Simon ticked his head to the side, smiling.

My heart raced as I called out, "Oh, punish me!"

"For what, dear mate? Why do I need to punish you?"

He ripped the decorative cloth from his waist, and his enormous cock hung out of his pouch. His come dripped onto the floor. My tongue poked out of my lips, licking them, just thinking of how much I wanted to taste him again.

"Because I'm a dirty little liar." I tried to think of all the naughty books I had read, and phrases that Simon might like.

Simon's horns gleamed in the dim light as his claws dug into my skin. The vines moved aside like an army of snakes submitting to their master, making way for Simon's massive hands to grip hold of my thighs.

Simon ripped the lace thong away with a swipe and dug his tongue between my folds, his long tongue rubbing my g-spot. Wetness pooled in his short beard, and I felt myself about to fall when he pulled away.

"No!" I screamed and fell back onto the mattress. The vines near my breasts slapped my nipples.

"Mmm, naughty thing."

The torture continued. Simon would lick my clit, even add his fingers with a thrust. He would deny me my orgasm and pull away. If I argued, his vines would slap my nipples. I was a whining, pathetic mess.

"Please, please, please!" I begged.

The vines must have decided I had enough. They let go of my breasts and lowered down my body. The vines parted my lower lips, exposing my needy core to him completely.

"Fuck, you are gorgeous laid out for me, Lucy."

"Please," I begged. "Let me come."

Simon shook his head, and his mouth latched onto my clit. His tongue swirled around the nub, and my body shook with the need to come.

"Don't come," he ordered. "Not until I say. This is your punishment."

Well, shit in a litter box.

The vines wrapped around my nipples, pulling and tugging. I groaned, feeling the wave of pleasure. "Simon, please, I can't anymore!"

Simon pulled away, and I whined for him to put his mouth back on me.

"I'm gonna take care of you, my queen." Then, Simon thrust into me with tremendous force. My walls clenched around him as he filled me completely and I came around him.

He growled, his hand fisting my hair and pulling me to his mouth. His mouth explored me, devoured me.

His hooves dug into the floor as he moved, each thrust brought us closer to our release. I screamed out with pleasure, releasing a wave of sound that bounced off the cave walls and echoed around us. The vines swayed above us like excited dancers, enjoying the sensual display below them.

Simon growled low in his throat as he continued his relentless pace. Our bodies slapped together, creating a symphony of lust that only we could understand. My breath quickened and my voice rose in pitch until I was screaming his name like a war cry in the night.

"Fuck, you are so tight. Such a suitable mate." My heart raced while I heard his hooves scrape against the floor. Another orgasm built up inside of me like a tidal wave about to crash upon the shore.

Simon's face contorted in pleasure as he neared his own release. "Do you want this? Do you want me to fill you up with my come? Fill you with my kid?" He asked between ragged breaths.

"Yes!" My voice echoed off the cave walls one last time before I erupted into a powerful orgasm that shook my very being.

With a roar of triumph and possession, Simon thrust one final time before collapsing on top of me. Our bodies became one in that moment of shared ecstasy as we lay there panting and sweating beneath the watchful eyes of our leafy voyeur above us.

The vines slowly retracted back to where they came from, leaving nothing but our mingled scents behind as a wild reminder of what we had just done.

Simon's breath was hot against my neck as he whispered, "I should punish you more often." I couldn't help but laugh, feeling the aftershocks of our passion still trembling through me.

He was still inside of me, and I didn't think he was planning on pulling out anytime soon.

Not that I was complaining.

"We should do more of this role-playing. This was fun." I wiggled myself against him. He groaned and pushed himself deeper.

"Is that what that was? You lied." He pushed his nose deeper into my shoulder.

I hummed and rubbed my cheek against his chest. "I was playfully lying. It wasn't real. But yes, role-playing, butt and tit slapping. I'm not sure if I enjoy edging, though. That wasn't very fun." I pouted.

Simon let out a bleat of amusement. "Is that what that was called? Yeah, I didn't think you would, that is why it is called punishment."

I narrowed my eyes at him and planted both hands on his face. "Okay, I'll do it to you next time. See how you like it."

Simon's eyes widened. "No edging! I get it!"

"I'll just make you come a lot. How about that?" I tilted my head and traced my finger along his lips.

Simon sucked my fingers into his mouth. "It will be a hardship I will have to get used to."

I giggled and rubbed his nose with mine.

Suddenly, the vines brought over a basket. The basket contained food and snacks, but it also held a device that I knew Simon wouldn't understand. Without jostling us, I pulled it out and held it in my hand.

"Oh, my gods." I snorted and covered my mouth.

Simon's jaw opened, and he stared in horror. "Is that a...? Why is it so pink?" His voice was high, and I pulled out the other device inside.

Straps.

Apparently, Calliope thought Simon would enjoy having his butt played with.

"Simon, so, uh, this is a 'for his pleasure' kind of toy." I gave him a Calliope wink.

Simon gasped and shook his head violently. "No! That is the no, no hole." One of his hands slapped behind him. "You will not put that anywhere." He grabbed the pink monstrosity and threw it into the waterfall.

Epilogue

Many, many years later.

Simon

My heart pounded in my chest, its rhythm echoing like the wings of a frantic pixie. The brilliant light sources, high above, bathed the landscape in a torrent of pink and golden beams, and seared my back with its warmth.

Beside me, my mate stood, our hands entwined, her touch like a gentle breeze that caressed my skin. As we ventured towards the heart of the freshly blossomed meadow, the scent of bloomed flowers enveloped us and mingled with the earthy aroma of dewy grass.

Fauns needed space to run, to prance and play. We had high energy, and while I enjoyed expelling my energy by rutting, when we'd had our kids, we quickly realized we needed them to burn off their own never-ending energy.

Three of our kids pranced in front of us. The eldest, Lark, was as tall as me at fifteen years old. His horns weren't as big as mine; he still had a long way to go to mature into adulthood. He still watched over his siblings, and he was the typical oldest child, as my mate would say. Strong, capable, and most of all, a leader.

Lark's favorite thing to do was whittle with knives and blocks of wood. When he was young, he created his first instrument, a single flute, and brought music to our home. He took books off the shelves of our thatchet and created multiple kinds, such as double triple and even a pan flute.

After our evening meals, he would play, but now that he was older, he preferred to help me ready the thatches for our new residences. In the evenings, he taught his younger brother, Canyon, the ways of music.

Canyon has added to the music, not just an interest in flutes but drums and a fiddle that Lucy gained from one of her fathers' frequent visits.

Our middle child, Clove, had the longest hair, that she wouldn't let anyone cut. It was as bright as Lucy's, always double-braided, so it wouldn't drag on the ground while she ran through the tall grasses of the meadow.

She looked so much like her mother; I knew I would have to protect her from any male that thought they were worthy of her.

I watched my family fondly while we took our time to reach the middle of the field to meet Sable.

Today was the day we had been waiting for.

Lucy squeezed my arm as her head leaned on my shoulder. "Everything is going to be amazing."

I swallowed heavily, but my chest felt like a boulder was sitting on it.

The orcs were at the tree line on the other side as a welcoming party. I told them they had to stay back until the initial welcoming to the Wood had happened. I didn't need the herd to scatter before we could officially welcome them and let them know they were safe.

The kings and queens of Bergarian stayed away. Thank the gods, because I didn't think I could handle the formalities, and I didn't think the other fauns could either.

"Simon." Lucy rubbed her hand up and down my arm. "Simon, you're trembling."

She pulled me to a stop just a few feet away from Sable, who was patiently waiting at the meadow's center. Our kids were keeping her company while panic overtook my body.

I had everything planned, down to the last thatchet. I knew of every family that would arrive. I knew their names, their faces, their likes and their dislikes. I knew how many fauns to each home, how many kids they bore in their absence from the Earth Realm while they stayed with Poseidon—which wasn't many.

They would know little of the home they had left. They would know that a god had saved them from a time when their species was in danger, but nothing more than that. My family, my mother and father, who had no more kids after me, had no knowledge I was missing to save their suffering, but once their hooves met the soil, they would remember.

They would know I had been gone for many years and that I had grown to be what I am today.

Emotions would swirl among my parents, they would feel many, and I would need to hold them together. I would because I was their son. I held no resentment toward them in any way.

In all of this, I was able to grow and be who I was supposed to be: the leader of the herd.

Would they see me as such a figure? Would they believe I could take care of them? Lead them in the dangers that were here? What of Bergarian; would they truly accept them? The orcs were still faced with wary glances.

I felt a warm hand on my chest, my rapid breathing slowed, and I looked down at my teary-eyed mate.

The female who had kept me calm all these years, the mate who had kept me grounded and told me I could do anything, wrapped her arms around me.

"You've done so well, my little faun." My body slumped and nuzzled into her shoulder. She smiled and pressed a kiss to my neck. "Poseidon and Sable wouldn't have brought your kind here if they didn't think we were ready."

"Our kind," I muttered, running my hand over her horns.

While she didn't have the hooves, she still walked barefoot, some days, I wondered if her feet were swifter than my hooves. She could even run faster than our energetic children.

Lucy pulled on my hand, leading me to the center. Sable perked up her head while all the kids were playing a fast round of Ring around the Rosie. A game that Lucy had taught them.

"Are we ready?" Sable asked. She appeared in much more professional attire, and her sleek dark-colored jeans clung to her legs. A flowing dark cape draped over her shoulders, swaying gently with each step she took. She'd neatly pinned back her hair, leaving a few soft curls to frame her face. In her hands, she held a clipboard, the sound of her pen scratching against the paper as she diligently checked off my arrival.

My stomach churned. I'd do anything to push this day off for a couple more weeks, but what Poseidon wanted is what he got.

Sable stepped back, and our children stood by our sides. We held them tight to us. Lucy stroked our youngest's hair and whispered to them quietly, while Sable cast a spell that would open the portal.

"Remember to be nice to the younger fauns. This will be their first time out in the open around so many trees, and they won't understand the surrounding dangers." Her voice turned serious. "Make sure they know the orcs are their friends, too."

The kids groaned and nodded.

"C-could one be our mate?" Lark asked, his face turning a bright red.

Lucy scowled and grabbed his ear. "Don't even think about it. You are too young to find a mate. Fifteen! You're only fifteen! You have to at least grow into your horns and know how to trim your own hooves." She stared down at his neatly trimmed hooves.

Lucy made sure all our kids' hooves were properly trimmed and groomed the night before, but Canyon, our eight-year-old, already had mud across his. Lucy scowled at him, and he stepped closer to me.

"Someone is in trouble." I winked at Canyon, and his ears lowered.

As soon as the portal opened, the light sources dimmed, and a bright light made us all close our eyes. We held up our arms to hide the brightness, and as quickly as the brightness came, it disappeared.

Sable looked proud of herself and panted, checking one box on her clipboard.

Lucy tilted her head and nodded for me to approach. While she was my foundation, I knew I had to step forward and be the leader I was. I squeezed her hand, and our whole family approached the bewildered-looking fauns in front of us.

They were an array of colors. They weren't just the brown, blonde, white, and cream like our family. Some were black, gray, red, and even deep purple I had not seen from my memories. Two of the fauns straight from my memories came trotting toward me. My heart nearly burst out of my chest when they slammed into me.

"You're here." My father pulled me tight into his chest. "I'd remember those eyes anywhere."

I heard my mother's sob beside me, her hand running through the loose hair at the nape of my neck.

"Hi." My voice was raspy, and I held out my arm to pull her in as well.

It felt like I was complete once more. My chest was about to explode. I could feel them, as my mate who was bursting with excitement to meet them.

I pulled away, seeing that they had tears in their eyes.

"We didn't mean to leave you," they both said at the same time.

I shook my head and put my hand on both their shoulders. "I know you didn't. It was fate that led me down this path. We have a home now, we"—I held my hand out for Lucy and pulled her to my side—"have prepared a home for everyone. For all the herd."

My mother's eyes filled with tears once more, and her hands covered her face. "Gods above. You have found a female." She held her hands out and pulled my mate into her arms.

My father wiggled his eyebrows. "She's beautiful. How was courting? I am sorry I was not there to help you." His voice was much deeper than mine, even his horns were larger.

I made a face of disgust and shook my head. "Stop." I cleared my throat.

Canyon tugged on my father's tail, and he yelped in surprise. "Hey, are you my grandpa?" He looked up at my father and scratched his ear.

My father looked from Canyon to me and back again. "Obviously, you figured it out just fine."

"I have grandkids!?" My mother bleated and jumped around Lucy to gawk.

This was not as awkward as I thought it would be.

I scratched the side of my face while I watched my father pick up my youngest, and my mother cupped Clove's face. Clove beamed up at her and smiled. "You are just stunning, love!"

Clove's face reddened, and a tiny bleat escaped her.

Lark had already walked closer to the crowd of fauns, introducing himself while they watched my parents and I reuniting. He was already explaining who he was and what our family had been doing here in the Wood these past years.

My chest puffed up with pride at his ability to take charge.

Lucy crossed her arms and nudged me, which caused me to automatically wrap my arm around her. "See, and you thought this was going to be a complete disaster."

I let out a sigh of relief and walked with her to the herd of curious onlookers. They weren't afraid; some even jumped in excitement when they saw the orcs on the tree line who waved excitedly.

"Who are they?" An excited young kid asked as he waved back.

I kneeled before the male kid, his eyes wide. "Those are the orcs. They have lived here far longer than I have. They are the Wood's warriors, and we are the nurturers of this soil." The kid blinked, and his lips parted. "Would you like to help the Wood grow, live amongst it, and play in its branches?"

The kid nodded furiously.

Canyon trotted closer to the kid and gripped his hand. "Well then, come on, let's go!" Canyon pulled the boy along toward the line of trees. The orcs slowly emerged, along with their families.

I rose to full height, and Lucy wrapped her arms around my waist.

"This is going to be an interesting entry in my research journal. Think this publication will take off?"

Since becoming my mate and queen of this Wood, she never stopped writing and researching every plant, animal, mushroom, light, whisp, bond, god and goddess legend she could. She had published fifteen different research books; they were distributed all over Bergarian, even to the curious packs and colonies on Earth.

And she showed no signs of stopping.

Clove was following in her mother's footsteps, except she had more of a desire to understand magic.

How that would favor her in the future, we were uncertain since she was a faun and did not harbor any magic in her blood.

Lucy was adamant her future mate would be of magical descent.

A growl rumbled through me as I watched Rune and James come through the clearing. They demanded they wanted to be here for the big event. They visited at least once a month and brought Clove a new book to study each time.

I narrowed my eyes at Rune, who felt my gaze. He knew I did not like Clove's insistent study of magic.

Lucy rubbed her nose into my shoulder while the fauns scattered, talking amongst themselves, the orcs and Sable for further instructions. "You worry too much. You know she loves to read. Leave her alone."

"You will change your tune when her mate is a warlock and grabs her up from the Wood and takes her away."

Lucy growled, and her claws dug into my arm. "She's only eleven. Would you stop!"

I chuckled and pressed a kiss to her cheek.

For the rest of the afternoon and into the evening, the orcs and the herd gathered together in celebration. While the orcs told them war stories of the past and tried to frighten the kids with blood and gore, this only spurred the younglings on. The kids and the fauns climbed trees, hunted through the thatches to find their names carved into their beds, and found food baskets and cloths for coverage if they wished.

The bonfire was lit in the middle of the small town that I had created over years of careful preparation. The flames crackled and danced high as the light sources dipped below the horizon, casting a warm glow over the herd and the orcs.

The scent of roasting meat filled the air, mingling with laughter and chatter. Lucy stood beside me, her eyes alight with joy as she watched our new community coming together.

I felt a sense of contentment settle over me, knowing that my family was here, safe and surrounded by those who would protect and care for them. The bonds that had been forged that day would only grow stronger with time. I was sure of it.

As the night wore on, the stars twinkled in the sky above, casting a gentle light over the revelry. I held Lucy close, feeling the warmth of her presence seep into my bones.

"You did it," she whispered, her breath tickling my ear. "You got your family back and made your own."

My lip twitched, and I pressed a kiss to her bond mark. "Never thought I'd have it all. Yet here we are."

"Tomorrow's agenda. Teach the herd about bonding."

I groaned and stood behind my mate to wrap my arms around her.

A baby orc's squeal pierced the air, and we both looked to our right to look at Valpar and Calliope. She sat on Valpar's lap as they held their first orcling. A baby girl, a beautiful shade of green with bright tuff of pink hair on top of her head.

Valpar rubbed noses with the little one and the orcling sucked on his nose while slapping his face.

For an orcling, it was... cute!.

And as the bonfire crackled and the laughter of our new family filled the air, I knew that Lucy and I finally had our happy beginning, as I rubbed her swollen belly.

The End

Don't wander off too far. Sugha has a story coming soon! Where did he and his father end up running off to??

And it would mean the world to me if you left a review or even recommended this book to a friend <3

BOOKS BY VERA

<u>Under the Moon Series</u>

Under the Moon
Clara and Kane's Story

The Alpha's Kitten
Charlotte and Wesley's Story

Finding Love with the Fae King
Osirus and Melina's Story

The Exiled Dragon
Creed and Odessa's Story

Under the Moon: The Dark War
Clara, Kane, Jasper and Taliyah's story

His True Beloved: A Vampire's Second Chance
Sebastian and Christine's Story

Alpha of her Dreams
Evelyn and Kit's Story

The Broken Alpha's Princess
Melody and Marcus' Story

Twinning and Sinning From Mutts to Mates
Dax, Dimitri, and Seraphina's Story

Under the Moon: God Series

Seeking Hades' Ember
Hades and Ember's Story

Lucifer's Redemption
Lucifer and Uriel's Story

Poseidon's Island Flower
Poseidon and Lani's Story

Thanatos' Craving

Thanatos and Juniper's Story

Saving Zeus—Coming soon!

Under the Moon: The Promised Mates of Monktona Wood

Thorn

Valpar

Simon

Sugha —-Coming soon!

Iron Fang MC Series

Grim

Hawke

Bear

Locke

Anaki— coming soon!

Bones— coming soon!

Visit authorverafoxx.com for updates and future books!